Also by Terry Spear

Heart of the Wolf
Heart of the Wolf
To Tempt the Wolf
Legend of the White Wolf
Seduced by the Wolf

Silver Town Wolf
Destiny of the Wolf
Wolf Fever
Dreaming of the Wolf
Silence of the Wolf
A Silver Wolf Christmas
Alpha Wolf Need Not Apply
Between a Wolf and a Hard Place

Highland Wolf
Heart of the Highland Wolf
A Howl for a Highlander
A Highland Werewolf Wedding
Hero of a Highland Wolf
A Highland Wolf Christmas

SEAL Wolf
A SEAL in Wolf's Clothing
A SEAL Wolf Christmas
SEAL Wolf Hunting
SEAL Wolf In Too Deep
SEAL Wolf Undercover

Heart of the Jaguar
Savage Hunger
Jaguar Fever
Jaguar Hunt
Jaguar Pride
A Very Jaguar Christmas

Billionaire Wolf
Billionaire in Wolf's Clothing
A Billionaire Wolf for Christmas

White Wolf
Dreaming of a White Wolf Christmas
Flight of the White Wolf

All's Fair in Love and Wolf

Terry Spear

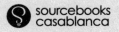

sourcebooks
casablanca

Published by Sourcebooks Casablanca, an imprint of Sourcebooks, Inc.
P.O. Box 4410, Naperville, Illinois 60567–4410
(630) 961-3900
Fax: (630) 961-2168
sourcebooks.com

Printed and bound in the United States of America.
OPM 10 9 8 7 6 5 4 3 2 1

*Beth Caudill, thanks for being a fan
and friend for so many years!*

May your writing always bring you joy!

Chapter 1

"WE'LL CAPTURE THE FUGITIVE, MOM. I'LL FIND HIM."
Jenna St. James was eager to locate Sarandon Silver,
promptly arrest him, and turn him over to the police
before her mom had to forfeit the bond she'd put up
to ensure he'd appear in court. He'd been charged with
numerous counts of identity theft, mail fraud, and pos-
sessing stolen property in Colorado Springs, Colorado,
and the judge had let him out of jail on bond. Afterward,
the suspect cut off his ankle GPS monitor and ran. It was
time for him to return to jail and stay there until his trial
date. Jenna just hoped she—or the police—could catch
him before her mother had to pay the bond in full.

She considered Sarandon's driver's license photo
again and thought it was a shame he was a crook—or at
least a suspected crook. He was a handsome guy, his hair
dark brown and wavy, his dark-brown eyes smiling, his
manly lips curved up just a hint, and his jaw sturdy and
square. She imagined that his good looks and smooth
moves could manipulate just about anyone. Good thing
he wasn't a wolf like her and her family, because she
was going to enjoy bringing him down.

"I don't want you to take any risks with this guy,"
her mom said. Victoria St. James had taken over as bail
bondswoman from her dad when he'd died, and she'd
run the business successfully for decades.

Jenna's triplet sisters, Crystal and Suzanne, and their

father, Logan, were all in other parts of the state on fugitive recovery jobs so Jenna had to do this on her own.

"I'll be careful, Mom. No problem." She continued to pack a couple of bags. "Piece of cake. He's never committed any crimes before this... Well, at least that we know of. His current charges aren't for violent crimes, just sneaky and despicable ones. I'll wear a bulletproof vest, just in case. I'll take my 9 mm semiautomatic pistol, rifle, Taser, boot knife, and pepper spray. I'll be ready." She figured Sarandon couldn't be all that dangerous, or her father would have insisted on handling the case.

Her family had one of the most successful fugitive recovery agencies in the state of Colorado—which made sense, since they each had a nose for tracking suspects. One with a gray wolf's keen sense of smell.

"Yeah, that's what your dad said when he attempted to bring that one man in. Logan was armed to the teeth, just in case. The bail jumper wasn't the problem."

"His brother was. I remember." Jenna had been ten at the time. Her dad had come home with the bullet stuck to his bulletproof vest. "I'll be fine. How many years have I been doing this now?" Jenna knew she didn't have to remind her mother, but they seemed to be having this discussion a lot lately.

"Nearly fifty. Your dad had been doing it for seventy years when he got shot. Thankfully, the bulletproof vest saved his life, but even then, the bullet broke a rib and bruised him badly. At least the bullet didn't tear through the vest and hit any vital arteries."

Bleeding out could be a problem for any of them. But being a wolf helped her father to heal faster than a human so he was able to return to work fairly quickly.

"That's why I'm wearing a vest. Just in case. I'll be fine, Mom. Really. If I get into trouble, I'll call on the local law-enforcement agency." Jenna already knew there was a sheriff's office in Silver Town. She gave her mom a hug. "You've posted a reward for information concerning his whereabouts, right?"

"Yes. First thing, always. We certainly would rather pay someone a reward for turning these guys in than have to pay the full bond."

"Okay, good." The fastest turnaround they'd ever had on one of their bail jumpers was an hour, when a mother called them about her son, picked up the reward money, and got him out of her house so she wouldn't be in trouble for harboring and abetting him. Best case ever.

Jenna wished that was the situation with this guy, but he'd already been gone for four hours. No one had turned him in, and he hadn't turned himself in. "I need to finish packing, Mom. I'll let you know when I'm on my way." Jenna already had a good lead, but she wondered if the guy had picked the name Silver as an alias based on the name of the place where she thought he was living. Silver Town. At least, that was the address on his driver's license.

No matter what, she didn't want her family to get stuck paying the $150,000 bond. A brother named Eric Silver had given them the title for undeveloped land as collateral for the bond. Once Sarandon Silver fled, further investigation revealed that the deed had been falsified, and there was no such property in Eric Silver's name. Sarandon was going down as soon as Jenna could catch up to him.

~~~

Eric Silver slapped Sarandon on the back as they met for lunch at the Silver Town Tavern before Sarandon took off for a vacation at the family cabin in the mountains. "Hey, Brother. I tell you, if you want to spice up your life a bit, you need to find a she-wolf to hook up with. Pepper has definitely made a world of difference in my life."

Sarandon was thinking more along the lines of finding a new and exciting adventure to take tour groups on. He was already booked for butterfly photo groups, bird photo ops, mountain climbing, wildflower hikes, whitewater rafting, and hikes into the backcountry. He was always trying to think up the next fun adventure. Which was one of the reasons he was headed to their mountain cabin retreat between tours. He often had returning customers who'd enjoyed his excursions but were looking for any new activities he might be offering.

"If you find a hot, sexy she-wolf who loves the outdoors and wants to visit me at the cabin, send her along."

Of course, Sarandon was kidding. Not that there weren't a few she-wolves like that, but any who lived nearby were seeing other wolves or too busy with their own lives. And he'd never met one he'd really connected with.

Eric laughed. He was the eldest of the quadruplet brothers, Sarandon the next oldest, and the two of them had always been the best of friends. They were close to their younger brothers too, but Brett and CJ, the youngest, always hung together. Their cousin Darien and his mate, Lelandi, were the pack leaders. Darien and his brother Jake had been pals with the older boys, while

Tom, the youngest of that set of triplets, had been Brett's and CJ's friend.

All in all, they were the Silver Town wolves, their ancestors having established the town in the beginning, and they continued to run the town as a pack.

Sam, the owner and bartender of the tavern, brought them roast beef sandwiches. "What I wouldn't give to go up into the mountains for a couple of weeks with Silva for a vacation. Now that she runs her tea shop in the afternoons, and we run this place in the evenings together, we just don't have the time to get away."

"You know, you'd have a ton of volunteers willing to take over for you at both places. And they'd do a good job. Just ask Darien," Sarandon said. That was one nice thing about having a pack-run town: they always had plenty of pack members who were willing to help out if they needed it.

"I guess I will. Do you need anything else?"

"No. Thanks, Sam. The sandwiches look as good as always," Eric said.

Sam nodded and headed off to another table, carrying a tray of drinks.

The door opened, and they saw the trio of men from the ghost-hunter show walk in with their cameraman. "Don't tell me they think the tavern is haunted," Sarandon said, still unable to keep from feeling animosity toward the brothers for wanting to take the hotel away from the three MacTire sisters who had purchased it.

"Sam will throw them out on their ears if they pull that in here. Who knows what story they're chasing this time."

The three ghost-hunter brothers waved at Sarandon and Eric, who inclined their heads in greeting.

"All right," Stanton Wernicke, the eldest and the darkest-haired of the three brothers, said to his blond-haired cameraman. "Listen, it's all right to take an emergency trip somewhere, but hell, let us know." They took seats near where Eric and Sarandon were sitting at the pack leader's table. The Silver cousins or Darien's brothers often used it when Darien and Lelandi weren't there.

"Sorry, man. I left a message on your voicemail," the man said.

Stanton narrowed his blue eyes at him. "That's not good enough, Burt. You need to clear it with us first, if there's a next time. We had a production schedule to meet, and we had to find another cameraman to fill in. You're the best at your job and you're a wolf, which is what we need, so just ask us next time, okay? If it's an emergency, we'll work around it. We've got a gig at that new lodge up on the slopes tonight, so no slacking off."

Sarandon wondered how Stanton and his brothers had found ghosts at the new lodge. No one had ever spied ghosts on the ski slopes or at the ski hut. And the lodge was brand new.

The men ordered hamburgers from Sam.

Eric cleared his throat to get Sarandon's attention. "You told Darien where you're going for the next couple of weeks, right?" Eric and his mate led their own pack located four hours from Silver Town. But serving as a park ranger in the state park nearby, Eric stopped in regularly to check on how things were going back home, as if he couldn't give up his old pack. Or felt the need to monitor what his brothers were doing.

"I told Darien. When would I not tell him?" Sarandon asked. He knew it was important to keep the pack abreast of where he would be.

Not that Darien or Lelandi micromanaged the pack. They just didn't want to send out search parties if they didn't have to. They had set up the protocol that anyone leaving the area for longer than a day would let Darien or Lelandi know. Even though Eric wasn't Sarandon's pack leader, he was still his older brother, and him looking out for Sarandon seemed to be something that would never change between them. That was okay too.

Sarandon sighed, thinking of the invitation Eric had given him. "Okay, sure, I'll come to the Spring Fling that your pack is having. No setting me up with a date. I'll come as I am." All the brothers and their cousins were mated now, and that meant everyone was trying to find Sarandon a mate, as if he couldn't be as happy as they were without having one of his own.

Eric smiled. "Good. Pepper will be thrilled. I've got to run to see Brett to make sure he puts the notice in the paper properly."

That meant outsiders—those who weren't members of either the Silver Town pack or Eric's Grayling pack—wouldn't have a clue where or when the Spring Fling was. Everyone else would know by the cryptic message in the paper. Sure, they could just email or text everyone, but they had fun sharing interesting tidbits without letting the humans in on the secret.

"Have fun," Eric said.

"I will. See you soon."

Sarandon returned home to finish his last-minute packing. His phone rang as he loaded the last bag into the Suburban. When he saw the call was from Lelandi, he figured she had pack-leader business to discuss with him. "Yeah, Lelandi, what do you need?"

"Jake's out on a wildflower shoot for a new art exhibit. He didn't realize you were going to the Elk Horn cabin this soon. The Bear Creek, Wolf River, Eagle's Nest, and Beaver Bay cabins are all booked. I just wanted to mention he might drop in on you for a day or two so you won't be too surprised," Lelandi said. "I couldn't get ahold of him to tell him about your plans. My mistake."

"No problem. I'd love the company. We can take a wolf run. Maybe he can help me brainstorm some ideas. We'll have fun. No worries."

"Okay, I just wanted to let you know in case he suddenly arrives."

"Thanks, Lelandi."

Looking forward to seeing Jake there, Sarandon climbed into the Suburban and took off. This might be even more fun than he had planned.

Sarandon headed into the wilderness, and after a couple of hours, he finally reached the Elk Horn cabin. He parked, got out, and stretched. Taking a deep breath of the pines and Douglas firs, he embraced the peace and quiet, the sound of a river flowing nearby, birds twittering in the trees, and the breeze fluttering the leaves.

Once he'd hauled all his supplies inside, he started a fire in the fireplace and planned to go for a run, something he couldn't do while acting as a tour guide. Not unless he was taking a wolf group out.

Within minutes, he'd stripped off his clothes and shifted, then pushed through the wolf door. He dashed through the woods, exploring and scent-marking, letting any animal in the area know a wolf was on the prowl and this was his claimed territory.

The sound of a car's tires crunching on the private gravel road, heading toward the cabin, caught his attention. He stopped and listened from the shelter of the trees and brush. There was nothing out here but wilderness. And the cabins and the land were private property. He could tell by the engine's purr that the car wasn't Jake's or anyone else's he knew in the pack. The car parked, and the engine shut off in the distance.

If the driver were a hunter, Sarandon didn't want to be caught in his wolf coat and end up getting shot. Cursing mentally to himself, he waffled about what to do. Hidden in the undergrowth in the woods, he could check out the person leaving the car, or he could run back to the cabin, shift, dress, arm himself with his rifle, and then see who it was and what he or she was up to.

Sarandon opted for returning to the cabin first and ditching his wolf coat. That way, he could tell the trespasser to leave.

When he reached the cabin, he dove through the wolf door, shifted, and rushed to dress. He removed his rifle from the locked gun cabinet and left the cabin, locking it behind him. Listening for any sign of where the person was, Sarandon headed down the road to where he'd heard the car park.

A quarter of a mile from the cabin, he stopped dead in his tracks. A woman was standing off the road, partially hidden in the woods, holding a rifle aimed at him. The way she was holding it, she looked like she knew how to use it. And he'd thought running as a wolf could cause him trouble!

"Hey, I'm just camping up here at one of my family's cabins. I don't have any intention of hurting you," Sarandon said, trying to put the woman at ease, even if she was in the wrong. "This is private property."

"Carefully, put the rifle down!" she commanded in an authoritative, no-nonsense way.

Well, *this* was bizarre. She was trespassing and pointing a rifle at him, and yet she was telling him to disarm himself when he belonged here? He considered her attire: black cargo pants, a black windbreaker, and boots. She didn't look like a half-crazed criminal or a hunter either. He wasn't afraid of her; he'd be much warier of a man holding a rifle on him than a woman. He just figured he'd spooked her.

"All right. All right. You don't have to be afraid of me." Being the nice wolf he was, Sarandon set his rifle on the ground, figuring the woman was going hiking, albeit on private property, and didn't know privately owned cabins were located here, though signs were posted in the area. But the fact that she was carrying a rifle made him suspect something else might be going on. "I run photo-op tours, hiking, mountain climbing, and white-water rafting guided tours, one-on-one tours, and group tours." He thought if he told her what he did, she would realize he was employed, not some mountain man living out here in the wilderness alone, and that his occupation meant he was one of the good guys who liked working with people. "Whatever customers might be interested in," he continued.

She was someone he was interested in. If she was a wolf and would put the weapon down. Something about her straightforward and confrontational attitude appealed. He swore it was the wolf in him.

"Sarandon Silver?" she asked, her brow arched.

Learning that she knew his name surprised him. If she knew who he was, why was she pointing the rifle at him? Then he wondered if this had something to do with his brothers. Maybe they'd sent her as a plant, a way to get him to meet a new she-wolf, believing the standard boy-meets-girl routine wouldn't cut it with him. Especially since he'd said he was trying to come up with an idea for a new adventure.

"Yeah, I'm Sarandon Silver. Do you want to tell me how you know me and why you're still pointing a weapon at me?" She had to be his brothers' idea, but he wondered where she was taking this.

If this was for real, he didn't recall anything he'd done that would have aggravated anyone to the extent that she'd pull a weapon on him. He hadn't taken a mate and pissed off her family. He hadn't lost anyone on one of his excursions. His dad was the only one who'd ever committed any crimes in the family, and he'd paid for his sins with his life.

"Come this way, nice and slow," she said, her voice firm and resolved.

He frowned at her. She sounded like a cop. He looked her over again, but her clothes didn't indicate that. He couldn't see what was underneath the jacket, though from the slight bulk underneath the material, it looked like she might have a sidearm holstered there. She hadn't said she was a cop though. Plus, if she were, she wasn't in her own jurisdiction. Her car was a silver Ford Expedition, with no indication it was a cop's vehicle.

She was a beautiful brunette, her hair cut short and bouncy, her eyes a crystal-clear blue. If his brothers—and maybe his cousins—had put her up to this... Well, he didn't want to appear as though he couldn't take a joke. She'd share with them how growly he'd been, and they'd all have a good laugh over it—at his expense.

"Am I under arrest?" he asked with good humor, smiling a little. He couldn't help it. He couldn't take this seriously.

She narrowed her eyes, looking warier than before, as if his acting like her actions were funny made her think he believed he had the upper hand. "Yes, you're under arrest, and I'm taking you in. I'm a fugitive recovery agent. Jenna St. James."

"Fugitive?" Bounty hunter? No way.

She smiled, albeit sarcastically. "Recovery. Agent. Wow, you're really good at this."

"At this?" He began to walk toward her as she'd ordered him to. If she wasn't a wolf, that would mean his brothers hadn't put her up to this. And she was for real. He had to smell her scent, and the breeze wasn't cooperating.

"Yeah—suave, polished, great at manipulation. If I hadn't been doing this for a number of years, I might even think you weren't the right guy, and you were innocent of any wrongdoing."

"I am. *Innocent* of any wrongdoing." Since she was still holding the rifle on him, he figured he should at least ask for her credentials. "Have you got some ID?"

"Hold it right there. Lie down on the ground and put your hands behind your head. I'll show you my ID once your hands are secured."

"You're serious." He still didn't believe this was anything other than a joke. "You have to play by the rules. You show me a badge, and I'll do whatever you ask of me." He was certain she wouldn't because she didn't have a badge.

"Down. On. Your. Belly. *Now*."

Every bit of his wolf nature rebelled at the idea that he'd get on his stomach for her or anyone else he didn't know. Even if it was a joke. "Or what? Are you going to shoot me? You can't. I'm unarmed, and I haven't done anything threatening. So then *you* would be guilty of a crime." Though he hoped it wouldn't go that far. "By the way, what am I supposed to have done?"

"All right, I'll play your game."

His game?

"You weren't supposed to leave the city. You removed your GPS ankle monitor. And you ran. As if you didn't know, you're wanted for identity theft and financial fraud." She gave him a wide berth as she tried to move behind him. "Keep your eyes straight ahead."

"I wasn't supposed to leave Silver Town?" He knew if she said yes, it was just a gag.

"*Don't* play dumb. You left Colorado Springs."

"Colorado Springs? I haven't been there in ages." He turned to watch her. "No ID, no can do. I know my rights. You could be a dangerous criminal, looking to steal from me."

As soon as the breeze caught her scent and carried it to him, he could smell her floral fragrance. And more. She was a wolf. He'd begun to worry that maybe this was a case of mistaken identity, and she *was* the real deal.

"I can tase you first, and then you'll be compliant," she warned, reaching for something around her neck, the object hidden by her T-shirt. When she pulled it out, he saw it was a Taser.

Okay, now she had him worried. For a second, he imagined her taking him down, but how would she be able to load him in her car? Still, he wouldn't be able to fight back, and she could confine his wrists in the meantime.

He lunged forward and tackled her, taking her to the ground before she had time to react. If this was the game, he was ready to play. If she was for real, he couldn't let her tase him and confine him. The fall knocked the breath out of her, but at least she hadn't hit anything except for leafy bushes that cushioned her fall.

Eyes wide, she took a deep breath, smelling his scent like any good wolf would, and struggled to get out from underneath him. "You're a wolf!" She sounded shocked.

What the hell was going on? If his brothers and cousins had put her up to it, she would have known just what he was. She wouldn't play dumb.

"My brothers didn't send you?" He breathed in her she-wolf fragrance, floral and woman, wolf and the woods. *She* could really spice up his life, if she wasn't trying to arrest him. "You really *are* here to take me into custody?" He couldn't believe it.

"Yes." Still lying beneath him, she read him his rights from memory as if she were in charge.

Smiling a little, he got a kick out of her gutsy actions. No woman, wolf or otherwise, had ever attempted to take him down like this. Feeling her heat and soft curves pressed against him, he felt his wolfish male interest in her waken.

She felt it too. Her eyes rounded and she tried to dump him off her, but he calculated the thrust with her pelvis and balanced himself to take the full brunt of her action so she didn't win the round. All her wriggling around underneath him turned him on even more, when he was fighting damn hard to keep that part of his wolf-ishness at bay. Hell, even his pheromones had leaped to the forefront, telling her in no uncertain terms just how intrigued he was with her. She couldn't deny that her own pheromones were reacting to his in the same fascinated way.

"Okay, so whoever the guy is you're supposed to arrest, do you know if he's a wolf?" The way she had reacted to learning Sarandon was one made him think she was clueless about that part. And that meant she had the wrong guy. Well, of course she had the wrong guy. He wasn't the one she was looking for, no matter what she thought. He needed to get this cleared up.

"I haven't met him—*you*—before."

"Well, that's for damn sure…about me. You would have known I'm not the one you're looking for, if you'd met the guy you're really after. You would know the difference in our scents, for one thing."

"You look just like your picture, and you have the same name."

"Which should tell you something right there. If I were on the lam, why would I be using the same name?"

"It's your MO? You're arrogant enough to believe you won't get caught?"

She was cute in an exasperating way. "I'm afraid you've got the wrong man." Damn glad too.

They heard something moving in the woods, and Sarandon turned his head to get a look at what it was, worried she might have backup and he'd *really* be in trouble. She took advantage of his distraction. Lifting her hip and grasping his shoulders with her hands, she flipped him onto his back, surprising him with her agility and strength.

She was seated on top of him, her hands holding his wrists against the ground, her jacket parted, her breasts close to his face in the formfitting black T-shirt. Her heart was racing, and he liked the way she was sitting on him, like she hoped to do more than just take him into custody. Which was why he didn't flip her onto her back to take charge of the situation.

That's when Sarandon saw Jake headed in their direction, camera bag slung over his shoulder, and Jake laughed. Hell, his cousin was supposed to come to his aid, not find humor in the situation. Though Sarandon had to admit if the roles had been reversed, he would have reacted in the same way.

Looking determined, Jenna pulled his arms forward to tie them. She wouldn't be successful, not without his cooperation, and he wasn't giving it. He flipped her onto her back again, straddling her.

"I didn't know you'd be up here," Jake said to Sarandon, smiling, watching.

"Lelandi told me you might come by," Sarandon said to his cousin. "Great timing."

Jake shook his head and joined them, looking down at the two of them. "I thought I might be interrupting something. I certainly never expected to see a she-wolf we don't know out here with you. I'm Jake Silver. Sarandon's my cousin. And you are?"

"I'm Jenna St. James, a *fugitive* recovery agent. And if you know what's good for you, you'll help me talk some sense into Sarandon. He has to come back with me to face criminal charges. We have offered a reward for his apprehension. Everyone will be looking for him so they can turn him in for the reward money. If you don't want to face tons of police and reporters and have to explain your own complicity in helping him to avoid being returned for trial, you'll do what's right."

"Well, Jenna, if you're not Sarandon's brothers' idea of a joke, you have to know that as a wolf, he can't be taken to jail." Jake folded his arms across his chest and smirked down at them. "He's right though. You've got the wrong man. The whole pack will vouch for him."

She scowled at Jake. "I knew there'd be a problem once I learned he's a wolf. A pack? Sure. Protect a pack member who's nothing more than a common thief."

"Listen, we'll take you to meet Darien and Lelandi Silver, the pack leaders. Darien's my brother and Sarandon's cousin. We'll help you in any way we can to straighten out this mistake," Jake said. "He's not who you're looking for, and if someone from our pack has committed a crime, he *will* do the time."

As if Jake had any authority over Sarandon, Jenna said, "Tell him to get off me."

Jake raised a brow at Sarandon, asking in his silent way if his cousin would agree.

Sarandon didn't trust her one bit. They'd have to disarm the lady and put the plastic ties on her, or he wasn't letting her up.

"She's armed and dangerous," Sarandon said, smiling. And she was one hot little firecracker of a she-wolf who had made the trip to Elk Horn cabin all the more worthwhile. As long as they cleared up this business of him being a fugitive.

Chapter 2

"I NEED TO CALL MY BOSS," JENNA SAID AS THE TWO WOLVES walked her toward a cabin, the smoke curling up from its chimney. She and her sisters never referred to the bail bondswoman as their mother. They thought it might not sound professional. Jenna couldn't believe the men had taken her hostage, or the bind she was in.

Once she realized Sarandon was a wolf, she should have known others in his pack could be lurking about. Were they all involved in the identity theft and financial crimes?

Even if they weren't, she knew they wouldn't offer him up to pay his debt to society. Not only because he was a wolf and going to jail could be problematic. Pack members often defended one another against outsiders. They took care of their own, including handling rogue wolves who were bad news for the pack and for humans.

The problem was that her mother would have to pay the $150,000 bond if Sarandon didn't show up for court. He could be looking at a fifteen- to thirty-year sentence if found guilty. Jenna wasn't going to allow the wolf to get away with this. At the very least, he'd have to pay the bond. Even if he did pay it, he'd still be a wanted man. Unless he could prove his innocence.

Wriggling her hands proved how futile it was to get rid of the ties on her own. She let out her breath in exasperation. She couldn't believe she was disarmed and tied up with her own plastic ties. *That* was humiliating.

How was she going to get herself out of this predicament? She had to convince them she was right and they needed to go along with her plan. Once she located a fugitive, she could often use psychology to control the suspect. Not all suspects could be influenced that way, but many could. She hoped it would work here. But given what had already happened, she suspected it wasn't going to be that easy. Not only did she have the problem with the two wolves, but she also had to deal with a whole wolf pack who would unite behind Sarandon.

Jake had taken her rifle, 9 mm pistol, and Taser, but they didn't have her pepper spray or boot knife. They'd confiscated her driver's license, badge, car keys, and phone too.

The fact that Sarandon was a wolf raised new questions. She needed to call her mom and ask more about him. Had her mom sent one of Jenna's sisters to get the bail bond paperwork from him at the jail when he had been arrested and confined for a few hours? If so, then whoever went to see him would know what he smelled like, and Jenna would be assured he was the right man when she brought him in. But if her mom had received the information in an email or fax, none of them would know him by scent.

Mainly, she needed to know if the man who had been arrested was a wolf. Then again, if her mother had known he was, she would have told Jenna. If Jenna had known that, she would have been even warier when trying to arrest him.

Since her mother didn't tell her the man was a wolf, that meant either he wasn't a wolf and Jenna had the wrong guy, or this guy was the right one, and no one had met him in person.

The suspect was a mastermind at identity theft. What if he wasn't Sarandon but had used Sarandon's ID to claim his identity? She couldn't have gone after the wrong man, could she?

"Is this really necessary?" she asked, raising her hands to indicate the plastic ties.

"Once we're at the cabin, we'll release you," Sarandon said. "And you can share everything you know with us."

"That you don't already know?"

"Absolutely. Because this is all news to me. In the business you're in, haven't you ever been tied up before?"

She smiled a little. Of course she had. So she could learn how to get herself out of a bind if this was done to her. Not that she'd ever had to. Until now.

"During your training? To know how it would feel to be the hostage? I mean, the captive suspect?" He smiled. Sarandon had the most devilishly disarming smile.

"No."

"Not even to learn how to get out of the tie if a suspect turned the tables on you? Am I right?" Sarandon lifted his brows. When she didn't answer him, he laughed. "Don't play poker."

She needed to school her expressions more. Or maybe he could read her so well because he was a wolf.

Jenna couldn't believe Sarandon had taken her down. Suspects had punched, kicked, and knocked her out, but not once had the wanted suspect taken her to the ground and held her there, acting…well, interested in her.

To top that off, he'd become aroused, as if he had

nothing to worry about as far as being arrested, and instead was just totally intrigued with her, which she attributed to them both being wolves. Even her attempt at overpowering him had seemed to be a turn-on. As far as her attraction to him, she couldn't help that he was as attractive as sin. No suspect should be that good-looking. Then their pheromones were singing to each other, which had to do with a wolf's biological need. She couldn't believe it. As if her wolf was telling her that no matter who this was or what he had done, that wolf part of her was eager to mate with him. Physical attributes came in at a ten. Willingness to have offspring with him? Check. That was her wolf's nature telling her what to do. Her human nature was in total conflict. Arrest him and turn him over to the police for their disposition. End of story.

Never had a perp taken *her* hostage either! If she made it through this okay, her sisters would *never* let her live it down. Not that she had any intention of letting the family know how he'd gotten the best of her, once she had him under control.

As they got closer, she could see that the log cabin sat near the river, with a dusty black Suburban parked beside it. She worried where Sarandon and his cousin intended to go with this, particularly when they had to know she wasn't leaving peaceably without taking Sarandon with her.

"I need to make a call," she said, her voice rising a bit in annoyance as she scowled up at Sarandon.

"To the bail bondsman you work for?" Sarandon's hand grasped her arm firmly, and he wasn't easing up.

At least her wrists were tied in front, which could

afford her a better opportunity to free herself, if she had the chance. All she'd need to do was reach her boot knife, make short work of the ties, and run. Then she'd have to get back to town, contact the sheriff's office, and have them help her take Sarandon into custody.

He was carrying his rifle over his shoulder. Jake walked beside them, a pack on his back, her rifle and Taser in his hand, her ID and cell phone in one of the backpack's pockets.

Irritated to the max, Jenna was trying to figure out a way to get all her stuff back. She had no intention of seeing the pack leaders. Trying to take on two male wolves at the same time and forcing Sarandon to return with her might be more than she could handle on her own though.

Yet she was making the attempt the first chance she got. She'd never let her family down before, and she wasn't about to now.

Jenna St. James truly was armed and dangerous. Not to mention that she was wearing a bulletproof vest beneath the black windbreaker, and a black fugitive recovery agent T-shirt underneath that. She must have thought Sarandon was really dangerous. She even had a badge, which surprised the hell out of him. They checked her driver's license and compared it with her badge and her appearance, verifying she was who she said she was.

She still had the wrong man.

She was petite, compared to Sarandon's height and his muscular build. He guessed the only way she would have been able to get the upper hand would have been to tase him. He was glad he'd taken her down before that.

He knew she didn't like the idea of meeting with Darien and Lelandi, but she didn't have a choice. He suspected that if she could, she'd try to get free, take him into custody, and drive him to Colorado Springs. The bond money was too important for her to risk losing him. He didn't blame her for what she thought she had to do.

"Do you have a sat phone?" she asked.

Sarandon glanced at her. She was scowling again. "In the line of work you're in, you ought to have one. The guy you're after could turn out to be really bad news—"

"Like you?" She arched a brow.

Sarandon smiled at her. "Like any of the real criminals you are after. *Not* like me."

"I don't have a satellite phone. Just a cell phone."

"There's no cell reception this far into the wilderness," Sarandon told her.

"Naturally."

"Well, I'm not the man you're looking for," he said. "Which means he's apparently still out there using my identity. Unless he's afraid of getting caught, in which case, he'll be using someone else's identity." That made Sarandon want to turn into his wolf and take the guy down permanently. Stealing someone's identify could cause problems with work, family, and friends—and for a wolf, real trouble if they were jailed. What if this guy impersonated a wolf who didn't have a whole pack to back him up? And who was more newly turned and couldn't control his shifting?

Sarandon wondered how the real suspect had managed to steal his identity. Was it someone he knew?

He unlocked and opened the door to the cabin for Jenna. She walked inside and glanced around at the living room furnishings, taking a deep breath to smell all the wolf scents left there. A large, velour-covered sofa bed sat in front of a warm fire, comfortable recliners on either side of it. A love seat was in one corner, and big pillows stacked on the floor offered ample seating for several people. Beyond the living room was a kitchen, and a table with eight chairs sat in the dining room between the two other rooms. "The cabins have four bedrooms and we can accommodate six to ten pack members, if we have guests. Like you."

"Where are the antlers or the poor dead elk head? It's Elk Horn cabin, right? At least that's what the plaque said on the door."

"We prefer steaks on the grill. No dead animals hanging on the walls. No wolves feasting on elk carcasses. Just photos Jake took of the elk in the forests or in the meadows full of flowers."

"They're beautiful, Jake," Jenna said, sounding like she really did admire them.

"Thanks. I'm a photographer. Mostly a wildlife photographer, but lately, I've been doing a lot of family portraits." Jake laid her weapons on the dining room table. Then he pulled out her ID, badge, phone, and car keys and put them next to the rifle. He slung his backpack with his camera equipment over the back of a chair.

"Well, they're wonderful."

Sarandon sat her down on the couch, then removed the plastic ties around her wrists and rubbed them gently, knowing the reddened skin would be perfectly fine in a few minutes because of their fast-healing wolf genetics. She frowned up at him. "You could make this easy on yourself."

"On you, rather? Why would you have an innocent man turn himself in, pretending to be a criminal? It's not happening. When the police learned the truth, you'd be embarrassed that you'd caught the wrong man, and a wolf at that. In the meantime, you would've let the guilty man go."

"I doubt that the police would deny I had the right man."

"That issue aside, how did you ever think you could take me down and haul me off?" He still couldn't believe her gumption.

"The Taser would have done the job."

He folded his arms and considered her slight build. "And then what? You would never have been able to get me into your car."

"I would have managed."

Sarandon highly doubted it. "You must be new at this." Either that, or he'd rattled her because she hadn't expected him to be a wolf.

"No, I've been doing this for years, and I've never had any trouble. The man, or woman, gives up without a fuss, or I have to use a little extra encouragement. But I've always caught my guy. You're the first who has been a real problem."

Jake was standing in the dining room, listening to them but staying out of the way. He knew two male wolves might intimidate her too much, and they had to learn what was going on.

"How many wolf suspects have you taken down?" Sarandon suspected none, or he wouldn't have startled her so.

"One."

Wondering how she'd managed that without getting herself in serious trouble, he raised a brow, wanting to hear the whole story. Maybe the guy had been a beta or omega wolf.

"Well, one still in progress. I'm working on it. Currently."

He smiled. "Me?"

"If you've got the situation under control, I'll bring her car up to the cabin," Jake said, smiling. He grabbed her car keys off the dining room table.

"Where's your car, Jake?" Sarandon asked, wondering how his cousin had gotten there.

"Alicia dropped me off. She was going to pick me up in a couple of days at the cabin." Jake frowned at Jenna. "If you've been doing this for some time in Colorado, you may know other bounty hunters. My wife is one. She was trying to hunt down some mobsters when I met her—and we fell in love. She was working for a bail bondsman while she tried to track the criminals down."

"Alicia Silver?" Jenna shook her head. "Never heard of her."

"Alicia Greiston, maybe?" Jake asked.

Jenna's jaw dropped. "She was human when I met her."

"Same here when I first met her. She was eyeing these mobsters in a restaurant, and I believed she needed some protection. Anyway, one thing led to another. One of the mobsters turned her, and eventually, we were mated. Best thing that could have ever happened to me. When the kids came, she wanted to be a stay-at-home mom. I was glad for that. Not that I wasn't proud of what she was doing, but I worried about her because she was so newly turned."

"And you needed someone to take care of your kids."

"We have a pack to help out. So no problem there."

Sarandon knew Jake preferred for Alicia to stay home and not risk her life trying to apprehend potentially dangerous suspects.

He caught Jenna glancing again in the direction of her Taser, making a calculated risk assessment. He didn't trust that she wouldn't make a go for it. Could she get it before he tackled her again? Not with two men in the cabin, but maybe when Jake left to move her car.

"Let me lock these away first." Sarandon hauled the rifles, Taser, and pistol into the bedroom where they had a locking gun cabinet.

In the meantime, Jake said to her, "You know that you have the wrong man. We'll help you track down the right guy."

"For a price," Jenna said skeptically.

"No. We're wolves, Sarandon's part of our pack, and someone's using his identity to break the law. This is something we would get involved in anyway."

Sarandon finished locking the weapons in the gun cabinet, then shoved the key into his jeans pocket. He rejoined them in the living room. "Weapons are secure." He smiled down at Jenna, but she looked so vixen-like that he wondered if she knew a secret he didn't. He reached down and took hold of her arm and pulled her to stand. "I didn't think we needed to pat you down, not after confiscating all your other weapons. I didn't figure you'd be armed with anything more than that. Maybe that's a mistake."

"Is that how you get your jollies?" she asked, sounding highly annoyed.

Ignoring her comment, he patted her down, having to admit that touching her sure stirred up his pheromones again, when he was trying hard to keep this impersonal. When he reached her jeans pockets, he found a can of spray. "Well, well." He handed it to Jake and continued patting down her pants legs until he came to her boots. He smiled to see a knife tucked inside. "Really, girls shouldn't play with knives." He pulled it free and gave it to Jake.

Jake tsked. "How did you miss those the first time?"

"We *both* missed them." Sarandon hadn't thought she'd be carrying anything more than what they'd already taken.

"I'll lock it up and then get the car." Jake took the knife and pepper spray and headed into the bedroom. All the Silver wolves had a key to the gun cabinet, just in case. And they never left their rifles when they weren't staying there.

Once Jake had locked them up, he left the cabin.

Feeling sure she wouldn't pull anything, Sarandon helped her to sit back down, then went to the kitchen. "Do you want something to drink?"

"A beer."

"You're on a job." Sarandon was amused she'd ask for a beer when she was working a case.

"It appears I'm taking a break. Can I have my phone back?"

"Sure." Since she couldn't call for reinforcements from her company or the police, he brought her a beer and her phone, then took a seat on a chair across from her.

"You're not going to join me in a drink?"

"When Jake returns."

"Okay, do you want me to tell you what I know?" Jenna took another sip of her beer and set the bottle down on the wolf coaster on the coffee table.

"Why don't we wait until Jake returns so he can hear the whole story."

"What are you planning to do with me?"

"Take you to the outskirts of Silver Town. We'll meet with Darien and Lelandi at their home out in the country to talk this over. For now, I want to know all about this, then you can ride with me in my car and Jake can take yours into town."

"Then what? Lock me up? You can't do that, because I'm a wolf too."

"Newly turned or royal?"

"Royal."

He smiled.

"Yeah, yeah, so my family has been wolves for generations, and we don't have any trouble with shifting. You still can't lock me up. If you tried to make up a story that I was tailing you, or pulled a gun on you and threatened to shoot you—"

"On my own property? We could charge you with trespassing, for starters."

"As a bounty hunter, I have the power to enter your home and even effect an arrest. Since Jake's married to a bounty hunter, he must know his wife can break into a home and arrest a suspect, when the cops can't do that without a warrant."

"True, but I'm not your suspect. And this business about a warrant? We run the town."

Her eyes widened. "A wolf-run town?"

"Yep. From its inception. We have no problem

incarcerating our own kind in the town jail. In your case, I don't think you have to worry about it though."

"The sheriff's office is…is wolf-run?" She let out her breath. "You're going to detain me?"

"You bet. You're not calling other law enforcement officials to tell them to come pick me up. Like Jake said, we'll help you find the right guy, but I'm not turning myself in and going to trial. Alicia became a bounty hunter to take down the men who killed her mother. How did you get involved in this line of work?"

She took a deep breath and let it out. "Okay, while we're waiting on your cousin, I'll tell you about us. My mom, Victoria St. James, is the bondswoman for the family company, but she was a bounty hunter before that. My dad, Logan, saw her on a case when he was an FBI agent. He fell in love with her, left the FBI, and got his bounty hunter accreditation so he could work for her family. By then, she was the bondswoman for the company. She hired him on the spot. Dad's great at the job. They make a wonderful team. You know, I kind of imagined I might meet a wolf like that someday. It's never happened."

"Maybe looking for a wolf bounty hunter isn't what you need. Maybe a potential suspect is more your style."

She snorted. "Like you? I don't go for the bad boys. I prefer taking them into custody." She took another sip of her beer.

"I take it you wanted to follow in your father's foot-steps and trained to be a fugitive recovery agent."

"Uh, no. Not exactly." Jenna had seemed proud of her parents and what they were doing when she'd been talking about them, but her expression had darkened when Sarandon mentioned how *she* got into this business.

He hoped that didn't mean she'd been forced into it and hated it. He didn't even know her, yet he was ready to rescue her.

"I...had a mate." She slipped some of her hair behind her ear. "And I was four months pregnant when the car my husband was driving was hit by a drunken driver. My husband died, and I lost the twins as a result of my injuries. A hit-and-run fifty years ago. Once I'd recovered physically, I was ready to take down the suspect. Emotionally, not so much though."

"I'm so sorry, Jenna. Did they catch the bastard?"

"Later. Yes. He was caught and given bail for another hit-and-run DUI case before they realized he was the one who had killed my mate and my babies. Will and I had been mated for five months after a whirlwind romance of a month. And then suddenly, both he and my babies were gone. I'll never forgive the man for taking them from me." She frowned. "Having Cavendish run off to avoid standing trial was my reason for becoming a bounty hunter like my father. And my two sisters. We're triplets, and while I was physically recovering from the accident, they immediately enrolled in fugitive apprehension training."

"And your mom was fine with it?"

Jenna shook her head. "Dad had to convince her that my sisters and I could do this. That it would be a family affair. Mom was worried it would be too dangerous, even though she'd been a bounty hunter earlier on. My sisters and I knew what was at stake, and we wanted to help. Since I completed my training and began working with my dad and sisters, I've always caught my man."

"The wrong one *this* time." Sarandon wondered if she'd ever picked up the wrong man before. "I hope the guy who hurt you is still in prison or died some time ago."

"I don't know. After my dad apprehended him, the perp stood trial, and a jury found him guilty, but he only received twelve years' incarceration."

"Hell. There's no justice in that."

"I agree."

Jake entered the cabin and said, "Okay, what did I miss?"

"Grab us some beers. Jenna's going to tell us what this is all about." Sarandon wasn't going to share the rest of what she'd told him. It wasn't his secret to tell.

Jenna turned on her phone while Jake grabbed a beer for him and for Sarandon. She began looking at her screen. "Okay, so you were in Colorado Springs when you were caught with five different credit cards, three passports, and three different driver's licenses."

"And he said he was Sarandon Silver," Sarandon ventured, ready to wring the man's neck.

"Right. The guy had never been fingerprinted before, and if you're not him but aren't in the police database either, no connection would have been made."

"So, he picked my name from one of his stolen identities. I've never been fingerprinted, so there's no way to verify I'm not him—unless I go in and prove my fingerprints don't match his."

"Exactly! If my mother had sent one of the other agents to get the forms from him, she would have smelled his scent. When she smells yours, she'll know you're not him. *If* you're not. I need to get ahold of her to learn if the forms were sent that way or if someone picked them up from the jail. Sarandon Silver is an unusual name. There isn't another one that I could find like that anywhere. Not online. Not in our database that we use for running people down. The guy in Colorado Springs didn't have any family or friends to speak of. He gave your address, which was verified by the driver's license.

"You own a house and an SUV, no mortgages. Everything was easy to check. The suspect paid for the bond himself. When I arrived at the home in Silver Town listed on your driver's license, I found you weren't there. A man saw me returning to my car, pulled into the driveway, and told me where I could find you. Here. At the family cabin…the Elk's Horn cabin."

"A man? A wolf, you mean?" Sarandon asked.

"I didn't smell his scent, but the way the breeze was blowing, he might have smelled mine and known I was a wolf." She smiled a little. "Maybe he thought you had a new girlfriend. Hope it doesn't get you in trouble with a real one."

"Hell." Sarandon didn't believe Jenna was all that worried she might have caused trouble for him with a girlfriend. He also couldn't believe one of his pack members had sicced her on him. The guy probably thought Sarandon's stay at the cabin had something to do with meeting the beautiful she-wolf up there.

"Since he doesn't have a girlfriend, that will sure start some tongues wagging," Jake said, amused. "I wonder who you spoke with."

"Hell, it'll probably be in tomorrow's paper,"

Sarandon said. "It makes me wonder when the person stole my identity. What did he have of mine, exactly? You said my driver's license. Anything else?"

"A credit card."

"And the police didn't suspect that all the identities he had on him were someone else's? That the real Sarandon Silver's ID wasn't his own?"

"His mug shot looks so much like you that I'm sure the police didn't give it a second thought." The more Jenna talked to Sarandon, the more her suspicions were raised that he really was a victim of identity theft. She finished her beer and said, "Okay, let's go to see your pack leaders. I'll call my…uh, boss, and learn if the man they incarcerated was a wolf."

"I'm not missing any credit cards. I only have one and have never applied for more." Sarandon pulled out his wallet. "And my driver's license is good." He showed her both.

She examined each of them. "That doesn't mean you don't have any more credit cards or a duplicate driver's license. The police have the others as evidence, so I don't have them to show you, but they said the items were legitimate."

"Let's go then. I have my name to clear." Sarandon went to the gun cabinet to retrieve the weapons, but he gave them to Jake to carry in her car.

Then Sarandon drove his car, with Jenna in the passenger seat, to Lelandi and Darien's house. Sarandon didn't confine her wrists this time. He suspected she realized she might have the wrong man after all. At least he hoped so.

"So your mom is really the boss, eh?"

"Uh, yeah. We don't usually reveal that to bail jumpers. It's a family affair."

"Makes sense with you being wolves. Do you live in Colorado Springs?"

"Outside it. So we have room to run in the forests. Have you always lived here?"

"Always. And I wasn't in Colorado Springs recently. The last time I was there, it was a few years ago. I went with Jake when he had a new photography exhibit at an art gallery in Colorado Springs."

Jenna assumed Sarandon would let her call her mother as soon as she could get a signal on her phone. "When will I get a cell signal?"

"Could be anytime now. Don't call the cops."

"Just my mom." Jenna kept calling, trying to get ahold of her mother until they were finally closer to town and she was able to reach her. "Mom, listen… Yes, I'm on my way to Silver Town. I have to know, did you send either Suzanne or Crystal, or Dad even, to the jail to pick up the bail bond forms from Sarandon Silver?"

"No, he emailed the forms to me. Why? What difference would this make? Have you located him?"

"I've located Sarandon Silver. And he's *all* wolf."

Sarandon smiled.

Chapter 3

SARANDON THOUGHT JENNA LOOKED A LITTLE RATTLED WHEN she ended the call with her mother as they headed to his pack leader's home. "Well?"

"Sarandon Silver emailed the forms to my mother from the jail and wired the money to her. Which means none of us met him."

"Which means you can't use my scent to determine if I'm him, so you have no way to identify him. Except for my forged ID. And no one knows if he's a wolf. What did your mom say about me being a wolf? There was such a long pause after you told her that either she was doing a lot of talking, or she was doing a lot of thinking."

"Both. She warned me that could be why you're so good at evasion—"

"Until this time."

"Yeah, like something threw you off your game. A woman, maybe? My mother said not to let you con me," Jenna continued.

Sarandon smiled at her. "Good to know you're not worried about me." Then he called Darien on his Bluetooth, in case Jake hadn't reached him yet. "Hey, it's Sarandon. Have you heard the news?"

"Jake just got reception on his cell phone and was able to reach me. I'm on my way back to the house. Lelandi canceled her afternoon patient sessions, and I asked CJ to listen in. He can report back to Peter so they can start an investigation into this guy pronto."

"Good show."

"Jake says you've got the bounty hunter with you."

"Yeah, Jenna St. James."

"Lelandi is eager to meet her. Jake said Jenna has met his wife before. Alicia called a sitter for the kids, and she's coming over to see Jenna too. I'll meet up with you in a bit."

"All right, Darien. Out here." So that Jenna knew all the players Darien was talking about, Sarandon told her, "Darien and Lelandi are our pack leaders. CJ's my youngest quadruplet brother, and he's a deputy sheriff. Peter Jorgenson is the sheriff."

"I still can't believe your whole town's wolf-run."

"Including our judge."

"Oh, okay. So, you're telling me you have a judge to back you." Jenna sounded like she realized taking him in was a lost cause.

"No. I'm just saying we have a judge in case we need one—not for our kind. We take care of our own. For humans who cause trouble in our jurisdiction, we needed a judge."

"I suspect if you needed his help, he'd back you up in this case. You're still going to have to return with me. To clear your name. You can't hide in your wolf pack in this town forever for protection."

"Hide?" Sarandon shook his head. "Hell, Jenna, I live here. And I haven't done anything wrong. I'm not hiding from anyone."

"Okay, so you say, and I'm sure half your pack or more would give you alibis for the time frame."

He couldn't believe she still thought he could be guilty of identity theft. "In other words, I'm guilty until proven innocent."

"You've already been arrested for the crimes, so yeah."

"And I've told you it wasn't me. Wait. You must have seen a picture of the guy."

"Yep. Your driver's license. Mine looks like crap. Yours is the perfect likeness of you."

"Hot, huh?" He smiled at her. He knew she was interested in him. "What about his booking photo?"

Jenna let out her breath. "Just a minute." She made another phone call. "Mom? It's me again. Jenna. Did you get a look at Sarandon's mug shot?"

Sarandon pulled into the pack leader's long country drive.

"You've got a copy of his driver's license. See if you can get a copy of his mug shot and determine how well they match. Then email it to me. If it's not really Sarandon, I need to find the right guy, and who knows what his name really is or where he's run off to." She glanced at Sarandon. "We're meeting at the pack leader's house. You know they'll cover for him, even if he's guilty."

Sarandon parked the SUV.

"Right. I don't know how big the pack is, but they run *all* of Silver Town. I know. Big surprise. They even have a judge. Exactly… Yes, I'll be careful… Okay, talk later." She ended the call. "Nope. She only has your driver's license, and it's the same as the one you have now. So, who could have stolen your credit card and your driver's license without you knowing it? And has anyone else in the community been targeted?"

"Not that I know of. Then again, I didn't know I had been either. Like I said, I only have the one credit card I showed you."

"Do you get credit card offers in the mail?"

"Hell yeah. All the time."

"Do you shred them?"

"No. We live in a wolf community. No one would pull crap like that here."

"The trash goes to a public dump site? That means anyone could go there and search for anything that would aid them in committing financial fraud."

"Okay, I'll have to admit you're right. What about my driver's license?"

"Did you renew it online? And did you shred the old one?"

"It was expired. It wouldn't be good to anyone."

Jenna cocked her head to the side a little, telling him his driver's license had worked for someone.

"Except for whoever needed to show an ID to get my credit card. Gotcha. Come on. Let's go inside and meet with Lelandi until Darien and CJ get here."

Jake pulled up behind them, and they all went to the front door. Opening the door before they had a chance to knock, Lelandi smiled at Jenna. She was a red wolf, unlike the Silver brothers and cousins who were gray wolves. She must have just had her hair cut, because she was wearing a short bob that framed her face instead of her usual long, red curls. Her green eyes were smiling as she greeted Jenna, while barely taking notice of Sarandon or Jake. "You must be Jenna St. James. How exciting that you're a bounty hunter! Come in and tell us all about yourself. Jake's wife is one too. She's on her way over."

Sarandon should have warned Jenna that Lelandi was always into matchmaking. Then again, Jenna was more interested in arresting him than mating him, so he knew that despite her psychology training, Lelandi wouldn't have any effect on Jenna. He suspected Jenna would be suspicious of Alicia joining them, as if she could convince a fellow bounty hunter that Sarandon was innocent of any charges.

Lelandi escorted Jenna into the high-ceilinged living room where twenty or more pack members could comfortably sit and visit on the velour couches and chairs. Lelandi offered to take Jenna's jacket.

"Thanks, I'll keep it." Jenna pulled it off and carried it over her arm.

Lelandi suddenly turned to Sarandon. "I guess this kind of messes up your vacation plans."

"For the moment, yeah." Sarandon had a group booked for a butterfly tour after his two-week vacation, so if he didn't get this straightened out pronto, he might waste his whole vacation trying to clear his name.

"Tell us about your pack," Lelandi said, seating Jenna next to her on a sofa, as if to show she would protect Jenna from all the men when they gathered. Lelandi was usually really good at making people feel comfortable around her.

Sarandon was glad for that, because Jenna was definitely uncomfortable. Her stiff posture and the way she was trying to put more distance between her and Lelandi indicated she didn't want to be influenced by the she-wolf leader.

"We don't belong to a pack," Jenna said. "My mother runs the bail bond office. My dad and my two sisters and I work for her as fugitive recovery agents." She glanced in Sarandon's direction as if to say he was currently her job.

"Oh my, I'm sure you have quite a few stories to share," Lelandi said.

Sarandon fought to keep from smiling at her, not sure Jenna was falling for the welcome-to-the-pack routine.

"Like Alicia does?" Jenna just smiled. She did have lots of fascinating stories to tell, but this wasn't the time to share them. She felt claustrophobic. The room was huge and comfortable for pack gatherings, but she felt like she was the center of all the wolf scrutiny, when Sarandon should have been instead.

They heard two cars pull up, and Jenna wondered what Darien would be like. A hard-nosed pack leader? Or more like Lelandi? Jenna didn't altogether trust her. She knew Lelandi was trying to make her feel welcome, part of the pack, as if she should have no reason to suspect Sarandon had done anything wrong.

"That's Darien's car and CJ's. Darien will have picked up Alicia. So, it looks like everyone's here." Lelandi smiled at Sarandon.

"I'll get everyone something to drink," Jake said. "What would you like, Jenna?"

"Water would be fine. Thank you."

"Tea, Jake, if you don't mind," Lelandi said.

"I'll take a beer," a sable-haired man said as he and another man headed into the living room to join them. "I'm Darien." He offered his hand to Jenna, and she stood and shook it, then sat back down. His dark-brown eyes studied her for a moment like a pack leader would, determining her strengths and weaknesses, seeing if she was easily intimidated. Which she wasn't. "And this is CJ."

CJ removed his deputy cowboy-style gray hat. He was wearing a denim jacket and cowboy boots and had a badge affixed to his belt. His hair was as dark brown as Sarandon's, but less wavy. His eyes were a lighter brown, but there was an obvious similarity between the two brothers. And Jake and Darien, for that matter.

Like Darien, CJ was unsmiling, but unlike the pack leader, CJ didn't offer to shake Jenna's hand. She suspected CJ was looking out for his older brother, and as far as the deputy was concerned, *she* was the enemy wolf, ready to arrest Sarandon. CJ wasn't going to pretend friendship, which she appreciated. She much preferred meeting everyone at face value. Otherwise, she felt like she'd stepped into a Stepford Wolves town.

Alicia hurried into the living room wearing jeans and a T-shirt and sandals. She had dark-brown curls hanging to her shoulders, and her dark-brown eyes widened when she saw Jenna. "Sorry, I had to take a call from the sitter. It's so good to see you again, Jenna. I'm Alicia, now Jake's mate."

"And a wolf." Jenna didn't know Alicia well, although she'd heard rumors the bounty hunter was going after a mob boss single-handedly. Jenna's family had talked about how they'd never take on a mob boss. They'd thought Alicia was either the bravest woman in the business or a little bit crazy. Jenna had met her at the El Paso County Jail and Criminal Justice Center in Colorado Springs when they were bringing in a couple of bail jumpers, but Alicia had been human then.

"Yeah, big changes in my life. I never suspected you were a wolf either."

"I was born a wolf." Jenna couldn't imagine how difficult it would be to not only have the issues with shifting while raising kids, but also those related to working a job. She could see the benefits of living in a wolf-run town if the wolf was newly turned.

"Don't you find that makes you see someone differently? When you learn the person you're talking to is a wolf and not just human? Like you have a secret you can share with him that you can't with others?" Alicia asked.

Jenna glanced at Sarandon. He smiled a little. "Yeah, but not as far as doing my job." She returned his smile.

His smile only grew. He was so cocky.

In truth, Alicia was right. Knowing he was a wolf made a lot of difference—but only because of the way he'd pinned her down and the physical interest they'd shown in each other. She was beginning to think he was innocent, and that meant she was even more intrigued with him.

"Honey, what would you like to drink?" Jake asked his mate.

"I'll have what Lelandi's drinking," Alicia said.

"I'm good," CJ said to Jake as he brought in the other drinks.

"Sarandon?"

"A beer."

Jake smiled at Sarandon. "Yeah, me too."

After Jake finished getting drinks for everyone, they all took their seats, except for CJ. He stood near the fireplace, arms folded across his chest, looking like he was ready to arrest *her*! He towered over everyone who was sitting, making him king of the forum. It was an act of intimidation any good deputy sheriff would use to ensure he had the upper hand. If he'd wanted to give the impression he was treating Jenna as an equal, he would have joined them on one of the couches.

From what she could tell, Lelandi was the easygoing pack leader, and Darien played the role of the tough pack leader.

She wondered if Lelandi was a family physician, since she had canceled on her patients. Jenna guessed none of the cases needed immediate care, or Lelandi would have taken care of them. It went to show how important Sarandon was to her. Jenna couldn't help but admire the pack for that.

"Okay, so what makes you think Sarandon has committed any crime?" Darien asked, getting the matter on the table.

To CJ's credit, he pulled out a notepad and began taking notes. Jenna had thought he might be totally arrogant and dismiss her concern completely, as if she had no say in any of it and they would take care of it.

She pulled her phone from her jacket pocket and began listing all the acts of fraud the perp had committed.

"So, let me get this straight," CJ said.

She knew he was going to be a hard-ass. Mostly because he was Sarandon's brother, but also because he was the law. And this was his jurisdiction. "Ask away."

"An identity thief uses one of the identities he has on him, and everyone believes that's his true identity. Why?"

"That's all the police have to go by until they can prove otherwise." She got a wolf's howl on her cell— letting her know her mother was calling—and pulled out her phone, noticing a few smiles. Her mother had insisted Jenna and her sisters use the wolf howl sound for her calls so they'd know the call was important. Their mom normally wasn't one to call just to chitchat. "Okay, my mom's sending the mug shot of the guy they've taken into custody." Since Jenna had already told Sarandon that her mom was the bondswoman, she didn't need to keep it secret from the rest of them. Being wolves and family-oriented, she assumed they understood why hers was a family-run business.

Jenna studied the picture while everyone was quiet in the room, waiting for her to share the photo.

"The suspense is killing me," Sarandon said, sounding annoyed. "Either he looks like me, or he doesn't."

"He's wearing a beard, so that makes him look different. He's got the same eye and hair color as you."

Sarandon got up from his chair and came over to look at the picture on her phone. "Well, hell, of course that's not me. My beard comes in red. And I'm a lot hotter than this guy. And I'm a wolf. I bet he's not."

Jenna fought chuckling at Sarandon. He was right. He was hot. And completely self-assured. The mug shot was too similar to dismiss though. The shape of the suspect's eyes and nose were similar, and the beard hid his jawline.

"Okay, have you got any pictures of yourself when you have a beard?" She wasn't going to take Sarandon's word that he had a red beard when it grew in. The rest of his hair wasn't red.

"He's right," CJ said, moving in to look at the mug shot. "This isn't him. And yeah, he has a red beard."

Darien took a look at the mug shot and agreed with them. "Similar, but not Sarandon."

Jake moved in to get a closer look. "I agree with everyone else."

"That he looks similar?" Jenna said, which was making her think of other possibilities. Was the man related to Sarandon? One of the men in the wolf pack living here even? That would be good news. The pack could help her take him in, if they would.

Lelandi looked at the mug shot. Her eyes widened. "He's a wolf."

"You know him?" Darien asked, sounding shocked.

"Well, not his name. I saw him in the tavern once. At first glance, I thought he was Sarandon. I didn't recognize the man he was with or him, once I really studied him. They are wolves because the tavern is only open to wolves," she added for Jenna's benefit.

"Great. More wolves." None of her family had had to deal with wolves in going after a bail jumper. She'd assumed that if Sarandon wasn't the suspect, the guy who was wouldn't be a wolf, unless he was related. It was good that she had a new possible suspect. Bad that no one seemed to know who he was.

"I'll get with Peter to see if we can learn anything about this man. If you can send the mug shot to me, I'll print up flyers and spread them around to the pack," CJ said.

"That would be great. Thank you." Jenna couldn't believe he'd want to help, but then again, if it got his brother off the hook, she guessed he would.

"In the meantime, you can stay with us until we get this straightened out," Lelandi offered, motioning to her and Darien's house.

"I'm sticking with Sarandon. He's the one I need to take back to Colorado Springs." When everyone looked growly because she was still sticking to the plan, Jenna added, "To prove he's a victim in this case." She had to agree the man in the mug shot didn't look enough like Sarandon to be him, as far as she could tell. But the police had been convinced enough to make a case against Sarandon. She still wanted to see a picture of him wearing a beard, but his fingerprints should eliminate him as the thief.

"I might have some photos at my house. I'm not big into picture taking, but as a professional photographer, Jake is, and he took some of me with my brothers."

"If your pictures look way different from the mug shot, we can use that to help prove your innocence," Jenna said. Though pictures could be touched up, so she wasn't sure the police would buy that.

"I can't believe a wolf would come to our town and steal the identity of one of our people," Jake said. "We need to catch him, but what do we do after that? If the guy who really did this is a wolf, we'll have to take care of him ourselves. We can't turn him over to the police."

"But we need to turn him over so he can clear Sarandon's name," CJ said.

"If he's not newly turned." Sarandon looked at Lelandi. "When did you see him?"

"Six months ago."

"Do you recall when exactly?"

"Around the first of the month. It was a Monday, because Sam was having a special on his fabulous roast beef sandwiches, but that's all I recall for sure."

"We could check out the moon phases for that date. It wouldn't tell us anything unless someone recognized his scent and saw him running as a wolf during the new moon," CJ said. Since only royals could run as wolves then, they'd know he wouldn't have any trouble being jailed in a human jail.

"We'd have to know what he looked like as a wolf first," Lelandi said.

"True," CJ conceded.

"My fingerprints can prove I'm not him," Sarandon reminded them.

Chapter 4

ONCE JENNA HAD SHARED ALL SHE KNEW, CJ AND THE REST of the men talked and handed out jobs to clear Sarandon. They wanted more evidence than just the suspect's fingerprints though, so they could get the bastard who had done this.

Alicia and Lelandi talked with Jenna. "The last I knew, you were trying to run down that mob boss. I can't believe you didn't get yourself killed," Jenna said, sounding impressed.

"Yeah, we took him and his cohorts down. He was a wolf."

"You're kidding."

Alicia shook her head. "No, newly turned too. He turned me by force. We had to take him down permanently."

"Okay, I understand." Jenna couldn't believe poor Alicia had been turned against her will. She'd thought Jake and Alicia had fallen in love and he'd turned her. Jenna could understand why Alicia wasn't still serving as a bounty hunter. It would be hard enough while raising kids, but ten times worse being newly turned and having to deal with young kids who shifted when their mother did.

"What about you? You were working on a murder case where the suspect cut off his ankle monitor and fled. I couldn't believe the judge gave him a $200,000 bond and then released him on bail."

"I told my mother not to take the case. But she was getting $20,000 for the fee, and she really didn't think the guy would run. He'd never committed a crime, which had prompted the judge to give him bail. What a mistake that was! The suspect's family had put up the money, so they were out the twenty thousand. And he's free. The bastard. Everyone knows he got mad at his girlfriend and strangled her."

"You never caught him?"

"Nope. We suspect he hid out in Mexico. We had to pay the bond. The collateral was some of the family's land, but it will take some time to sell. It was an expensive lesson in accepting risky cases. Worse than that, the guy got away with murder, and he's never paid for his crime. And might never, if no one ever takes him into custody. The victim's family was devastated. We had a more recent case where the suspect had been in and out of jail for years for kidnapping, sexual molestation, indecent exposure, you name it. The judge released him on a bail bond, and he ran. While he and the police were in a high-speed chase, he totaled another car and now is charged with felony hit-and-run. Luckily, the two women in the car weren't killed. We have to apprehend these guys the best we can. I feel sorry for the victims and their families and the police who work hard to put these suspects behind bars, only to have them be released on bond."

"Yet that's the way you earn a living," Alicia said.

"Sure. It's good for the ones who really *aren't* a risk. That way, they don't have to be incarcerated in jails that are already overcrowded. And for those who are innocent of the charges. In some cases though, the suspects should never have received bail." Jenna drank some of her ice water. "Have you ever missed the work?" she asked Alicia. Jenna didn't think she'd ever want to settle down with a wolf and give this up. She loved apprehending bail jumpers and felt she helped society by putting those guys where they belonged.

"Nah. I love being home with the kids. I have thought of doing it when they are older though."

Both Jake and Sarandon glanced at Alicia. She smiled at them.

"Looks like you haven't discussed it with the pack." Jenna wouldn't like it if she wanted to do something and the pack, or her mate, didn't agree.

"I've talked to Jake about it, sure. He said whenever I want to do it, it's fine with him. He's going with me."

"What about taking the training?" It was one thing for Jake to say he'd help out, quite another to take it seriously. Jenna had never considered having a wolf partner in this business. Oh sure, she'd fantasized about meeting a man like her mother had met her dad, but she'd never seriously considered working with a mate who was also a bounty hunter.

"Oh, Jake has already taken the training. He's all set to go when I decide it's time to work again."

Jenna smiled. *He* was a wolf mate to love.

"What are your plans?" Lelandi asked Jenna.

She had wondered when Lelandi would jump into the conversation. She would want to feel Jenna out to see if they were dealing with an alpha or beta wolf. Someone they could easily influence or not.

The men were talking about who had been at the tavern the day Lelandi was there. They were trying to come up with a list of suspects. Jenna felt she should be listening in on their conversation instead of chatting about nothing of importance with Alicia and Lelandi. Still, Jenna wanted everyone's cooperation, and she knew it was better to handle the situation like this. Particularly when a whole pack was united behind Sarandon. Maybe they could actually help her apprehend the right guy, if Sarandon was innocent.

"I'll stay with Sarandon and see if he can prove he didn't commit the crimes. It's the only way we can clear his name and get the police to look for the right man," Jenna said.

"We will have as many witnesses as you need to get him off the hook," Lelandi said, sounding dead serious.

Lie if they had to? "You don't think that will look a little suspicious?" Jenna asked.

"Not if what our pack members have to say is true and it clears Sarandon's name. He didn't do what the police claim he did, and we will find the man who did this," Lelandi assured her.

"I'm sorry. I've taken up so much of your time when I'm certain you need to see to your patients." And Jenna needed to get out of here and do her job.

"This is just as important, and I wasn't handling any critical cases." Lelandi turned to Darien. "Why don't we have a cookout before Sarandon takes Jenna to his house to gather whatever evidence she needs to help prove his innocence?"

"All right. Could you tell Peter everything you remember about the man you saw so he can make up a police sketch?" Darien asked his mate.

"We have the guy's mug shot," Jenna said.

"He wasn't wearing a beard when he was at the tavern." Lelandi set her empty teacup down on the coffee table. "I still say the guy I saw looks very much like this man, without the beard. And he did look like Sarandon. I was about to say hello when I realized he wasn't Sarandon."

"All right," Darien said.

"You don't have any look-alike relations you rarely see, do you?" Jenna asked.

The Silver men shared glances.

"None that we know of," Darien said.

"That doesn't mean there aren't any." Sarandon sounded bitter about it.

Jenna wondered what that was all about. "If there is someone, how would he be related to you?"

"Maybe Sheridan, my dad, was seeing someone after our mother died."

Jenna didn't press for details. Something about the tension in the air told her their dad was a troublesome wolf. She would ask Sarandon when they were alone.

She had envisioned taking a confined human to Colorado Springs as soon as she could nab him—certainly nothing like having a cookout with a pack of wolves, then accommodating the suspect while he tried to prove his innocence.

CJ was on the phone to someone. "Okay, Peter. Thanks." When he ended the call, he said, "Peter should be here in a couple of minutes so you can give him the details of what the guy looked like, Lelandi."

"Okay. It's been six months, but I'll do what I can."

"Steaks and shrimp sound okay to everyone?" Darien asked.

"Yeah, that'll hit the spot." CJ headed out with Darien.

"Coming?" Jake asked Sarandon.

Sarandon's arms were folded across his broad chest, his dark eyes taking Jenna in. He finally nodded to Jake and left with him.

"Do we need to do anything?" Jenna wanted to finish this business and get on her way, as much as she was trying to be cordial so the pack would help her and not hinder her.

"No, the guys love to grill, and any excuse works for them," Alicia said.

The front door opened, and Lelandi said, "Jenna St. James, this is our sheriff, Peter Jorgenson." He was fairer than the rest of the men, his eyes amber, cool, sheriff-like.

Peter shook her hand, breathed in her scent, and was all business. "Jenna." He didn't tell her he was glad to meet her, but she didn't blame him.

She realized at once that if she'd gone to the sheriff's office for help in taking Sarandon down, she would have had a rude awakening. Pack members looked out for one another, and Sarandon was obviously someone everyone liked.

"Do you want to tell me what the suspect looked like?" Peter asked Lelandi, pencil and art pad in hand as he took a seat next to her.

"Sure." Lelandi gave him the mug shot of the guy they'd taken into custody.

Peter was frowning hard as he studied it.

"The man I saw wasn't wearing a beard. He did look similar to Sarandon, and I had to take a second look to make sure it wasn't him. The man had a pointy chin and a narrower face, and he was wearing a billed cap that shaded his eyes."

"The man in the mug shot might not be the same one you saw at the tavern," Peter said.

"Maybe not, but the shape of his eyes and his nose were the same. And similar to Sarandon's."

Peter was studying the photo. "Sarandon's beard is red. This guy's beard matches his hair, same dark brown, not red. Does anyone know if Sarandon's father had any other offspring?"

"Not that they know of," Lelandi said. "The guys mentioned it was possible."

Peter sketched the man's eyes and nose, copying the nose in the mug shot because Lelandi said it was so similar.

"Can you add a billed cap?" Lelandi said.

"Describe it."

"Just a regular baseball-style cap with a long bill that shaded his eyes a bit. It was denim, had a marlin caught on a fishing line embroidered on it."

Peter added the hat, then worked on the shape of the face.

"He had a pointier chin. Oh, and a cleft in it. That was a real giveaway when I saw that. Sarandon doesn't have one."

That meant if the pack could get ahold of this guy, they'd need to shave off his beard to see if he matched the man Lelandi had seen. Still, his fingerprints would match the ones the police department had taken, if he was the real suspect. They would need to determine who he was, if he had been here before, and how he'd come by Sarandon's ID.

"What about his physical build? Not for the sketch, but to have some idea how big he is to add to the flyer."

"He's about Sarandon's size, six foot, broad-shouldered, muscular, as far as I could tell. He was wearing jeans, steel-toed workman's boots, and a gray wool sweater."

Once Peter had the sketch the way Lelandi thought it should be, he told her he'd send it to everyone in the pack.

"Have lunch with us first, Peter. The guys are all out back grilling, if you'd like to join them."

"Sure. I'll show them the picture and see if anyone else recognizes him. I'll have to check with Sam too, because he most likely served him. Unless this guy dropped by at night and Silva was also there serving the meals and drinks."

"She was."

"Okay, I'll show it to both of them. You never go there alone. Were you meeting Darien or anyone else?"

Lelandi said, "Darien. He hadn't arrived by the time the two men left."

"Two men."

"Uh, yeah. I guess I should have mentioned there was another one too."

Peter took his seat on the couch again. "Okay, what did he look like?"

"His hair was blond. He had a reddish-blond beard and gray eyes. His face was much squarer, more angular. He was wearing black sweats and sneakers. Since the two of them were quiet and didn't cause any trouble or seem to behave suspiciously in any way, I didn't check what vehicle they'd come in or where they went after that. Or alert anyone."

"Did they talk to anyone?"

"Not that I noticed. They were already at the tavern and had ordered food before I arrived. They seemed to keep to themselves. Not like wolves who wanted to join the pack. Not beta exactly, but they kept their heads down in conversation. Alphas who were interested in joining the pack would have been talking to everyone. Betas would have been more introverted but would still have tried to talk to the others in the tavern. These guys were looking around. So they weren't totally ignoring everyone. But they weren't catching anyone's eye either…you know, to nod in greeting. They just appeared to be passing through."

"They didn't focus on any particular person?"

"No. Well, me, for a moment, when they realized I was watching them."

"How did they react when they realized that?"

"Nonchalantly. They continued to talk occasionally, eat, drink, and look around a bit more when they stopped talking."

"You're a beautiful wolf, Lelandi."

"Why, thank you, Peter."

Peter's cheeks reddened. "If I visited the tavern and I didn't know you, and you acted interested in me, watching me, I would have smiled or something. A woman who watches a man means she's intrigued. *Usually*."

"Unless they figured I was a pack leader and they knew I was only watching them to make sure they didn't cause any trouble for our people. I wasn't smiling at them. I was pack-leader serious."

"True. What about Sarandon? Was he there?"

"No. I don't remember who all might have been.

Since I first thought the man was Sarandon, he couldn't have been there already. I remember wanting to ask Darien if he knew the men, but they left before he had a chance to see them. We're always wary when wolves we don't know come through here."

"What about this guy's build?"

Lelandi looked at the sketch. "Yes, this looks like him, the best I can recollect. He was shorter than the other man, maybe by an inch, not much. And he was a little less muscled, wirier looking."

"Anything else?" Peter had his pen ready to write.

"That's it."

"Okay, I'll join the others and get this out as soon as I return to town."

"I'd like to tag along when you ask Silva and Sam about the men," Jenna said. "Sarandon will have to come along too, because I'm not letting him out of my sight." She really wanted to hear any details Silva might have picked up about the man, if Lelandi was right about him looking like the one in the mug shot. Sam might give other details. Jenna wished the tavern sighting hadn't happened so long ago so that Lelandi might have remembered everyone there that night.

Peter frowned at Jenna. He probably didn't like her treating Sarandon as a suspect. *Tough.* He was, until she could clear his name with the police.

"She's just doing her job," Alicia told Peter.

Lelandi agreed. "Tell the guys what I told you, and see if it rings any bells with them, Peter."

Peter inclined his head, cast Jenna a look that said he was watching *her*, despite what Lelandi and Alicia thought, and then headed outside.

Lelandi sighed. "Peter's just protective of all of us. It's nothing personal."

"I completely understand. We've never been part of a pack, so seeing the dynamics is interesting. I envisioned what it might be like once I knew Sarandon was a wolf and Jake said we had to meet with you and Darien. Imagining and seeing the pack in action are two different things. I'm used to dealing with the human police in Colorado Springs. I never believed a pack would have their own law enforcement agency."

"It helps to police our own."

"No need for bounty hunters even," Jenna said, thinking that she'd be out of a job here.

Chapter 5

WHILE GRILLING THE MEAL OUTSIDE, SARANDON AND THE guys had been talking about the case, trying to figure out when his identity had been stolen and how to clear him of the charges. Jake had to tell all the guys how Sarandon had tackled Jenna before she'd tased him, and that had everyone but CJ smiling.

"I should have arrested her on the spot," CJ said, frowning.

"She was just doing her job," Sarandon said, trying to appease his brother. He wasn't bothered by it. He didn't want anyone else to see Jenna as the bad guy in all this.

"You know she believes you're guilty," CJ insisted.

"She'll come around. As soon as the fingerprints and everything else clear me."

"You think she's hot. That's the problem." CJ still looked annoyed.

"Well, she is." Sarandon was amused that his brother was so irritated about her. He knew that before long, they'd get it all sorted out.

"*Only* if she didn't want to arrest you. That really takes the hotness factor to zero for me."

Jake smiled as he held a platter for Darien so he could dish out the grilled steaks, shrimp, and grilled vegetables.

"At least Lelandi's not trying to make a match between the two of you." CJ leaned against a stone pillar and shoved his hands in his pockets.

"Oh, she's trying. Believe me. She's handling Jenna with kid gloves, but don't think that will stop Lelandi from planning her next move." Darien finished dishing up the food.

"What if I'm not interested in the little lady?" Sarandon asked.

Jake laughed. "All I can say is when I saw you take the she-wolf down, I thought you might have a secret lover. You weren't keen on releasing her, and she wasn't making a huge effort to unseat you or ask me for help when you both realized I was there. I was glad you took her down before she had the chance to shoot you with the Taser. I believe, once she realized you were a wolf, she began to have serious doubts about whether she had the right man."

"And Sarandon thinks she's hot," Darien added. "In my book, that means there could be a lot more to it."

"At least when Alicia was working as a bounty hunter, she was going after the genuine bad guy. I can't believe anyone would have thought a man with a bunch of fraudulent IDs would show the police his real one. They should have assumed he was using one of the stolen IDs," CJ said.

"They should have, but Sarandon and the suspect look enough alike that the police just assumed it was him," Darien said.

"Hey, Eric said you were going to the Spring Fling with the rest of us, Sarandon," Jake said. "Maybe you should ask Jenna to go with you."

Sarandon chuckled. "She doesn't live here. Colorado Springs is about six hours away, which makes Eric's pack's location ten hours away, so I don't believe that's a viable option."

"See? You're already considering it," Jake said.

Sarandon hadn't, not until his cousin brought it up. Sarandon and Jenna lived too far apart to consider courting each other. Still, taking her to the Spring Fling would have really made a difference, he thought. No one would be trying to fix him up with another she-wolf. And going with her would be more fun than going solo.

Peter cleared his throat. "We'll run by the tavern and talk to Sam and Silva about these two men." He showed the sketches to Darien and the others. "Lelandi was waiting for you to arrive at the tavern the day she saw the men, but she said they left before you got there. They did see her watching them."

Darien looked over the two sketches. "I don't recognize either of the men."

Everyone else concurred.

"Silva's got a pretty good memory, even if that was a few months back. She might remember something about them," CJ said.

"Agreed. Jenna wants to come with us," Peter warned CJ.

CJ grunted.

"And, Sarandon, she insisted you go too. I'm sure you would want to anyway. She said she's not letting you out of her sight, no matter what." Peter smiled a little. Then he grew serious. "Taking her to the Spring Fling might still be in the works." He smiled again.

Sarandon shook his head. "Not unless Eric and Pepper moved the date up to this evening and I took her there by force. On accompanying her to your office? Fine by me. I'd just as soon stick close to her so she doesn't decide to call for reinforcements from her agency or other law enforcement officials, in case she still believes I'm the real culprit. Besides, I want to learn what's going on as much as she does." Sarandon's cell rang, and he pulled it out of his pocket. "Yeah, Eric?"

"Hell. Jake told me you're in trouble. Why didn't you call me?"

Sarandon knew he should have. He just hadn't thought of it at the time, not when he was concentrating on what they were going to do about this situation. Even though Eric was running his own pack and Sarandon was part of Darien's, his older brother still felt everything the brothers did should be shared with him. Sarandon loved him for it, really.

"Hey, sorry, Brother. We've been working on where to go next with this. Lelandi thinks she's seen the guy— whose mug shot we have—at the tavern. CJ's going to send everyone an email and texts with the suspect's picture and that of the man he was with. No one here recognizes him."

"Okay, good. Let me know what you find out, and we'll check into it from here too."

"Thanks, Eric. I'll let you know."

Jake called out, "He might be bringing the wolf to the Spring Fling."

"Hell, you've got some explaining to do. Call me when you can. I've got to chase off a bear at a campsite. Just call me with updates." As a park ranger, Eric seemed to be doing a lot of that lately.

"I will. Good luck with the bear."

"Pepper will be thrilled you're bringing a date." Then Eric ended the call.

Sarandon would have to straighten him out about the date issue later.

"Eric's chasing off another bear at a campsite?" CJ asked.

"Yeah. They're drawn to the food." Sarandon's phone rang again. He knew that it would be his other brother, Brett, the reporter in the family, wondering why Sarandon hadn't called him too. "Yeah, Brett?"

"I've heard the news. I was thinking we could make an announcement in the paper about the identity theft. That way, everyone can check their financial records and make sure they haven't also been victimized."

"That's a great idea. Peter drew sketches of the men who visited the tavern. One of them might be the guy. Maybe you could run those with the announcement. Someone who reads the paper might have seen these men. We also have a copy of the mug shot of the man who was arrested, claiming he was me."

"I'll clear it with my boss, but I'm sure it will be a go. Did Eric call you?"

"Yeah. He's going to see if he can learn anything there."

"Well, let me know what else I can do to help. Jake said the bounty hunter is a wolf and she's a real knockout."

"She is. But I don't think she's convinced I'm not the suspect."

"We'll convince her," Brett assured him.

Peter got the door for Jake and carried the food inside.

"Thanks, Brett. We're eating now. I'll let you know if anything else comes up."

"I'd sure like to know who did this to you."

"We all would. Hey, I should have asked Eric, but... You don't think we have a half sibling running around, do you?"

After the meal, Sarandon climbed into the driver's seat of Jenna's car to drive them to Silver Town Tavern, not trusting that she wouldn't attempt to drive him to Colorado Springs. At least, that's what she suspected when he wouldn't let her drive her own vehicle. She couldn't help but be highly irritated. What did he think? That she would chance having the whole pack of wolves come after her?

CJ and Peter had already gone ahead of them.

"By the way, do you have a brother named Eric?"

"Yeah, he's a park ranger and leader of another pack. Why?"

"He's the one who put up the collateral for your bond."

"No way."

"Well, whoever did it was impersonating him."

"Well, hell." Sarandon got on his Bluetooth and called Eric, but only got his voicemail. "He's chasing a bear from a campsite." He left a message telling Eric how his name had been used too.

If Jenna still suspected Sarandon was guilty, she'd slip off tonight with him, when he least expected it. The police would be looking for him too. She didn't have anything to do with that. Since he—or rather, the guy they'd caught—had been wearing the court-ordered ankle monitor, the police were alerted when he cut it off.

"As easy as it was for me to find you, based on your driver's license, you do understand it won't take the police long to locate you here, right?"

"We all figured that," Sarandon said.

Normally, Jenna had nothing to do with trying to learn whether a suspect was guilty. Her only job was returning the suspect to the police so the judge could determine whether to revoke his bond. If the judge did, the suspect would be incarcerated. Or the judge might apply more restrictions to ensure the suspect showed up for his court date. She didn't want to take Sarandon to Colorado Springs and learn he wasn't the right guy. She'd never had a case where she was in doubt.

"What's the deal with your father?" she asked. "Every time he's mentioned, there are a lot of negative vibes. If you don't mind talking about it."

Sarandon let out his breath. "Our dad was the sheriff, but when our mother died due to a hunter's carelessness, Dad lost it. Suffice it to say, he went to the dark side. He murdered Lelandi's twin sister, who was Darien's first mate. As pack leader, Darien had to take him on and put him down. The pack is family and means everything to us, but we had to leave after that. What our father had done was unforgiveable. We were ashamed of him and what he'd done to the pack.

"At first, we didn't believe he had any hand in it. When he confessed, we were devastated. Eric, our oldest brother, felt he was responsible. He had taken care of Brett, CJ, and me once our dad became an absentee father. Eric felt he should have known what Dad was up to. He couldn't know that. No one had.

"My brothers and I left the pack for a while, but our youngest brother wanted to return."

"CJ, the deputy sheriff?" Jenna asked.

"Yeah. We all did, really. We had to find a way to rejoin the pack that wouldn't make us look like we had returned with our tails tucked between our legs. We knew someone was causing trouble for the pack, and we were trying to learn who."

"You were trying to prove your worth to the pack."

"Yeah. In the end, we returned, that case was solved, and we were glad we were back with the family. Eric found his mate, Pepper. That meant helping to run her pack. CJ and Brett also found mates, Laurel and Ellie. We needed to be here. Fortunately, no one blamed us for our father's criminal behavior."

"I'm so sorry. I know what family means to wolves. And to have to give up the rest of your family because of the sins of your father... I'm sorry." For the first time, Jenna saw a man who had been really hurting. Yet despite that, the pack was completely galvanized to take care of him. "You seem to think you might have some unknown half siblings who could have stolen your identity."

"It's possible. I never thought it would be, but if a wolf who looks similar to me stole my identity, the possibility exists."

"Your dad mated with another wolf?"

"He was seeing a wolf named Ritka, but she died. She never had any children that we know of, unless she gave one up for someone else to raise. It usually doesn't happen, but that whole part of our lives should never have happened. Not as wolves."

"Okay."

"Since you insist on 'sticking' to me so I don't sneak off, what are we going to do about tonight? Did you want to borrow some of CJ's handcuffs so we can be handcuffed together?"

She smiled. "You're so hilarious."

"I'm serious. What are you going to do if the police show up to arrest me, and they discover you're sleeping with me?"

She laughed. "I *won't* be sleeping with you."

"You know what I mean. We'll be in the same house. *Cohabitating*. No telling what else."

"We *won't* be doing anything else."

He smiled so charmingly that she felt her whole body warm. "Yeah, as wolves we know that. As humans, *they* won't. You haven't alerted them that you've caught me, have you? They'll think you've fallen for the suspect and are trying to hide the fact that you've caught him because you have the hots for him."

"Hots for you?" She laughed. "Are you trying to convince me to turn you in?" Or leave him here with his pack and pretend she hadn't found him?

"I don't want you to get in trouble over this."

She studied him, surprised he'd feel that way when she had intended to turn him in pronto. Was he just kidding? He didn't seem to be. "Okay, the truth of the matter is that I've never had a case where I was unsure whether the suspect was the right one. I certainly wouldn't want to turn in an innocent man. It's not my job to learn whether someone is guilty or not, but in your case, if you're not the guy they already arrested and fingerprinted, maybe…maybe we can have Peter send your fingerprints to the police department in Colorado Springs and prove you're not the one they're looking for. That would clear you without you even having to go to Colorado Springs."

"Are you sure that will suffice?"

"Well, as long as the sheriff's department is

contacting them. I'm not sure, but it's worth a try. Peter can send them a copy of the sketch he did of the man Lelandi saw. And another thing. If you have an alibi for when the suspect was detained at the jail and while he was wearing the ankle monitor, you should have a truly verifiable, airtight defense."

"You know I can come up with one. Or, for that much time, several alibis."

"So, what are they?"

"I don't know."

Smiling, she shook her head.

"Off the top of my head? I wouldn't venture a guess. I'll have to look at my schedule to see what I was doing during that time. I had taken a tour group out right before that. That may have overlapped with when the police picked him up. If I was still running the tour, those on the tour would be witnesses. I'm with them all the time when I'm conducting one. After that, I would have been here. I didn't go to Colorado Springs."

"His court date isn't for another couple of weeks. I wonder why he ran when he did and not earlier," Jenna said.

Sarandon smiled at her.

She let out her breath. "Okay, all right, I believe you. No matter whether you have airtight alibis or not. I can't imagine you having been gone from here and your pack not coming to your aid. You wouldn't have needed a bail bondsman. Your pack would have handled the matter personally, as much as they appear to care about you."

"They do. As to why he wouldn't have run earlier, maybe he was trying to get ahold of a friend to help him skip town."

"That could be." She kept going back to the man looking similar enough to Sarandon that he could use Sarandon's driver's license and fool everyone. It would have been one thing if the driver's license picture had been faked, but it hadn't been. "Back to the eerie way that he resembles you. What if Ritka had a kid with your father? Where would he be? Do you have any idea?"

"No. And I don't know why he wouldn't come to see us instead of doing something like this."

"Well, if he was sent to another pack, maybe he never knew who his mother and father were," Jenna said. "Maybe it was safer for him like that, considering his mother had died and his dad was guilty of murder. This is all speculation, of course. What if somehow he finds out who his real family is—and comes to Silver Town to learn what he can. He brings along a friend from his current pack to bolster him."

"What about the theft of my ID?"

"Maybe like father, like son, at least in his case, because he feels neglected by his real family. Or maybe he's pissed off that his father had to be put down by the pack. Something like that."

"Could be. Then why target me? Why not Darien? He's the one who had to kill him. Though Leidolf, Lelandi's brother, wanted the honor because my dad had killed their sister. They're red wolves, and Leidolf was much smaller than my dad, a big gray. Leidolf was badly injured in the fight, and Darien took over."

"Hmm, not sure. Maybe you're the first and he had plans for the rest, or something happened and he was able to get your ID more easily because you threw it in the trash without cutting it up."

"It won't happen again. I still figure he would have gone after Darien first." Sarandon motioned to the Silver Town Tavern as they pulled up to it. "Here we are—the local watering spot for our wolves and others far and wide." Sarandon pulled into the lot where several cars were already parked.

Jenna sure hoped Sam and Silva would be able to shed new light on the wolf who had visited the tavern and help her catch the real suspect.

Chapter 6

"THIS LOOKS LIKE A POPULAR PLACE. I LOVE THE OLD WEST feel of the town," Jenna told Sarandon, thinking it would be fun to live in a wolf-run town like this.

"We won't allow anyone to construct anything that doesn't fit with the period. Even the brand-new ski hotel is built in Victorian style." Sarandon left the car.

"That's really nice." Jenna got out of the car and met him on the boardwalk. She took a deep breath, smelled all the delicious steaks grilling, and noticed the deputy's and sheriff's cars parked nearby.

Hand-carved bears stood on either side of the doorway, a wooden covered boardwalk giving the place even more charm. A beautifully carved sign with a gray wolf and a red wolf said this was a Members Only Club. She loved it.

Across the street was a beautiful Victorian hotel with a white picket fence, and several other shops were located in Victorian-style buildings. If she wasn't here on business, she'd love to check out the shops.

Peter and CJ had already headed inside. Jenna hoped they weren't prepping Silva and Sam on what to say. She couldn't help being wary of a pack that would do anything to protect its own. Not that they wouldn't make pack members pay for their crimes. That had become clear when she'd learned Darien had put Sarandon's father to death for murder.

Sarandon opened the door for her, and she entered. When she saw the wooden floors, tables, and chairs, ceiling fans, and long oak bar, Jenna felt like she had slipped back in time. A smoky black mirror covered the wall behind the bar, and a piano sat in one corner of the tavern. Someone dressed in a barbershop quartet outfit was playing tunes on the piano, his straw hat sitting on the top of it.

Most of the tables were filled with patrons, and everyone looked in their direction, inclining their heads toward them—or rather, toward Sarandon, Jenna suspected. Some raised their frosty mugs of ale. Absolute silence took over, and then murmured conversations started up again.

One older man said to his companions, "Hell, if a bounty hunter came for me, I would have done just what Sarandon did." He smiled and winked at Jenna.

Her cheeks heated. Had Jake told the whole pack what had happened?

"Wasn't me," Sarandon said, smiling down at her and appearing to get a kick out of it. "That's Mason, our bank president. He gives our wolves the best deals at the bank."

Then they saw CJ and Peter standing nearer to the back of the tavern. Peter was showing a man and woman the sketches and mug shot, but as soon as the woman saw Jenna and Sarandon, she broke off from the others and hurried to greet them. She was all smiles.

"I'm Silva, and so pleased to meet you." She had sable curls tied up on top of her head, and she was wearing short shorts and high-heeled boots, her red tank top fitting a well-endowed bust. Jenna imagined that if her mate wasn't the bartender and watching over her, Silva would have received lots of attention from the bachelor wolves in the place.

Jenna hoped having her meet more of the wolves in the pack wasn't an attempt to sway her into thinking they saw her as one of them and she'd fit right in.

A black-bearded man joined them, his black hair tied back in a tail. "I'm Sam, Silva's mate, and if no one told you, we own the tavern and the tea shop in town." He looked like a wary wolf as his amber eyes took Jenna in.

"Yes, good to meet you both." Jenna hadn't known what to expect. Most of the patrons seemed curious about her, talking to themselves about who she was and why she and Sarandon were questioning Sam and Silva about people they'd seen in the tavern. Others, like Sam and CJ, weren't happy she was here. And then some were going overboard to make her feel welcome, especially Lelandi, Alicia, and Silva.

"You've met Jake's mate, right? She's a bounty hunter too. It's so exciting to meet you. I just waitress here and at my own tea room; nothing exciting about that," Silva said.

"Don't let her kid you," Sarandon said. "She's seen plenty of excitement here over the years. She even helped search for Lelandi in the woods before she was part of our pack and was being hunted down by a killer. Silva was the only woman in the pack to insist on going, even though Darien didn't want her to, for her own safety."

Instantly, that made Jenna's mind up about the woman. "Sounds like you'd make a darned good bounty hunter." And she meant it. Not everyone would be willing to risk their life for someone who wasn't even part of the pack.

Silva laughed. "If I didn't have so many jobs already, I'd love to."

Sam growled a little.

Silva smiled at him and patted him on the chest. "Don't worry. I'm not giving up my tea room for anything. And you need me here."

"Do you remember anything about either of these men?" Jenna asked.

"I see a lot of men, but most are pack members and well known to me," Silva said. "These men stood out, not in anything they did, but just because they didn't belong to the pack. They were quiet, not really speaking much except to order food and drinks. Every time I was near their table to serve food or more drinks to other patrons, I'd either try to hear what they might be saying, or I'd turn and ask if they needed refills. They just shook their heads and didn't talk whenever I was near. They ordered the food and drinks, and that was it."

"Isn't that unusual in itself?" Peter asked.

"Yes. Even if they didn't want to talk to me, though I tried to engage them a few times, they didn't say anything, like they didn't want to be bothered. Then again, my growly wolf of a mate might have had something to do with it. I'm sure he was eyeing them the whole time."

Sam grunted. "You're damn right. If some horny male wolves come in and don't know you're my mate, I want them to know you're not on the menu."

Silva smiled so sweetly at him that Jenna thought they made a cute couple.

"Between Lelandi keeping an eye on them, and my mate too, they might have felt ill at ease."

"Did they look that way to you?" Sarandon asked.

"No. Not really. I figured they'd dropped in for lunch, just passing through town. That would explain why they weren't friendly. On the other hand, no one was really friendly toward them either. You know how wolves can be wary of other wolves, particularly if they're males, afraid they could be trouble."

"Were they watching the other wolves in the tavern? As if they were looking for anyone in particular?" Jenna asked. Even though Lelandi had said the men only looked around casually, Jenna wanted Silva's take on it, in case she had seen something differently.

"Well, they were wolves. Truly, anyone in the tavern glances at the entryway when someone comes inside. It's just a natural tendency. Even when you and Sarandon came inside, we all looked. Partly, it's to make sure no humans are just walking in. You probably noticed the sign out front that states you must be a member. Membership is $150,000 a year. Wolves are free. Humans don't know that. We've had a few who want to join, until they hear the price. It's a private club. We set the rules. If anyone asks, those who come here are members.

"Sometimes we have guests, wolves we don't know who come in. Anyone sitting close to the door would have smelled those men's scent. We have a fan near the doorway to help send newcomers' scents to the wolves already in the tavern. Word of mouth has spread to other wolf packs about the tavern, and even my tea shop, so we've been getting new wolf patrons all the time. My tea shop is open to anyone though. Taverns can get away with being private clubs. And we need a social gathering spot in town where we can be ourselves. So this is it."

"You'd know the men by scent then if you met them again." Jenna thought they might have a real break if she could locate the men and bring them here. Then again, if Silva and Sam could remember strangers' faces well enough, they'd probably recognize the man if they saw him again.

"I'm sure several of us smelled them. Mason, our bank president, was here with a bunch of his usual friends. They were sitting closest to the men's table. I'm certain they would recognize the men's scents if they ran across them again. If someone doesn't smell like a wolf, they're out of here."

"What about you, Sam?" Peter asked. "Would you recognize the dark-haired man by scent?"

"Yeah. I delivered a couple of beers to their table."

"To intimidate them," Silva said, running her hand over Sam's chest. She pointed her finger at the sketches. "Lelandi and Peter did a great job. I couldn't have described them any better." She considered the mug shot. "He does look like this man." She pointed to the sketch of the first man Lelandi had described to Peter.

"You didn't happen to see what they were driving, did you?" CJ asked.

"No. I must have been busy. The next thing I knew, their table was empty. I probably wouldn't have looked out the window or door anyway. No real good reason to."

"Did they leave a good tip?"

"No. Cheapskates."

"I should have charged them with something," CJ said.

Everyone smiled.

"You shouldn't return to your home," Jenna said to Sarandon, beginning to worry that the police might pick him up before she and the pack could prove beyond a doubt he wasn't the suspect. Yes, she was changing her mind about him. "If the police are headed here, you need to go somewhere else to stay." To Peter, she said, "Can you fingerprint Sarandon and send the sheet to the Colorado Springs Police Department to let them know the Sarandon Silver they thought committed the crimes isn't him? That he's a victim as much as anyone else? That the address the suspect used is Sarandon Silver's, but Sarandon doesn't know the man they arrested?"

"Yeah. We'll get right on it," Peter said. "They may not go along with it. It's their jurisdiction, and they'll probably insist he go there. But we'll give it our best shot."

"Did you want to stay at my place?" CJ asked Sarandon. "Nobody would try to take you into custody there."

"The Elk Horn cabin belongs to the family, you said?" Jenna asked.

"The title is in Darien's and Lelandi's names," Sarandon said. "We have several cabins, actually, but that's the one I usually use. They're all in the pack leaders' names, and anyone can use them. Lelandi usually makes a note of who's going to be at which one at which times."

"Why don't we stay there? When I came in search of you, I didn't have any idea you'd be at a cabin in the wilderness, and you can't get there by GPS. The guy who told me where you were gave me directions. If the police do show up, they won't learn about it. Right?"

"No. No one will tell them. So, you're saying you want me all to yourself." Sarandon gave Jenna a big smile.

Jenna rolled her eyes, but she felt as if her cheeks were aflame. She couldn't believe he kept twisting her words. Then again, he was a wolf. She wasn't going with Sarandon because she wanted to be his girlfriend. She wanted to find her suspect but stop the police from taking the wrong man into custody. What if Sarandon was incarcerated until they could prove he wasn't the right man? Then the real suspect would think he was in the clear.

What if that was his whole plan? Not to just steal from Sarandon for his own gain, but to make it appear Sarandon was the criminal himself so he would be arrested.

Silva laughed. "Sam and I've got to get back to work. If we think of anything else, we'll let you know. Take good care of him, Jenna." Silva winked at her.

"Thanks," Peter said, and everyone else chimed in to thank Sam and Silva too.

Jenna didn't think telling Silva she only wanted to keep Sarandon from getting into trouble would convince her that was all there was to it. Sarandon was just teasing her, so no sense in setting him straight.

"Ready to head over and give us your fingerprints?" Peter asked. "CJ and I have some work to do after that, if you and Jenna will be safe where you're going," Peter said.

Sarandon slapped him on the back. "Yeah, thanks. Let's get it done. As soon as Peter sends in my finger-prints and they accept them, I should be in the clear. That will be the end of that."

Jenna should have been eager to get on her way and go after the real suspect so her family wouldn't have to pay all that bond money. So why was she hoping this was going to take longer than that?

When they were heading over to the sheriff's office, she got a call from her dad. "Yes, Dad?" She assumed he was worried about her because Sarandon was a wolf.

"Your mother told me you have a whole wolf pack to deal with. I'll get there as soon as I can clear up the case I'm working on."

"No. I'm fine, Dad. Really. The local sheriff's department is going to send Sarandon Silver's fingerprints to our police department. If they learn he's not the man they arrested, we'll have to locate the real suspect. In that case, I have a couple of leads from the pack members. They've all been really cooperative."

Sarandon smiled at her, then parked the car at the sheriff's department.

Yeah, when he had tackled her, he hadn't been cooperative in the least. Though she didn't really blame him. One time, one of the suspects she was after had tased *her*! So she knew just how it felt and was glad Sarandon had stopped her when he did.

"All right, well, if you have any trouble, let me know right away."

"I will, Dad. Thanks." She wouldn't mind her dad helping her to track down the other guy, but she really wanted to deal with Sarandon on her own.

Her mother had warned her and her sisters never to fall for the charms of a suspect, but Sarandon wasn't really a suspect anymore. So that meant it was okay to spend a little more time with him. *Right?*

He certainly seemed to believe so.

Chapter 7

EVEN THOUGH SARANDON HAD NOTHING TO WORRY ABOUT, he hated having to submit fingerprints to prove he was innocent. He didn't like having them on file anywhere because wolves lived such long lives. Five years for every human year now. Still, if giving his prints helped clear his name, he had to do it.

"Okay, we'll take it from here," Peter said once Sarandon had finished giving them his fingerprints.

"If you need anything, just call me," CJ told Sarandon, casting Jenna a wary look. CJ pulled a satellite phone out of his desk drawer. "Here, take this to keep in touch."

"All right," Sarandon said. "Once I see what I was doing during the last few days, I can let you know. That's how long this guy was being monitored before he took off."

Looking serious, Peter nodded. CJ glanced at Jenna, and she knew he planned to tell Sarandon he'd vouch for him if he didn't have an ironclad alibi.

When they left the office, Sarandon said to Jenna, "We still need to drop by the house."

"And look at your schedule to see what your alibi happened to be." She raised a brow.

He only smiled. "I'll have one. And more."

"Oh, I'm sure you will."

—◦◦◦—

Once they were in the house, Jenna kept watching out the window and looking back at Sarandon while he searched through drawers in a bureau in the living room where he threw stuff he meant to organize someday.

"Are you worried the police will show up?" Sarandon finally found where he'd put some of the pictures Jake had taken of the brothers. He needed to get more organized.

"Yes. Aren't you?"

"Not really. I have you to vouch for me. Here it is. One Jake took of me and my brothers on the ski slopes last winter. We stopped at the lodge to have hot drinks."

Jenna walked over to look at it. "You have a fairly red beard." She considered the stubble starting to appear on his chin. "It's coming in even now."

"Yeah. There must have been an Irishman or a Scot in the bunch. At least, that's what everyone always says. One of our grandfathers also had black hair and a red beard."

"Okay." She pulled up the mug shot on her phone and compared the photo of Sarandon with it. "His eyes and nose still look similar, but the beard and coloring are not at all the same. Unless you dyed your beard, or it comes in different colors at different times."

"Nope. And I'll prove it to you, if you hang around long enough."

She laughed. "I can imagine hanging around just to watch your beard grow."

"It would be all right by me. Besides, all you'd have to do is have me shift. If I were dyeing it, the shift would knock the dye right out of it."

"True, but humans wouldn't know that."

"You can come by later to check out my beard's progress." He rubbed his whiskery chin.

"I could, but I have to catch this guy. Besides the fact that he'll steal from others, the business of us having to pay his bond is too important not to."

"As a wolf, he's not going to go with you willingly." Sarandon already didn't like that she was handling this on her own. What if this guy was a wolf and had a pack to back *him* up? If he was related to Sarandon, he was a wolf.

"Yeah, if he is one. If he's the same man Lelandi thought he was. What about your schedule? The one that shows where you've been every day for the past several days."

Sarandon went to his office, Jenna following him, and when he reached his oak desk, he pulled an appointment book out of a drawer.

"Not high tech, eh?" she asked.

"Some things I prefer doing the old-fashioned way. Like reading a book. I still prefer paperbacks. I guess you read only ebooks and use online calendars." He handed her the book.

"Most of the time, sure."

"Don't tell me you're a young wolf."

"What? And have never used a typewriter before? Don't worry, Pops. I'm probably as old as you are. Maybe even older."

"Good, because I wouldn't want to be accused of robbing the cradle."

She was thumbing through his appointment book, pausing to read appointments on dates that weren't even relevant. She glanced up at him. "You would only be accused of that if I were a young wolf and you were trying to court me. Which you're not doing."

"Hell, I thought we'd already accomplished phase one of the courtship ritual."

"In your dreams." She kept skimming through the date book. "I wore Victorian gowns when they were the required fashion of the period."

He smiled. "Me too. I didn't wear the gowns, but that was a good era for me."

"Good to know. Back to your alibi." She kept flipping through the pages, and he thought she would have reached the right time frame way before this.

"We have a grand Victorian Days celebration in the fall. A ball too. You should come. Everyone who lives here dresses up for the occasion. Some visitors to the area dress up in Victorian-style clothes too, just to enjoy the festivities." He reached for the appointment book, and she frowned at him. "Here, let me have it for a second." He took it and set it on the desk, then took her hands in his.

"What are you doing?"

He placed a hand on her waist and held her free hand with his. Then, to the nonexistent music, he waltzed her around the office.

Following his lead, she danced beautifully, not pulling away, not even when he pulled her closer.

"That is not the way the Victorians dance," she said.

He smiled down at her. "Victorian wolves did, and in this day and age, it's perfectly acceptable."

She pulled her hand free of his and wrapped her arms around his neck while he resettled his hands on her hips. "And like this."

He glanced down at her softly parted lips. Then he lifted her chin and brushed his mouth against her jaw, moving his lips across her lips. "And like this." He kissed her mouth, gently. "You are so beautiful."

She smiled against his lips and licked them. "So are you."

And she kissed him right back. Parting her lips for him. Taking him in. He was in heaven.

"Wow," she said and separated from him. "I haven't danced like that in decades. And never without music."

"And the kiss?"

She only gave him a dark smile. "No more interruptions, unless you have something to hide."

He didn't. If his schedule didn't show he'd been in Silver Town with verifiable witness accounts, he wasn't going to sweat it. His family and friends, and the law even, would provide him with witness statements proving he had been here or close by.

"Okay, so when you were arrested"—she frowned at him, and he was frowning at her—"*supposedly* were arrested, you were on the last two days of your butterfly photo op. You were at the state park with seven people. You can contact them and have them state for a fact you were with them the whole time?"

"I can try to get ahold of them to verify my whereabouts. They're human and have returned to other cities and their jobs."

"Okay, well, the police might want to verify this themselves if the fingerprints don't prove to be enough."

"That's fine. I can provide names, phone numbers, and email addresses. I'll see if they can email statements to me or to the sheriff's office."

"Good. You had a luncheon date with Laurel on the second Monday after your arrest. The suspect's arrest." Jenna glanced up at him to hear what he had to say for himself on that account.

He swore she thought he was dating a woman. She was way more interested in him than she was trying to let on. "Laurel MacTire. I'm sure she has the lunch date listed on her calendar too. She's a lot more organized than me. She's part owner of the Silver Town Inn, and she's CJ's mate."

"Oh." Jenna's cheeks flushed a little.

"We were discussing an anniversary gift for CJ. She wanted to ask me if I'd fill in for CJ at the sheriff's office so she could take my brother to some exotic place for their anniversary. I said I would."

"And when was this supposed to happen?" Jenna was taking notes.

"December."

"Okay, so it looks like you had an appointment with…" She looked up at Sarandon. Her confused expression made him look down at the book to see what she had read.

He smiled. "Ghost hunters. The three men are Laurel's cousins. All-around nuisances. They document haunted places and showcase them on their TV series. If you ask me, I think they're frauds. Laurel says she thinks one really has some abilities."

"Why were you meeting with them? Just curious."

"Darien asked me to speak to them about what they were doing hanging around Silver Town. He wanted them to find haunted places far from the town. We don't want a lot of outsiders coming here to see the haunted places."

"Does Silver Town have a lot of haunted places?" Jenna sounded surprised.

"Mostly, no."

"Colorado Springs is purported to. It always fascinated me. Not that I've ever experienced anything. Did the ghost hunters leave?"

"Yeah, for a little while. Now they're back, and they're checking out the new ski lodge."

"Is it haunted?" Jenna asked, skimming through the calendar book further.

"I can't imagine that it is. It's brand new."

"Can you have the ghost hunters verify you met with them then?" She wrote down some more notes.

"I can, but, you see, all this has to be true, because I didn't have time to create a calendar of alibis for you. So, it has to all have been real."

"Unless you're the suspect and already had this set up in case anybody checked what you've been doing and where."

He shook his head.

"Hey, I'm just saying if someone really believed you were the suspect, that's what he might assume."

"Have you seen any cases of someone using someone else's identity during an arrest and getting away with it?" Sarandon asked.

"Unfortunately, yes. Not any I've worked. Not like this. My dad had one where the guy had stolen his friend's expired driver's license."

"Hell."

"Yeah. You need to destroy those. Anyway, it turned out the man whose ID he used was a lawyer who had proof he'd been in court during the time of the crime—DUI charges—and subsequent booking of this man. I would think that would be one hell of an irrefutable alibi! Nope. The attorney had to fly to the location a thousand miles away to appear at a hearing. He was fingerprinted but not booked. If he hadn't appeared, they were going to try to have him disbarred. If that wasn't bad enough, they never went after the real criminal."

"Hell."

"Yeah. Life isn't fair sometimes. It looks like you have an alibi for several of the days you were supposed to be wearing the GPS monitor in Colorado Springs. We need to drop by the sheriff's office and have him verify this information so you'll be covered in case you have to go to the CSPD. I'm ready to go. Are you?"

Sarandon really thought she was concerned for him now. He was a little surprised she wanted to stick with him, but he was glad she seemed to be changing her mind about him.

They dropped by the sheriff's office, and CJ made copies of Sarandon's calendar. "You still go by this old thing?" his brother asked.

"Yeah. Look how it can help clear me as a suspect in this case. If I had one online, I could just go in and change everything. And since I've been in Jenna's custody all along, she knows I didn't make this stuff up to cover my whereabouts. At least, you can verify with everyone I met with who's listed on my calendar."

CJ flipped through Sarandon's appointment book, looking at the relevant dates. "Okay, you'll need witness statements that you've met with all these people. The bad news is that the CSPD won't accept you're not the suspect unless you appear at a hearing there. They'll fingerprint you... Yeah, I know, like we're not able to properly fingerprint you here. You can provide witness statements that we'll take here at the office so they'll be more credible, witnessed by Peter and me. I'll start calling everyone to come in and do this. You'll have to give your statement under oath in Colorado Springs. The issuing jurisdiction is the only one that can clear you of the charges, they said."

"Hell."

"Sorry, Brother. On second thought, I might have Trevor take my place as a witness so it doesn't look like collusion between family members."

"Yeah, sounds good. I'll call the folks on the tour, if you can call our local people," Sarandon said, irritated to the extreme over this. He swore he'd make this guy pay for all the trouble he had to go through to clear his name.

"Can I help in any way?" Jenna asked, looking like she'd do anything to help him clear this matter up.

"Just call your mom, I guess, and let her know the problem. Tell her we're still all going to help with trying to track down the suspect," Sarandon said.

"Okay. I don't usually have this much trouble tracking down a fugitive. I thought I had it made, once I found you, and would be all set to go after the next bail jumper."

"You know what they say—if it sounds too good to be true, it probably is."

She scoffed. "Yeah, don't remind me." She got on her phone. "Okay, Mom, Sarandon has airtight alibis for the time he supposedly was arrested and for every day that the real suspect was in Colorado Springs being monitored. We're returning to Colorado Springs right after Sarandon gets witness statements to that effect. We're not sure how long that will take, but we probably won't arrive until tomorrow evening."

CJ was calling Lelandi to tell her about getting witness statements and that Sarandon would have to go to Colorado Springs to clear his name. Sarandon wasn't able to reach five of the seven people on his tour. But he did have gas receipts from Silver Town before he took the group out in the wilderness and a grocery receipt for the food he had provided for the lunches and snacks on the trip.

Two of the people on the tour said they'd email statements to the sheriff's office and gave their phone numbers and addresses so the police could verify their statements with them. Sarandon hated to tell clients he was wanted by the police, but one of the women was so angry about the injustice that she said she'd go to Colorado Springs herself and testify.

"Thanks, Lisa. I appreciate it. I think I'll have enough statements, but if I need you to, I'll be sure to contact you."

"Well, my husband's a lawyer. So if you need one, just let me know."

"Thanks. Hopefully, it won't come to that. I'll sure keep it in mind." The woman had taken three excursions with Sarandon, and her husband had come on the whitewater rafting one last summer. Sarandon was thankful they were eager to help him. When they ended the call, he emailed the other people on the tour to ask them for written statements, just in case he needed them.

What he really hadn't expected was for pack members to start pouring into the sheriff's office—Mason,

the bank president; Mervin, the barber; Silva, with a box
of pastries for him and Jenna; Lelandi; Darien; Laurel;
and even her ghost-hunter cousins. It didn't matter if
he hadn't had a scheduled lunch or dinner or other date
with them. They were here to say they'd talked to him at
the grocery store, or the bank, or the tavern, or any place
where they'd seen him during that time.

Jenna looked in awe, and he smiled. He'd told her
he'd have an alibi.

Chapter 8

JENNA COULDN'T HAVE BEEN MORE ASTOUNDED TO SEE ALL the outpouring of love for Sarandon. The hugs and smiles—and a few growls when some mentioned they'd love to tear into the guy who had stolen Sarandon's identity. She watched as wolf after wolf made statements and another deputy sheriff, Trevor Osgood, arrived to be a witness.

"Did you want me to go with you to Colorado Springs?" Lelandi asked Sarandon.

"No, thanks though. If the witness statements and my fingerprints don't prove I'm not the man they booked, then everyone can arrive together to help me out. Until then, hopefully this will be enough."

It was nearly midnight by the time all the statements were given. Sam had even brought over dinner for Sarandon and Jenna and the sheriff and his deputies. *Unbelievable*. And it was really wonderful too.

After the last of the witnesses arrived and four more of the ones on his butterfly tour sent statements to him, Sarandon had forty-two witness statements in hand. Jenna just couldn't believe it.

"Where to now?" he asked her. "It's a two-hour drive to the cabin, which means an extra two-hour drive tomorrow when we head to Colorado Springs. Or we can stay at my place. I doubt any police officers are going to arrive to arrest me, now that CJ has contacted them and sent my fingerprints. They know I'm headed in, so no need to waste time and money to come get me."

"Right. I agree."

When they arrived at his house, Sarandon opened the door and let her inside, then locked the door. "So tomorrow, I'm thinking I could just ride with you to Colorado Springs and then fly back home and someone will pick me up from the nearby airport. That way, we don't have to take two cars."

"Okay, that works for me. I have to admit I was surprised to see so many people come forth to make statements."

"We're wolves, a pack, a family. Humans won't understand. They'll probably figure it's because we're a small, friendly town. It's a lot more than that. Everyone knows everyone. We all help each other out. And we run into each other all the time while we're running errands. Nobody's making false statements. We all have known each other for decades, so it's not like we would make a mistake about having seen one another. When we see each other on the street, we wave. We're also wary, so we watch whoever's wandering around town. It's not like with humans who don't notice the people all around them. Plus, we live so long that we've known one another forever."

"And the woman who said she'd swear she was having hot sex with you when the suspect had been arrested?"

Sarandon smiled. "Meghan MacTire is dating Peter. She was just joking, trying to get a reaction out of Peter."

"Well, he was keeping his cool, but I saw the look he gave her. Besides the fact that having hot sex with her would mean you were mated wolves."

"Yeah, if we'd been together, Peter would have had

me strung up, no worry about identity theft charges. And as sheriff, he'd say he was completely justified."

She chuckled. The Stepford Wolves did have that darker, wolfish side to them. They were totally territorial.

"Did you still want to sleep with me? You said you needed to stick to me." He looked hopeful.

Smiling, she shook her head. "I'd say you were in the clear."

"Okay, well, I don't have a guest room. Just an office and a junk room and an empty room."

"Empty room?"

"I'm trying to keep it from becoming a second junk room."

She smiled. "I can sleep on the couch."

"Wouldn't think of it. You can have the bed. Let me just change the sheets."

"It's really not necessary."

"Changing the sheets?"

She laughed. He was already stripping the bed, so she helped him. "You're all right with sleeping on the couch?"

"If you insist."

"Well, you can sleep anywhere, as long as it's not with me. Cohabitation between a suspect and the fugitive recovery agent is strictly forbidden."

"I proved beyond a doubt that I'm not this guy."

"Right. Now you have to prove it to the police and get your name cleared."

"And I suppose you want me to catch this guy for you too."

"That's my job. Though my mother put up a reward for tips leading to his arrest." The thought did occur to Jenna that if there was an added incentive, Sarandon might help her with the case. Not as in just clearing his own name or looking for the guy on his own, but actually going with her to track down the guy. Then again, she thought he had the best lead—his dad had possibly fathered a child that was his half brother, and he might want to help her locate him for that reason alone. She really wanted to work with Sarandon. Still, he hadn't had any of the kind of training she'd had. Yet he did say he was going to take his brother's place as deputy sheriff while he and his mate had their vacation. She was certain Sarandon must have had training to be able to substitute for CJ.

She helped pull the fitted sheet onto the mattress.

"I don't need any money to give me an incentive to take this guy down."

"I don't blame you. I wouldn't either. You said Ritka was having an affair with your dad. If she had a baby by him, no one knew, correct?"

"She had a couple of female friends, but they're dead." Sarandon changed out the pillowcases, then hauled the used bedding out of the room.

She followed him. "I keep a diary."

He looked back at her, his face brightening a bit.

"Do you journal?" Jenna asked. She only said it because she wondered if Ritka had mentioned having the baby in a diary. Maybe not, if she wanted to keep the shame of having a baby secret when she and Sheridan hadn't agreed to reveal they were mated.

"Uh, no, I don't journal. If Ritka and my dad had a child, they would have been mated."

"Right, but if he was trying to hide the fact that they had mated, she'd have to keep the child secret."

"Gotcha. Ritka had a diary."

"Oh? Where is it?"

"It was for the period of time that Sheridan had been involved in several illegal actions. That's how we verified the truth about him. It didn't go beyond three years. If she had more diaries, Darien didn't mention them."

"If Sheridan made her get rid of the baby, he might have made sure she didn't keep any record of it."

"Possibly. I'll call Darien and see if he knows of any other diaries. They wouldn't have been relevant to the murder case, so no one probably read them."

Sarandon could believe anything where his father was concerned. In the beginning, he'd fought against believing his father had done anything wrong. Now, nothing surprised him. He started the load of wash. Then he pulled out his phone and called his pack leader. "Hey, Darien, did you find any other diaries of Ritka's?"

"We have them in storage for evidence, though we never used the others, just the one that convicted Sheridan of his crimes. What are you looking for?"

"A half brother."

Darien didn't say anything for a moment. "Hell."

"Yeah, my thoughts too. What would be the likelihood that a near-clone likeness of me would steal my ID and not be related?"

"Slim, I would think. We have a special code to get into the warehouse. CJ can get you in, and he'll know where Ritka's things are stored."

"Thanks, Darien. I'll call him now."

"There were a lot of diaries and journals. We live a

long time. She didn't have any relatives to pass them on to, so we just kept them in storage."

"Good."

"If you do really have a half brother, he might have been born at any time."

Sarandon knew that. Which was why he wanted to get started on it tonight. He knew he wouldn't be able to sleep, thinking that a half brother may be the one who'd stolen his identity. If he had, then what? The guy must have been given to another pack to raise. He might have only recently learned who his father and mother were.

"Did Ritka have any siblings? Or other relations living with another pack that we know of?"

"None that I know of who are living. Which is why we couldn't give her property to anyone. She had a twin sister, but she died years ago, according to Ritka."

"Do we know if her sister was mated?"

"No, we don't. She didn't stay with our pack, so she could have mated someone and have a different last name than Ritka. Jackson is common enough that looking for an Evie Jackson who mated and changed her name won't be easy."

"You don't know when she was supposed to have died?"

"No, but it was years ago. Dad was running the pack back then."

"Okay, maybe I can find in a diary whether she had a son by my dad. Maybe she wrote who she gave the baby to."

Darien sighed. "All right. Talk to you later."

"Thanks, Darien." Sarandon called CJ next. "Hey, I

need you to help me locate Ritka's diaries. Darien said they're stored at the evidence warehouse."

"For?"

"I'm trying to find out if Dad had a son by Ritka and she recorded it."

"Ah, hell. All right. I'll meet you over there."

"Thanks, Brother." Sarandon hated making CJ help, but this was too important not to look into. He figured finding the information quickly would be too much to hope for. He envisioned staying up all night and reading through diary after diary. He just hoped Ritka's handwriting was legible.

"We're going to a warehouse to look at years of diaries, I take it," Jenna said, grabbing her purse.

"You don't have to go with me."

"Are you kidding? If this is a lead to my suspect, I definitely have to."

He hadn't wanted her to do this for him, but he realized from her words that she wasn't. She still had a job to do. He swore he was such a sap sometimes when he thought a she-wolf he was interested in might be interested in him.

"Hopefully, we'll find it right away," she said, following him out to the car. When they drove off, she added, "We still need to leave first thing tomorrow for Colorado Springs so we can get your name cleared. That means we need to get some sleep tonight."

"You don't need to go. Your priority is finding this guy. Not proving my innocence."

She smiled a little at him.

He wasn't sure how to take her smile, but he suspected it had something to do with how growly he was feeling.

"You'll need me to back you up if you get arrested. I can

arrange for help for you right away, if that happens. You might not get to make a call immediately. Besides, if we learn a name and where he might be located from a diary, he could be my suspect. I need all the leads I can get."

"What if there's nothing in Ritka's diary to say she had a son? This is all pure speculation."

"I'm sure someone from your pack could keep looking while we're gone."

Sarandon was sure he could solicit someone's help to do that, but he really wanted to learn the truth before they left in the morning.

When he reached the warehouse, no one was there.

"CJ's on his way." Sarandon parked, wishing CJ had already opened up the place. If the building hadn't had a special secure lock, Sarandon would have used his standard *lupus garou* lockpick on it. He fought pacing back and forth in front of the building, not wanting Jenna to see how impatient he could be. As much as he wanted to pull out his cell phone and call his brother, he wouldn't.

"He'll be here," Jenna assured him.

Sarandon glanced at her.

"No telling what he might have been in the middle of when you called." Jenna folded her arms and smiled.

He hadn't considered that. Then he heard his brother's car engine. "That's CJ."

As if it would be anyone else.

CJ pulled up in his Land Rover and greeted them both. "Sorry it took me so long."

"No problem," Sarandon said, hoping he hadn't interrupted anything. "If you'll just let us in and show us where Ritka's stuff is stored, we'll get to work on this."

CJ unlocked the door, then turned on a light and led

them down a hallway. The evidence was either secured in lockers or, as in Ritka's case, in a caged area. "A table and some chairs are in there. All her stuff is in that cage."

They walked inside the eight-by-ten room and looked inside the secured area. Everything was in boxes. They saw several marked with her name, some of them listing the contents as diaries.

"Okay, this is it. Thanks, CJ. We'll call you when we need to lock up."

"It'll lock automatically. And no problem."

"On a guess, I'd say there are around a hundred diaries in here," Jenna said.

"I'll be back in a few minutes," CJ said.

"You don't need to stay." Sarandon hadn't expected him to help. Tomorrow, if they didn't find what they were looking for, maybe, but not tonight.

"Always the jokester." CJ walked back down the hallway and left the building. They soon heard his engine turn on, and he backed out of the parking area and drove off.

"So you're a jokester?" Jenna said, unloading the first box of diaries and setting them neatly on one end of the three-by-six-foot table.

Sarandon chuckled under his breath. "Hardly. CJ was making a joke."

She laughed. "Okay. I kind of wondered. You have a fun sense of humor, but I really couldn't see you as a jokester, and I'm usually good about profiling people."

"Like you thought I was guilty?"

"Well, you have to admit your face was on the ID and you did get caught—even if it wasn't you."

He set another box on the floor at the other end of the table to give them room to work. Instead of emptying his box and piling the diaries on the table like Jenna did, he pulled one diary out of the box, not wanting to crowd his space. She studied his work flow and smiled.

He began reading and groaned.

Jenna was already reading a diary and didn't look up from scanning the content, searching for anything about Ritka's association with Sheridan. "What?"

"Can you read her handwriting? I can see a case of major eyestrain coming on."

"Yeah, I can. You'll get used to it and begin to recognize words after a bit." She went back to reading, but they both stopped when they heard a car drive up.

"Brett's vehicle. Either Darien or CJ must have called him to see if he could help."

Then another vehicle pulled up. Jenna smiled.

"Jake's car." And another parked outside. "CJ's back," Sarandon said.

Then people started coming into the building. Not just Sarandon's brothers Brett and CJ and his cousin Jake, but at least three or four other pack members with each of them.

More cars pulled up.

Sarandon smiled. He loved his pack.

After a while, fifteen pack members had boxes spread out on the floor, and some were sitting at the table with Jenna and Sarandon. Others sat on the floor, going through every diary, page by page.

"Thanks, everyone. You don't know how much this means to me," Sarandon said, not believing CJ or Darien had notified so many in the pack to help him and Jenna out.

"We sort of do," Eric said, joining the group and bringing five members of his new pack with him.

Sarandon was surprised to see his older brother. "Hell, Eric. You had a long drive."

"Well, you'd sure as hell do the same for me. Besides, we were on the way here already. If Ritka had a son, he'd be my half brother too. If he'd been living with us, I would have whipped his ass into shape, and he would never have been in any trouble. Or created trouble for you."

Sarandon chuckled. He was sure that was true. Eric certainly had kept the family together and had been responsible for his three brothers when their dad had quit caring about them.

Eric made a pack member move so he could sit at the table. Even though he wasn't a member of this pack any more, he had always been a pack leader at heart, and he wasn't changing the way he did business when he returned here.

"Do you really think Dad had another kid?" Brett asked. "Usually, it's hard to keep much secret in a pack."

"Ha!" CJ said. "Look how many secrets our dad kept from us that we've only recently uncovered. So yeah, I'd say it was possible. Even likely."

"It's way too much of a coincidence that this guy steals your ID and looks so similar to you," Brett said.

Another car pulled up, and then another. That was Darien and Peter.

Sarandon looked up at them as they walked into the caged area.

"How's it going?" Darien asked.

Sarandon looked back at the diary he was trying to read through. It was giving him eyestrain and a major headache. "Still looking. No one's found any mention of Dad and Ritka yet. Or of Ritka being pregnant."

Before Darien could take a seat on the floor, another wolf at the table quickly gave up his chair. "Thanks, Mervin," Darien said.

Another pack member let Peter have his seat. As sheriff, Peter was well respected and everyone liked him.

"Any word from any law enforcement agencies about the sketches you sent to them?" Sarandon couldn't imagine writing notes in a diary every day when Ritka really had nothing to say—what she was going to cook, a few things about patients she'd taken care of as a nurse at the clinic, but nothing novel-worthy. And it was the same thing day in and day out. Sometimes he'd get a break when she skipped a day or more and didn't write anything.

"Not yet," Peter said.

Sam and Silva arrived, bringing sandwiches, sodas, tea, coffee, and water.

"How much do I owe you?" Sarandon asked, standing and pulling out his wallet.

"Nothing," Darien said. "It comes out of pack funds."

"Thanks," Sarandon said.

"If the pack hadn't paid for the food, we would have given it for free," Sam said.

"Now you tell me." Darien smiled and continued to read one of the diaries.

"I found something," Jake said. "She doesn't say who she was seeing, but she said she'd hooked up with a wolf and she was in love. Then several pages later, a couple of weeks, and she admits he's mated."

Sarandon gaped at Jake. "Don't tell me it was my dad and it occurred before my mother died."

Chapter 9

Jenna heard the anger and hurt in Sarandon's voice when he asked if Ritka had been fooling around with a mated wolf before they'd lost their mother. True, the mated wolf might not have been their father, but Jenna could see how upset he was just at the thought.

All the Silver men were waiting to hear the truth. So were others, while some continued to read as if they didn't want to look like they were sitting on the edge of their seats to hear the news.

Jenna hoped the wolf Ritka had been seeing wasn't Sheridan, for Sarandon's sake. She wished she wasn't sitting so far from him. She'd never expected pack members to fill chairs on either side of the table, and she'd wanted to have room to spread out the diaries she was going to read.

"The year before you were born," Jake said.

"If he wasn't already dead…" Sarandon growled.

"She might have been seeing someone else," Jake reminded him. "Not Sheridan."

Sarandon just grunted, and Jenna swore he looked like he wanted to slam the diary he'd been reading against the wall.

Everyone who had finished with a diary, including Jenna, began looking for the ones closer to the date Jake had been reading to learn who the mystery male wolf was.

Sarandon looked like he was still having a time

deciphering Ritka's handwriting. He was turning the pages so slowly, as if he were wading through molasses to get to the end of a page. She figured he couldn't set it aside or he might miss something. Or make someone else go through Ritka's boring commentary, just to ensure every page was read.

"She mentioned him in this one also, no name," Darien said, frowning. "I have the diary for the year after Jake's. That's the year you were"—most glanced up at Darien—"hell, you were born."

Jenna glanced at Sarandon. He was staring at Darien but only nodded and went back to reading the diary. Sarandon was still trying to finish his first diary. *Poor guy.* He must really be having trouble deciphering Ritka's handwriting.

Darien kept reading.

Jenna had found mostly entries about Ritka's nursing duties. Jake was still studiously reading the diary that told about how she had fallen for a mated wolf. He suddenly cleared his throat.

This time, everyone looked to see what he had to say.

"She learned she was pregnant."

Jenna felt sick to her stomach. No one flipped through any more pages. All were quietly waiting to learn more.

Jake took a deep breath. "Ritka said she never thought she'd get pregnant, but she'd only been with the man who was the love of her life, no one else. She wished he'd leave his mate, yet she knew he wouldn't. Not only because he was sheriff and had a position to uphold— which, hell, he should have thought of before he started screwing around with Ritka—but he said he loved his mate and Ritka was a mistake. She wanted to kill him.

She doesn't know if she's just pregnant with one baby or more. She's clearly upset. Devastated. Not sure what to do. She's thought of exposing him for the fraud he is. She's afraid he might kill her."

"They were together later, weren't they?" Jenna was confused.

"Yeah," Sarandon said. "She must have given up the baby to another pack and kept it secret from ours."

"She would have been showing." And Jenna thought if Sheridan had been close enough to her, he might even have heard the heartbeat.

Darien said, "In this diary, Ritka said she moved into her sister's pack and told Sheridan she couldn't stay with the Silver Town pack, not when he was going to have babies and wouldn't leave his mate. He was furious with her, and she was furious right back. She didn't tell him she was pregnant. She was afraid he'd kill the baby, even if she got someone else to take care of it. She knew he wouldn't want any 'damning' evidence of his adultery."

"Her sister was Evie, but does anyone know what pack she was with?" Sarandon asked. "Or her last name if she'd mated?"

"Maybe an earlier diary would have that information," Brett said. "I've got one that's about ten years before the one Darien has. I didn't think I'd find anything relevant in it, but you never know when one little bit of information might yield what we need to learn most."

There were several who agreed.

Sarandon kept eyeing the diaries Jake and Darien were reading.

CJ tossed the diary he'd been reading into a box. He looked pissed.

"It's two in the morning already," Darien said, raising a brow as he eyed Sarandon. "You and Jenna have a long drive ahead of you, and I don't want either of you falling asleep at the wheel."

She appreciated that Darien worried about them, but she was also amused he was treating her like she was a member of the pack.

"I'm good," Sarandon said. "Maybe someone could drive me back home tonight. Jenna can go to bed now and drive the first part of our trip tomorrow while I get some shut-eye."

She didn't blame him for wanting to learn all he could about this business with Ritka and his father. She was even angry with Sheridan for hurting his own sons, and the cousins too. In fact, it must have had an impact on the whole pack because of the position he'd held in Silver Town.

If they couldn't trust the sheriff to do what was right, who could they trust?

"I'm good," she said. As long as she got five hours of sleep, she could manage. So if she went to bed around three and they left around eight, she'd be fine. Besides, this was too interesting to give up right now. If they hadn't found any clues about Ritka and Sheridan's past, she would have gladly gone to bed.

Sarandon looked growly at her, but she didn't think he was upset with her. "Another hour," she said.

He shook his head and looked back at the same diary. Maybe he'd made it halfway through it. He might just be an incredibly slow reader. She suspected Ritka's penmanship had a lot to do with it.

Sarandon let out his breath in a huff and said, "Anyone else have anything more?"

"She says she moved in with Evie, and she was so angry Sheridan didn't give a damn that she was leaving. In fact, he seemed relieved. She wanted to hire a hit on him. She wonders if she should just hire one on your mom," Darien said, his words spoken with a darkness Jenna hadn't heard before.

CJ swore under his breath. "What if the 'hunting accident' that was the cause of our mother's death wasn't an accident after all?"

"Sheridan wanted the hunter strung up for accidentally killing her," Eric said. "So we know he had nothing to do with it."

Darien shook his head. "Hell, my father was the one who convinced Sheridan it was just a hunting accident."

"Here I had always felt sorry for Ritka because she had loved our dad—some years after we'd lost our mom, but he'd been too heartbroken to take a mate again." Sarandon looked down at the diary he was trying to get through. "If she did have Mom murdered because she wanted to get her out of the way and thought that was the only way Dad would consider mating her, then she deserved what she got. Karma's a bitch."

"Yeah," several muttered.

"We were eight when the hunter shot and killed Mom as a human," Brett said. "Does anyone have Ritka's diaries before that incident, during, and after? It was in the fall."

"I've got it," Sarandon said. "I'm just into June. I'll fast-forward."

"Wait," Jenna said. "If she had anything to do with it, why wait all that time before she hired a hunter to kill your mother?"

"He was leading her on," Eric said. "I've got the

diary for the year before. She says here over and over that Sheridan promises to make an honest woman of her." Though, with wolves, that was an impossibility. They didn't divorce or leave their mates. "And he was good to Mom whenever I saw him interact with her. So I believe he was having a fling on the side with Ritka because she was easy and he had no intention of leaving Mom, even though such behavior is unacceptable. Ritka might have been fantasizing he'd abandon Mom but knew he couldn't desert her. Certainly, he would have been drummed out of the pack, lost his job and his family, and been completely ostracized."

"And when Ritka thought the only way to take your mother's place was to hire a hit on her?" Jake asked. "It would have been too obvious if Ritka had paid him to get rid of you all too. This way, it appeared to be an accident. If it had looked like a hit, Uncle Sheridan would have known who had the most to gain from killing his mate and getting rid of his sons. No matter how he behaved, he still loved you."

Sarandon was still reading, not fast-forwarding like he said he would. "Hell."

Everyone looked over at him.

"She said she didn't want to do it, but if she was ever to get her kids back and raise them as his children, she'd have to take some drastic measures."

"Kids," Darien said, flipping through the pages of the diary. "Yeah, here it is. She learned at the end of the year that she was pregnant with twins, was living with her sister, and no matter how much she wanted to raise her son and daughter, Alex and Faye, she couldn't stand being apart from Sheridan."

"She returned then and left the kids with her sister?" Eric asked.

Darien gave a sad nod. "Yeah, at Christmastime. It says her sister pretended to be their mother so Sheridan wouldn't ever suspect they were his kids and want to kill them. Ritka hoped that in time, he'd be thrilled to know he had a boy and his first little girl."

How awful that must have been for both Ritka and the kids.

"Does it say anything about how she longed to see them in the years after that?" Jenna asked. "I don't see her mention them at all in the diaries I've read, and they were written after the shooting incident."

"She says she's moving back to Silver Town and leaving her sister to raise the twins. Evie never had children, and Ritka said that was the only way Evie and her husband agreed to take the kids in. No interference from Ritka. They didn't want Sheridan showing up on their doorstep and killing them and the kids because he didn't want any evidence of his adultery. Ritka agreed—for the same reason, but also because she couldn't give up Sheridan and thought he'd change his mind about them when the time was right," Darien said.

"Never. Dad was as hardheaded as they come," Eric said.

"Okay, well, I understand why she might not see her kids, but I'm surprised she really didn't seem to care about them. Even if I had to do something awful to protect my kids, I would have been writing how I felt about it. She already wrote about them, so it's not like she was afraid he'd find her diaries and read them, or she wouldn't have written what she did and kept them," Jenna said.

"The diaries were hidden under a floorboard in her bedroom closet," Peter said. "Sheridan never found them."

"Good thing for her," Darien said. "I just wish we'd found these sooner. We've got to learn where her kids are now and offer for them to join us or at least get to know us."

Sarandon's jaw gaped. Eric and CJ looked just as shocked.

Brett was the first of the brothers to speak up. "There's just one little problem. If this boy is the one who stole Sarandon's ID and then framed him for the identity theft—"

"He's dead meat," Eric said. "No welcoming him into the family, damn it. And this 'boy' is a year older than us."

Several grumbled in agreement. Darien said, "We need to learn what this is all about before we hang him for what he's done, if he's done this."

"You have any doubts?" CJ asked, sounding just as angry.

"No," Sarandon said, opening the diary to the back. He pulled out a photo and passed it down the table.

Jake snorted. "That's the guy. Dead ringer for Sarandon when he was that age."

When the photo reached Jenna, she was looking at a little boy of about two, his mouth downturned, sulky, and a little girl, also dark haired, with a happy-go-lucky smile. Jenna hadn't seen a picture of Sarandon at that age and now she wanted to. She turned it over to find it said *Alex & Faye, 2 years old*.

Silva began going through all the diaries no one had touched yet, and Jenna suspected she was looking for older photos. Some had gone back to reading the diaries.

Sarandon said, "If no one has found anything else important to share, we're going to bed."

Everyone looked at Sarandon, most wearing surprised expressions, a couple of the men smiling. Silva winked at Jenna, as if *going to bed* meant she and Sarandon were sleeping in the same bed.

Jenna wanted to set everyone straight, but she figured they'd know before long she wasn't coming back. "Do you want to take our diaries to your place for a little late-night reading?" Jenna was too OCD not to finish hers.

"Yeah, but only if you finish mine too," Sarandon said.

She chuckled. "Sure, I can do that." And much quicker than he was getting through it. She felt really bad about the business with his father. She could tell everyone was upset about it. At least, everyone sympathized, and they didn't see the Silver brothers in a bad light for the sins of their father.

Everyone said good night to Jenna and Sarandon, and Darien added, "I'll let you know if we learn anything further. I'll text it to you. You need to get your sleep."

"Yeah, thanks, Darien."

"Good luck with catching your suspect," Darien said to Jenna, "but let us know first if you do."

"All right." Only because their half brother could very well be the man impersonating Sarandon. Was he just like Sheridan? A troublemaker?

What about the other man who had been with Alex in town? Jenna suspected he was in the same pack as Alex and Faye, and that's why they were together at the tavern. Alex had to have learned his father's people ran this pack. Maybe that his "mother" was his aunt instead, and his birth mother was dead.

She could understand why Darien wanted to reach out to him. And why Sarandon and his brothers wanted to strangle him. Would Darien have felt differently if the suspect had targeted him instead? She suspected not, and that's what made him a fair pack leader.

"You think it's him, don't you?" she asked Sarandon on the way home.

"It's him. When I was looking at that photo of him, it was like staring back at myself. I was a handsome devil back then."

She smiled. "You still are."

He glanced at her and smiled.

She was glad she could cheer him, after all they'd learned about the family secrets tonight. "You don't really want to kill him, do you?"

"Yeah, I do, in a manner of speaking. Look at the mess he's gotten me into. And the mess he'll be in when we catch up to him. I keep thinking of how we had a pack to help raise us after our mother died, even if our father hadn't been there for us. Alex did too. His aunt and uncle raised him. So why come after anyone in the pack? Revenge? Why? After all these years?"

"He must have only recently learned of all this. Wolves like to belong to a pack. Really fit in. Maybe others in the pack knew the situation. Think of it. His aunt wasn't pregnant, but his mother was. She's suddenly not pregnant, and two babies are being raised by the aunt and uncle, so you know that the rest of the pack had to have figured it out."

"True."

"And even though your pack didn't treat you poorly because of your father's actions, who knows how the kids would have been treated in that pack? Maybe the adults were okay, but we believe in permanent matings. So how do you tell your kids that those kids are the same as their own?"

"Are you trying to convince me the guy deserves a second chance?"

"No. Just that he deserves to be heard. If he's as corrupt as your dad was and there's no hope for rehabilitation, that's another story. What about the hunter?"

"He's got to be long dead, unless he was a wolf," Sarandon said. "Darien told us his father had it investigated and said he was human. It could be that Ritka intended to hire someone and it never happened. And the man who shot my mother coincidentally did so around the time Ritka was spouting off in her diary."

"Or she did hire him."

"If so, he's dead, with as many years as we live. So there's no one to take down, or I would have been the first on his doorstep to do so. Though Eric would have wanted the honor. I can just imagine us capturing Alex, bringing him home, and Lelandi questioning him with all her psychological reasoning. Maybe she can reach him. Maybe we can speak on his behalf and get a sentence reduced, make him pay back the people he stole from, do community work. And try to see if he'll fit in."

"And his sister?"

"His sister too, but she might be mated in another pack and not be interested in getting to know us. I wouldn't be surprised, given the circumstances."

"I agree."

Sarandon pulled into his driveway and then into the garage. "Sorry about the going-to-bed business. I was just thinking it, but after I said it, we got so many smiles that I figured I should have worded it differently."

"I assumed trying to explain what you meant would just cause further speculation." When they walked into the house, Jenna said, "Listen, Sarandon, why don't you just sleep on your bed. I'll be fine on the couch."

"You mean I changed the sheets for nothing?"

"They probably could have used a wash." Though they had smelled of sexy male wolf and springtime fresh.

"I changed them yesterday."

"Oh. They did smell good."

"Me, or the sheets?"

She smiled, not about to tell him the truth.

"You're not feeling sorry for me, are you?"

"No."

"Yeah you are. I'd rather you were still eager to chain me up and take me as your captive."

She laughed. She was glad he could joke about it, because she was feeling bad about him. "You would, would you?"

"Yeah." He winked at her and headed to the laundry room.

She followed him in there, still holding onto the two diaries she would finish reading before she fell asleep tonight.

He removed the wet clothes and put them in the dryer. "You probably never accidentally leave your clothes in the washer, do you?"

"And they sour? Yeah, on occasion, get to doing

other things and forget about them. Then have to rewash them."

"I'm glad I'm not the only one. My brothers swear that never happens to them." Once he was done, he got sheets and a comforter out for the couch.

She helped him make his bed. "Are you sure you're all right, curled up on the couch?"

"Are you offering the bed?"

"Yes, and I can sleep here."

"Only if you were to join me in there." He began stripping off his clothes. "Holler if you find anything in either of the diaries, will you? I'll drive first thing in the morning so you can get some more sleep."

"I will. Night, Sarandon." She headed for the bedroom before she did anything foolish like kissing him good night or dragging him to the bed with her. She entered the room and shut the door, then set the diaries on top of the oak dresser.

She quickly stripped off her clothes and took a shower in the master bath. When she left the shower stall, she realized her overnight bag was still sitting in the living room. She could holler for Sarandon to bring her bag, sure he wouldn't be asleep yet. Or she could dress in her street clothes again. Or she could slip down the hall and across the living room in a towel and grab her bag, hopefully not disturbing him, and return before he ever knew she'd been there.

She was a wolf. Slipping into the room would be easy to do, and he'd never know. Towel secured around her body, she opened the door and gave a startled cry to see the hot wolf in his boxer briefs, her bags in hand, his free hand raised to knock on the door.

He smiled at her in such a wolfish way that she wanted to laugh. "Thank you."

"No problem." He handed her the bags and waited.

She took the bags and quickly leaned over and gave him a sweet kiss on the cheek. "Night."

"Night," he said on a heavy sigh, then closed the door for her. She hung the towel in the bathroom and dressed in a long T-shirt.

Grabbing the diaries off the dresser, she took them to the bed and slipped under the covers and continued reading the rest of the diary she had started. After skimming the rest of the diary and finding nothing, she started reading Sarandon's.

Two pages into it from where he'd left off, she read:

> *I could kill my sister! All these years, she's said she's been taking care of my son and daughter, but a friend in the pack told me the truth. Alex was given up to another childless couple because Evie only wanted to raise my daughter, even though she knew I wanted them to be raised together. What must he have felt like, raised for a while with his sister and what he thought were his parents and then given to another family at my sister's whim?*
>
> *I want to bring them here. I do! I don't chance bringing the kids home. Sheridan said he wants no more kids and he's happy with our arrangement. What can I do but go along with it because I hopelessly love him. He keeps saying when the time is right, we'll announce we're mating, but not before then.*

Jenna read the rest of the diary, but Ritka didn't say another thing about the kids. Only about Sheridan coming to see her when he could and hoping that no one would get suspicious.

Jenna wondered how that had worked out for them. She couldn't imagine keeping something like that secret from a pack. Wolves were too curious by nature. Yet from everyone's shock from learning about this, at least among those who were there tonight, she assumed Sheridan and Ritka had pulled it off.

She bookmarked the section about the kids with a piece of paper from her notepad. Should she tell Sarandon now or wait until morning? He said he wanted to know if she learned anything tonight. How would she feel if he didn't tell her what she'd wanted to learn right away?

She sighed and crawled out of bed, grabbing the diary and heading for the door. She hoped the news was important enough for her to wake Sarandon. For her, it would have been. Maybe he wasn't sound asleep yet.

When she opened the bedroom door, he called out from the living room. "Did you learn anything important?"

Glad she had decided to tell him, she joined him in the living room where he'd turned on one of the lamps and patted the couch for her to sit down and tell him the news.

Since the couch was made up for bed, she felt she was joining him in bed. Why did that appeal?

He actually wrapped his arm around her shoulders and said, "So what's the news?"

She read him the passage.

"Okay, so it sounds like Alex could have some family issues. If he ever learned that not only did his 'mother and father' give him up to another couple, but they were really his aunt and uncle, and his real mother had given him up. Not because she wanted to, but because she wanted to stay with Sheridan more than she wanted to be with her kids."

"That's all I found in the diary. Nothing in the one I was reading. I'm getting some water. Want some?"

"Thanks, no. You'd better get to sleep too. Darien's orders."

She smiled. "Good thing I don't belong to the pack."

When she didn't get up right away, he said, "You heard my sob story. Do you have one? I feel I've bared my soul to the world tonight, confiding in you."

"And you need me to reciprocate, or you'll feel you've revealed too much about yourself?"

"Something like that. It can cause terrible anxiety, sleeplessness…"

"I hate to mention it, but other than my father being shot and surviving it, I don't really have any dark secrets to share."

"Only some you don't want to share."

"True." She didn't want to discuss her dead mate and babies any further. "Darien's orders." She patted Sarandon on the chest. "Get to sleep. You're driving first thing." Then she left the couch to get some water.

"You don't think you'll come up with some ideas in the middle of the night and need to bounce them off me, do you?"

"Why do you ask? Do you think it would be better if you joined me in your bed?"

"You wouldn't have to go so far to tell them to me."

She laughed and got a glass of water. "Night, Sarandon. We have a long drive ahead of us. I hope everything goes fine and your name is cleared and you don't land yourself in jail."

Then she went to bed, but she kept worrying that the Colorado Springs police would arrest Sarandon because he looked so similar to the other man. She just hoped the witness statements and his fingerprints would be sufficient to clear him, and he wasn't incarcerated for any length of time.

Chapter 10

DESPITE THE LATE HOUR WHEN THEY FINALLY WENT TO SLEEP, Sarandon hated to admit he couldn't have slept any later this morning if he'd wanted to. He wanted to get on the road as early as possible so they could prove to the police that they were looking for the wrong man.

Wearing only his boxer briefs while cooking breakfast, he realized he should have brought out a set of clean clothes before Jenna had gone to sleep last night. He'd have to dress after he woke her this morning.

He made scrambled eggs, sausage, hash browns, and coffee, hoping the delightful aroma of the food cooking would wake Jenna enough to rouse her, and she could eat and then go back to sleep in the car for a while as he took the wheel for the first few hours. What he hadn't expected was for a wolf to bound through the wolf door—a beautiful gray wolf with white facial hairs and a gray and black mask that gave her an elegant look. He smelled her scent—a mixture of peach, fresh air, her own feminine allure, and the piney woods—and smiled, never having heard her leave this morning. He must have been sleeping more soundly than he'd imagined.

He shook his head. "Here I thought I'd wake you while cooking breakfast. I never heard you sneak out at all."

She wagged her tail as if delighted she'd slipped out

without waking him, woofed, and ran back into the bedroom. A few minutes later, she came out wearing black cargo pants, a different black fugitive recovery agent T-shirt, and black hiking boots. She looked like she was ready to conduct official business, and he wondered then what she'd look like in something soft and feminine and huggable. Deep down, he had to admit that what she wore didn't really matter. All he had to do was look into her vivid blue eyes, and he was lost.

"You should have woken me, and I would have gone for a run with you." He started dishing up the eggs, hoping she was fine with what he'd fixed.

"I *tried* to wake you. I licked your face even. You just smiled." She sipped from a coffee mug.

He looked up from serving up the sausage links. "Really?" He couldn't believe she'd been teasing him with her wolf's tongue and he'd missed it completely. That he hadn't left the couch, stripped out of his boxer briefs, shifted, and licked her right back, telling her in no uncertain terms this was only the beginning between them.

"Yeah. I waited, figuring you would get up, but you must have just been dreaming about being with a wolf and getting wolf kisses." She smiled. "I tugged at the comforter you had pulled over your waist. Licked your bare chest even."

He laughed. "Hell, now that you mention it, I was dreaming about being with you as a wolf. And you were stealing my covers. No wonder. I just incorporated your wolf kisses into my dream. You should have tried harder."

She carried the plates to the table. "You were really tired and needed the extra sleep. Are you going to make it all right with driving first? Or do you want me to drive?"

"I'll be fine. I never fall asleep at the wheel. We can always switch off later if I get sleepy and vice versa."

"Wow, great breakfast. I usually just grab some cereal."

"We've got a long drive ahead of us. I figured we needed some real food before we hit the road."

"Well, this is great."

He was glad she liked it. Anything to make the point that he was a good catch.

After they ate and packed the car, they headed out. She curled up in the back with a pillow and a patchwork quilt. "I don't really know if I can sleep."

"Just try, and if you can't, I'll stop for gas in an hour and you can ride up front with me."

"Or drive."

For an hour, they drove down the interstate, and Sarandon swore a black SUV was following him. Though he'd known other drivers to follow him, slowing down when he did and speeding up in the same way, as if they were mesmerized by the car in front of them. He wanted to stop and get gas so they could fill up, but also to see if the black SUV drove on past or pulled into the station too.

When he pulled up next to one of the pumps, Jenna was sound asleep. Glad she was getting some sleep, Sarandon pumped the gas and watched the SUV continue on down the road. He breathed a sigh of relief. He couldn't catch sight of its license plate so he could have CJ run a check on it—in case he wasn't being paranoid.

Then he went inside to use the restroom. When he returned to the car, Jenna was gone. He felt a bit of a panic, then told himself she must have run inside too.

He went back inside to get them cups of coffee, and she came out of the restroom and smiled at him. "Thanks for letting me sleep. I really didn't think I'd be able to."

"I'm glad you got some. Hey, if you're not busy and you don't mind the long drive from your place to Eric's pack's location, he and his wife are having a Spring Fling in about three weeks, and I'd like to take you to it."

"If I don't have a case."

He paid for the coffee. "That's a yes?"

"A maybe. There are a lot of variables," she said, walking back out to her car with Sarandon. "Like whether or not you're still free."

"I'm not dating anyone."

She laughed and took the wheel this time. "You haven't been jailed."

"Not happening."

"And if you're not taking a bunch of people on one of your excursions."

"Not that weekend."

"And I'm not chasing down a fugitive."

"Okay, so it's a definite yes, if you're free."

She smiled and pulled out of the gas station. "I never expected that the man I was trying to apprehend would want to date me."

"Are you kidding? You're the most exciting she-wolf I've ever met."

"I bet you didn't think that when I was ordering you to put down your weapon and get on the ground."

"Oh yeah. That was just the beginning."

"I have to say, when I realized you were a wolf, the situation got a whole lot more complicated."

He laughed. That's what made her so fascinating. "You're wearing your gun, badge, and bulletproof vest on you, aren't you?" Sarandon still wasn't sure about the black SUV. Then again, there were tons of black SUVs, so he could have spied different ones at different times and thought they were the same one.

"I'm not wearing the vest right now. I only wore it to apprehend you in case you were armed and dangerous. Why do you ask?"

"I'm not positive, but a black SUV that I saw shortly after we drove out of Silver Town could be following us. I could be mistaken. There are a lot of them on the road."

"Okay." She glanced back over her shoulder. "I don't see any cars."

"He passed us and kept going when we stopped at the service station."

"So he can't be following us."

"Maybe not."

"You sound like your gut instinct is telling you he's someone to be concerned about. I always listen to my gut instinct. Why don't we pull off and wait for him to see if he returns? If he suspects you know he's following us, he might have driven on past, then pulled in up ahead to wait for us. If he doesn't return, we'll continue on our way, and we'll both keep an eye out for him."

"Sounds like a good idea. If we don't see him, it will prove I'm just being paranoid."

"If you're right, we'll have to do something about it."

"Hell yeah. What about parking right up there?" Sarandon motioned to a church.

Jenna pulled off onto a side road and parked in the church's parking lot. A few cars were there, along with a sign announcing that the preschool graduation date was coming up. What appeared to be three- and four-year-old boys and girls were outside playing on a playground, a couple of women watching them. The other cars would give them some cover as they watched the main road for any sign of the black SUV returning.

The problem was they saw several: one with a couple and two kids, and then another, a woman driving it. Then what looked like a teen driving a third black SUV.

"Maybe we should head out. I must have been mistaken. There are tons of them on the road. He couldn't wait this long to follow us, or he'd risk losing us completely," Sarandon said.

"You know, he probably figured where you're headed by the route you're taking. If it's Alex or his friend following us."

"True. So he could just meet up with us at some other juncture. Why would he be following us?"

"If someone is keeping an eye on you, I'd lay odds it's either Alex or his friend."

"I can't imagine anyone else tailing me."

"Unless it's an undercover cop?" Jenna asked.

"He would have pulled us over, checked my ID, and learned who I was, don't you think?"

She sighed. "Yeah, I agree. Why in the world would the identity thief follow you? Wait, what about *that* black SUV headed toward us? It's going way faster than the speed limit in this little town."

"Yeah, where's a cop when you need one?"

The vehicle approached them and drove on past, never seeing Jenna's car sitting in the church parking lot. Jenna quickly wrote down the license plate, then called it in to someone. "Yeah, we think he's tailing us." She glanced at Sarandon. "Uh, yeah, I'm bringing him in. I told you already, he's not our suspect. The real suspect is still on the run. Sarandon's just coming in to clear his name... Uh, let me ask him." She paused. "Thanks, Mom." Jenna ended the call and said, "Okay, my mom wants us to go to their house and have dinner after we clear everything up for you."

"What if I end up in jail?"

"She'll get you a lawyer to make up for sending me after you, armed to the teeth. Um, she said she got a call from Lelandi."

"What?" He couldn't imagine why Lelandi would call Jenna's mom. Maybe to tell her in no uncertain terms that he was innocent, and if they had to prove it, the whole pack would show up.

"Yeah, surprised me too. Lelandi just wanted to make sure Mom knew your wolf pack was trying to run down the suspect as they spoke. And that—of course—you're innocent. So my mom wants to make it up to you. At *least* I didn't tase you."

"You didn't because you thought I was too hot and sexy."

She chuckled and pulled out of the church's parking lot. "Good to know you're not modest. I was just in shock to learn you were a wolf and knew the trouble that could mean for me."

"I was shocked to learn you were one too. And intrigued. Not often does a beautiful she-wolf point her rifle at me, commanding me to give up my weapons and allow her to take me prisoner."

"I have to admit you were funny. I almost felt sorry for you when you thought I might be your brothers' idea of a joke. I did consider that was just playacting on your part though."

"I'm not much of an actor. What you see is what you get."

"Same with me. Mom said she wants to put you up for the night at their home before you fly back to Silver Town."

"I still have two weeks before my next outdoor tour takes place. In the meantime, I have every intention of helping you take down this guy."

"Good. So, Mom and Dad want you to stay with them," she repeated.

Sarandon swore the tone of Jenna's voice indicated she wanted him to decline and stay with her. At least that's how he was taking it. He didn't think she was hoping he'd stay with them in an attempt to make a good impression. "They're probably worried you'll offer to put me up at your house and have to fight off the big, bad wolf."

She smiled broadly. "They're probably worried I'm not being nice enough to you after coming for you like I did."

"Well, you'll have to let them know that with great regret, I'll have to decline their generous offer so you can make it up to me."

"Oh, I will, will I?"

"Yeah, I insist."

She got back on her phone. "We're coming over for

dinner, as long as Sarandon isn't jailed before then. About the bed arrangements, he wants to stay at my place. I'm afraid he thinks staying at your place might mean you're thinking he might be my forever mate and Dad might bring out his shotgun to ensure this goes the way it should."

Sarandon raised his brows.

Jenna cast a self-satisfied smile at him. "I'll tell him. I'll call when we get to the police station, and then after we get this cleared up, I hope, I'll let you know we're on our way over to your place for dinner. Did you get anything back on the SUV's license?" She paused. "It's registered to a Burt Dreyfus? Okay, thanks. Talk to you later, Mom. Bye." When she hung up, she asked Sarandon, "Do you know a Burt Dreyfus?"

"No. Guess it was just a random black SUV. Let me touch base with CJ, just in case." When Sarandon reached his brother on the Bluetooth, he said, "We're still headed for Colorado Springs, but someone appeared to be following us. Jenna gave her mom the license tag number, and she ran the plates. The owner of the black SUV is Burt Dreyfus. Do you recognize the name?"

"Hell, that's Stanton Wernicke's regular cameraman's name."

It was way too much of a coincidence that the guy was working around Silver Town and was now driving in the same area where Sarandon was traveling. "I didn't know his last name and hadn't remembered his first until you mentioned it. I saw him in the tavern while Eric and I were having a meal. Stanton was giving him grief for leaving and not getting permission to take off for an emergency. Stanton had to hire another cameraman to substitute for him."

"I'll check with Stanton to see how long Burt has worked for him and exactly when he missed work. I'll also learn where he is now and get back with you."

"Good deal." When Sarandon ended the call with CJ, he explained to Jenna that Stanton was the guy in charge of the ghost-hunter crew who had the TV show.

"So this Burt Dreyfus is a wolf too."

"Yeah."

"Okay, so Lelandi and Sam and Silva didn't know the two guys who were in the tavern. That means it can't be the same guy as they saw."

"The Wernicke brothers aren't part of our pack. Nor is their cameraman, or whoever else works for them. I've only seen Burt twice. At the tavern and with the Wernicke brothers one other time. He wasn't wearing a beard either time I saw him. I couldn't say for sure if he was the man in the tavern with the guy who is probably Alex. Lelandi, Sam, and Silva may not have ever run into him before. Let me call CJ back and mention he might want to check with them, just in case he doesn't think of it." Sarandon knew his brother was good at his job, but he didn't want this to slip through the cracks. "Hey, CJ, one other thing. If Stanton can get a picture of the cameraman and send it to you, you could check with Lelandi, Silva, and Sam—"

"Already on it," CJ said. "Thanks for reminding me. I just thought of it."

"Okay, I'll let you do your job then. Talk soon." Sarandon thought back to the conversation Jenna had with her mother, while watching for any sign of the black SUV. "What did your mom say about *your* version of why I don't want to stay with them?" He couldn't believe what she'd told them and hoped they knew she was just joking.

"Dad mentioned something about getting his shotgun ready. You think *I'm* bad."

Sarandon laughed. "I guess that means we ought to get to work on the next part of this relationship."

"We have a relationship?"

Hell yeah, they did. "Yeah. I'm going to help you find the suspect and save your family a fortune."

"I allowed you to make your case—"

"After I took you down." He wasn't letting her forget that part.

"Well, there is that. And I didn't take you into custody like I planned. Instead, I was cohabitating with the suspect."

"Exactly. So is it a deal?"

She raised a brow.

"Courting. You know you want to." Sarandon smiled. He wasn't taking no for an answer. Not when they had such great chemistry.

Chapter 11

WHEN THEY FINALLY ARRIVED AT THE COLORADO SPRINGS Police Department, Sarandon was a little worried he would be arrested on the spot. He was glad Jenna was there to vouch for him. When she took his hand, he looked at her in surprise, thinking she would want to be hands-off.

"I'll turn all wolf if they pull out handcuffs."

He loved how she could make a serious situation feel less ominous. He had a stack of witness statements in a large manila envelope—the originals, while the copies were all safely at the sheriff's office in Silver Town. Before they entered the station, she let go of his hand.

He assumed it was because she wanted to look professional.

When they entered the building, Sarandon identified himself to a police officer and gave him the details of the case of mistaken identity. Likewise, Jenna explained her business there—to verify Sarandon's claims and to state she still needed to apprehend the real suspect.

A dark-haired, black-eyed Officer Calvin Meissner had smiled at Jenna and greeted her in a way that said he admired her and was interested in her. Sarandon was glad he knew her and was on friendly terms. Though Sarandon's wolfish need to protect a single she-wolf from a human male came to bear. He fought the urge to growl when the officer drew too close to her or showed more than a professional interest in her.

"Come this way with me to get your fingerprinting done," the officer said and took them to the Police Operations Center.

After the fingerprinting was done, the officer had them return with him and sit in an interview room. In the interim, he made some calls to verify the witness statements. When that was done, the officer began to really read the witness statements. Looking up from the fifth one, he said to Sarandon, "You seem to be a really popular guy. I'm surprised you could get so many of these together on such short notice. Usually, getting this many people's statements together would take weeks or more. In a day would be impossible."

"You should have seen it," Jenna said, confirming she was there to witness the whole thing. "The townspeople are a tight-knit community. Everyone knows everyone, and they were eager to ensure they gave the sheriff the statements Sarandon needed before he came here to clear his name. They didn't want Sarandon to take the rap for what someone else did."

Officer Meissner agreed. "If the fingerprints don't match, I'm sure he can be cleared." He studied the witness statements further. There were over thirty more to go through. And he considered the mug shot of the suspect against Sarandon, whose beard was just starting to appear and was red. "I still say he looks awfully similar."

"Sarandon's beard is red, and it looks a lot different from this man's," Jenna said, pointing to the mug shot. "They do look similar otherwise. Sarandon and his brothers think maybe there's a half brother out there who has done the crime. They didn't know one might exist, but after conducting an investigation into the matter, they discovered their father had a son by another woman. Both the father and the woman are dead. We're trying to locate the son now."

"We?"

"It's my family's business. We have a lot of money riding on this."

Meissner nodded. "Which is why I know you're being honest with me about this guy, or you'd just turn him in to get your family off the hook."

"True," Jenna said.

"How long will it take to get the fingerprints back?" Sarandon asked, wishing it was done pronto.

"Up to forty-eight hours. We'll need you to make a statement under oath in the meantime. We won't be booking you. There's enough verifiable evidence here— the word of the local sheriff and deputies that you were in town for most of the time that the real suspect was here, wearing his GPS ankle monitor, and the statements from the people who were on your tour—to help to prove you're the victim of identity theft."

"Thanks. I appreciate it."

"In the meantime, I need to know where you'll be staying."

Which sounded a hell of a lot like Sarandon was still in the hot seat.

"He's staying with me while we wait to hear about the fingerprint results," Jenna said.

Meissner's eyes widened a smidgeon.

She shrugged. "It's the least I can do after hunting him down and threatening to tase him."

Meissner laughed. "Yeah, I wouldn't ever want to get on your bad side. Okay, folks. You're free to go, Mr. Silver. Just check in with us in a couple of days." He got both their cell phone numbers. "If we hear sooner, I'll give you a call."

"Thanks," Sarandon said. They all stood, and he shook the officer's hand.

"If I didn't love it here so much, your town sounds like a good place to raise a family," the officer said.

"Silver Town is special," Sarandon said. "Born and raised there. No complaints."

"Sounds like it." The officer said goodbye, and with a sigh of relief, Sarandon and Jenna returned to her car.

"I was afraid they would have to book you. I'm so relieved." Jenna took hold of Sarandon's hand and smiled up at him.

"Now that I'm almost not a wanted criminal, are you ready to date me?"

She chuckled. "I think going to my parents' for dinner means we're definitely headed that way. I have never brought a suspect home for dinner."

"Or a male wolf recently?"

"That either. Are you ready?"

"Yeah, let's do this. I've got to make a good impression on your parents. Can we stop at a florist shop on the way there? Maybe a liquor store?"

Jenna laughed. "What about for my sisters?"

"They're going to be there too?" He already had enough to deal with.

"Yep. You thought the police officer questioning you was all you were going to have to go through tonight?"

Sarandon wrapped his arm around her shoulders.

"I'm ready for this." In truth, he wasn't. He'd never had to make a best impression on a family while vying for a she-wolf's affections. Everyone knew him in Silver Town, so they knew his faults and his strengths. He didn't have to prove anything to anyone there.

He'd never imagined he'd be going far outside his hometown to find a mate either. Not that Jenna and he were quite there yet.

"What would appeal to your sisters?" He hadn't expected he'd have to bribe her sisters too.

"I hate to tell you this, but you're on your own. It will mean a lot more to them if you pick out something of your own for them."

"Hell, that's not fair. I don't know them at all. Their likes, dislikes, hobbies, anything. I could get myself into real trouble here."

"Believe me, if I told you what they like, they'd know it was 'from me' and not from you. Be creative."

He checked his GPS to locate an army surplus store. When he directed her into the parking lot, she frowned. "What are you going to get for them here?"

"I have no idea. When I see what I think will work, I'll get it." When they entered the store, he looked at the personal defense weapons—batons, pepper spray, daggers, knives, and tactical pens. He was thinking more in the line of something they could use that might protect them that they didn't have already. He smiled when he saw a pair of pink handcuffs.

"Don't even think of it," Jenna said next to him as she looked down at the glass case.

"I was more amused than anything. I don't think those are for apprehending anyone. I imagine they're more for sexual bondage. Besides, I didn't think you were going to help me."

She slid his arm around her waist. So she was going to help him only because she didn't want to lose out on dating him?

When he began studying body cameras, she shook her head. "Way too expensive."

"Do you have one?"

"No."

"Well, you should, for your own protection." He waved to the clerk. "I'll take three of these."

"Okay, well, what if this doesn't ever lead to a mating? You'll be out of all that money," she said for his hearing only.

"It's a sure bet." He smiled.

"You are so sure of yourself." She snuggled closer to him, smiling, and he knew he'd made big points with her.

They went to the florist shop after that, and he picked out a bouquet of lilies and roses for her mom, boxes of chocolates for each of the women at a candy specialty shop, and then her dad's favorite scotch.

"I don't know what the rest of the family will think, but I'm wondering what you're giving everyone for Christmas."

"Hot damn! That's a good sign."

"What if you don't care for my family?"

"I would be a fool not too." He did hope that they would all get along. Wolves were family-oriented by nature, though some of the wolves in a pack would disperse to start their own packs when the pups grew older. So if they were perfect for each other and the family didn't exactly suit, he hoped she would be agreeable to just leave and make their own way in the world.

When they reached her family's home in Woodland Park, he wondered what homes like this cost, immediately loving the wooded acreage backed up on the mountainside. She parked her car next to two other vehicles sitting in front of the home. Her parents' house was a two-story, brick-and-vinyl-sided home with tall sloping rooflines on the various segments of the house and a long circular drive out front. There was no sign of any nearby homes, so they had complete privacy.

"I love the woods."

"We go cross-country skiing out here, mountain biking, hiking—"

"And running as wolves?"

"Especially. We can go for a run after dinner, if you'd like."

He'd love that. "What if everyone else wants to go running too?"

"They might."

He'd much rather just run alone with Jenna. From a wolf's perspective, that would be the perfect way to start the wolf courtship.

She took his hand and led him to the front door, while he carried the packages, hoping they didn't think he was overeager to court her. Even if he was.

She motioned to the other two vehicles. "My sisters are here already."

"Do you have family get-togethers often?"

"We do."

He sure hoped he liked her family. He wanted a mate, but he really wanted to stay in Silver Town near his family. He hadn't ever considered living anywhere else. How would she feel about leaving her family and joining his?

She opened the door and called out, "We're here. Dad must be out back grilling shish kebabs already. Why don't you join him?"

"Thanks. Just point me in the right direction."

She took the packages from him and pointed to a dining room that had expansive windows all across the back of the house. "Door is that way."

"Okay, see you in a bit." He hoped her dad was a likeable guy. He'd never given much thought to mating a she-wolf and then having to deal with the family. They all had their own quirks. Just like his did.

"I'll go look for Mom and my sisters," she said.

"Okay."

She was still watching him, and he smiled. "I'll be all right. I promise I won't get myself into too much trouble."

"Okay. It's not you I'm worried about."

Maybe he should have asked her more about her father.

Sarandon found the door to the outside and stepped onto the deck. Her dad looked to be about sixty and had graying temples. The rest of his hair was dark. "I'm Sarandon Silver. And you must be—"

"Jenna's dad, Logan St. John. Sorry about the mix-up on what you've done. We'll do everything in our power to make this right."

"That wasn't your fault. The police shouldn't have believed the suspect's lies. Not when he was already an identity thief."

"I agree. Jenna said you want to stay with her for however long this takes to clear your name." The dad was eyeing him as if trying to get a feel for him.

"Yes, sir." Sarandon wasn't surprised. All wolves did that—judged another wolf, took in their scent, attempted to determine what kind of a wolf they were. He knew if he had a daughter of his own who began courting, he'd be just as interested in learning everything he could about the prospective wolf mate.

Logan turned the shish kebabs over to grill the other side. "Did she tell you she lives next door?"

"Uh, no." The vixen.

Her dad smiled. "All the girls do. We have four homes here right together."

Well, that sort of answered his question about Jenna moving back home with him. He might be getting ahead of himself here, but he figured if she had children, she'd want to be near her mother and sisters so they could help out. Not that his own pack wouldn't all love on their babies, but he assumed it wouldn't be the same for Jenna.

He and Logan heard squeals of excitement coming from somewhere deep in the bowels of the home, and Logan looked at Sarandon. "It appears the girls are excited about something."

The cameras he'd bought for them? Sarandon hadn't expected that much of a reaction.

Then two women who looked similar to Jenna rushed onto the deck and gave Sarandon hugs and kisses. He *really* hadn't expected that. He glanced back at the door and saw Jenna and another woman, most likely her mother, smiling at them.

"If Jenna doesn't want you, you can court me. I'm Crystal," the one woman said. She was the fairest haired of the women, her eyes a little more greenish-blue than Jenna's.

"Nah, me first. I'm Suzanne." She gave him a warm smile.

Logan moved the shish kebabs onto a platter, then served up the rice. "Looks like someone sure made an impression."

"Yeah, Dad. You should see what he got us. Body cameras!" Suzanne flipped her ash-blond hair over her shoulders and showed hers to him.

Logan took it and looked it over, then turned his attention to Sarandon. "Me too?"

Jenna laughed. "He picked up your favorite bottle of scotch for you. We can get you a camera for your birthday."

"The flowers and candy are lovely. Thanks, Sarandon," Jenna's mother said.

"I had to do something to thank my hosts."

"Mom and Dad will have to have you over a lot," Suzanne said.

"Come on, girls. One of you can get the silverware and some water for everyone, and someone can pull the cake out of the oven," their mother said, and the women all disappeared inside the house.

"You probably don't have a lot of time for home-cooked meals," Logan said.

"I actually like to cook," Sarandon said.

"Good. Jenna says you live in a great town. That it's wolf-run. And your cousin is the pack leader. That you have three brothers and all kinds of other relatives there.

I suspect you're probably not interested in moving from there," Logan said, glancing at Sarandon.

"It's been home forever for me. And yes, my whole family is there."

Logan let out his breath. "We want our daughters to stay in this area."

Sarandon suspected Jenna might feel that way, but he hadn't expected her father to bring this up now.

"You know, when the pups come, the girls' mother and I want to be there for them."

"I understand." Sarandon wasn't sure how he felt about that.

"Of course, it's completely up to my daughters what they decide to do—find a mate and move to his pack, or bring him here to increase our own pack size. We'd strongly prefer she stay here with her mate."

Logan handed the platter of shish kebabs to Sarandon while Logan carried the rice side dish. "Hopefully, Jenna has told you already, but she was in an accident some years ago with her mate and unborn children and lost all of them. The doctor said she could have more children, but, well, she and her mate had been living in another state when the accident occurred, and we just don't want to see her living so far away again. It was really hard for her to adjust with moving home and all. It was decades ago, but you understand how we feel."

"Yes, she told me. I was so sorry to hear of it. The guy who caused the accident should've received life." Sarandon didn't know what else to say, but he knew the family still had to worry about her. And about their other daughters.

"You just met Jenna, so I'm probably getting way ahead of myself on this."

"Yes, sir." *Not really*.

"Come on. Let's eat. And then we can go for a wolf run."

He knew it. The whole family would all run together. One big, happy family.

They walked into the house, and Jenna's mother had everyone take a seat at the table. Jenna glanced at Sarandon. He reached over and squeezed her hand.

After dinner, they went running as wolves, as a pack. And then the parents stuck together and headed in one direction, the sisters taking off in a different direction, while Jenna stayed close to Sarandon. He was glad he could run with her alone for a while, and he appreciated that the rest of the family understood the need for them to be wolves together.

He thought he saw something moving in the woods quite a distance from them. He swore it was a wolf. He woofed at Jenna to wait for him and ran through the brush to locate whatever it was. He heard something behind him and turned to see Jenna following him. *Damn it*. He didn't want her in harm's way if the animal he thought he'd seen was a male wolf.

She nipped at Sarandon's cheek, telling him he wouldn't leave her behind, and started sniffing the area. He was smelling the scents in the area too. A male wolf. Not her father's scent. Did the family know any other wolves in the area?

Jenna woofed at Sarandon, and he assumed they didn't know this wolf. He still wanted her to wait for him.

He ran again, searching for the wolf, and saw it

moving fast through the brush, a brown wolf, no other markings. Just brown. At least Sarandon knew the wolf's scent now. The wolf disappeared over a hill.

Sarandon raced through the trees, trying to reach the hill, but when he topped it, he didn't see any sign of the wolf. He continued searching for him while Jenna searched nearby, the two of them working together to track the wolf. He realized then that they could do this. Work together as a team. He was so used to being with his brothers or cousins, protecting the she-wolves and pups in the pack, that he'd never considered working with a she-wolf who had his back.

They'd lost sight of the wolf, then heard a vehicle's engine running and raced through the woods to see what it looked like. Maybe they'd get the license plate number. They reached the dirt road and saw the black SUV, with the same license tag they'd learned belonged to Burt Dreyfus.

Now they knew his scent and what he looked like as a wolf. And they knew they hadn't been wrong about him following them. Why else would he be sniffing around Jenna and her family's territory?

With Burt gone, Jenna howled, warning her family they'd found trouble.

A male wolf howled, then a female, followed by two more females. Sarandon howled to let them know what his wolf's voice sounded like. She licked his face, and he licked hers. He loved running with her, and he realized everything he did with her was a test of their friendship and whether they would be suitable wolf mates.

Jenna and Sarandon headed back to the house. They saw her parents a little way off and her sisters after that. They ran together as a pack of wolves, just as though he were family. He thought he could really fit in. That it wouldn't hurt her family to have another male wolf in the pack.

Once everyone entered the house, they went off to their respective rooms, shifted and dressed, and then returned to the dining room where Victoria fed them cake and coffee.

"We saw a brown wolf named Burt Dreyfus running on our property," Jenna said before Sarandon had a chance. "He's the cameraman for a ghost-hunter show. The TV personalities are wolves and are related to Sarandon's sister-in-law." She didn't know if CJ and Laurel were married. Even though wolves mated for life and didn't need to prove their fidelity by marrying, many did for the kids in the event they needed it. "He had been following us on the interstate. Mom, you looked up the license plate."

"Right. A black SUV."

"Yeah, it was parked on the old dirt road. We lost him before we could reach him," Jenna said.

"At least you learned what he was driving," Victoria said.

"I think we need to get ahold of the ghost hunters' management and learn what is up with this man," Logan said.

"I agree. I'll call my brother CJ, who is a deputy sheriff of Silver Town, and let him know what's going on," Sarandon said.

"Why would he be running around here? Following you?" Logan asked.

"I think this all has to do with the other guy stealing my ID. I think he was in on it," Sarandon said.

"He's a wolf? And the TV show personalities are too?" Logan asked.

"Yes." Sarandon finished his chocolate cake.

Jenna eyed Crystal and Suzanne and the way they kept smiling at him and offering him more cake and coffee or anything else he wanted.

"Are you sure you don't want another slice of cake? Another cup of coffee?" Suzanne asked Sarandon again but not anyone else.

"No, thanks. It was great." Sarandon patted his rock-hard stomach. "I'd have to do a lot more running if I ate any more tonight."

Jenna wasn't sure about her sisters' attentions toward him. Were they being nice because he gave such great presents to them? Or because they thought they had a chance with him? They'd never been interested in her boyfriends before. But Sarandon wasn't like any wolf she'd ever known. Certainly, none had brought presents for her family.

"Oooh, I like the guy in charge of that TV show," Suzanne said, finding an episode on a search on her phone. "I watch that show all the time. He's the cutest. Totally in charge. A real alpha male. I didn't know they were all wolves."

"I'll have to watch the show. I figured it was all a put-on," Crystal said. "And like you, I had no clue it was run by wolves."

"Right, well, this Burt Dreyfus needs to be picked up and questioned," Logan said, getting the subject back to the crux of the matter.

"I agree," Sarandon said.

"If we're all finished…" Jenna began carrying plates into the kitchen.

Her sisters helped her with the dirty dishes.

Jenna was ready to take Sarandon home with her. She was annoyed at him for being overly protective and wanting her to return home and stay out of harm's way when the wolf was running in their territory. Burt. What was he up to?

Yet Sarandon had irked her when he treated her as though she couldn't defend herself or help him search for the wolf. What did he think she was doing in her line of work? She captured fugitives all the time. Just because she didn't manage to take one wolf in because he had a whole wolf pack to back him—and besides, he was innocent—didn't mean she couldn't take another wolf down.

Especially when Sarandon was there to help.

Sarandon had been quieter than usual, and she hoped her dad hadn't said something to upset him. She knew her dad well enough to guess he might have told Sarandon something. Then again, what if it was all about her staying with Sarandon to locate the brown wolf? And he was annoyed with her? Maybe, seeing her in action, he didn't care for the kind of wolf she was. Well, tough. That's the way she was. If he didn't like it, that was his problem.

"Night, all. We need to be ready when the police call about Sarandon's fingerprint results."

"Night, Jenna, Sarandon," everyone said, and after hugs, Jenna and Sarandon got in her car and drove back to the main drive that would take her to her long driveway next door. The properties had ten acres apiece, so nice and spacious.

When they pulled into her garage at her home, she said, "Okay, spill. What did Dad tell you?"

"About this," Sarandon said, motioning with both hands toward the house. "That you live right next door. That your dad expects you to stay here if you find a mate."

She groaned and got out of the car. "He's not supposed to sabotage me courting a wolf like that."

"Well, isn't that what you'd want?"

She hesitated. "What I want is what my mate and I mutually agree upon. It's not a one-sided affair."

"Uh, yeah, okay. Sorry," Sarandon said. "I'm getting way ahead of myself on this. I'm not usually this way."

She slipped her finger into his belt loop and tugged him toward the house. "Apology accepted. I figured you've never done this before."

"He did mention one other thing."

She closed the door behind him. "What's that?" She was afraid her father had talked about her mate and losing her unborn children. "Forget it. He told you about Will, right?" She led Sarandon into her living room, and they sat down on the couch. "I know my dad's heart is in the right place, but still, it was for me to say. And besides, I already told you about it. He didn't think I would?" She shook her head. "He thinks the reason I haven't mated again in all this time is because I'm still pining away for them. I still think of them, of course—I loved them dearly—but I'm not giving up on having a mate and a family. I just haven't found any wolf I was interested in like that. Sure, I've dated tons. I don't know. You threw me for a loop from the beginning.

First, from being my suspect, to being someone I could see lasting longer than the other guys."

"As in a mating."

"That remains to be seen."

"I'm sorry about what happened to you. It never should have."

She nodded. "What was the deal with Burt Dreyfus? I got the distinct impression you wanted me to return home or go to my parents' place. Or stay put, not help you track the wolf."

"Jenna…"

She frowned at him.

He pulled her onto his lap and wrapped his arms around her. She couldn't help liking the way he was trying to make it up to her. Or at least she thought that's where this was going.

"My brothers and cousins and I have always been there to help out the she-wolves and the kids, the elderly, anyone who needs protecting."

She raised her brows.

"I know you're a fugitive recovery agent, well trained in apprehending fugitives, well trained in searching for them. In that instant, I saw a male wolf. An unknown male wolf snooping around your family's territory. You told me in your way that he wasn't a wolf you knew. He wasn't a friend. I acted on instinct. Protect you. Go after the wolf."

"Okay," she said, running her finger down his chest, "what if we see the wolf again, or another wolf you don't know lurking about?"

"Can I help it that my first thought is to protect you? That's better than me tucking my tail between my legs and running to get behind you, isn't it?"

She chuckled and pulled him down for a kiss. "I couldn't even imagine such a thing, but truly? Yes, I much prefer you trying to protect me, only know I will be doing the same for you."

Then she kissed him long and hard, his hands sliding down her arms, his hot mouth molded to hers.

She realized just how addictive he was and how hard it would be to let him go. How could they really date if he lived so far away? Even though he had invited her to his brother and sister-in-law's Spring Fling, that was a ten-hour drive.

She knew he didn't like the idea of her family wanting her to stay here, just as she was certain he'd prefer living with his pack in Silver Town.

So why did she give in to his hot, molten kisses, writhe beneath his fingertips as he molded his large, warm hands to her breasts, cup his face, and close her eyes to soak in every bit of the sexy way he was making her feel? And want even more?

The wolf's howl on Jenna's cell phone startled her, and she glanced at the phone, surprised her mom would be calling her after she'd just seen her. Jenna considered ignoring it, but what if her mom had news, good news for Sarandon? She kissed Sarandon's cheek, then answered the call. "Yes, Mom?"

"Tell Sarandon we retained a lawyer for him. His hearing is scheduled for tomorrow afternoon, but the lawyer wants to meet with Sarandon in the morning. He wished Sarandon hadn't seen the police first, but our lawyer will get this straightened out right away."

"Ohmigod, that's great news. You're talking about Jeb Booker, right?"

"Yes."

"Good. He's the best. I'll let Sarandon know, and he can call to make arrangements. Thanks, Mom."

"Well, we need to get Sarandon's name cleared so the police are looking for the real suspect. *And* so you can court the wolf. Your sisters are saying if you don't want him, they do."

Jenna laughed. "They're not getting him." She watched Sarandon's dark expression brighten. "Talk to you later." When she ended the call, she smiled at Sarandon. "Good news. My parents hired the best wolf lawyer in town. Best lawyer, period. He'll clear your name and—"

"You'll court me."

She chuckled. "You have a one-track mind."

"*Only* when it comes to you."

"Good." She pulled a card out of a drawer in a side table and handed it to Sarandon. "You have a hearing scheduled for the afternoon."

"Sounds good." He called the number for the lawyer. "This is Sarandon Silver, the wolf accused... Yeah, that one. All right, sir... Ten? Okay. See you there." He smiled at Jenna. "Yes, she's coming with me... No, she didn't tase me to bring me in, but that had been next on her agenda." Sarandon laughed. "See you then."

"What did Jeb say about me attempting to tase you?" Jenna asked Sarandon.

"He said that was your specialty."

She smiled. "Yeah, and yours is taking down armed assailants...me. Okay, I'll let you get some sleep. See you in the morning."

"Night," Sarandon said, but he pulled her into his arms for a hug and kiss.

She cherished the feel of his hands sweeping down her back, his lips parted, his tongue spearing her mouth, but she knew they had important issues to discuss before they let things go too far.

"Guest bedroom is in there." She pointed to the room, smiled, patted him on the chest, and hurried to her room before she changed her mind.

Chapter 12

SARANDON FELT LIKE HE'D MADE GREAT STRIDES WITH Jenna on the courtship business. He hadn't been able to quit thinking about her half the night, wishing they were further along with it and that he'd wake with her in his arms this morning. He hadn't even been worried about clearing his name.

He was sitting on his bed, slowly waking up, when he finally heard her in the master bathroom. He was glad she hadn't gone on a run without him—at least, he didn't think she had. Maybe he was mistaken.

Jenna woofed at Sarandon's guest-room door. *Hot damn*. Wearing just his boxer briefs, he opened the door and smiled. "I take it you want to run with me this morning."

She woofed again and wagged her tail. He ditched his boxers and shifted. She raced off for the wolf door, and he followed her outside.

He loved running with her in her own territory. And claiming it for his own. *Again*. He couldn't help himself. He was going to ensure everyone knew she was off-limits to them and all his. Also, that this was their territory, so beware. He'd enjoyed seeing all the new scenery in this area, realizing he rarely saw anything new in Silver Town. Most of all, he loved just being with Jenna on these runs. Seeing her darting through the trees and brush in a game of hide-and-seek, showing him the creeks, a river, and ponds. He wondered about cross-country skiing in the area, which she said she and her family liked to do. And he thought it would be fun to see the fall colors here and the summer flowers blooming all over.

She had hidden behind some rocks and he came around to find her, but this time, she paused and was smelling the ground, not waiting to nip at him in play.

He joined her to see what she was smelling. Another wolf had passed through here, not scent-marking with a urine trail, but his paw pads had left his scent just the same. Sarandon wondered if Jenna knew who it was. He nudged her to see what she thought—friend or foe—and she growled a little.

Someone's scent she didn't recognize, he suspected.

They began following the scent trail and explored a new area of woods—with no human hiking trails, so they should be fairly safe—but they lost the wolf's scent at a river. They ran for about five miles, one of them on each side of the river, trying to locate where the wolf had crossed, but they didn't find his scent trail. Maybe in the other direction? They needed to head back to her house so Sarandon could get ready to see the lawyer. He was sure glad Jenna's parents got him one to expedite things and make sure he didn't get railroaded.

Jenna had the same idea, and when he crossed the river to join her, she licked his wet cheek, then they loped all the way home together.

When they reached the house and went inside, they raced each other to the bedrooms. He shifted and took a quick shower, then dressed, and was ready to fix them breakfast.

She met him in the kitchen. "Okay, so I didn't recognize the wolf who's been in our territory. It wasn't Burt."

"Which makes me feel it's still related to the case. How often do you get stray wolves up here near your home?"

"Rarely. It just seems too coincidental to me."

"I can't imagine what these guys hope to accomplish by following us. He has to know I'm about to clear my name so whoever is responsible takes the blame."

"Why not try to stop you? If he didn't want you to clear your name, I would think he'd have wanted to stop you before now."

"Financial fraud is one thing. Murder, quite another. Maybe he doesn't have the stomach for killing anyone."

"Or he's afraid of you if he knows I tracked you to Silver Town, armed to the teeth, *and* you took me hostage instead."

"If you must know, I was as gentle as I could be with you, given the circumstances." He began looking through her fridge. "Scrambled eggs or omelets okay?"

"Omelets, bell peppers, ham, and cheese." She began pulling out the other ingredients, while he grabbed the carton of eggs.

After finding the skillets and olive oil, he cracked some eggs and started cooking them, while Jenna cut up the bell peppers and ham. The cheese was already shredded.

"Coffee or tea?" she asked.

"Coffee, milk, and sugar."

She began making a pot of coffee, filling a teakettle with water and heating it. "I'll call Mom and let her know we've got another wolf in the area. Dad will go out and check on it, as long as he isn't working a case this morning."

"I would have continued to search for the wolf in the other direction if I didn't have to meet with the lawyer this morning."

"Well, that's *our* priority. I agree. I wanted to know where he got out of the river and took off to." She got ahold of her mom and said, "Sarandon and I took a wolf run this morning and smelled the scent of another male wolf in the area. We followed him to the river, but he must have swum in it for some time to hide his scent. We searched south on the river but couldn't find where he got out. We had to return home for the lawyer's meeting. Did you want to ask Dad if he could check it out? Okay, thanks, Mom. We're just having breakfast and heading over to see the lawyer after that."

She got off the phone and fixed the coffee and orange tea.

Then Sarandon served the omelets.

"You're a really good cook."

"We had to fend for ourselves after our mom died and my dad gave up on raising us. Now I think I know why. He was off seeing Ritka but trying to keep it secret. Eric, my oldest brother, learned how to cook from several of the women in the pack. Bertha Hastings runs the bed-and-breakfast in town, and she taught him how to make all kinds of different meals. He wasn't about to be our full-time mother, so he taught us how to cook too and we took turns making meals. We learned to do the laundry, yard work, and everything else we needed to do so our pack members wouldn't feel obligated to come by to see us all the time."

"So you lived by yourselves in your home?"

"Yeah. It worked out fine. As long as we didn't roughhouse and end up injuring one another."

"Did you?"

"Sure. Four boys? What do you expect."

She smiled and set the table.

When they sat down to eat, he hoped he hadn't left any shell fragments in the eggs. Sure way to ruin her impression of his cooking.

"These are delicious."

"Thanks. I make a great pot roast too."

"Hmm, sounds heavenly." She forked up some more eggs. "Okay, so after we go to the hearing later this afternoon, what's next on the agenda? We've been focused on clearing your name, but after that's done?"

"We're going after this guy. Or the two guys. We need to locate both Alex and Burt Dreyfus." Sarandon's phone rang, and he saw it was his brother CJ. "Yeah, CJ? I'm putting this on speaker so Jenna will hear what's going on too."

"Stanton sent me a picture of Burt Dreyfus, and I ran it over to show to Sam, Silva, Lelandi, and Eric. Sending it to you now. Was this the guy you saw at the tavern?"

Sarandon looked at the photo. "Yeah, looks like him. What did everyone else say about him?"

"They all confirmed it was him," CJ said.

"What about the dates he was missing that Stanton was angry about?"

"He was gone about the time the suspect cut his GPS ankle monitor off."

"He could have helped the suspect leave Colorado

Springs," Sarandon said, carrying his empty plate into the kitchen.

"He could have. I'm interviewing Burt this afternoon. They're filming a show right now."

"At the ski lodge?"

"No, another location. I'm on my way there now."

"Okay. Someone's been running as a wolf here, so if Burt has been in Silver Town all this time, it's not him. But the wolf is driving Burt's SUV." Unless the wolf had been here in the middle of the night, but then he probably wouldn't have made it back to Silver Town in time for the filming. "Where are they filming?"

"In Colorado Springs, so he *is* in your area."

"All right. Then he's definitely a possibility. Where are they exactly?"

"They're at a fast-food hamburger place, one of the major chains. An employee fatally shot her manager some years back, and strange happenings continue to occur there. Chairs put on top of tables are mysteriously placed back on the floor when the cleanup crew isn't there, according to employees. Some have seen a ghostly woman in the kitchen and other things moved around that no one can explain. Stanton said he wants to do shows on a dozen places in the Colorado Springs area—two haunted high schools, a hotel, an old cowboy night club, tunnels, a school for the deaf and blind, just all kinds of places. Which is good, because that means the ghost hunters won't be here sensationalizing any of our haunted spots for a while."

"That's good. We're not sure about the wolf who was near Jenna's house. Logan, Jenna's dad, is trying to track him down. We lost his scent at a river and had to stop tracking him because I have a meeting with the lawyer this morning. The wolf has to be a shifter if he's trying to hide his scent."

"Yeah, sounds like you're right. You're only about fifteen minutes from Colorado Springs, correct?" CJ asked.

"Yeah."

"I'm going to try to get to Colorado Springs early. I left Silver Town at three this morning."

"Jenna's family got me the lawyer, so we'll be in town for that first thing," Sarandon said, helping Jenna put the food away, though she kept waving him away so he could talk freely with his brother.

Then they headed out to the car.

"That doesn't sound good," CJ said.

"He's a great wolf lawyer, and he's only going to be there in case I run into trouble. We have the hearing this afternoon too. I'll let you know how it all goes."

"Okay. Let's get together once I get in. I won't be able to interview Burt until this evening now. I'm trying to track down his family to see if they belong to a pack. Stanton says he has no idea if Burt belongs to one."

"He doesn't even know where Burt's from?" Sarandon couldn't believe it.

"You know Stanton. Prima donna. He's only interested in himself."

Why wasn't Sarandon surprised?

"I've told Stanton not to tell Burt I need to talk with him or anything about this business. I don't want him running if he's involved," CJ said.

"Okay, sounds like a good plan. Talk to you later, CJ. And thanks."

"You've got a whole pack here waiting to hear the results. So let me know soonest."

"Will do."

When Sarandon ended the call, Jenna asked him, "Do you ever feel overwhelmed by your pack? Like everything you do or say is being monitored? Or that you have to keep them posted at all times?"

He laughed. "I've grown up with it, so it feels right. I guess for an outsider it would seem that way. If anyone's in trouble, everyone's there to help out."

"How are you feeling about seeing the lawyer and the hearing?"

"Ready to get all of it over with."

Chapter 13

WHILE SARANDON WAS IN THE PRELIMINARY COURT HEARING, Jenna waited outside the courtroom, praying everything would go well for him. Jeb, the lawyer, had gone with him, and she knew Sarandon was in good hands. She wished they'd learned about the fingerprint results though.

Jenna began searching Google on her phone for anyone named Dreyfus who lived in the area. She found a few who lived within an hour's radius of Colorado Springs. She called several of the numbers, pretending she was trying to locate a Burt Dreyfus who had won some contest money, stating this was the phone number he had given, but so far, no one knew of a Burt in the family tree.

"Are you sure the name you're looking for isn't Bernard?" one elderly woman asked. "I'm sure Bernie must have won it. Maybe he used his Burt nickname."

Burt? "I thought Bernie was his nickname."

"Uh, well, he goes by both."

"How old is he?"

"Oh, he had to give his birth date?"

"Yes." Jenna knew the man they wanted was about thirty, and she was certain it wasn't anyone named Bernard or Bernie.

"June 15, 1943."

"Sorry. That's not it."

"Are you sure? Maybe he gave the wrong birth date. He's always doing that."

Jenna smiled. "No. Sorry. Thanks for your time."

"But—"

Jenna ended the call and checked with the next Dreyfus listed, this one in Cañon City, thirty-five miles from Colorado Springs. Lots of woods for running as a wolf out there too.

"Hello, I'm calling from Johnson and Johnson Contest Winners, looking for a Burt Dreyfus. Is he home?"

"The younger or the older?"

Yes! Jenna's heart was pounding with excitement at possibly finding the right family. She quickly said, "The form doesn't ask for a birth date, but he had to share a photo for verification purposes, and he looks like he's about thirty."

"Okay, well, my son works for a TV personality, and he's on an important assignment. I can't tell you what it is about exactly, but he even did a program at the St. Cloud Hotel here in Cañon City. It's haunted, you know. I don't know why he would have entered a contest. Then again, he does a lot of things I don't know about. I'm surprised he gave our number and not his own cell number."

"I wouldn't know. Do you have his cell number so I can get ahold of him?"

"Sure."

The woman gave it to Jenna, and then they ended the call. Jenna was so excited that she wanted to burst into the hearing and tell Sarandon she'd found where Burt's parents lived. If Alex was part of the family's wolf pack, maybe they could discover where he was now.

The door to the room where the hearing was being

held opened and Jenna stiffened, holding her breath while she waited to see Sarandon emerge. She prayed he'd look ecstatic or at least relieved.

Jeb was on his phone as he left the court hearing but ended his call. He came to stand beside her and patted her on the back, smiling. "That was a call from the police. Sarandon's fingerprints came back and are definitely not the same as the suspect's they had in custody."

Sarandon came out of the hearing and smiled broadly at Jenna. Then he scooped her up in his arms and swung her around, stopping only to lean down and kiss her.

She hadn't expected his exuberance to go this far, not in the courthouse, but she totally understood it and was glad he showed it. She was over the moon for him. She kissed him right back and heard some chuckles as people passed them in the hall. Sarandon set her on her feet, put his arm around her shoulders, keeping her close, and shook Jeb's hand. "Thanks for everything."

"You were innocent, Sarandon. You had enough verified witness statements, all from credible witnesses, and your fingerprints proved you were not the same man. You did it all on your own. I'm glad to take the credit. And the payment for my services."

Sarandon smiled at him. "I hope I never have to have a lawyer in the future, but if I need one, I'll give you a call."

After they said their goodbyes, Jenna gave Sarandon the good news about locating Burt Dreyfus's parents. "They may know where Alex and Burt live."

"That's great news. We need to speak with them in person."

"When is your brother going to see us?"

"I'm here," CJ said, stalking down the hall. "Sorry I didn't make it any sooner than this." He eyed the way Sarandon had his arm around Jenna's shoulders.

"I'm cleared of any wrongdoing," Sarandon said, smiling.

"Hot damn!"

"And Jenna found Burt Dreyfus's family's home. Should we all go out there and pay them a visit?" Sarandon asked.

"Hell yeah." CJ was wearing his deputy sheriff uniform, probably to impress Burt with how serious this was when CJ interviewed him.

Jenna was impressed.

"Do you have enough time to go with us to Cañon City and then return for your interview with Burt?" Sarandon asked his brother.

"Yeah, and dinner with you before we head back. That way, you don't have to fly back," CJ said. "You can ride back home with me when we're ready to leave."

Jenna had forgotten that part of the plan—that Sarandon would fly home when he was done here. She really didn't want to see him go. Besides, he'd said he would help her track down the suspect. Alex might still be in the area. She was about to say so but then held her tongue. It was up to Sarandon to tell CJ what he was going to do. Stay or leave. She sure hoped he'd want to stay.

When had she started wanting a partner to help her recover fugitives? When Sarandon thwarted her from taking him in and took her hostage instead. She smiled.

"I promised Jenna I'd help her find the suspect and turn him in. Besides, I have to make her pot roast. Thanks for the offer."

She took a relieved breath, and Sarandon rubbed her shoulder, giving her a smug smile. He knew she wanted him to help her on this.

"Pot roast?" CJ asked. "You're staying with her?"

"Yeah. Her parents live right next door, so she's safe."

CJ smiled a little at that. "You didn't tell me you were getting serious."

"I'm surprised you couldn't have guessed. Besides, it was all on the condition that I cleared my name first."

Still smiling, CJ just shook his head.

"So, if Burt is here, why was he following us?" Sarandon asked.

"Maybe he wasn't. The Wernicke brothers left Silver Town about the same time you did to get here for their show. Maybe he was just headed in the same direction around the same time and seemed to be following you. The route you took was the fastest to reach Colorado Springs."

"Okay, that's plausible. But he returned to the town we stopped in. And what about the wolf we smelled in Jenna's family's territory? He was driving Burt's SUV. We didn't know the wolf's scent, but the St. Jameses don't usually have unknown wolves running in the area. The wolf was brown. Can you ask Stanton if he's ever seen Burt as a wolf?"

"Your guess is as good as mine. I can ask his boss if he's ever seen him as a wolf. I thought you'd seen Burt before."

"I've seen him twice, but I've never been close enough to catalog his scent," Sarandon said.

"Okay. So it could have been him. Or Alex, for that matter. Or anyone else. A real wolf, even."

"Neither were real wolves. The one was driving the black SUV, and the other tried to hide where he was going by swimming in the river."

Jenna got a call from her mom and felt bad she hadn't called her right away to let her know how the hearing went. "Sarandon's name has been cleared, and we—"

"Mate him."

Jenna glanced at Sarandon as they walked outside the courthouse with CJ. "We're officially courting each other. He's making me pot roast for tomorrow. We're on our way to check out a man's family who might be with a pack that the suspect was staying with. Or raised by."

"Oh, that's good news. We want you to come over for supper again, if you'd like to."

"Sarandon's brother CJ is here. He's a deputy sheriff in Silver Town, and he's going with us to Cañon City to check out the lead we have. Sarandon and his brother might have plans for tonight."

"Tell them they're coming over for supper. Dad is grilling steaks."

"Okay." Jenna told the brothers, "My mother has invited you both over for steaks on the grill. Dad's cooking, if that's all right with you."

"We'll be there," Sarandon said. "It has to be after CJ interviews another person of interest."

"Did you hear that, Mom?"

"I sure did. We'll wait to hear what time that will be. I'm so glad for Sarandon too. I'll tell the rest of the family."

"Thanks, Mom. Oh, and did Dad locate the wolf's trail?"

"Oh, yes, well, it led to a dirt road and then it was gone. Tire tracks were in the dirt next to the road."

"So, it was a shifter, like we figured."

"Yes. The wolf is no one we know."

"Okay, see you later." They ended the call.

"I'd say we should drive just my vehicle, but if I have to take someone into custody, it would be better to have two cars," CJ said.

"I agree. Is having supper with Jenna's family all right with you?" Sarandon asked, even though Jenna had already ended the call with her mother.

"Steaks? When have you ever known me to turn down grilled steaks?"

Sarandon smiled. "Thanks."

"No problem. Sounds to me like you've gotten yourself hooked into this, and you'll need someone who's level-headed to check out the situation," CJ said.

"Ha. As if he needs you to check out my family," Jenna said.

CJ actually smiled, shocking her.

Before they headed to Cañon City, she told them exactly what Burt's mother had said. "The phone number is listed for Sarah and B. Anton Dreyfus."

"Okay, let's get there and get this done so I can get on with the interview of their son. Both of you can come with me when I question Burt. If Burt sees Sarandon, he might be even more rattled than if I spoke with him alone," CJ said. "And if he knows what you do, Jenna, he might be just as worried."

She hoped Burt spilled his guts.

They left for Cañon City, and Sarandon said to Jenna,

"I think we shocked my brother when he learned about us. He doesn't shock easily."

"How do you think he feels about you living with me here, so far from your family? If that's what happens?"

"I think what's most important is that the mated couple is together."

"You're close to your family, and I'm close to mine."

"Yours wouldn't consider moving to Silver Town, would they?"

She hadn't thought of that possibility. "They're pretty set in their ways. I doubt they would."

"I can see the benefits of living at your location. In Silver Town, the whole place is wolf-run. Everyone there is ready and willing to help you out."

"I saw that. Even for newcomers to the area?"

"Absolutely. When CJ's wife and her two sisters moved into the Silver Town Hotel to renovate the place, we were all over there to help them out. I'll admit we kind of got underfoot."

"Four brothers interested in three sisters?"

"Two brothers. Brett wooed Ellie, CJ courted Laurel, and Megan's seeing Peter, the sheriff."

"Aww, so that left you and Eric out."

"Eric needed his own pack to lead, and Pepper, an alpha she-wolf who was running her own pack after having lost her mate, had property north of the park where he works as a ranger. Eric was perfect for the job—and to be her mate. Even though she emphatically said she didn't want an alpha male taking over. They're perfectly suited and perfect as the leaders for their pack."

"And they still live close by?"

"Four hours away."

"So not all the Silver brothers live in town or on the outskirts."

"No. We can move to other locations. It just depends on what we agree on. I'm flexible."

She really hoped he was.

CJ called Sarandon, who put the call on speaker-phone. "We're almost there. They live on the outskirts of town, and I'll go first. You just wait for me."

"Are you sure you don't want all of us to go? What if they know Alex really well, and they see Sarandon and the expression on their faces gives them away?" Jenna said.

"Good point. Just park behind me, and we'll go to the door together."

They got out of the two cars and headed up the long, curving front walk to the door of the brick house. CJ knocked on the door, looking official and imposing.

The man who answered the door looked like an older version of the police sketch Lelandi had Peter draw.

"Mr. Dreyfus?"

The man immediately smelled they were all wolves, but his eyes widened when he saw Sarandon, and his jaw gaped. "Alex?"

That was the proof they needed.

"I'm Sarandon Silver. I'm trying to locate my brother," Sarandon said.

The man paled.

"Who is it?" a woman asked. "Alex?" She wore the same puzzled expression.

"Sarandon Silver, ma'am. I'm looking for my brother, Alex. We share the same birth father, Sheridan Silver."

The woman looked so pale that her husband quickly

took hold of her arm to steady her. "We never told Alex who his father was. Ritka's sister, Evie, gave us the boy to raise. We didn't have a child of our own and were convinced we could never have one. Not until we began caring for Alex, and then lo and behold, we had a son. Why…don't you come in?" Anton glanced at CJ and frowned. "Why would a deputy sheriff need to come too?"

"He's my brother. And Sarandon's. I'm CJ Silver."

"I'm Sarandon's mate," Jenna said brightly.

Sarandon and CJ looked shocked. Then Sarandon smiled, leaned down to kiss her cheek, and wrapped his arm around her shoulders. "You sure are."

She'd only meant to give a reason why she was here with the two brothers looking for their half brother. She was good at improvising. Sarandon seemed to be taking her declaration as a statement of fact.

"Well, come in, come in. My wife needs to take a seat. This is all a little too much for her."

CJ closed the door after them, and they followed Anton into the living room where he eased Sarah into a chair. "Would anyone like anything to drink? I need to get my wife something."

"Can I help you?" Jenna asked.

"Uh, yeah, sure." Anton smiled at her. "We always wanted a daughter too, but we were lucky to have our two sons." He muted the WWII movie on the huge, curved TV mounted on the wall.

Jenna had never seen one of them in someone's home, and this one was over six feet long. And curved? Amazing.

"Are either of your sons mated?" Jenna wanted to

assure him they weren't here to break up the family unit. They weren't trying to get Alex to leave his adoptive home to join the Silver pack.

When he and Jenna were in the kitchen, Anton said, "They've both dated a lot, but neither has found the right woman." He brought out glasses, and she began to fill them with ice and water. "What are you doing here, really? After all these years, Sarandon and CJ suddenly are checking up on a half brother they didn't care anything about before?"

"The truth?"

Anton hesitated to respond. She swore he looked like he was aging several years just standing there, worried about what he would hear. "Yeah. Tell me what's going on."

"The Silver brothers—there are four of them, quadruplets—didn't know anything about their father having an affair with Ritka. He wouldn't have left his mate for her or any other reason, but Ritka ended up having twins by Sheridan."

"So that's the story. We always wondered, and Evie wouldn't tell us the truth. Evie, Ritka's sister, raised Alex's sister, Faye. We didn't know Sheridan was having an affair with Ritka."

"I understand. Wolves mate for life. Ritka was so in love with Sheridan that she returned to him to have this secret affair. She hoped she could change his mind about mating her and taking the kids in to live with them."

"What about Sheridan's mate?"

"She was killed in a hunting accident when the boys were young. So, she was out of the way, as far as Ritka was concerned," Jenna said.

"But Sheridan had four boys he was raising."

"Right."

"That doesn't explain why you've come to see him now."

"They didn't know about Alex or his sister. Not until…well, until I went after Sarandon, believing him to be a suspect in an identity theft."

"You're a police officer?"

"Fugitive recovery agent."

"Don't tell me. Sarandon wasn't involved."

"He wasn't."

"And you're not his mate."

"That's how we met—me trying to arrest him. Now we're courting. But"—she pulled out her phone and showed him the picture of Alex's mug shot—"you can see how similar Sarandon and Alex look. The same with CJ. Especially Sarandon. His discarded, expired driver's license was stolen, and Alex used it when he was arrested, stating that he was Sarandon. Neither men had their fingerprints on file. Sarandon cleared his name today in Colorado Springs based on his fingerprints and witness statements that verified he's been in Silver Town the whole time. We need to find Alex and learn the truth. Is this a case of revenge against one of the brothers for not being raised as one of the Silvers? We don't know. Only Alex will know what's really going on."

"You want to arrest him."

"The police already have a warrant out for his arrest. He's going to get caught. It's only a matter of time. They have his fingerprints. They have his mug shot. He cut his GPS ankle monitor to slip out of the city, so he's on the run now. My family has one of the best lawyers in the state, a wolf like us. We'll pay Jeb to represent him."

"You're a bounty hunter." It was taking the poor dad forever to get the gist of the situation.

"Yes. My mother is the bail bondswoman. We'll have to pay the $150,000 for the bond if we don't turn him in to make his court date, because the deed he gave us as collateral was forged."

"He didn't do this. I know Alex. He wouldn't have done this."

"He had passports and other IDs on him that belonged to other people. He impersonated Sarandon. He didn't have any ID of his own on him. Why wouldn't he? Why would he say he was Sarandon and get him in trouble? Like I said, we'll have a lawyer represent Alex."

"Why? He ran out on the bond, and you could get stuck for it. What's in it for you?"

"I really care about the Silver family. And they really care about their half brother, despite what he's done. They didn't know about him before they started investigating Ritka. They learned about him, and about his sister, in Ritka's diaries."

"This news will break my wife's heart."

"We have to do something, Mr. Dreyfus. He's a wanted suspect."

Anton nodded. "All right." They carried the glasses of water into the living room, and Anton told it like it was. "Dear, Alex is in serious trouble."

Chapter 14

WHEN CJ, JENNA, AND SARANDON SAT IN THE LIVING ROOM with Alex's adoptive parents, Sarandon hoped they would learn where Alex was now.

Sarandon couldn't have been prouder of Jenna for soothing the dad's concerns and convincing him this was best for their adopted son. He was glad she'd offered her lawyer to represent Alex.

Once Anton had explained everything to his wife, Sarandon said, "The lawyer is really good. He helped get my fingerprints expedited, and he was there at the hearing to help clear me. We'll all do what we can to help Alex with this situation. I won't press charges against him for using my ID to impersonate me. We just want to ensure he knows he has family in Silver Town. We don't mean to take away from the importance the two of you have always had in his life, since you've served as his real family all these years."

Sarah had been quietly crying off and on but finally raised her hand to speak as if she were in school and needed permission. Sarandon thought she was going to offer something about Alex, but instead, she said, "Ritka killed her."

"We don't know that," Anton said, rubbing her back, looking alarmed, and glancing from one brother to the other.

"Ritka did. She'd been talking about hiring a hunter

to shoot something that was getting in her way." Sarah sniffled and wiped her eyes. "I didn't know what she meant by that. I knew she was seeing Sheridan and that he had a mate. I never told Anton. Then suddenly Sheridan's mate was shot in a hunting accident."

A cold sweat washed over Sarandon. Seeing his mother accidentally killed in front of him and his brothers had been devastating enough. If it had been murder and Ritka was behind it? If she wasn't already dead, he'd want to take her down himself. CJ was clenching his fists, his face red with anger.

Jenna's eyes were filled with tears, and she reached over to take Sarandon's hand in a comforting manner.

"I didn't really put all the pieces together. Not until after Ritka had died and your pack leader, your cousin, put Sheridan down. By then, it was too late to mention it to anyone. Ritka's sister knew we couldn't have children, or so we thought. We'd been trying for years, and nothing came of it. Evie didn't want the boy, just the girl. We were thrilled to take Alex in, though it was on the condition that we never told Ritka about the arrangement. She never came to see the kids anyway, so it really wasn't a problem. Then I got pregnant right away with Burt, and we were filled with joy that we had two little boys to raise. I don't believe Alex would do what you said he did. Not unless he was coerced, maybe. Can you really clear his name?"

Sarandon couldn't imagine any woman doing anything more hateful than what Ritka might have done. On the other hand, Alex was the product of Ritka's and his father's deceitfulness, and their son didn't deserve to be treated as though he was in any way responsible for their crime.

"We'll do our best," Jenna said, squeezing Sarandon's hand.

He appreciated her concern and wrapped his arm around her shoulders.

Sarah tried to get ahold of Alex on her phone, but she couldn't reach him. "I haven't talked with him in a couple of weeks. Which isn't unusual. He gets busy with his job and calls when he's through."

"What kind of work does he do?" CJ asked.

"Construction work. He makes good money at it. He's building some new homes in Colorado Springs. At least, the last we heard from him," Sarah said. "I'm really proud of him. We both are."

Since he was being GPS-monitored, maybe that's why he stayed in Colorado Springs as long as he did and didn't run off right away. The only other thing Sarandon could think of was that Alex had been forced to leave.

"Do you think someone at his workplace could have put him up to it?" Anton asked, sounding hopeful.

"We'll check. What's the name of the company?" CJ asked.

Anton ran his fingers through his hair. "J and R Construction."

"What about pack members? Could any one of them have put him up to it?" CJ readied his notepad to take a list of names.

Sarah and Anton exchanged looks, as if revealing any pack member names would be a cardinal sin.

"We have no intention of accusing anyone of anything. We just need to make some headway with the case." Sarandon really hoped they could find someone else who was responsible, but Alex had used Sarandon's

ID at the police department, so it would be hard to explain that away.

"This is all a real shock to us. We had no idea," Anton said.

"Same with me." Sarandon stood.

Sarah began to list off names. "Christina DeWitt. She's at the top of my list."

"Why is that?" Jenna asked.

"She's his girlfriend, but she's not right for him," Sarah said.

Sarandon glanced at Anton to see his take on it. He remained silent, and Sarandon suspected the only one who didn't like the woman was Sarah. Was the woman not good enough for her adopted son?

"Why do you think she's not right for him?" Jenna asked.

"She works in a motel. Cleaning. You know. He needs someone who has a better job."

What difference did that make if she was working hard? Sarandon thought Sarah was a bit of a snob. "What do you do for a living?"

"Me? I'm a homemaker."

Anton offered, "I worked construction too, which is why Alex works at it. He loved to come on jobs with me, from the time when he was about ten years old. Way before he was old enough to get a job on his own, he used to bring me tools and help me out and make his own birdhouses."

"And Burt?" Sarandon asked.

"He liked to do other things," Sarah quickly said. "He didn't like the loud noises the power saws made."

Sarandon could tell Anton felt a closeness to Alex. He wasn't sure about Burt.

Sarah gave them the names of nine males, and Christina was the only she-wolf on the list.

"What about his birth sister, Faye? Would she know where he's gone?" Jenna asked.

"Once Alex was given to us, his aunt never wanted to have anything to do with him, so the daughter never got to see her brother. Later? There was no interest. He never spoke of her, so I doubt she would know where he is," Sarah said.

"Where is she now? Where are her aunt and uncle? Just in case they have made contact," Jenna said.

"They lived on the other side of town. They cut themselves off from the rest of the pack. I don't know if they're living or dead," Sarah said. "I would imagine their niece is mated and who knows where she is. Their name is Fennimore." Sarah gave their last known address.

"Okay, thanks." Sarandon wasn't about to discount that the brother and sister might have been close all these years and never shared that with either of the families who had raised them. "What about your pack leaders?"

"Monty Matthews," Sarah said. "He's a good man."

"I say we stay in the pack area of Cañon City. We talk to the pack leaders and get a list of pack members, in case someone else could be harboring Alex. They may believe he's staying with them for some other reason. We haven't alerted the police about his identity yet," Sarandon said. "And we still need to find Alex's sister, Faye."

"Can you give us the number for your pack leaders?" Jenna asked Sarah and Anton.

"Yeah. Monty is our only pack leader. He lost his

mate last year. I should speak with him about this, but I hope you can locate Alex and not involve the pack," Anton said.

That was the importance of having a pack. To deal with issues that could involve all of them. "Don't you think Monty will be upset with you for not telling him?" Sarandon asked.

"After losing his mate, he hasn't been really interested in what's going on with the pack. All of us have been talking about asking another wolf to take over. No one wants to if Monty steps in again. He's been a great leader all these years," Anton said.

Sarandon nodded, though he didn't agree with their tactics. He couldn't imagine keeping Darien and Lelandi in the dark about something this serious. "Okay. Well, we still need to ask Monty if he knows where Alex could be. I can say you just learned of it, which you did."

"Thanks. I can give you a list of the pack members' names though. We have an emergency roster." Anton left the living room, and a few minutes later, they heard a printer running. He came back with a piece of paper that he handed to Jenna.

The list included twenty names with phone numbers, email addresses, and snail mail addresses. They could begin to canvass the surrounding area to see if anyone knew of Alex's whereabouts. Not wanting anyone to warn him and let him slip away if he was staying in the area, they didn't call anyone first.

Even then, they figured anyone they talked to could alert Alex and he'd be on the run.

"We'll let you know if we learn anything," CJ said.

"Thank you," Sarah said.

Anton escorted them to the door and shook Sarandon's hand and then CJ's. Finally, he took hold of Jenna's hand and squeezed. "Take good care of Alex for us when you find him."

"Thanks so much," Jenna said. "We'll let you know if we find anyone who knows where he is."

The three of them left Anton and Sarah's house and stood by Jenna's car while she called Monty as a courtesy to the pack leader. "Hello, we need to speak to you about a couple of your pack members. Sarah and Anton Dreyfus gave your name to us. I'm Jenna St. James, and CJ and Sarandon Silver are looking for Alex Dreyfus and his sister, Faye. May we visit you, and we'll let you know what this is all about?"

"Yes, of course. Are they in trouble?"

"Alex is. We'd rather talk to you in person about it, if that's okay with you."

"Sure. Come on over."

"Thanks."

When they arrived at his one-story brick home, Monty walked out to greet them. He was in his sixties, gruff, his black hair graying, and he was frowning at Sarandon.

Sarandon suspected he'd get the same wary response from everyone in the pack because he looked so much like Alex, but not exactly.

"Monty Matthews?" Sarandon said. "I'm Sarandon, and this is CJ Silver of Silver Town. We're Alex's half brothers."

"Half brothers? When did that happen?" Monty asked, looking genuinely perplexed.

When Alex used Sarandon's ID and Jenna hunted the wrong man down!

"We just learned about him, and we're trying to locate him," CJ said.

"Because he's wanted by the police," Jenna said. She explained what was going on, not only with him, but with Burt too.

Monty shook his head. "Why don't you come inside."

When they entered the house, Monty motioned to the living area. "Have a seat. Would any of you like coffee? A beer?"

"Coffee, cream, and sugar, if it's not too much trouble," Jenna said.

"Same here," Sarandon and CJ said.

"So tell me about Silver Town and how you are Alex's half brothers." Monty went into the kitchen that was open to the living room, making it easy for him to keep talking to them.

Sarandon gave him an abbreviated version of how they came to be related, leaving out that their dad had died.

Monty returned with four mugs of coffee. "And you're his mate?" he asked Jenna.

"Working on that," Sarandon said.

She smiled at Sarandon. Then she explained about going after Sarandon, thinking he was her suspect, and about the lawyer who would represent Alex.

"All right. Well, I haven't heard a thing about any of this. I guess his parents hadn't known about it either, from what you say."

"They hadn't. We just learned about all of it ourselves," Sarandon said. "What about his sister, Faye? Sarah said she didn't think he ever was close to her, but we were thinking since they're twins, they might have been in touch without anyone knowing."

"It's possible. I don't have any knowledge of it. We have gatherings, or had, until my mate died. She was always organizing the social gatherings. I don't recall ever having seen the twins at the affairs."

"Is she mated?"

"Faye is. And she's got a set of twins herself."

"And her aunt and uncle?"

"Died a few years back." Monty pulled out his phone. "I'll see if I can get ahold of her." Monty shook his head and then tried another number and spoke to someone. "Is Faye there? Okay, has her brother been there? Alex?" Monty looked up at Sarandon. "Okay. Um, has he been by to see her? Recently?"

Sarandon hung on every word, watching Monty's expression—which revealed that whoever he was talking to knew Alex. Which meant Faye must too.

"Okay, thanks, Bill. Can you…have her call me when she returns? Thanks." Monty put his cell phone on the coffee table. "Faye's on a camping trip with her girls. Her husband said she has no cell reception where they are. He had to work, or he would be there with them."

"He knows Alex?" CJ asked.

"Yeah. He said he isn't there."

"He knows him," Sarandon said. "Which means Faye does too." He ground his teeth. "Where are they camping?"

Monty let out his breath and made another call. "Hey, Bill, can you tell me where Faye and the girls are camping? Yes, it's about Alex. I need to get ahold of him. It's really important… Thanks."

They ended the call again, and Monty told them, "They're at Wild Wolf Run. It's a private camping ground, the property owned and operated by our pack for pack members. I'll give you the directions. You can't find it with GPS."

"Cabins?"

"Yeah. Number five." Monty wrote down the directions for them on a script map. "I suspect Bill and Faye know something about the trouble Alex is in. Bill wouldn't say, but he sounded worried they'd be in trouble for not having told me. Keep me informed about this, will you? Seems I've been rather out of the loop of late."

"We will," Jenna said. "And we'll let you know, or we'll have him call you, when we locate him."

Then they left the house, and CJ said, "Why don't we head out to the campsite first? Afterward, we can split up and each take five of the people on the list of names Sarah gave us who she suspects could know something."

"Just as long as Sarandon and I get to speak with Alex's girlfriend," Jenna said.

Sarandon was still surprised Sarah had added her name to the list. Maybe Christina didn't like Sarah and felt she was interfering in her relationship with Alex.

First, they caravanned out to the camping area where seven log cabins were set around a picturesque lake, the firs and pines between each of the cabins giving them enough privacy from their neighbors to make for the perfect camping experience.

Sarandon, Jenna, and CJ went to the fifth cabin on the dirt road, but when they reached it, they noticed the place was dark, and no vehicle was parked beside it. They sure hoped Faye's husband hadn't lied that they had no cell reception or that she had a satellite phone and was warned that someone might be coming for Alex—or to question her about his whereabouts—and she took the kids and left.

"Maybe they went on a wolf run," Sarandon said, hoping that was the case as they got out of their vehicles and looked around the cabin for signs of anyone outside grilling or playing near the lake. Though that didn't explain the absence of a vehicle.

Before Jenna could knock on the door, Sarandon saw movement in the brush and turned to look. Five adult wolves were watching them from the woods. They wouldn't have shown themselves unless they had smelled Sarandon, Jenna, and CJ's scents and known they were wolves.

The wolves growled, baring their teeth. It didn't seem to matter that CJ was wearing his deputy sheriff's uniform.

"Hey," Jenna said, frowning at them. "We're here looking for Alex Dreyfus. We want to help him. Has he been here with Faye? She's not in trouble. He is, and we want to ensure the human police don't arrest him before we can talk to him and make sure he has the best wolf lawyer there is to represent him."

They didn't even know if these wolves knew anything about Alex or the kind of trouble he was in, but Sarandon agreed that they needed to set them straight.

"We're his and Faye's half brothers," CJ said. "I'm CJ and this is Sarandon Silver, from Silver Town."

Then a smaller wolf appeared behind the larger male wolves. Faye?

She paused for a moment, then headed for the cabin and ran through the wolf door. Sarandon, Jenna, and CJ waited, hoping she was shifting and getting dressed and would speak to them, while the other wolves watched them, ensuring they stayed put in the meantime.

A few minutes later, she opened the door and said, "I'm Faye Emerson. My brother, Alex, isn't here. Come in and tell me what this is all about." Her hair was a lighter brown than Alex's, and she had blue eyes. She didn't look like Alex at all.

"I'm Jenna St. John, a fugitive recovery agent. I'm looking to take Alex in to meet his trial date, but we've got a good wolf lawyer to represent him. Do you know the trouble he's in?"

"He wouldn't talk about it. He said he was in trouble, but he didn't do it. He trusted Burt to help him leave Colorado Springs, but now he's in even more trouble."

"We're here to help him," Jenna insisted.

"You're here to arrest him. You don't care about anything else."

"That's not true. He has to go in though, because he has a warrant out for his arrest," CJ said. "It's not going away."

"He didn't do whatever they've charged him with," Faye said.

"Fine. Let him explain himself in court then," Sarandon said. "With a good wolf lawyer representing him."

"I don't know where he is."

"He's been in touch. Recently," CJ said.

They'd smelled all kinds of male wolves in the area, and any one of them could have been Alex's scent. One of them smelled like the paw prints left behind near Jenna's home.

"Yeah, I've seen him since he got into trouble." Faye sat down in the living room, and they joined her.

"He was staying here." Sarandon was only guessing, but he suspected that's why she left with her kids and returned with some of the male wolves camping here.

"Tell me about this wolf lawyer." Faye tilted her chin up.

Jenna explained who he was, and Sarandon corroborated that he had helped him out.

"All right. He ditched his phone, knowing he could be tracked. As soon as I can reach him, I'll tell him what you've told me."

"You don't have any idea where he went?" Jenna asked.

Sarandon was sure Faye knew where he was, but she only shook her head.

"Okay, well, we're out of here then." CJ stood. "I just wanted to say you're family too. And we'd like to get to know you, if you'll let us."

Sarandon and Jenna joined him.

"We'll help him," Jenna said, and then they left the cabin.

The other wolves were hanging around outside but looked up at them as they walked down the steps of the deck.

They didn't say anything to the wolves; no sense in repeating what they were there for. Sarandon, Jenna, and CJ were trying to take in the wolves' scents, but all of them had been in Sarah and Anton's house at one time or another. He couldn't smell Alex's scent among them, if the wolf who'd been in Jenna's territory had been him.

"We have a wolf lawyer for Alex, if he cares to talk to us." Sarandon figured he'd give it his best shot.

None of the wolves came forward.

A car tore down the gravel drive and parked off to the side of Jenna's car.

"Looks like someone's in a growly wolf mood," Jenna said.

"How much do you want to bet it's Bill, Faye's mate." CJ had his hand on his holstered gun.

The man threw open his door.

"You're probably right." Jenna moved closer to Sarandon. He figured she thought she'd protect him because he didn't have a weapon on him like she did.

"Where's my—" the guy said.

"I'm here, Bill. I'm fine. They just wanted to talk to Alex, but he's not here," Faye said, coming out on the deck. "They're leaving."

"Yep, we sure are," Sarandon said, irritated, but he knew if anyone had come to Silver Town accusing him of being a crook, his people would... Well, they did stick up for him. So it was understandable.

"Okay, let's take care of interviewing those on the lists," CJ said. They hoped none of the wolves here were on Sarah's list.

"Sounds good." Sarandon got into Jenna's car. She drove while he navigated for her, and CJ followed them out of there.

"Do you think Alex was there?" Jenna asked Sarandon.

"I suspect he could have been," Sarandon said. "Either he took off when Monty called Faye, or he was standing there with the rest of the male wolves, maybe shielded by their scents. I was trying to watch Bill's face when he glanced at the wolves, but I couldn't tell if he spied Alex among them."

"Alex must be a beta wolf, don't you think? Or he would come forth and just deal with this."

"That could very well be."

Armed with five of the names, Sarandon and Jenna went to see Christina first. She was living in a one-story, white brick home on the south side of Cañon City. When they arrived at her red door, the blond, blue-eyed woman gaped at Sarandon.

"We're looking for Alex. I've just learned he's my half brother and wanted to touch base with him and welcome him into our family and our pack. Is he home?" Sarandon asked.

"Ohmigod, I can't believe it. He only recently learned his father was the sheriff of Silver Town, except he learned Sheridan is dead now. Along with Ritka, his mother. He was upset to learn that but couldn't understand why his family gave him up. You look just like him. Did they give you up too? Or did they raise you?" Christina asked.

He hadn't expected her to question him about all this, but if she and Alex were going to be mated wolves, he could understand why she'd want to know. "He was more of an absentee father after my mother was murdered. Ritka was not my mother," Sarandon said.

"Oh. I'm sorry to hear it. I guess Alex should be grateful his adoptive parents raised him."

"He would have enjoyed being with us," Sarandon said. "Four brothers and three cousins to include him in all our shenanigans." Not that Sheridan would have liked it if Alex had come to live with them, but Sarandon knew his brothers and the rest of the family would have accepted him into the family.

Jenna said to Christina, "Are you mating Alex?"

Christina frowned at her. "Why? Are you interested in him?"

"No." Jenna took Sarandon's hand. "Sarandon is the one I'm courting. I've never even met Alex."

Sarandon was surprised Christina would even think some other she-wolf was interested in him if he was planning to mate her.

"Okay, listen," Jenna said. "Alex is in a lot of trouble. The police are looking for him after he skipped bail. If you know where he is, we need to get in touch with him. My family has a really good wolf lawyer, and we want to help him clear his name, if we can."

"Why?"

Sarandon thought it was interesting that Christina didn't appear shocked or surprised that Alex was in serious trouble. And she hadn't asked what he was in trouble for. Which meant she knew all about it.

"We want to help him because I'm courting his half brother, and he wants to help him out. If you don't know already, Alex impersonated Sarandon when they caught him and charged him with identity theft. Do you have any idea where he has gone? He can't hide forever, and he'll have a warrant out for his arrest until we take care of this."

"He's been in Colorado Springs on a job."

Old news, but the cavalier way Christina said it made Sarandon think she knew where he was. "When was the last time you heard from him?"

Christina chewed on her lip. "Last night. He called me and said he wasn't coming home for a couple of weeks. That's not unusual. It just means he's got another construction job."

Which Sarandon thought was odd. If he was courting the she-wolf, like Sarandon was courting Jenna, he'd be seeing her all the time. It wasn't that far to Colorado Springs. "Did he tell you for sure where he was going to be working?"

"Nah. It's not something that would interest me, so he never really talks about his jobs."

Again, that surprised Sarandon. He didn't think they would become mated wolves at that rate. "Not even where he'll be staying?" Sarandon asked.

"No. Not unless I ask."

And why wouldn't Christina ask Alex where he was going to be? Sarandon would certainly know where Jenna was going if she was trying to track down a fugitive and he wasn't riding shotgun. He'd probably be making a nuisance of himself, calling her for updates constantly if he couldn't be with her.

"So, he lives with you normally?" Jenna asked.

"Yeah, but we're not mated. His mother doesn't like me, and he's trying to ease her into the idea that I could make a good mate for him."

Which made Sarandon really believe Alex was a beta wolf. Otherwise, he would have done what he felt in his heart was right. Even though families were often close, choosing the woman who would be his mate was just as important. Either that, or one of the two of them wasn't that eager to mate.

"Why does Sarah think you wouldn't be a good mate?" Jenna asked.

"Are you kidding? No one would ever be good enough for her golden son."

"Golden son?" Jenna asked.

Sarandon was confused too. Burt was their real son. Why would Sarah consider their adopted son to be so special? He thought the dad was the one who really connected with Alex.

"Sure. Alex is so dutiful to his parents and loves them like they were his own. He's always going over there to help them out. Burt is a different story. He's the black sheep of the family. I think they were so thrilled they'd have their own flesh-and-blood son that they spoiled him terribly. Alex was thrilled to have a little brother. Burt is always getting into difficulties and trying to get Alex into the same messes as him. He wants Alex to be in trouble with his parents too, so they won't think of him as the good son. Not only that, but Burt keeps pulling crap and then blaming Alex for it."

"Are you sure?" Sarandon figured Christina felt an attachment to Alex so she most likely was biased, but her claim was certainly something they needed to look into.

"Yes, I'm sure. Just ask Alex."

"If we can get ahold of him, we will. How does Alex react to Burt's actions?" Jenna asked.

Christina shrugged. "He cares too much about his younger brother to give up on him, no matter what he pulls."

Sarandon gave her his card. Jenna didn't give Christina one of her own. She might feel Jenna was there to take him into custody, if Christina didn't already know she was a fugitive recovery agent. "Call me if you hear from him. Give him my number and tell him there are no hard feelings. We'll get it straightened out," Sarandon said. "I want to get to know him. All of us do."

"Yeah, sure." Christina sounded like she didn't think they really wanted to help him.

"We either are able to aid him—and as wolves, that means something—or it's strictly a police matter, his choice," Jenna said.

"I'll tell him, if I hear from him." Then Christina shut and locked the door.

They waited until they were in Jenna's car, and then she said, "Do you think Burt could be the reason for all this?"

"Alex was caught with the stuff, but if for some reason Burt set him up to take the fall, there's still the business of Alex using my ID and claiming to be me instead of telling the truth and saying he'd been framed. We have to remember Christina will probably say anything to keep Alex out of jail."

"True." Jenna sighed, then looked at the list. "Okay, so what did you think about the way she reacted when we told her he's wanted by the police?"

"Like she already knew about it. If he's really planning to mate her because he loves her, I believe he'd tell her he was in trouble. I think she could be hiding him."

"Or knows exactly where he's staying right now and wants to discuss our offer with him first," Jenna said. "What did you think about the way she doesn't care where he is for weeks at a time and doesn't bother to keep in touch?"

"Like they're not that committed to each other. You'd have a devil of a time going off on your own without me knowing where you're going to be," Sarandon said.

She patted his leg. "Good to know."

"That's good, isn't it?"

She laughed. "Believe me, I feel the same about you. Are you ready to see the next person on the list?"

"I sure am."

After about a twenty-minute drive, they located the white vinyl-sided home. The man who answered the door was gray-haired and wearing a leather motorcycle jacket, leather boots, and a leather hat. When they told him they needed to find Alex and offer him help before the police took him into custody, the man couldn't believe Alex would be in any trouble. "No, not young Alex. Burt? Yeah."

"Burt, his brother?" Sarandon asked, clarifying that's who he meant and not the dad.

"Hell yeah. Burt was always goading Alex on, trying to get him to do things that could get him in trouble. Even when they were kids."

"Why, do you know?" Sarandon asked.

"Alex was always the good son. He did what he was told, and he was always there for his parents. When he learned they weren't his real parents—though he didn't know until more recently who his biological father and mother were—he wanted to show them how much the Dreyfuses' love for him meant to him. Burt was spoiled rotten, their only flesh-and-blood child. I really believe he didn't feel he had to prove anything to them."

"Sarah said you might know why Alex is suspected of stealing identities," Jenna said.

"She would say that. She's never liked me because I ride bikes. She believes they're evil, and motorcyclists are evil. When her sons wanted to take up riding bikes, she was furious with me and ranted that I was going to get them killed. Anyway, they both rode bikes for a while, until they got in accidents and gave them up. The boys still talk to me when I run into them in town on occasion, but Sarah has never forgiven me for nearly getting both her sons killed…her words. Their bikes were totaled, but they weren't badly injured. Shaken was all."

"Do you have any idea where Alex might be?" Sarandon asked.

"No. Sorry. I'd let you know if I knew. If you're going to get him that high-powered wolf lawyer, I'd advise him in a heartbeat to go with you."

Sarandon gave the wolf his card and thanked him, and then they called the next man on the list, but he wasn't available until the next day. They called the last two people and got the same result.

"It sounds like Sarah's got grudges against people that are unfounded," Jenna said.

"I agree." Sarandon made a call to CJ. "Sarah seems to resent the people on her list. The two witnesses we've seen believe that, of the two boys, Burt is more likely to have done criminal activities."

"That's what I'm finding with the list I'm working from. Three of the five people I've interviewed said Alex is great to work with, but Burt, and Sarah, are beastly," CJ said.

"Sounds like that is the consensus of opinion," Sarandon said. "When did you plan to see Burt for the interview?"

"I can't get ahold of the remaining two people on my list until tomorrow morning. Stanton should be wrapping up his ghost-hunter show by six, and he's going to make sure Burt stays put so we can talk to him."

"Okay, we have three to go, but we're in the same

boat as you. The men we need to talk to won't be home until tomorrow. It's five thirty now, so if we head back to Colorado Springs, we'll be there just in time to talk to Burt." Sarandon wondered how Burt was going to react to seeing them. He was glad they knew more what others thought of Burt before they spoke with him.

"Okay, meet you at the hotel where they're staying. The Antlers Hotel, another place listed as haunted in Colorado Springs. Three ghosts are reportedly living there and appear to staff and guests from time to time."

"Well, if you don't get too spooked, we'll see you there."

"Not me, Brother. Ghosts don't bother me. See you there."

Then they finished the call.

"Sounds to me like a lot of people have trouble with Burt, not just the two we talked to. I wonder if Sarah knows how people feel about him, and about her," Jenna said to Sarandon.

"She probably does. Unless she's in denial."

"What if Burt egged Alex on to do the identity theft?" Jenna asked as they drove back to Colorado Springs.

"What if he had everything to do with the crime and Alex didn't have anything to do with it?" Sarandon was beginning to wonder who was really at fault. Either Alex wasn't as innocent as he appeared, someone else had talked him into it, or he was being framed. "What if he is innocent of stealing the passports and credit cards?"

"He still used your ID to impersonate you, no matter what else he did or didn't do. And if he didn't have anything to do with the rest of it, why wouldn't he have said so?" Jenna turned onto the highway.

"He was caught with it, and who would believe someone else had stolen all that stuff?" Sarandon really didn't know what to think. "Besides, he looked just like my driver's license. Or close enough. Even if he denied that was him, do you think they would have believed it?"

"You're probably right about that. It seems irrefutable. Maybe, though, he didn't want to give up the name of the person who really did it."

"Burt?" Sarandon asked.

"Yeah. Because he feels some unswerving loyalty to him. Others said he really cared for his younger brother."

"Or Alex felt the loyalty to their parents. Maybe Alex feels it would kill them if they knew Burt had stolen all that. Or make it worse because Burt's always in trouble."

"That's possible. We really need to know how the thief stole everyone's stuff." Jenna turned onto another road. "That might help us to nail down who did it. Who had the easiest access? A guy who works construction? One who is a cameraman for a ghost show? Or someone else who might be close to Alex?"

"His parents, but I doubt they would have done this to him. They seemed totally clueless."

"A girlfriend?" Jenna asked. "Who…works in a hotel, cleaning rooms."

Sarandon frowned, thinking how she didn't seem concerned about Alex at all. "And if anyone left passports or driver's licenses in the rooms? Credit cards? While they're swimming in the pool maybe? But wouldn't the police have been notified, and she would have been caught? Because she cleaned those particular rooms? Or even if she hadn't but had access to the rooms, I would think all the hotel staff would have been questioned.

Which means we need to learn where the items were stolen from. I wonder if anyone else in the pack could be involved in this."

"Like an identity theft ring? I doubt it. Not with them being wolves."

Chapter 15

WHEN THEY REACHED THE ANTLERS HOTEL IN COLORADO Springs, Sarandon and Jenna met CJ in the lobby. Shimmering crystal chandeliers cast shadows across the tile floor. The hotel had been rebuilt twice, once due to a fire and the other time to modernize it. It was elegant and the perfect place for the ghost hunters to put on a show.

Sarandon mentioned to CJ some of the suspicions they had about who else might be involved.

"Is the girlfriend mating him?" CJ asked, knowing close friends or family were always suspect.

Jenna folded her arms and shook her head. "To me, that's the oddest part. She wouldn't say. Does that mean Alex hasn't indicated he's that interested in her? Or maybe they're both just waiting. Maybe she's the one who is balking about the mating. I just thought it was odd that she wouldn't say."

"Not to mention that other red flags were raised," Sarandon said.

"Oh?" Red flags were CJ's specialty.

"Yeah. She didn't seem surprised he was in trouble, and she doesn't care where he is or what he's doing. To me, that says a lot," Sarandon said.

"Okay. Sounds to me like their relationship isn't going far. I called Stanton to tell him I had arrived, and he said he's on his way down to meet us. Burt is in the suite," CJ said. "Stanton's brothers are making sure he's staying put."

"Good to hear it."

"I agree. Another thing, with your law enforcement background, can you check with the police and learn where everything was stolen? If we have some idea where the stuff disappeared, we could start checking alibis," Sarandon said.

CJ made a note of it. "Next on my list."

Then they saw Stanton headed for them. He looked angry, his gaze taking in CJ and Sarandon, and then he considered Jenna, the only person he didn't know. Sarandon was certain CJ would have told him who she was and the stake she had in being here to question Burt.

"He's still here, right?" CJ asked, sounding growly.

Sarandon felt the same way, wanting to learn as much as they could from Burt about Alex or even Burt himself.

"Yeah. My brothers are watching him. There's really nowhere private to meet except one of our rooms. So we'll meet in my suite. It has a sitting area and bar." Stanton motioned to the elevator, and they all went up to the fifth floor. "You don't really believe Burt is guilty of anything, do you?"

"We don't know. That's why we need to question him," CJ said.

"He's a damn good cameraman, and I'd hate to lose him."

"He may have nothing to do with it." Though Sarandon had his suspicions.

When they reached Stanton's suite, his brother Vernon opened the door. He was a little blonder than his brothers and a little shorter, but just as muscled and serious.

Yolan looked sheepish about something and motioned to Burt, who was passed out on the floor. "We had to knock him out."

"What?" Stanton growled.

"He must have assumed something was up. He took a phone call, and then he said he had urgent business he had to attend to. He'd talk to you later," Vernon said. "Of course, we knew you wouldn't okay his leaving for *any* reason, short of dying."

They looked at the man lying on the floor, his eyes closed. He looked just like Sarandon remembered— lean, wiry, blond haired but not wearing a beard now, his face angular with a cleft in his chin.

"Who called him on his cell that prompted him to want to leave in a hurry?" Sarandon asked, wondering if it was Alex. Or maybe his mother to warn him about his brother, or to learn where he might be.

"I didn't ask, and he didn't say. I told him he couldn't leave, and he said he'd make it up to Stanton, but he really had to run. That it was an emergency."

"Then you knocked him out? Couldn't you have just confined him or something?" Stanton sounded like he wanted to knock some sense into his brothers.

"I knew this was important to you," Vernon said, frowning at Stanton.

"All right. Wake him up so they can talk to him and get on their way."

Yolan splashed some icy water from the ice bucket onto Burt's face, and the man sputtered and threw his hands up to fend him off. "Hell, what did Vernon go and hit me for?"

"I told you Stanton wanted to talk to you. If you want your job, you stay and talk to him."

Not that they would have let him go if he had wanted to quit his job. The Wernicke brothers were still trying to get into the Silver Town wolves' good graces, and they knew if they wanted to ever join the pack, this is what it would take. Working with the Silver Town wolves in crises like this.

Burt rubbed the red spot on the side of his head, but when he saw Sarandon, his eyes widened. Because Sarandon looked so much like Alex? Or because he had something to do with the theft of Sarandon's ID?

"Tell us all you know about Alex and this mess he's gotten himself into," Sarandon said before CJ could do so. Before Burt could say anything—not that he was jumping at the chance to offer anything—Sarandon added, "And your involvement in him leaving the city."

Burt's lower jaw dropped. "Hell, I don't know what you're talking about."

"We caught you on a street cam leaving with Alex," Sarandon said, not that they had. Luckily, CJ folded his arms and nodded, as if what Sarandon said was the truth.

"That was *you. You're* the one the police wanted." Burt sounded growly about it, as if Sarandon was trying to pull a fast one on everyone.

"I thought you said you didn't know anything about it. And if that's true, why would you have helped me leave the city? I didn't even know you."

Burt didn't say anything and just glowered at Sarandon.

"For your information, my name has been cleared. Want to try again with another bullshit story? Or the truth this time?" Sarandon asked.

Burt glanced at Stanton.

"Tell them the truth. They need to find Alex and help him beat this," Stanton said, his words a command.

Burt threw up his hands in defeat as if he had no choice but to come clean. "Alex begged me to come get him and take him out of the city. I told him it was a mistake for him to leave. Christina had left him off in the city on the job he'd been working, and when he got caught, he didn't have any transportation. Then again, he couldn't go to prison, not as a wolf. You understand that, surely," Burt said.

So it was just like they'd suspected. Alex didn't leave on his own. And Burt had been the one to help him. Had it happened the way Burt said it had? Was it just that Sarandon wanted his half brother to be innocent? Or had Burt forced Alex to leave when he had wanted to do what was right by continuing to work his job and remain in the city?

"Wait a minute," CJ said. "The police said the suspect was found with the goods in his vehicle. Care to change the story again?"

"Hell, that's what he told me!" Burt said.

"Where did you go after you left the city?" CJ asked.

"We went to Cañon City, and he stayed with his girlfriend for a little while, but we were afraid if you cleared your name, the police would check Cañon City because he's from there. In the meantime, I returned to work on a job with the Wernicke brothers."

"Sounds like a stretch to me. How would the police know we had a half brother and learn his name?" When Burt didn't respond, Sarandon asked, "Why did you do it?"

"He's my brother, and he begged me to come get

him. He figured his truck would be picked up too easily. No one would be looking for me. If he was your brother, you'd have come to help him out too."

"He *is* our brother, and we *are* here to help him out," CJ said. "You've changed the story again. You said Christina had driven him to Colorado Springs and left him off at the job site. Now you're saying he didn't want to drive his truck because the police would be on the lookout for it and you knew about it."

Burt glanced at the door. Wishing he could escape?

"I have a lawyer to represent him. A wolf lawyer," Jenna said.

Burt's mouth gaped.

"If he'd stayed put, none of this would have been necessary," Sarandon said. Though that wasn't really true. Without Jenna coming after Sarandon, they would never have known Alex was a wolf or that he was related to the Silver brothers and cousins. And the St. Johns wouldn't have hired a lawyer for him.

CJ put Burt on the spot. "We've learned you've been in some trouble with the law yourself."

"Minor things. Nothing big. Not like Alex is in trouble for."

Sarandon narrowed his eyes at Burt. "Several of your pack members say you were always trying to get him into trouble. Why? So that you weren't the only one who disappointed your parents with your actions?"

"Hey, you can't pin Alex's actions on me. Hell, he's just never been caught before, that's all. Besides, he's my older brother. Who do you think put me up to everything I did? Except he's a lot better at not getting caught at it."

Sarandon smiled. "You're good at this. The perfect con man. Who's to say you didn't do all this—steal the IDs and the rest? Then frame Alex so your parents wouldn't think their adoptive son was a better son than you. What about Christina? If Alex went to prison, maybe you wanted to court the she-wolf in his place?"

"Did she say that?" Burt looked a little panicked all of a sudden.

Sarandon and CJ exchanged looks. Sarandon wondered if there was more to the situation between Christina and Burt than they'd suspected.

"Yeah. That she didn't want to hurt Alex by letting on she was really interested in courting you," Jenna fabricated. "What is up with that? She's more into the bad boy? Then what would you say to Alex? When he went to jail, well, she couldn't wait for him to return for all those years and things just happened. You were there to comfort her, take care of her, and voilà, the mating just happens."

"She wouldn't have told you that."

"She cares about Alex. Not as a mate, but like a brother," Jenna added. "She didn't want to hurt him, even if she wants to be with you."

"She wouldn't have said that. I just got a call from her."

So that's who had called him, warning him to get out of there. Sarandon smiled. "Telling you that you'd better get the hell out of here because we were coming to talk to you next? That we were on to you? That Alex wasn't at fault for any of this?"

"You'd say so because you don't want Alex to be your real brother if he's been in trouble with the law.

Well, get used to the fact that he's a rogue wolf. That he's going to spend time in jail. If I end up hooking up with Christina, it happens. We hadn't planned any of this. Alex is the sneaky kind of wolf that everyone thinks is so good, but in reality, he's not. He's just gotten away with it all, conned everyone else all along. Even me."

Sarandon didn't believe him for an instant. Vernon had his arms folded across his chest and was shaking his head. None of the rest of them looked like they believed Burt either.

"Why were you and Alex at the Silver Town Tavern a short while ago, having a meal?" CJ asked. "We have several witnesses who identified the two of you."

Burt didn't say anything for a moment, and Sarandon knew he was trying to come up with a story. "We were just in the area and needed a bite to eat. It's open to wolves passing through, isn't it?"

"Yeah. It just seems too convenient that you come to town, my ID is stolen, and then a fugitive recovery agent comes after me because Alex has used my stolen ID," Sarandon said.

"That's all we were doing. Eating a meal. How do I know how Alex came upon all those passports and other IDs? I didn't ask, and he didn't offer an explanation when I came to help him leave the city."

"The two of you were together the whole time you were in Silver Town?" CJ asked. "You didn't split up for a time?"

Burt paused before he responded. Sarandon figured he was trying to come up with a way to incriminate Alex further—and make himself seem completely innocent of any wrongdoing.

"Okay, look, we did go our separate ways for a while. I had my camera with me, and I wanted to take some pictures of the ski area."

"Have you got those pictures?" CJ asked.

"Nah. None of them turned out. Way overexposed. Still learning my camera settings. Alex had learned he was Sheridan Silver's son and wanted to see Silver Town, since he would have lived there if his father had accepted him. How was I to know he planned on stealing your information? I was just as shocked as you were to learn what he'd done. You think you know someone, and you don't at all. I was surprised he didn't ask for my help, like he was always doing so I'd end up taking the fall. I guess he was just angry your dad had raised you and not him, and he wanted to get back at you. He didn't even tell me what he'd done wrong when he begged me to come get him and take him to see Christina."

"If I'd known he was my brother, I would have asked him what he'd done wrong so we could help him out," Sarandon said. "We wouldn't have ignored the situation. He has a warrant out for his arrest now."

"I didn't feel it was any of my business."

"You're wolves, and you grew up together. You should have made it your business, unless you already knew all about it," Jenna said. "Or you didn't really care."

"I'm not the one who did any of this. Damn it, just like usual, everything gets twisted around and I'm the one who will take the blame. Who the hell are you anyway?"

"I'm Jenna St. James, the one who intends to take Alex into custody. He's skipped his bail. I'm a fugitive recovery agent. I believe you know all about what Alex has purportedly done. Especially since he was begging you to come rescue him. And I believe you had a lot more to do with this than you're saying."

"Okay, all right. I knew what he'd done. I told Alex I couldn't help him unless he told me everything that had happened."

"How did he get ahold of the passports, credit cards, and driver's licenses?" CJ asked.

"That part he didn't tell me about. He said I might be considered an accessory to the crime."

Sarandon laughed. He couldn't believe the guy could twist the truth so much.

"You are, for aiding and abetting his escape," CJ said.

"He didn't want me to get in any deeper than I was by helping him out."

"So where is he now? He's going to be arrested, and it will go worse for him if we don't reach him first and have the lawyer counsel him," Jenna said. "If you care."

"Of course I care. I told you I dropped him off at Christina's place. If he left there, I have no idea where he went next. I guess he didn't want me to know either, so I wouldn't be in more trouble."

"Or so you couldn't tell anyone where he is?" Sarandon texted Brett to call him, just to pretend he had some information for them. His phone rang. "Yeah, Brett?" He raised a brow at Burt. "You did, eh? Okay, that information is invaluable."

Brett chuckled. "I'm glad to hear it. How's it going?"

"We're questioning Burt now. Glad to know you have the evidence against him."

"Burt was involved?" Brett asked, sounding surprised.

"Even aided and abetted Alex in his escape. We've

spoken to several people in their pack and know a lot more about the two men now." Sarandon didn't take his eyes off Burt and hoped Brett understood he was making up stuff as he went along.

The guy squirmed to get comfortable on the sofa.

"That's good news. I've got to get back to fixing dinner. Have you been able to reach Alex yet?" Brett asked.

"No, not yet, but we're not stopping until we do."

"Good. If you need my help, I'll take off from the paper for a few days and be there for you. I hear you've got another supper date with Jenna's family."

"Thanks, I knew I could count on you. Yeah, you're right on supper with Jenna's family."

"Well, you know how Eric is. He always wants to hear the news first, so if you and Jenna decide to mate, let him know first. Then me."

Sarandon chuckled. "What about Darien and Lelandi?" The pack leaders were supposed to hear from the pack members first.

"Yeah, sure, after Eric and me."

Sarandon laughed. "All right. Thanks for the information. I'll talk to you later." Sarandon and Brett ended the call.

"Good news?" CJ asked, looking hopeful. Sarandon suspected his brother really thought he had information.

"Yeah, for us. Not for them." Sarandon motioned to Burt. He wished Brett had known more that would help them.

"We've got a supper to go to," Jenna reminded Sarandon and CJ.

"I'm going to have to skip it," CJ said.

Sarandon was surprised, but he shouldn't have been. He assumed his brother was going to arrest Burt, and CJ, Peter, and Trevor would take turns questioning him back at the sheriff's office. If Burt was influencing Alex in any way, or responsible for any of this, Sarandon hoped they'd learn the truth. In the meantime, he had every intention of finding Alex and hearing his story.

"You don't have any legal right to arrest me," Burt said, as if he thought he might be able to talk his way out of this.

"Yeah, we do." CJ read him his rights and handcuffed him. "Not only for aiding a suspect in fleeing the city, but also because I imagine you know a lot more about this than you're letting on."

"That would be the Colorado Springs Police Department's jurisdiction. Not some deputy sheriff's from Silver Town."

"We're wolves. You know how this works."

"Prove I had anything to do with this," Burt snarled.

"Oh, I aim to," CJ said.

"Why were you running through my territory as a wolf?" Jenna asked.

"I don't have any idea where you live, lady."

Stanton said, "So how soon before we get Burt back so he can video record our program?"

"Could be a while, for however long it takes to learn the truth. If I were you, I'd call your backup guys." CJ hauled Burt out of the suite, with him protesting the whole time.

Sarandon shook Stanton's hand, then thanked him and his brothers for helping them out.

"I hope you find your brother soon and can help him

beat this," Stanton said. "I hate to lose a good cameraman, but from the guilty look on Burt's face and all the lies he told when he took off during that job, I don't trust him."

"I agree with you on that, but you've been working with him, so you'd know him even better than we would. Still, the more we talked with him, the more it appeared he was more involved in this than he's letting on," Sarandon said.

"I agree with you there. I don't believe I've ever seen him squirm so much."

After saying goodbye, Sarandon and Jenna left to have supper with her parents. She called them on the Bluetooth to let them know CJ was returning to Silver Town with a suspect.

"Your sisters are disappointed they had to leave to track down another bail bond skipper, but we look forward to the meal and visit. Sorry to hear CJ couldn't make it, but you know he could eat here first and then leave," Logan said.

"CJ and Burt already left," Sarandon said. "I'll call him anyway, in case he hasn't traveled too far and would like to join us." They ended the call, and Sarandon immediately called his brother. "Hey, Jenna's dad suggested you come over for supper. You've got to eat anyway and you've got a long drive ahead of you. We can help keep an eye on Burt while we all enjoy the meal."

"I'll take you up on it. I'm still here in the city, just getting gas."

"Okay, give us your location, and we'll meet up with you and lead you over there." Once CJ did that, Sarandon called the construction company Alex worked for and got the manager. "I'm looking for my brother, Alex Dreyfus. I spoke with his adoptive parents, and they said he was working for you. Is he there, per chance?"

"He had to take time off for family business. He's a good man. I hope he gets it sorted out and comes back to work soon."

"Did he finish the job he was working on?"

"Yeah. Despite being anxious about getting on his way, he stayed until he finished what he needed to do."

"I figured he would." Sarandon had suspected that was partly why Alex had stayed in Colorado Springs as long as he did. "So, you don't have any idea where he is now."

"No. He has a girlfriend in Cañon City though."

"We've already spoken with her. She thought he was working a job."

"Not with me. I hope he didn't start working for some other company before he let me know he was quitting."

"I'm sure he wouldn't have. He's a good man," Sarandon said, repeating the manager's words, as much as he was questioning the validity of the statement. "I'll ask him to give you a call when I find him."

"Thanks."

They ended the call. Sarandon hated to stir up more problems for Alex when he was already in trouble. But they had to explore every avenue. He hadn't meant to give Alex's boss the notion that he might have quit his job without giving notice and started working for another company.

As soon as they joined CJ at the service station, he told them, "I picked up a sandwich for Burt here. You can let Jenna's family know they don't need to feed the prisoner."

"Will do."

When they arrived at the St. Johns' house, Logan came out to greet them. He shook CJ's hand and Sarandon's, then scowled at Burt. "So where is Alex? Have you got him hidden away somewhere?"

Burt's eyes widened fractionally. "If I knew where he was, I'd damn well say. After all my parents have done for him too."

"What about all they've done for you? You don't have a squeaky-clean past," Jenna said as they walked into the house.

"Oh my," Victoria said, giving CJ a hug and then Sarandon too. "We're so glad you could come and have supper with us. The steaks are ready."

When they went into the dining room to eat, CJ uncuffed Burt but made him sit next to him at the table to ensure he didn't go anywhere. "Behave yourself, or I'll cuff you and you can skip eating."

"I'll eat. It isn't right that you've taken me prisoner when I haven't done anything, without a warrant for my arrest or anything." Burt eyed the steaks.

"Eat and be quiet," Logan said. "Unless you're willing to tell us where Alex is."

Sarandon figured Burt thought the St. Johns might come to his aid. He probably didn't know the whole family was in the bounty-hunter business and had put up the bond for Alex to ensure he showed up for his trial.

"What's it to you?" Burt asked.

"My mom is the bondswoman who has to pay the bail if Alex doesn't show up for his court date," Jenna said. "You know what? Since you helped him run off, I'm sure you can be charged and have your own trial date set."

"I take it you're not going to help me get out of jail free." Burt removed the wrapper from his turkey sandwich. "Got any beer to go with this?"

Jenna got him a glass of water. "Fat chance. I wouldn't trust you to honor your obligation."

CJ cut off a piece of New York strip steak. "No worry about getting bail where you're going. The local judge doesn't set bail for wolves. If we arrest you, you can wait there until we hear what we want to hear."

"Hell, that's not right. What are you charging me with?"

"Aiding and abetting and obstructing justice," CJ said. "For starters. I'm sure we can add to the list with a little more digging." He turned to Victoria and Logan. "I'm glad you caught me before I left the city. Great food, great company."

After dinner, CJ took Burt in hand, and Sarandon said, "I'll walk you out to the car."

Jenna stayed inside with her parents, and after CJ put handcuffed Burt into the back seat of his car, he shut the door, and Sarandon said, "Just call me if you have any trouble."

"Will do. Good luck finding Alex, and we'll work on getting the truth out of Burt. I don't trust him one iota."

"I agree. And I'll check with the other two people you were going to talk to on Sarah's list tomorrow. Let me know when you get in."

"I will. What's the deal with Jenna? Her parents?"

"Jenna and I are officially courting."

"What about the living arrangements?"

"We haven't decided yet."

"Hell, we'll miss you if you move out here. You

know if she starts having babies, she'll want to be by her parents."

"I kind of figured that. Even if she agreed to live in Silver Town, I would imagine it would be a hard adjustment to make."

"For the right she-wolf?" CJ asked.

"Moving anywhere is the only choice, really."

"I hear wedding bells then." CJ slapped Sarandon on the shoulder. "Good luck with that, Brother. If you learn where Alex is, let me know right away."

"Will do."

Chapter 16

AFTER DINNER WITH JENNA'S PARENTS, SARANDON AND Jenna returned to her home. "A wolf run, right?" Sarandon asked.

"Absolutely," she said, and before long, they had stripped naked in the living room, shifted, and were racing out the door.

She wondered if they'd smell any sign of the wolf who had been here earlier, and they found themselves going in the same direction as before. She was thinking more and more about how it would be if Sarandon was her mate and they lived here together. How they would enjoy these wolf runs, just the two of them, and then sometimes with her parents and sisters. She tried to think of how it would be if she lived with Sarandon in Silver Town. Everyone—well, mostly everyone—seemed to love her. They'd be good about trying to make her feel welcome. She knew her parents and sisters would visit when they could.

If Sarandon was really set on living in his hometown, with his wolf pack, she'd give it a try. She'd mate him. Love him. Because that's what mated wolves did. They were there for each other, no matter the circumstances.

Once they'd run through acres of forest and made sure no wolves had intruded on their territory, she and he played for another hour. Wolf play—all the growling and chasing, nipping and biting—was part of the courtship ritual. Even during the quiet times when she stopped to drink from the river, she saw him watching her and wondered what he was thinking. Maybe the same thoughts she was having—where would they live and raise their pups.

He drew close and brushed against her, his body needing to touch her, to share his scent with her. She drew closer, saying she thought they were together, just as much as he did. She turned her head a little, and he licked her muzzle. She licked his back. Then he nuzzled her cheek.

He was being sweet, and yet there was more to it than that. A female and male wolf in courtship. The pheromones letting them know just how interested they were in each other. She decided that she wasn't letting him go. She wanted him in her life for good. No matter where they ended up, they'd do this together.

Then she wondered about the job. Would he be her partner in that too? She would be thrilled. Then she frowned. She hoped he wouldn't be overprotective, worried she couldn't handle fugitives on her own. Especially if he didn't want to work with her. And what about his own business?

She sighed, nipped at him, then bolted for the house. They needed to discuss everything. At least she wanted to. She hoped this wouldn't be a disaster.

After the wolf run with Jenna, Sarandon chased her all the way to her house. They were getting to the mating stage, he knew. The quiet times together, just breathing each other in while out in the wilderness, contemplating

their lives together—both as wolves and as humans—
the playing part of getting to know each other. He knew
from the way she kept close to him that she was ready
for more.

Inside the house, he chased her all the way to her
bedroom, ignoring the fact that their clothes were in the
living room.

She turned around and nipped at him, and he tackled
her to the floor as a wolf. She growled in a playful way,
and when he let her up, she tackled him right back.

He loved it. And he loved her.

He let her take him down to the floor and nipped at
her ears and cheek as she grabbed his neck in a play
bite. As soon as she moved off him to let him up, panting, he shifted and got to his feet. She studied him for a
moment, making his cock stir. He wanted to be with her
tonight in the worst way, if she wanted the same as him.

She ran her tongue up his leg, and he smiled at
her before she shifted. Then she shifted and tackled
him, knocking him back onto the mattress. He could
have withstood her maneuver, but he wanted to be just
where she was sending him—backward onto the bed.
Beneath her.

She pinned him down. He quickly wrapped his arms
and legs around her, pinning her to him. "Now, this is
the way to end a wolf run."

She began to kiss his chin and cheeks, her mouth sliding across his mouth. "I so agree."

He kissed her back, their lips synced, their hot
bodies molded together. He wanted this, and he wanted
her. Not just now, but for a lifetime. He knew it in his
heart. He hoped she was feeling the same way about

him. He thought she was, or she wouldn't have made this maneuver.

He gloried in the feel of her soft curves and skin pressed against him, her soft mouth moving across his lips in a gentle sweep back and forth, her mons pressing against his engorged cock.

She rubbed against him and grabbed his wrists, holding them against the mattress, pinning him down as if she were in charge. He still had his legs wrapped around her, holding her tight to him. Proving he was just as much in charge.

She smiled against his mouth and licked the seam of his lips.

He parted his lips to take her in. She hummed against his mouth. "Delicious."

He twisted his hips and rolled her onto her back, and in the same smooth move, he was on top of her, grasping *her* wrists, holding them against the bed. Now she was open to him, her legs spread, his body in between, his tongue in her mouth, stroking, tasting the sweet, spiciness that was Jenna.

"Hmm, Sarandon."

Even the sultry, sexy way she said his name made him hotter.

―⁓―

Sarandon moved off her to caress her breast and kiss her jaw. Jenna cherished the way he made her feel loved, the tenderness of his kisses, and the touch of his fingers sliding across her breast. They tingled, and her nipples stretched out to him.

She pulled him down to kiss his mouth and moved

her tongue inside to stroke his tongue. She loved this between them, but she wasn't ready for a mating all the way. Not yet. They hadn't decided on anything. Where to live. What he would do if he joined her here. What she would do if she joined him in Silver Town.

He cupped a breast and touched his tongue to her nipple, scorching her. Wrapping his lips around it, he suckled and she slid her fingers through his hair, wanting all of him.

"Hot," she said. He made her hot, made her want to go all the way—at least her body was craving having him deep inside her. "Hurry." She reached down to stroke his cock, and that encouraged him to stroke her between her legs. "Ohmigod, yes."

They continued to kiss, their pheromones going crazy.

He rubbed her clit, then slipped a finger into her, and she wanted his cock inside her, stretching her, deeply thrusting. He slid his tongue between her lips. So enraptured with his touch, she lost her grip on his cock. Climbing the peak, she felt the end coming. She dug her fingers into his shoulders, saw him watching her strained expression, his eyes smoky with desire. She gripped him harder, just as the climax ripped through her and she cried out in wonderment. Sinking against the bed, she was awash in pure bliss, cognizant that she should help him come but wanting to soak up the glorious way she was feeling.

He rubbed his cock against her belly, his mouth kissing her mouth, jaw, and cheeks. Her fingers dug into his buttocks. And he rubbed more vigorously, but she wanted to help. She pushed at him until he was lying on his back and she climbed onto his legs and began to stroke.

He groaned, running his hands up her thighs with solid strokes, his expression tightening. "Don't stop," he ground out, as if she had any intention of leaving him hanging.

She drew in the heady scents of him and wolf, of musk and sex as she watched his eyes darken. He sucked in his breath as she continued to pull on his emotions, milking him until the wolf couldn't hold back even if he'd wanted to. He released, his expression brightening.

"Aww, Jenna honey, you're amazing."

"So are you." She slid her leg off him so he could climb off the mattress. He left the bed and held his hand out to help her up from the bed. Once she was on her feet, he swept her up in his arms and carried her into the bathroom so they could shower together.

"We need to do something about this soon," he said, getting the water hot. Then he pulled her into the shower and shut the glass door.

She turned him around so his back was to her, then squirted jasmine soap into her hands and began soaping him down, working on his chest while she pressed her body against his back. She appreciated that he wasn't complaining that the scent of her body wash wasn't manly enough. "We need to talk." She kissed his wet back and nuzzled her face against his warm skin.

"About us?"

"Yeah. I don't know about you, but—"

"You can't quit touching me?" Sarandon pulled her hands lower to wash his cock.

She laughed and began soaping up his cock that was

beginning to grow of its own accord. "Yeah, that too. We've got to make some decisions."

"I've got tours booked up for the next six months. Maybe you could come on some of them with me?"

That's *not* what she wanted to hear. She made him turn and face her. "I have a job to do. I couldn't let my family down. If we have bail bond skippers, I've got to help apprehend them. That's what I'm trained to do."

"I understand completely. I've received payment for all these tours. I'm contracted to do it, which means I have a legal obligation."

She soaped his shoulders while he ran his soapy hands over her neck and shoulders, making her inner core tighten again. Jeesh, he was going to make her come all over again!

She had been afraid of this business with their jobs and a long-distance relationship. Their jobs were important to each of them, and they lived too far away from each other to make it work. She felt saddened that they could be the right wolves for each other, at least physically and emotionally, but the business of her family versus his pack could always be an issue. She couldn't see living without close family nearby, so living halfway between Silver Town and her family's home, three hours in either direction, probably wouldn't be the solution.

She let her breath out on a heavy, frustrated sigh and set the container of body wash on the shower shelf. She quickly rinsed off and left the shower.

He hurried to rinse off and turned off the water, exited the shower, and grabbed another towel to gently towel-dry her hair, even though he was dripping wet, and damn it, she wanted to lick every water droplet dribbling down his skin, starting at his nipples.

He leaned over to kiss her neck. "We'll work it out, Jenna. I'm not giving you up for anything."

She felt tears well up in her eyes. She had left her family before because her mate hadn't cared for them. She'd been so worried that when her babies were born, Will would be awful to live with if she'd wanted to see her family, to give them time to spend with her and her children. She didn't want to feel that way again. Yet the pull to have a mate who was so perfectly compatible in other ways drove her need to take more drastic measures. She knew by the way her family had treated Sarandon, and the way he seemed to genuinely like them, that he wouldn't act the same as Will. Her husband had been a lone wolf, while Sarandon was a wolf who loved his family and would do anything for them. She knew he would also do anything for her family—but maybe not live by them.

He kissed her cheek, then grabbed another towel and dried himself off. "I love you. We'll figure this out."

"I guess you wanted in the worst way to rejoin your family after you'd left the pack, didn't you?" She had to remember how hard it had been for him to leave his pack after all his father had done. She'd been fortunate to have a family who had always been there for her. Now that Sarandon was back with his pack and accepted by them, would she want to rip him away from them?

Jenna ran her hands up his chest with a tender caress. She couldn't help loving him. Maybe he needed more time with his pack because of how hard it had been for him and his brothers to return to them.

He touched her cheek. "Yes, I did want to go back. All my brothers did. We would have done anything to prove we were worthy of returning to the pack. This business between you and me... This is just as important."

She took his hand and led him back toward her bedroom. "I think I've fallen for the suspected fugitive. Maybe I'm in the wrong line of work."

"No, you're good at your job. I've been thinking about it. A hell of a lot. Every waking moment, in fact."

She hoped that meant he was contemplating joining her in the family business.

She climbed into bed, and he joined her. "I need to practice some maneuvers with you so another human, or wolf, doesn't take you down like I did."

She sighed and cuddled against him. "It won't happen again. You were just a...shock."

"And hot. And you love me for it."

She smiled and kissed his cheek. "We have to decide how we are going to work this before we can go any further."

"We'll work it out, Jenna. For now, I'm here to help you find Alex and sort this all out. After that, I'll stay with you until I need to be the guide for my butterfly tour group."

And then he'd be back in the fold with his pack, his brothers, his cousins, and his extended family. Without her to distract him, would he feel the gnawing need to return here? To be with her forever?

She knew saying goodbye would be heartbreaking, but if they couldn't come to a compromise, she'd have to give him up.

—〰—

They'd fallen asleep in Jenna's bed, and she was still snuggled against Sarandon, just where he wanted her to be, when his phone woke him. Still half asleep, he'd been thinking about how he could resolve the situation with his tours by finding someone else to take his place. He would have to make sure his tour group members agreed to the change. He'd been doing this for so many years that he had regulars, and several paid for his excursions because *he* was their guide.

He peered at the caller ID. Gillies's Travel Center. That was three hours out of Colorado Springs on the road to Silver Town.

He sat up in bed, immediately worried something had happened to CJ, since that was the direction he was headed.

"This is Sarandon." Before he even heard what was going on, Sarandon quickly got out of bed and began to dress.

"Will you accept a collect call from CJ Silver?" the operator asked.

Collect call? What the hell? "Yes." Sarandon knew it had to be bad news if CJ had to call him collect.

Jenna got out of bed next and began dressing in jeans and a T-shirt.

"Hey, Sarandon, I'm in a real bind," CJ said, breathing hard.

"What's wrong, Brother? You sound like you're having a hard time breathing." And why was he calling collect this late at night? Something was really wrong.

"We made a pit stop, and I filled up on gas."

"CJ, are you injured?" Sarandon didn't think he sounded like himself. Sarandon pulled his shirt over his head.

"When I went to uncuff Burt so I could place his hands in front of himself to pee, he got the better of me."

"Hell. Okay, I'm coming. Are you all right?" That's what really mattered. Sarandon knew CJ couldn't be, or he wouldn't be calling him.

"He stole everything. The car, my gun, my badge, my uniform, my wallet."

"I'm getting dressed, and I'll be there as soon as I can."

Jenna was hurrying to finish getting dressed, and then they headed outside to her car. Sarandon hadn't expected her to go with him, but then he remembered he didn't have a car here. He put his cell on speaker.

"Hell, I had to borrow shorts and a T-shirt since I have no money," CJ said.

"Jenna and I are coming. I'll bring some clothes… Uh, got to grab a bag." Sarandon raced back into the house to grab a bag he hadn't unpacked yet and headed back outside. Jenna had slipped into her room to also grab a bag. She got into the car and started the engine while Sarandon tossed his bag into the back seat and climbed into the passenger's seat. "I'll alert Peter and Darien right away. Are you okay?" He quickly gave Jenna the name of the service station, and she looked it up on her GPS. Then she drove out of the driveway and headed to the main road.

CJ didn't sound okay. He was having to pause for a long time before replying to Sarandon. And he hadn't once said how he was feeling. Burt had to have knocked him out. It was the only way he would have had the opportunity to take CJ's clothes and everything else and stolen his car.

"I'm seeing double, feeling nauseated. I'm sitting on the floor next to the checkout counter. In the way of customers."

"What the hell." Someone should have already called for help! "Is there someone there I can talk to?" Sarandon had to get someone to call for an ambulance.

"A man's taking pictures of me."

Sarandon scowled. "Tell him I want to talk to him."

"K."

"Hello?" a young man said.

"Are you local to that area?"

"Passing through."

"Hand the phone to the clerk."

"Hello?" another man said.

"Do you live in the area there?"

"Yeah. Just about a mile away."

"Do they have a hospital nearby?"

"A clinic."

"Call for an ambulance. I'll pay for it. I'm Sarandon, CJ's brother. It sounds like he's got a concussion. I'm still two hours and forty-five minutes away. What's the name of the clinic?"

"Providence."

"Call an ambulance. I'll be there as soon as I can."

"Yes, yes, sir. Right now. I've got to hang up to do it."

"Just do it."

"Okay." The call ended.

Sarandon felt sick about it. He should have helped

his brother transport Burt to Silver Town, but he really hadn't thought the cameraman was dangerous. He called Peter, waking him up.

"Did you find Alex?" the sheriff asked, sounding half asleep.

"No. CJ was transporting Burt Dreyfus to Silver Town when he knocked CJ out and stole everything. CJ is at a service station, and the clerk is calling an ambulance for him now. I'm on my way there, but it's about three hours from where I was staying. About the same distance for you."

"I'll call the state police about the stolen car and the injury to CJ. You take care of him. I'll notify Laurel that her mate has been injured and call your brother Brett to see if they can join you. I'll take care of the search for Burt."

"I'll call Darien so you can alert everyone else in law enforcement. If the guy thought he could get away with this, he's gravely mistaken."

"We'll catch him. Out here."

Sarandon called Darien next and told him what was going on.

"I'll call Mason about the alert roster, and everyone will be notified. We'll get Burt. The bastard."

"Agreed. Thanks, Darien."

"Let us know when you get there, and tell us CJ's status."

"I will. Talk soon."

As soon as Sarandon ended the call, Jenna asked, "Where do you think Burt's headed?"

"Away from Silver Town, for certain. He has to know that the whole pack will be out for blood. His blood.

He'll probably be driving the deputy sheriff's car off some dusty side road somewhere, not on the main roads. If I were him, I'd ditch the car and everything in it and run as a wolf."

"Okay, I think that's what he'll do also. CJ's car would be too noticeable. I'm so sorry about your brother. I need to call my dad and let him know what's up. He'll let Mom know I can't take any other case, in the event they need me."

"You're going to call him now?"

"Yeah. I'll ask if he can talk to the rest of the people on our list concerning Alex. We don't want to drop the ball, not when time is running out on paying the bond in full."

"At this hour?"

"Yeah. I also need to let him know what's happened to your brother." When Jenna called her dad on the Bluetooth, she explained where they were headed and what had happened.

"I'll see the people on your list first thing in the morning. What else can I do?"

"That's it for now. Thanks, Dad."

"How's Sarandon doing?"

"I think he's ready to take the wolf down permanently."

"I don't blame him. I am too."

Then Laurel called Sarandon. "Tell me exactly what happened." CJ's mate sounded like she was ready to turn wolf and chase Burt down herself and take him out.

When Jenna and Sarandon finally reached the clinic

where CJ had been taken, they hurried inside. Sarandon asked the receptionist where his brother was.

"Visiting hours—"

"We're the ones who had to get an ambulance for him. We've been driving for three hours to get here. And if you need payment for his bill, I'm here to do it. I'm seeing my brother."

The woman looked at Jenna.

"He's my brother too. I'm his sister."

"Okay, well, he's in room six, second floor."

"Thanks." He headed for the elevator. "Sister, eh?"

She took hold of his hand. "Just so I could get in to see him. If I were his sister, I would be yours too, and no way would I want that."

He smiled and squeezed her hand.

When they reached the second floor, there were no nurses at the station. They made their way to CJ's room, and Sarandon hoped he wouldn't have to fight with any nurses about visiting hours.

"Hey, Brother," Sarandon said, seeing CJ lying in the bed, his head bandaged, the lights still on in the room. Sarandon had been worried sick about him, hoping he was going to be okay.

"Hey, I'm fine. They're keeping me here overnight for observation, but my stomach is settled and I'm feeling much better. Not seeing double or anything." CJ looked sleepy, but he was still awake.

"We'll stay here the rest of the night with you," Sarandon assured him.

CJ's gaze drifted to Jenna.

"Hey, Deputy," Jenna said, coming farther into the room and smiling at him, though she still looked concerned. Sarandon knew she was trying to put on a good show for him.

CJ frowned at her. "Hell, Sarandon dragged you all the way out here to sit with me?"

"I wouldn't have been left behind. How are you feeling?"

"Truthfully? Like shit. My head is pounding with pain. I'm angry. I couldn't believe that Burt knocked me out. He dragged me into a damn stall and locked the door. When I came too, I managed to stand and struggled to unlock the door. Took me forever. Then I made my way out of the bathroom. A woman screamed, and I realized I was wearing only my boxer briefs. At least he left me with those."

"I should have gone with you," Sarandon said again.

"I've never had a problem like this. No wolf—or human, for that matter—has ever gotten the best of me." CJ narrowed his eyes. "What time is it?"

"Two in the morning," Sarandon said.

"Ah, hell, Sarandon. What are you doing here? Why don't you two get a room? The nurses are taking good care of me. You can come back in the morning after we've all had some sleep. Just one thing though. What about someone running down my car and everything else? Well, Burt too."

"Peter is on it. I've notified Darien, and he's having the alert roster called. Peter's calling Brett to see if he can come with Laurel to pick you up and take you home. What did the doctor say?" That was the most important consideration.

"Mild concussion. I'll live. And you know how we are. I don't want to stay here too long."

"I agree. We'll come and get you tomorrow, if the doctor says you're okay. We'll take you home if Brett can't come." Sarandon got a call from their brother Brett. "Yeah, we're at the clinic now. He's in bed, trying to get rid of us. He has a mild concussion. Jenna and I are going to a hotel, and we'll come back for him in the morning."

"I've taken off work. Laurel and I are on the way. You need to find Alex. The state police are looking for Burt," Brett said. "We'll take care of CJ."

"How much do you want to bet they won't find Burt because he's running as a wolf?" Sarandon asked.

CJ agreed.

"Yeah, you're probably right. The police would pick up on the stolen deputy's car too fast. Well, I'll be there at around six, and I'm bringing him a set of his clothes. I'll see you around six or seven, and then I'll bring CJ home. So you can do your job."

"Thanks, Brett. See both of you soon." Sarandon hung up on his brother and pocketed his phone. "Okay, CJ, if you think you can manage without us, we'll leave you to sleep and return first thing in the morning. Brett and Laurel are coming to get you then, and the state police are looking for your car and Burt. We've got everything covered."

"Okay, good. Yeah, the two of you get a room." CJ closed his eyes. "I need to sleep."

"Come on, Jenna." Sarandon took her hand.

"Night, CJ. Hope your head feels better soon," Jenna said.

"It will. Thanks. Night."

As soon as they left the room, a nurse frowned at them.

"I was seeing my brother. We're headed out to get a hotel room."

"He's doing well. He should be released tomorrow."

"Thanks." Sarandon gave her his card. "If there's any trouble, call me, will you? Another of our brothers is coming to pick him up tomorrow. Brett Silver. We'll square away the bill."

"Okay, thanks."

Jenna and Sarandon took the elevator down.

"There are two hotels near the clinic," Jenna said, looking at her phone, "and both have vacancies."

"Okay. Anything is fine with me." Sarandon didn't care as long as they got some sleep and saw CJ before he left for Silver Town.

"All right," Sarandon said, looking at the screen. "This one looks like it will be the better one because it's closer."

When they finally arrived at the hotel, Jenna parked the car and they grabbed their bags.

"Two rooms or one?" Sarandon asked her.

She slipped her arm through his as they walked inside the lobby. "You have to ask?"

"Well, I don't want to take things for granted. Thanks for coming with me tonight."

"I wouldn't have done anything differently. And I know if someone in my family had been injured, you would have been there for me." She figured they should resolve the issue of where they were going to live before they got too much more involved, and they did need to sleep, but slipping into bed with Sarandon and just cuddling wasn't enough.

Chapter 17

THE NEXT MORNING, AFTER HAVING UNCONSUMMATED SEX again—since consummating the relationship would mean a permanent mating, though Sarandon was certain she nearly gave in to her inner wolf and went for it—Jenna and Sarandon showered together.

"We're going to do it, you know. Sooner or later," Sarandon said, making her a promise, soaping up her breasts and kissing her forehead. He loved running his hands over her soft skin and kissing her all over.

She seemed to take just as much pleasure in rubbing her hands over his soapy chest and kissing him back. She slid her hands down to his aroused cock. "Just hold that thought." Then she began to stroke him, every movement designed to make him come, their hearts beating faster, their breathing more ragged.

"You're sure hard on me," he ground out. And he treasured her for it. He couldn't imagine anything better than making love to Jenna any time or place.

He tilted her head back and kissed her soft mouth, enjoying anything he could have with her for now, even though he was ready for so much more. It wasn't just the sex but the commitment to each other. To be there for each other through thick and thin, and for wolves, they meant it.

Her hands slowed on his cock, which was fine with him because he wanted to get her in the mood for what he would do next to her.

He deepened the kiss, and her response was fiercely urgent. He couldn't keep this up—having her part way. He wanted all of her on top of him, underneath him, him all the way inside her. He'd been completely under her spell from the moment she had tried to take him down as a fugitive recovery agent. She'd taken him hostage all right, when here he thought he'd had everything under control.

He slid his hand between her legs and began to stroke her. Her hand loosened on his cock and he concentrated on bringing her to climax, stroking her, kissing her, the desire to take her filling him with urgency. She released his cock and grabbed his hips, as if she needed to hold on to him to keep from slipping to the floor, as if she felt boneless. Then she was bucking against his hand, and he slid two fingers between her feminine folds, her mouth hot on his.

"Ahh," she breathed against his mouth, clinging to him. He smiled down at her and was afraid she was too weak to finish what she'd started on him. But then she began to stroke him again, and she quickly brought him to completion. He'd wanted to lift her up against the tile wall, spear her with his cock, and bring her to climax with him inside her this time. But what a way to begin their day. If only every day could start this way.

He hated that he was already regretting he'd have to return home without her when the time came. She was an addiction he couldn't wean himself from.

After drying off and dressing, he suggested a pancake restaurant and called CJ. He was awake and wanting out of the place.

"We're having breakfast. Did you have yours?" Sarandon asked, putting the phone on speaker.

"Yeah, and Brett and Laurel are here."

"Good show. How are you feeling?"

"Like normal. Just waiting for the doctor to release me."

"Okay. We'll be there in an hour or so."

"See you then."

At the pancake restaurant, Jenna and Sarandon ordered plates of pancakes and maple syrup. She was glad to hear CJ was feeling well enough to leave.

After eating, they ran over to see CJ at the clinic. Laurel was sitting next to CJ's bed and smiled at them when they walked in the door. Brett was sleeping in a chair next to CJ's bed, while CJ was wide-awake, dressed, and sitting on the edge of his bed, waiting to be released. Sarandon and Jenna smiled at Brett.

Jenna loved seeing how the brothers took care of one another, just as she and her sisters did if any of them were hurt.

CJ sighed. "I'll have to drive us home, since Brett drove all those hours in the middle of the night to come get me."

"Like I can't drive?" Laurel said.

"You're not driving anywhere," Sarandon said to CJ. "Only Laurel or Brett. Or I will, if they both need to rest."

Jenna hoped Sarandon didn't have to, but if he did, she was following Brett's car so she could take Sarandon back home with her. He had a job to do—help her find his half brother—and he wasn't getting out of it, not when she wanted to spend more time with him. He was completely addictive.

Brett stirred, and then his eyes popped open. "Oh, you're here."

"Watching you sleep. Are you sure you can help Laurel drive CJ home?" Sarandon asked.

"Of course. I was just getting a bit of a snooze until the doctor comes in and releases him. You know how they are in these places. They make rounds, like, late afternoon, making the poor patient wait forever to be released."

"Yeah, I know what you mean," Sarandon said.

Brett raised a brow at CJ. "Hell, how long have you been dressed, Brother?"

"An hour. I'm ready to go. Can't you just pay the bill and get me out of here?"

"I could, but I'm not going to. What if you began having seizures or something on the way to Silver Town? I'm not risking it."

"I'm not going to have seizures. My head isn't even pounding any longer. I feel perfectly fine."

"Okay, so explain to us what happened," Sarandon said, and Jenna knew he wanted to hear CJ tell the story again to ensure he was all right and hadn't left anything out.

"Aw, come on, Sarandon. I already told you once, and I had to tell Laurel and Brett everything too," CJ said.

Sarandon folded his arms and frowned.

"All right."

Once CJ repeated the story he'd told late last night, Sarandon nodded. "Okay."

"Did I pass?" CJ asked, though he was giving him an "I told you so" look.

"With flying colors," Jenna said, and she was glad for it.

"Great, then once the doc says I'm good to go—"

"We'll take you home, and our doctor will check you out." Brett got up to stretch and then sat back down.

"Not another doctor's opinion," CJ said.

"One that will make more of a difference," Sarandon said, "because he's a wolf doctor and will have a better idea about your injury."

"You have your own doctor?" That was one thing Jenna had always worried about—getting pregnant again and having a wolf doctor deliver her baby, or multiple babies, as the case might be. Then she worried… Would she end up with lots of babies? Four, as in Sarandon's case? Three as in Darien's case? Three in her case? She was thinking more like two, max.

"Yeah. We have a veterinarian too," Laurel said. "Depending on which doc you need at the time."

Jenna laughed. "Good to know."

"Yeah, if anyone in your family ever needs a doctor, he'd be willing to see you," Sarandon said.

"You don't need to hang around here," CJ said. "Go, take Jenna home and find Alex."

"If you're sure," Sarandon said, looking like he felt he needed to stay at least until the doctor released CJ.

"Yeah, you've got important work to do."

Laurel agreed. "We'll take good care of CJ."

After saying goodbye to CJ, Laurel, and Brett, Jenna and Sarandon drove back to Cañon City to talk to the remaining people on Sarah's list. Jenna was glad they were returning. The time was quickly running out on finding Alex and returning him for trial.

"CJ will be fine, Sarandon. He remembered everything he told us when you talked to him before."

"Yeah, you're right. I just wish I could be at the forefront of the manhunt for Burt. He won't be fine when I get ahold of him."

"I'd be glad to be right there when you do. I need to see if my dad managed to contact everyone left on Sarah's list." Then she got on the Bluetooth and called him. "We're on our way back. We can interview some of the people in the pack if you haven't had a chance."

"I didn't make any headway with the one I spoke to. Now I have to go on a case. How's CJ?" Logan asked.

"He's going home to see their doctor, but he seems to be better. One of Sarandon's other brothers and CJ's mate came to take him home."

"They have a wolf doctor?"

"Yeah, and they said if we need one to help us out at any time, he would. Isn't that great?"

"It sure is." Her dad paused. "I was only able to get ahold of the one wolf before your mom put me back to work." Logan gave them the three names he hadn't contacted yet.

"Be careful with the case you're on," Jenna told her dad.

"It's a deadbeat ex-husband who swore he has to keep working to be able to pay the child support he owes for the last three months. The judge took him at his word, not able to make the man pay when he doesn't have any earnings. But instead of going to work, the guy took off his ankle monitor and ran. Not paying child support is his only run-in with the law, so he shouldn't be dangerous."

"Just be careful anyway."

"The same with the two of you. I've got to get on the road. Good luck finding Alex."

"Thanks, Dad. Good luck to you too."

When they ended the call, she said to Sarandon, "I think we need to get ahold of Faye again and see if she has been in touch with Alex."

"I agree. For now, let's finish speaking with the people on Sarah's list."

When they arrived in Cañon City, they met with one of the men on the list, but he wasn't a bachelor male like they'd thought. "We don't know anything about what is going on with Alex, only that he has a job in Colorado Springs working in housing construction. We haven't heard anything bad about him," the husband said.

"What about his brother, Burt?" Sarandon asked.

"Oh yeah, he's been in trouble a lot over the years. Nothing really major, just tons of petty stuff," the guy said. "Sorry we couldn't help you any further."

The wife said, "Yeah, if we hear from him, we'll let him know you're here to help him."

"And Burt?" Jenna asked.

"We don't know where he is either. We figure he's staying wherever the ghost hunters are filming a show," the man said.

"Okay, thanks," Sarandon and Jenna said at the same time.

They left to look up the next man on the list. When they finally tracked him down in a coffee shop, he motioned for them to take a seat with him. "Yeah, I know Alex. Is he really in trouble? He stayed with me yesterday."

"Where is he now?" Sarandon asked, hating that they'd missed him.

"He left. I assumed he had a construction job to work on. That's his business."

As soon as they left, they talked to Alex and Burt's dad on the phone. "CJ was taking Burt to Silver Town for questioning concerning Alex's whereabouts, but Burt knocked him out and stole his car, clothes, and everything else. Burt's in a lot of trouble."

"Are you sure about all this?" Anton sounded shocked to learn of it.

Did everyone know about Burt's criminal activities but his parents? "Yes. CJ had to see a doctor for the concussion after Burt knocked him out. Burt stole CJ's badge, car, and gun, and now the state police are looking for him. Why would Burt be afraid to speak with another deputy sheriff and the sheriff of Silver Town if he had nothing to hide?"

Anton swore. "You think he's been involved in the theft?"

"Yes. If Burt turns up there, let us know. We'll try to protect him, but we can't guarantee anything, not after what he's pulled."

"Have you had any luck locating Alex?" Anton asked.

"Not so far, sir."

"My wife is at the grocery store now. I'd rather... Well, I'd rather she didn't know this latest news. It's bad enough that Alex is in so much trouble. I'd rather wait until Burt's picked up by the police and charged."

"All right. Just let us know if you hear from either Burt or Alex."

"I will. Thanks. I'm...sorry."

"It's not your fault."

"They're my sons. I raised them. We were much too lenient with Burt, I'm afraid. Let me know if you hear anything."

"We will."

After they finished the call with Anton, Jenna called her mother. "We're still looking for Alex, and now Burt. Did you change the reward poster to say Alex was pretending to be Sarandon? We don't want to have people reporting sightings of Sarandon."

"The men look so much alike that I'm sure if anyone sees Sarandon, they will still think he's the suspect," her mom said.

"I guess that's so. I'll have to protect him."

Sarandon smiled.

"What? You don't think I can?" Jenna asked him.

He chuckled. "Yeah, truthfully? I do."

"Okay, Mom. I'm out here."

"How are we doing on time?" Sarandon asked Jenna.

"Alex needs to be at the court tomorrow afternoon, so we really don't have much time left." Jenna kept thinking they'd catch up to Alex, but at this rate, she wasn't sure. They'd had to pay bonds in the past—a hazard in this business. But they'd never come this close to the deadline without being sure whether they'd have to pay one off. Well, the deadline hadn't run out yet. "Let's have a late lunch at my place and figure out where to go next. You know, I keep wondering why Alex or Burt would have been roaming around my family's territory as wolves."

"If Alex is a beta wolf, maybe he was trying to get up the courage to approach your family. He would know they put up the bail bond for him. Maybe he's running scared. Not sure what to do. Maybe he allowed Burt to convince him he had to run. And now Burt's not there to tell him what to do."

"Not according to Burt."

"And you believe anything Burt has to say?" Jenna asked.

"Not a word."

When they arrived at Jenna's home, she made them grilled ham and cheese sandwiches.

"These are great. Something I never fix."

She smiled at him while he scarfed his down fast. "Want another?"

"Yeah, sure. Can't eat just one."

When she went into the kitchen to make a second sandwich, she washed her hands in the kitchen sink and saw something out the window. A wolf. "Don't look now, but I see a gray wolf in the woods, watching the house. Because of his bigger size, I'm sure it's a male."

"Not a brown wolf like Burt?"

"Gray."

Sarandon started to move toward her.

"Sarandon, don't move. If he sees you come to the window to look out, he's bound to bolt."

"I have an idea. And a very good reason to move in your direction. I know what I'm doing." Sarandon slowly joined her and rested his hands on her shoulders, then nuzzled her cheek with his. Then he leaned over further and kissed her neck. "What's he doing?" he whispered against her hair.

"Still watching. What you're doing is distracting me even more."

He smiled. "That's the plan. At least to keep his attention. Not to distract you." He slowly pulled her T-shirt up and over her head and then tossed it aside.

"*What* are you doing?"

"You'll see. Just some heavy necking, removing our clothes, and then we'll move this to the bedroom. Or appear to be moving this toward the bedroom," he said as he ran his hands over the silky bra covering her breasts.

She melted to his touch, trying to keep her eyes open so she could keep an eye on the wolf but wanting to lose herself in having Sarandon touching her, making her feel loved, needed, and sexy.

"We need to do something about him before he runs off," she warned, but her voice was ragged with desire.

"We will," he mouthed against her neck, his hands massaging her breasts. He turned her around so she was facing him and he could see over her shoulder, though he continued to kiss her neck to make it appear he was caught up in turning her on and not getting a glimpse of the wolf. "I wish we knew what Alex looked like in his wolf form."

Jenna pulled off Sarandon's shirt and tossed it to the floor. She began kissing his cheeks, then his bare shoulders as he ran his fingers through her hair.

"We're on a mission here," he groaned.

She smiled. "You can't make me all hot and bothered and…distract me a bit from the mission, and then not expect me to reciprocate." She licked a trail down to his navel and began unbuckling his belt.

He slid his hands around to her back and unfastened her bra.

"Is he still there?"

"Yeah." Sarandon tossed her bra in the air so the wolf would see it too.

The window was too high for the wolf to see any lower than their chests, but Sarandon figured the wolf would get the gist of what was going on, or at least be hoodwinked into believing the wolves were getting it on.

"We are going after him as wolves, right?" Jenna felt that Sarandon's moves were a prelude to sex, not to shifting. Not to mention he was fully aroused as she pulled down his pants. Gloriously aroused.

"Yeah." His response was husky and needy. "I'll sweep you up in my arms as soon as we're naked and carry you in front of the dining room window and into the hallway to make it appear we have every intention of taking this to the bedroom. Once we're out of his view, we'll shift and make a mad dash for the wolf door. If we're lucky," he said, pulling off her jeans, "we'll catch him before he can outdistance us and learn who he is."

"Okay, damn it."

He smiled at her. "We can finish this later."

Once they were completely naked, he swept her up in his arms, carried her through the dining room, pausing to kiss her, while she wrapped her arms around his neck and kissed him deeply back. She didn't want to end this!

Which was totally wrong! She was always focused on the mission first. And if the wolf in the woods was Alex, they had to get him. But, man, did she not want to give this up.

Then Sarandon hurried her to the hallway as if he was

in a rush to have sex with her. As soon as they were out of view of the windows, he set her on her feet, briefly kissed her, and they both quickly shifted.

They raced for the wolf door, and he let her go first, though she suspected from the way he'd dashed for it, it was killing him to let her out first. He wanted to take the wolf down. Probably to protect her. So for him to hesitate and allow her to take the lead meant everything in the world to her.

Would he always do this, or only when he was trying so hard to please her? She loved him for it, no matter what.

The wolf was still in the woods, sniffing around, not paying attention until they crashed through the wolf door and tore off in his direction.

His ears perked up, his head swinging around to observe them, his expression startled. He quickly turned and ran off.

And the chase was on.

Jenna couldn't believe how Sarandon played the game. God, the wolf was hot, and she definitely wanted him in her life for good. Not only was he the sexiest wolf she'd ever known, but his ploy had actually worked! She really hadn't thought the wolf would stay glued to his spot in the woods, observing them the whole time.

Because she knew the woods better than Sarandon, she ran the wolf toward a small box canyon, the cliffs only climbable if the animal was a mountain goat or a cougar. The wolf wasn't from this area, but he was the one they'd smelled the second time they'd recognized a wolf's scent out here, so he didn't realize she was chasing him right where she wanted him to go. Sarandon seemed to remember the location and helped her steer the wolf in that direction.

The wolf looked up at the canyon walls and realized he couldn't go that way. He whipped around but saw Sarandon and Jenna approaching cautiously.

He stopped in place, panting, his tail tucked between his legs, his ears down. If it was Alex, Jenna almost felt bad for him, except for the fact that he'd led them on a merry chase, created trouble for Sarandon, and was only now looking defeated when he had no place to run.

At least he didn't appear to want to fight them.

Sarandon shifted, and she growled at the other wolf to let him know if he attacked, she was taking him down.

"I'm Sarandon Silver, your half brother, if you didn't know."

Was Sarandon guessing? She didn't have a clue if it was Alex.

"I'm not pressing charges against you for using my ID and claiming you were me, but you have to come with us and clear everything up. Now. We'll do everything we can to help you out. All of us. Jenna and her family, me and my brothers and cousins. You're family, and family takes care of their own. Will you come with us willingly? Or am I going to have to injure you so you have no choice but to comply?"

Jenna figured Sarandon would have to threaten the wolf. It appeared to be the only way to get him to agree.

The wolf nodded.

"Okay, I'll tell you right now, I've taken down wolves much bigger than you, and I've dealt successfully with more than one at a time. So don't test me."

Now that, she was surprised about.

Sarandon shifted back into his wolf form and motioned with his head for the wolf to go toward the house.

To Jenna's relief, the wolf acquiesced and loped back with them.

When they reached the wolf door, they waited for the wolf to enter. Jenna followed him, and Sarandon came in after that.

Sarandon woofed at her, and she nodded, grabbed her clothes with her teeth, and dragged them to the first room she could reach, the guest room. In there, she quickly shifted and dressed. She left the room and stalked down the hall to her bedroom to get her Taser and gun, then returned so Sarandon could shift and dress.

He didn't leave though, just shifted right there as if he wanted to keep an eye on the wolf, not trusting him not to try to escape or attack Jenna, despite the fact that she was armed. Sarandon had to know that this time, she'd use the Taser on the wolf.

"I'll get you a pair of my boxer briefs, and you can wear them while we talk," Sarandon said, pulling on his own briefs. He glanced at Jenna and she nodded, letting him know she really could handle this.

Then Sarandon left, and she waited. She swore the wolf was sweating this out, glancing at her and her Taser and the hallway where Sarandon had disappeared. When Sarandon returned, he dropped the boxer briefs on the floor in front of the wolf. The wolf shifted and hurried to pull them on.

Jenna closed her gaping mouth. Man, did he look like Sarandon.

<p style="text-align:center">~~~</p>

Alex stared at Sarandon before he took hold of his hand
and shook it. "You're my brother."

Sarandon saw Jenna's jaw drop when he pulled Alex
in for a hug. "Hell yeah. We're brothers, and we shouldn't
have had to wait this long to discover the truth."

Alex looked so surprised that he didn't respond at
first, but then he hugged Sarandon back. He could see
Jenna's eyes welling up at the sight of the first meeting
between him and his half brother.

Sarandon motioned to the living room. "Why don't
you take a seat, Alex."

Jenna offered him a glass of water as he sat.

"We need to get you to Colorado Springs so you can
turn yourself in," Sarandon said.

Jenna explained who she was. "We have a wolf
lawyer who will represent you, which means I need to
turn you in before my mother pays the bond for you."

"All right."

"Did you steal the passports and ID?" Jenna asked.

He shook his head.

"Who did?"

"I-I can't say."

"Why do you want to take the rap for this?" Sarandon
asked, not understanding why Alex was willing to face
prison time for the theft.

"I...really can't say."

"Fine. Let's go. We'll take you to the station, and
they can decide what to do with you. Jail time? Maybe.
Another opportunity to wear a GPS monitor and stay
put? It's up to the judge." Sarandon let out his breath
in exasperation.

Jenna's eyes were wide. She seemed surprised

Sarandon was throwing in the towel and letting Alex take the blame for this, but he was done trying to convince Alex it was in his best interest to tell the truth. If he refused to do it, what could they do about it?

"I'll get you some of my spare clothes. They'll fit you just fine. We can't take you like this."

"What about the lawyer?" Alex asked, sounding a little panicked.

What did he think? That Sarandon and Jenna would just let him go? That he was a wolf, and they couldn't allow him to be jailed?

"He'll be waiting to see you when we take you into Colorado Springs," Jenna reassured him. "Sarandon's right. You need to tell us the truth."

"You're not my lawyer. Anything I say could be used against me in a court of law. Right?" Alex said to Sarandon.

"I'm your brother. I'm here to help you. Whatever you tell me is between the two of us." Sarandon needed him to come clean so they could sort this out.

"Like you helped our dad?"

Now that pissed Sarandon off. Alex didn't know anything about it. And yeah, Sarandon wished he could have saved his dad, but not when he learned he had murdered one of their kind. "He killed our cousin's mate," Sarandon growled. "And he was involved in other criminal activities. We even left the pack for a time over it. But no. We didn't try to save him. We felt terrible about what he'd done. Like somehow it was our fault. When it wasn't."

Sarandon could have brought up the possibility that Alex's mother had hired a hunter to kill Sarandon's mother, but he didn't believe it would help matters.

"You might have felt you were denied belonging to your blood-related pack, and we certainly will rectify that. All your half brothers and cousins will want to meet you. We need to clear up this matter first. If it means you'll have to spend some time in jail, then that's the way it's got to be."

"Did Burt frame you for stealing this stuff? Is he blackmailing you?" Jenna asked. "Or did he push you to steal?"

Alex looked down at his lap.

"What about Christina?" Sarandon asked, suddenly wondering if Alex was protecting her.

Alex's gaze shot up to Sarandon's. *Ah, hell*. Had he hit a nerve or what? And completely understandable. Sarandon would do the same for Jenna.

Alex was a royal—all the Silvers were, including their dad and Ritka—so Sarandon knew Alex could control his shifting at any time. Maybe Christina had more humans in her family tree and couldn't control her shifting during the full moon. Which meant going to jail for several years would be dangerous for her and their kind.

"Hell, Alex. You know she did it! Or you suspect she did it. Is she not a royal wolf?" Sarandon asked.

"She's not a royal."

"Alex, did she tell you she did it?" Jenna asked.

"No." Alex looked down at the floor.

"Okay, so how do you know she did it?" Sarandon asked. "We were thinking Burt was the one who was responsible."

Again, Alex looked up so sharply that Sarandon knew his brother was surprised to hear it.

"Why do you think that?" Alex asked.

"Did you ask him to come get you? To take you away from Colorado Springs?"

Alex ran his hands through his hair. "No. I didn't ask him to do it. He…he told me Christina would go to jail. All right? She would never last. She'd shift during the full moon. Don't you see I had to do this? For her? And for our kind? There's a hell of a lot more at stake than just me paying for the crime. It's not safe for her to go to jail. For us either. That's what wolves do for each other. Make sacrifices. There's nothing else I can do about it."

"So why did you leave with Burt?" Jenna asked.

"He convinced me to leave and said he'd find a way to clear my name before I went to trial."

"And did he?" Sarandon asked, knowing Burt hadn't.

Alex shook his head. "I've…I've been trying to figure out a way to see Jenna and turn myself in without the police shooting me. That's what Burt kept saying, that word was out that I was armed and dangerous. I think Burt was afraid I'd try to see Jenna. I smelled his scent in the area, but I hadn't come here yet."

"The police don't think you're armed and dangerous. What about Burt taking the blame for the theft?" Sarandon asked.

"I couldn't do that to him."

"He didn't offer to take the rap either, did he?" Jenna asked.

"No. He said he'd find a way to clear me. Besides, Christina's my girlfriend, not his."

"So why did you run?" Sarandon asked.

"Burt convinced me it was the only thing to do and said he'd find a way to clear me because he knew I hadn't done it."

"And the fugitive recovery agent would come for me, not you, because you used my name and address," Sarandon said.

Alex let out his breath. "I didn't tell the police that was me. I wouldn't tell who I was. I know it sounds crazy, but I didn't want to lose my job, and if my boss had heard I was in trouble, he would have fired me. I didn't want my parents, who have been so good to me, to learn of it either. The police just took one look at your ID and assumed that was me. I look so similar to you; I just didn't confirm or deny it."

"That's the same difference," Sarandon said. "Okay, well I've got another question for you then. You and Burt were in Silver Town. Why?"

"He wanted to check out the place, since that's where my dad was from. I did too. That was all there was to it. He kept egging me on, saying he couldn't believe my blood parents could have been so cruel to throw me away like that. I never felt that way. Not when the Dreyfus family had been so good to me. Yet, you know, it's hard not to wonder what it would have been like to be a member of a pack as large as yours. To have several brothers and cousins who were blood-related to grow up with. Or to have my birth parents raise me. And your family founded the town. I-I wished I had been part of that growing up."

"Okay, I can believe that. So how did you get my ID?"

"I didn't. I didn't steal it, and I didn't use it."

"Except when you were caught and didn't deny the ID was yours," Sarandon reminded him.

"Hell, you think they would have believed me? I look too much like you to claim it wasn't me. And I didn't have my own on me that day. I did, but when I reached in my pocket to grab my wallet, it was gone."

"Your wallet was stolen? That is precious," Sarandon said, wondering if he was as much a con artist as Burt.

"It's true. I hadn't needed to look for it before then."

"When was the last time you'd seen it?"

"I don't know. I guess…I guess it was when I had breakfast with Christina and Burt that morning. Then I went to work and didn't think anything more of it."

"You pulled out your wallet to pay for breakfast?" Sarandon asked.

"Yeah, to pay for mine and Christina's. Burt paid for his own."

"And you don't recall any situation that seemed suspicious, someone on the street or at the restaurant bumping into you?"

"No."

"When you were in Silver Town, did you go by my house?"

"Yeah."

"Why?"

"We drove by several of the Silver homes. Burt wanted to see just how well off all of you lived."

"And you?" Sarandon asked.

"Well, yeah. I won't deny I was curious too."

"Was the garbage out that day?" Sarandon asked.

"What?"

"The garbage? I'd thrown out my old driver's license. It had expired. The one you had on you. And I'm always throwing out credit card offers. I never cut them up either. So I'm thinking mine were stolen from the garbage can. My place is surrounded by trees, so it would be easy for someone to grab something from the garbage and no one would notice. Someone could have learned when the garbage was picked up and watched to see when I left it out the night before. Maybe looked in it that night and grabbed the license and credit card application. Then used the application to request a card. And voilà. A credit card in my name with my birth date, and insta-credit."

"We weren't there the night before when you put out your garbage. I don't recall seeing any garbage cans there." Alex was looking steadily at Sarandon, which made him think he was telling the truth.

"Okay, maybe you didn't, but what if Burt returned and made it his business to check my garbage. Maybe he was checking everyone's garbage. I don't recall if I threw out a credit card application the same day I tossed my old driver's license. I might have, but I don't remember. Why me? Maybe he looked in all our garbage cans, but he got lucky with mine."

Alex was watching Sarandon now, listening, his brow furrowed a bit.

"So if Burt had been there, he might have had the opportunity to try to grab my ID. What about Christina? Would she have gone there to do it?"

Alex rubbed his forehead.

"Well? Burt told you Christina did it, didn't he? Did you ever talk to her about it? Ask her why? Or how she did it?" Sarandon asked.

"No. I just assumed…" Alex quit speaking, as if he realized Burt could have been lying to him all along.

Sarandon said, "Why don't you call Christina. Tell her what Burt said. See what she has to say. If she denies all of it, you might be in hot water for thinking the worst of her, but that might indicate Burt's the one at the root of all the crime. If Burt is a royal, and if he committed the crimes, he can go to jail for them."

"Hell. Yeah, he's a royal. His parents are. They were glad I was too, though they'd wanted to raise me so badly, I don't think it would have mattered. I still can't believe Burt would do that to me."

"He's been in trouble before. He even knocked my brother CJ out when he was transporting Burt to the jail in Silver Town for questioning."

Alex's eyes widened.

"If he had nothing to hide, why would he do that? We've done a lot of investigating on our own, talking to several of your pack members, and everyone we've spoken with said he's trouble. And you're not. Has Christina ever been in trouble for anything?"

Alex shook his head.

Sarandon waved his hand in the air. "Well, there you go. Call Christina. See what she has to say about this."

"Why would Burt do this to me?"

"Maybe he's jealous of your relationship with your adoptive parents," Jenna said. "You've followed in your dad's footsteps in the construction business. He's proud of you. Your mother is too. It sounds to me like Burt is acting out, angry you're always the good son, and you're not even their flesh-and-blood son. Did anything happen between you two around the time the thefts occurred?"

"From what the police said, I've been doing this for six months. The first time using a credit card was..." Alex looked at the floor, appearing to be deep in thought. "Hell, that occurred two days after I told Burt I was seeing a pretty she-wolf. He wanted to meet her, but he's always had a way with women, and I didn't want him meeting her right away. Not until I thought for certain she and I had a connection.

"Then a couple of weeks later, after I felt it was more of a sure thing with Christina, I brought her home. Mom didn't like that she worked on the cleaning staff at one of the local hotels. Dad thought she was nice, but Burt made all over her like he was trying to prove he was the better wolf to court. I just figured Burt was being Burt, always wanting the attention. As much as it irritated me that he was making a fool of himself over Christina, I figured if she could fall for him, she was too shallow to be the one for me."

"And?" Jenna asked.

"She didn't fall for him. When we left my parents' place, I took her home. She said my mom didn't like her, but she liked my dad. And Burt was a jerk. I fell a little in love with her right then and there. I just had to convince my mom that Christina was the right wolf for me. Not to mention that I had to make sure Christina and I had what it took to make it long-term."

"Do you?"

"I think so. I'm still working on my mom. I really care about my parents, and I want them to love her too. If it doesn't happen, it doesn't. Christina always wants to know what I'm working on and where I am. She comes to see me when she can get away from her job."

Jenna and Sarandon exchanged glances. That wasn't what Christina had told them at all.

"What?" Alex asked.

"She said she never asked about your job," Jenna said.

"Sure she does. You can ask the guys who work on the crews with me. They joke about me being hen-pecked, and I'm not even married to her. Truth is, the other guys wish their girlfriends or wives took more of an interest in what they did. They just give me a hard time because she's always kissing on me, bringing me lunches—whenever she can get away to do it."

"So why would she tell us anything different?" Jenna asked.

"She was afraid if anyone questioned her, they would realize she always knew where I was. So if she said she didn't, that would sound like we weren't all that close. I guess you told my parents about the trouble I'm in."

"We had to locate you. You weren't easy to track down," Jenna said.

"I imagine I'm a real disappointment to them."

"They don't believe you did it," Sarandon said, and he was glad they supported Alex. He did wonder if Burt might still be interested in Christina. Or at least in making sure Alex and Christina wouldn't be together—because if Alex went to jail, that's what would happen.

"If Burt did it to spite me? And we convinced the police he was the one responsible for the crimes? Then what will my parents think of me? That it's my fault? That I am the one who's accountable for sending him away?"

"The alternative is you take the blame, and if you're found guilty, Burt's free to comfort—and court—your distraught girlfriend. Is that what you want?" Sarandon wanted Alex to wake up and grow some alpha balls.

"Hell no."

"Good. Then call Christina and square it with her."

"I...don't have my phone with me."

"Here, take mine," Sarandon said.

Alex let out his breath and then called Christina. "Hey, honey, it's me, Alex. I'm using Sarandon's phone." He paused. "Yeah, I'm okay. I'm talking to my brother and trying to sort all this out."

With that one little declaration, Sarandon felt an overwhelming kinship with his half brother. He would do anything to help him beat this rap and place the blame where it truly belonged.

Jenna reached over and squeezed Sarandon's hand. He leaned over and kissed her cheek. Alex caught the interaction.

"I didn't do what I'm accused of doing," Alex said over the phone to Christina. "I... Burt... Ah, hell, how do I say this without making it come out sounding bad, no matter what I say?"

Sarandon felt his pain. If Alex said he believed Burt when he told him Christina was a thief, she could be furious with Alex.

"All right. You're not a royal, and Burt told me you had stolen all this stuff. That's why it was in my car when the police pulled me over for my left turn signal light being out. Then they saw something that I didn't see, sitting on the floor of the passenger's side of the car. They asked me to step out of the car, and they were going to look through my car, if they had my permission. I haven't done anything wrong, so I said sure. That's when they found a bag of passports and credit cards and other IDs, including Sarandon's. I denied any of it was mine, but they booked me as Sarandon. I didn't...didn't want you to know I'd been arrested. So I didn't call you. I called Burt. And he said he knew all about you and what you'd done."

"What?" Christina's voice was so loud, even Sarandon heard it with his acute wolf's hearing.

"Yeah, I'm sorry, honey. He convinced me you had done it, and he reminded me you weren't a royal. That you could go to prison and cause all of us real trouble."

"You believed him?" Christina shrieked.

Well, that wasn't going well, but Sarandon had suspected it wouldn't. Still, they had to know that she hadn't had anything to do with this. What if she was in league with Burt? Maybe they were afraid they were going to get caught, and they needed someone to blame, so they used Alex to take the heat.

"I'm sorry."

"You sure are!"

"Sarandon and Jenna said they'd help me to learn the truth. I don't know why I believed Burt. I'm truly sorry. I'll do anything to make up for it. Christina? Are you there?" Alex's eyes were misty. "She hung up on me."

"You can sort it out later. All that matters is that we clear you. If Christina really loves you, she'll understand how much of an influence Burt has had over you and that you were only thinking of protecting her. How more noble can you get than that? You'd go to prison—possibly for fifteen years—for her, if convicted? If I were her, I'd think you were total hero material. I might have to think about it a bit to realize that," Jenna said.

Alex took a deep breath. "Okay, I'm ready to go, speak to the lawyer, and turn myself in. You promise me you'll learn the truth."

"Hell yeah, Brother. You have the whole Silver pack behind you on this."

"Thanks," Alex said.

"No problem." Sarandon got him some of his clothes, and Alex dressed.

Just as Alex finished buckling his belt, Sarandon got a call from Christina and handed the phone to Alex.

"Christina." Alex looked at Sarandon and Jenna. "Um, yeah, Sarandon said he and the Silver pack will help me with clearing my name." He paused. "Thanks, honey. I love you."

Jenna took a deep breath and exhaled.

Sarandon patted her back.

Alex ended the call, handing Sarandon his phone, and stood. "Let's get this done."

"Is everything okay between you and Christina?" Jenna asked, sounding hopeful.

"Yes, thanks." Alex smiled. "She forgives me for believing Burt and thinking she did anything criminal. She wants to help me in any way she can, and she's glad I haven't done anything illegal."

"I'm glad for that." Sarandon thought if she could offer to help him that quickly, they stood a chance. "You wouldn't have any idea where Burt took off to and is hiding out, would you?"

Jenna slipped into the driver's seat of her car, and Sarandon sat beside her. Alex climbed into the back seat. "I don't know." He gave a bitter laugh. "Hiding. From you. And from me. And if he knows what's good for him, from Christina too. So, tell me, what did Burt do to CJ?"

"Our brother CJ is a deputy sheriff in Silver Town.

He was on his way there with Burt to question him before Burt overpowered CJ and took off with his car, badge, clothes, wallet, and gun," Sarandon said.

"Is CJ all right?" Alex asked.

"Yeah. We're having our local doctor check him out. Burt's in a hell of a lot of trouble. The state police found CJ's car hidden in the woods with everything else inside. Thankfully, no one else took off with CJ's gun or anything else."

"The clothes too? Burt's clothes were left behind?"

"Yeah. Burt must have run as a wolf. So he had to have gone someplace where he could get clothes to blend in and then hide out. Do you know where that could be?" Sarandon asked as Jenna drove them to Colorado Springs after getting ahold of the lawyer to tell him they were on their way.

"Staying with any one of the pack members. Maybe Mom or Dad. I don't know. Dad would have been mad at him. Mom always forgave him for anything he did that he shouldn't have."

"Like?"

"He had sticky fingers."

Sarandon looked over the seat at Alex.

Alex shrugged. "It was when he was younger. He stole money from Mom's handbag, lifted money from his friends' homes, shoplifted. He swore he hadn't done any of it. He had the evidence on him. The money he shouldn't have had. The same dollar amount that was missing from Mom's purse. Not to mention his scent was on the inside of her purse. Then he said he'd needed the money and she wasn't around so he could ask for it."

"He needed the money for what?" Sarandon asked.

"I don't remember. It was years ago, and I believed it was just a kid thing. I didn't think he was still pulling that crap. The stuff he stole from friends? I saw a couple of the items in his room. Later, he was shoplifting. Stuff I know he didn't pay for but that he was bragging about having. And he was always trying to get me to steal something, as if I was too scared. I wouldn't be goaded into it."

"Well, maybe he's been doing the credit card and passport theft all along. For years. If that's the case, I'm wondering if the passports were stolen some years apart. Had any of them expired?" Sarandon asked.

Alex shook his head. "I don't know. I never even saw them. They were in a bag stuffed under the passenger seat, but a couple of the passports had slipped out onto the floor. That's what the police officer saw and why he took me into custody. I had no idea any of that was in there, and when they found your ID, I was shocked."

"Did you see Mom's TV?" Alex asked. "Burt bought it for her last week. She was thrilled, but Dad and I knew it was just Burt's way to try to make up for never getting her anything for her birthday or Mother's Day for years. She loved listening to a CD player, and I'd given her a new one that had room for over a hundred CDs for her birthday. When she was thanking me for being such a wonderful son while Burt had forgotten her birthday again, he took off. She felt bad, thinking she'd shamed him."

"He returned with the TV?" Sarandon asked.

"Yeah. I knew he was making pretty good money as a cameraman for the ghost-hunter show, but the TV was really expensive."

"Are you sure he really wasn't trying to make up for the years of not getting your mom anything?" Jenna asked.

"And to show me up. I just didn't think he could afford anything quite that expensive, nor would he get her anything that cost that much. For himself, yeah, and then go into debt over it."

"Unless he was using someone else's credit card," Sarandon said.

"Yeah. That's just what I was thinking. The TV came from a computer and office supply store near us. Office Warehouse. I was in there shortly after that, like the next day, looking for some printer paper, and I checked out the TVs for curiosity's sake. I wanted to find out the price of the brand he bought. It was the 4K HDR Elite, curved panel, 75-inch screen, and cost nearly $7,000."

"That's a lot of making up to your mother," Jenna said.

"And not like Burt at all."

"Why were you running as a wolf around here?" Jenna asked.

"I wanted to talk to you and Sarandon. I was afraid to. I couldn't get up the nerve to call. I had to see you in person. To see if you could really help me out."

"We will. We'll do everything we can," Sarandon assured Alex, damn glad they'd finally caught hold of him.

Chapter 18

WHEN SARANDON, JENNA, AND ALEX ARRIVED IN COLORADO Springs, they met with Jeb at the Antlers Hotel. The lawyer spoke with Alex about everything. Sarandon and Jenna went with them afterward to turn Alex in to the police, and he was locked up until the trial the next morning.

Jenna couldn't believe how much she hated that Alex had to be locked away, when from the beginning, that had been her only goal. She was glad she could let her mother know they wouldn't have to pay the bond.

"Okay, thanks, Jenna. Let us know how the trial goes," her mom said.

That was a first, but Jenna realized if Sarandon was going to be family, so were Alex and his twin sister, Faye. And Christina, if she mated Alex. And Faye's husband and kids.

They were there too, staying at a hotel nearby, along with Alex's parents. Jenna was glad they had all come to support him.

In the meantime, they got a call from Monty. "I presume you want to stay and learn what you can about the trial. Some of Alex's coworkers are going to testify on his behalf. His boss even. Several of his pack members too."

"Oh, that's wonderful. Thank you," Jenna said.

Sarandon agreed.

"The Silver pack isn't the only one that takes care of its own," Monty said, sounding proud of his pack.

"What about Burt?" Sarandon asked.

"He's the Silver pack's problem. We don't have a jail of our own here. If I learn of him being in our territory, I'll turn him over to you because of what he did to CJ Silver. No word on his whereabouts yet."

"Okay, thanks." Jenna really hoped they'd catch up to him soon.

———

The next afternoon, during a break in the trial, Jeb came out to talk to them, looking reasonably pleased.

Sarandon asked him, "How do you think it's going for Alex?"

"It appears to be going well. His financial records show the only deposits he's made have been from his construction job wages. He wasn't anywhere near the location where several IDs went missing, and he has witnesses to verify he was working during the time. His fingerprints weren't on any of the stolen items. Not on your driver's license or credit card either. The items weren't wiped down. They still had several sets of fingerprints."

"Hell, that's good news." Sarandon was relieved, not having considered that possibility, though Alex might have worn gloves. "What about Burt's fingerprints?"

"That's the thing. If Burt swiped the stuff and his fingerprints are on them, would anyone even have his fingerprints on file to compare them to?"

"Maybe not. Most of us have never been finger-printed," Sarandon said.

"He's not in the police database. I've talked to Stanton Wernicke about the wages he pays Burt. Sarah

Dreyfus is listed on his bank account, so she checked the bank balance and discovered he's made some hefty deposits into his account. She's also on Alex's account and found nothing of the sort there. When your brother CJ and I began cross-checking missing credit cards and passports with the locations Burt was at when they went missing, we found a pattern. Seventeen matches—all hotels where the victims had stayed—and the ghost hunters were at each of the locations filming a show."

"And Burt was serving as their cameraman," Sarandon said.

"Yes. The police checked guests and the staff at the various locations. No one thought of investigating the ghost-hunter group. They had left by the time guests discovered the items were missing."

"Could it have been any of the ghost hunters?" Sarandon asked, really hoping none of them had been involved.

"It could have been, but Burt seems to be the most likely suspect because of his past criminal behavior and the extra-large deposits in his bank account."

"How are Alex's parents holding up?"

"They're hopeful Alex's name will be cleared. We have two wolves on the jury."

"I'm glad to hear Alex's parents are doing well. And that's great that we have wolves on the jury." Sarandon thought there couldn't be better news than that.

"The only problem I see is that the wolves could work against us if the two jurors suspect Alex is a wolf who is involved in criminal activities. I'm hoping everyone sees the situation for what it is. Someone else has framed him. The only good thing is they could worry that he couldn't keep from shifting during the full moon and not want to convict him. They don't know him, so they're not part of his pack. I asked Alex."

"Don't let on that he's a royal. Will you defend Burt if we can catch him and learn he's the one responsible for all this?"

"Yeah. My goal would be to get him off on all the charges and turn him over to your pack or Monty's, whichever feels the greater need to deal with him."

"We have a jail. And the charges of assault and battery and stealing CJ's car and gun and everything else is in our jurisdiction. We won't be dismissing those charges. He won't get a jury trial, but even if he had one, you know how that would go. I'm not sure Monty would be able to incarcerate him properly if we turned Burt over to his pack for disposition. Monty has already said he'll turn him over to us if he catches him in his pack's territory. We have another option, a jaguar police force that has facilities for jaguars and wolves who need long-term incarceration."

"We've heard of them. Haven't met any of them yet though. Okay, that sounds like it might work well. I've got to go back in."

"Good luck."

Jenna took Sarandon's hand. "We need to find him. Burt."

"Your job is done," Sarandon said, pulling her into his arms, surprised she wanted to continue with this case.

"I don't have another case right this minute. This situation with Alex and Burt made me realize that I want to see real resolution. Normally, we only make sure the fugitive is returned for trial. And that's it. We might see the news of the verdict—guilty, not guilty—and, if guilty, the sentencing phase. But this time..."

"This time, it has to do with me."

"Well, true."

"And maybe because they're wolves."

"True. And Burt hurt your brother. I'm involved. I want to see it through."

Sarandon understood and agreed.

Three hours later, the jury found Alex not guilty, and he came out with his family and Jeb, all of them smiling. Sarandon knew the parents would be upset if Burt was the one responsible for all this. It would be bad enough if someone they didn't know had tried to implicate Alex, but their own son, his brother?

Sarandon offered his brother a hand, which Alex took, and pulled him into a hug.

"Thank you, for everything," Alex said. "I would never have proved my innocence if it hadn't been for your help."

"You're welcome. And don't be surprised if you hear from the rest of your brothers and your cousins," Sarandon said.

"I'll welcome it."

Faye gave Sarandon a hug too. "Thanks for being such a good brother to Alex when Burt hasn't been." She hugged Jenna next. "And to you and your family for providing a lawyer and helping so much."

Alex's boss joined them. "That means you're ready to come back to work for me."

Alex smiled. "I sure am."

"I'll see you at this address at eight tomorrow morning," his boss said.

"I'll be there. Thank you."

When his boss left, Sarah asked if Alex would come home for supper with them.

"I will, thanks." Alex thanked his lawyer, Jenna, and Sarandon one last time before he left.

Sarandon was glad his brother had been cleared of all charges.

"Now what?" Jenna asked.

Sarandon settled his hands on her hips. "I have another week and a half before I need to take the tour group out. Do you want to come with me when it's time?"

"I would, if I don't have a case. What about in the meantime?"

"I'm on vacation."

"Good. I'm not, but while I'm not chasing down fugitives, we can have fun."

"A run after dinner tonight?"

"You've got it." They headed for her car, and he thought this was the best vacation plan ever. As long as he got to spend the time with Jenna. "What about us?"

"You have six months of tour groups to guide. Once they're done, we can think of us."

He groaned. "Not happening."

"I know it's important to you."

"*You* are what's important to me."

"What about Burt?" she asked.

"We'll keep looking for clues of his whereabouts."

They arrived at her house and planned to run next. But the wolf's howl rang out on Jenna's phone.

She groaned.

"It doesn't mean your mom's got a case for you," Sarandon said.

"Yeah, well, the ringtone says it's important." She sighed and took the call. "Yes, Mom?"

"I have a case for you. Maybe you can take Sarandon."

"I'll ask him. Is it a bad case?"

"Jerome Jeffries is suspected of stealing a coin collection. The man he stole it from is missing, but no evidence of foul play, no body, and no crime scene. He has no priors, so the judge set his bail at two fifty. And he's run. I'm sending you a copy of his driver's license and mug shot. And the location of his parents who put up the bond."

"Okay, thanks, Mom. I'm on it."

"And Sarandon?"

She smiled at Sarandon. "I'll ask him. This is supposed to be his vacation."

"Tell her I'm helping you, if this is a case you're on."

"You hear that, Mama? He's going."

"Good. You mate him. He's the one for you."

Jenna let out her breath and smiled. "All right, talk later. Hopefully, I'll catch Jeffries quickly."

"So who are we after now?" Sarandon asked, pulling Jenna into his arms.

She showed him the mug shot and driver's license. "His parents are in Cañon City."

"Maybe some of the pack members who live there will know him. Is he a wolf?"

"Mom would have told me." She sighed. "Just a minute." She called her mom back. "Was he a wolf?"

"We need to start going to the jail to get paperwork from the suspects in person so we can catch their scent," her mother said. "We've never had a wolf to track down before, and it's still such a rarity that he's most likely not one. Identifying a suspect's scent right away would also help us know he's the right one when we pick him up. This suspect faxed the paperwork to us. So none of us have actually seen him. We don't know if he's a wolf."

"Okay. We'll check with the Cañon City pack and see if anyone knows whether he's a wolf."

"Sounds like a good idea."

When they finished the call this time, Jenna started removing her clothes.

Sarandon raised his brows.

"I still want to go for a run. Don't you?"

"Hell yeah."

They stripped off their clothes and shifted, then ran out of the house and into the woods. Sarandon chased her, and she turned and leaped at him, both of them rising on their hind legs, playing with each other. She'd never had so much fun playing with another wolf. She couldn't take him down, as much as she tried. He wouldn't let her either, which she appreciated. She didn't want him to make it easy on her. Jumping back, she turned to run but then turned around and jumped him. That time, she caught him off guard enough to knock him to the side.

He nipped at her neck, and she nipped him back. She tore off, and he chased after her. She loved playing chase with him. She was superfast and could keep out of his reach for the short term, but no way could she keep the pace for long.

She made a quick turn, and he didn't turn fast enough. She woofed with joy, but he quickly caught up to her. She loved running with him as a wolf, and after they returned home, they made spaghetti together, ate, and then went for another wolf run, looking again for any sign that Burt had been in the area. They didn't find any, but they were certain Burt was behind all the thefts. They raced all over the woods and swam across a river, but when they returned home, she got a call from her mother.

"Jeffries is now wanted in connection with the murder of the coin collector. They've just found the man's body," her mom said. "Ask Sarandon if he can carry a concealed weapon. We want him armed and wearing a protective vest."

Sarandon nodded.

"We'll be right over to pick up the vest and the gun. And then we'll head on out."

They'd been trying to track down Jeffries for a week when they finally got a lead. They'd already called the police on two other "leads" that didn't pan out. Jenna's police friend, Calvin Meissner, was good-natured about it, hoping to take Jeffries into custody before he was gone for good, but this time, Jenna and Sarandon wanted to be sure.

They'd picked up Jeffries's scent at a motel in an isolated area four hours from Colorado Springs, just a run-down place on a highway, and they hoped they'd be successful this time. The problem was there were no close towns, just a nearby gas station and lots of farms.

They pulled into the parking area in front of the motel lobby. There wasn't anywhere to park where they could remain hidden from view. They were both wearing bulletproof vests, black cargo pants, boots, and T-shirts with *Fugitive Recovery Agent* imprinted on them. Her sisters had ordered Sarandon one when they knew he was going to be helping Jenna with her cases.

Jeffries had no criminal record, at least that anyone knew of, so Jenna and Sarandon didn't know how he would react to them wearing uniforms. The alternative was to pretend to be civilians, but that could get dicey too.

Sarandon remained outside watching the motel while Jenna walked into the lobby. A man smoking a cigar looked up at her. "Don't tell me. You're here to arrest one of my paying clientele."

Jenna showed him Jeffries's mug shot. "He's wanted for questioning in the murder of a coin collector. Jeffries was found trying to fence the coins. Is that the kind of clientele you want?"

"Room ten. Don't break down my door." He tossed a key on the counter. "And yes, he's still there. As far as I know."

"Thanks." Jenna hurried outside to join Sarandon. "Room ten."

They studied the front of the motel, a black number one on the blue door of the room next to the office, and the last unit at the end, room ten.

They saw the curtain in the room's window move. "He saw us," Sarandon said. "If that's him and not someone staying with him."

As Jenna pulled out her gun, the door opened. A man inside shouted, "Don't shoot. I'm coming out. Don't shoot."

"We're fugitive recovery agents. Come outside with your hands up," Jenna shouted.

The bearded man did, his hands held up high. He was wearing nice clothes—leather loafers, trousers, and a shirt with a button-down collar. Not exactly what she was expecting.

"Down on the ground, now!" Jenna ordered.

The guy quickly complied.

Sarandon moved forward to handcuff Jeffries and read him his rights before Jenna could. She recalled Sarandon sometimes worked as a deputy sheriff. He was perfect for her.

"I didn't do it like they're probably saying," Jeffries said as Sarandon hauled him to the car and set him inside.

"You'll have a chance to explain what happened at trial," Jenna said and called the nearest county sheriff's office. She identified herself and said who she was bringing in, and then they ended the call.

"It was self-defense," Jeffries insisted.

Sarandon said, "You were selling the guy's coin collection, and then he's found murdered."

"He tried to kill me. I was going to buy the coins from him, but he wanted the coins and the money."

"You can prove that at your trial," Jenna said again before driving to the sheriff's office and dropping him off.

She was glad she and Sarandon had recovered one more fugitive together before he had to leave. His butterfly tour started the next day. She would miss him.

"Mate me," Sarandon said. "We'll work everything out somehow."

"You're leaving tomorrow. What if you get home and decide you can't give up what you love doing? That you want to stay there with your pack, your family? If we're separated for six months and find we can't live without each other, that will be a sure sign this is right between us."

He sighed. "Jenna, come home with me tomorrow. You can go on the tour with me, and then I can keep trying to find someone else to take over the tour groups. I've been helping you out with your work. Come have some fun on mine."

"All right." She wanted to. He was right. She wanted to see him doing this. "Let's wait on a mating until—"

"I find someone else to take my tours. You drive a hard bargain, but I'll do whatever I need to do."

When they arrived home, Jenna knew how the night was going to end, them in bed making love to each other. First, she had to tell her mother she was going to go home with Sarandon for a few days. She called while Sarandon was in the kitchen making them a pizza.

"You haven't mated him yet?" her mother asked her.

"Mom, you said I jumped into the last situation without really knowing what I was getting into. I told him six months or, well, sooner, if he finds someone to lead his tour groups. I don't want him to change his mind about us while he's guiding his tours and away from me."

"All right. Thanks on returning Jeffries to custody. Have a good time with Sarandon."

She would. Every moment she could be with him.

Chapter 19

LATER THAT NIGHT, JENNA GOT A CALL FROM HER MOM. "We've got a fugitive on the run. Everyone else is out on jobs. I'm so sorry, Jenna. I really wanted you to take the time to be with Sarandon."

"Of course, I'm on it." Jenna couldn't go with Sarandon on his butterfly tour, as much as she wanted to. She'd even spent several hours last night reading up on the various butterflies they might encounter, so she'd appear to be as knowledgeable as everyone else.

"I should cancel on my tour and go with you," Sarandon said as soon as she hung up with her mom.

She pulled him in for a hug and kissed him. "No, you can't. You're contracted to do this. It's not good for business, and I'll have this done in a couple of days. Then, if we don't have another case in the meantime, I'll join you."

"The next one is a bird-watching group. They bring cameras and take pictures."

"I'll bring my cell phone and take pictures."

"I don't want to leave you," Sarandon said, speaking from the heart.

"I don't want you to either, but this can make getting together again even more special. Don't you agree?" She didn't really believe it. Being with Sarandon all this time had been like a beautiful honeymoon. What if when he returned to Silver Town, he felt at home—more so than when he was here with her, living next to her parents.

"You know I'm trying to get ahold of everyone on the tours to get them to agree to having a different guide. And I'm still trying to find someone who wants to take over the business as a whole."

Jenna understood he couldn't just advertise for someone to take his place. That person would have to be a wolf, if the guide was to live in Silver Town and work from there.

Sarandon smiled and pulled her into a tighter hug, kissing her deeply. "We'll get this covered. Hopefully sooner rather than later."

"Yes," she said and tried not to show her distress at the notion that he was leaving her to return to his home and his pack and his family in the morning.

The next morning, Jenna took Sarandon to the airport and they said their goodbyes. She hated to see him go, as much as it appeared to be killing him to leave her.

"You'll wear your bulletproof vest and be armed to the teeth? Tasers all powered up?" Sarandon asked, kissing her cheek and then her forehead.

"Always."

"You'll call me when you locate the suspect and after you've successfully taken him down?"

"Yes, I will."

"You'll call for backup if you run into any trouble?"

"Of course. Don't worry, I've been doing this forever."

"All right. While I'm back in Silver Town, or at least

after I finish this tour and before I start the next one, I'll try to get someone else to take over the rest. Be careful." He kissed her deeply.

When he let her up for air, she tried to fight the tears welling up in her eyes. She didn't think she'd ever feel this way about another wolf.

He hugged her to his breast. "I'll be back, Jenna. This isn't forever."

She had a job to do. A meaningful job. So why did she not care about anything but seeing Sarandon again? She knew when he left, he'd be taking her heart with him.

She kissed him back and let him go.

As soon as he was out of view at the airport, Jenna felt lost. She hadn't felt that way since she'd lost her mate and unborn children. She had it bad where Sarandon was concerned.

She had to get her mind on the job. The man she was searching for was from Cañon City, which, of course, made her think of Burt and his pack. She knew the chance of running into Burt while tracking down Herman Schofield was miniscule. Herman was wanted for aggravated assault and battery, and her mom had been worried that Herman was more violent than most suspects Jenna had brought in. The man used his fists to terrorize people. He didn't use weapons. But Jenna was carrying a small arsenal, knew how to use the weapons, and had no qualms about doing so, though she had to be careful to protect herself from being charged with a crime. She loved that Sarandon had bought her a body camera to protect herself from that.

As she drove out to Cañon City, Jenna couldn't stop

worrying about Burt. She couldn't stop wondering why he had been prowling around their territory as a wolf, unless Alex's supposition was correct and Burt hadn't wanted Alex to turn himself in to Jenna.

Cañon City was small, and it hadn't had any special meaning for Jenna before this. Now that she'd met so many people who were wolves living in the area, it wasn't just another town. It was special. Important. Yet she kept wondering if the reason they hadn't had any clues to Burt's whereabouts was because other wolves in the pack were hiding him, covering for him.

She got a call from Sarandon, and she smiled. "Hey, you. Did you leave something behind?"

"You. And I've got this awful itch that needs scratching."

She chuckled. "Hurry up and find someone to take your guided tours so you can come home."

"I'm working on it. I have so many tours, and they're so varied that I haven't located a wolf who could handle all of them as a business who doesn't already have a job. So where is your first lead on this guy?"

"He's in Cañon City." She was certain Sarandon wouldn't be happy to hear it. "His whole family lives there. So it's my best lead."

"Cañon City."

"Yeah."

"Can you check with Monty and see if he has any idea what's happened to Burt?"

She was surprised Sarandon wanted her to stir up that hornet's nest when he wasn't there with her. "Yeah, I can do that."

"Okay, but if you get a lead on him—"

"I'll call you."

Sarandon growled. "Call law enforcement. Even though we wanted to handle Burt on our own, he's a royal, and he can go to trial and jail. Better that happens than that he takes you down while you're on your own."

"I doubt Monty will know anything, or he would have notified us. I'll be careful."

"If you don't call the local police, I will."

"I will. Sheesh, Sarandon, you're not here to do this job. I am. Let me do it."

"I don't want you getting hurt. Or killed."

"I understand. I'm going to get off here and call Monty. I'll be in Cañon City before I know it."

"All right. Tell me what he says after you speak with him."

"I will." Jenna hoped Sarandon didn't think he was going to tell her how to run her business, not after she'd been doing it on her own for so many years.

She called Monty next. "Do you have any idea where Burt could be? We haven't had any leads. Sarandon asked me to check with you, though I told him you would have called if you'd known anything."

"Yeah, I would have," Monty said. "I haven't heard anything to indicate Burt is here and staying with anyone. You don't think he returned to see his boss, Stanton, for help, do you?"

"No. Stanton likes Burt and thinks he does a good job, but he wants this matter straightened out. Stanton wouldn't have Burt working for him, if he knew what Burt had done to CJ. He's married to Laurel, Stanton's cousin, so they're family by marriage."

"Ah. I understand. So Stanton and his brothers are part of the Silver pack?"

"No," Jenna said. "They haven't asked to be part of the pack, yet."

"All right. Well, I'll check into this right away."

She felt bad for Monty because he'd lost his mate, but she realized that if he couldn't gain the confidence of his people or be strict enough that his pack members would tell him when there was trouble with any pack member, he should step down.

Monty called her back. "I'm going to call a pack meeting for two hours from now. Can you come to it?"

"Sure. I'll be in town in a few minutes. I'm trying to track down another fugitive, and if I don't locate him by the time you're having your meeting, I'll be there."

"Good. Hope to see you soon."

Jenna was glad Monty seemed to be taking over his pack again. Or he'd have to give it up to someone who would. Packs needed strong leadership.

She went to Herman Schofield's home first. No one appeared to be home. She listened for any sign of movement inside the house, but there was none. Next, she asked at the neighbors' homes. They seemed to be afraid to say. Because of the violent behavior that had already caused him trouble?

Next, Jenna drove to his parents' home. They emphatically denied he was there or had been in touch, not for months. She didn't believe them. Both of them looked way too nervous, the father casting glances at the mother, who kept pulling at a strand of hair as if she had a nervous tic.

Jenna gave them her card, then left. Herman had three

grown brothers she was going to check out next, but the time had slipped away, so she went to Monty's pack meeting instead.

Monty greeted her and said, "Alex is on a job in Colorado Springs, and two other families are on vacation, but everyone else showed up for the meeting. We haven't had one of these in a while, so I wasn't sure how the turnout would be."

"I'm glad everyone showed up that could."

"Well, of course, Burt didn't, but his parents are here."

"Okay, good." She knew this had to be difficult for Monty and how hard it had to be for the parents. She wondered if Anton had told Sarah what had happened concerning Burt. Jenna hoped so.

Once everyone had something to drink in Monty's large living room, he said, "Some of you know Jenna St. James. She was looking for Alex Dreyfus to help clear his name of charges pressed against him in the case of ID theft and other crimes. We're grateful to her and her family and the Silver pack, who worked hard to help him out and successfully cleared his name."

Christina was biting her lip, sitting across the room from Anton and Sarah.

"We have a new problem. Deputy Sheriff CJ Silver was taking Burt Dreyfus to Silver Town for questioning, on suspicion of him being involved in the actual theft instead of Alex. Burt knocked the deputy out, giving him a concussion, stole his weapon, clothes, and car, and ran. He's still on the run. You know we can't harbor a rogue wolf. He has to pay for his crimes. And if he was the one who stole the passports and credit cards and framed Alex for that, he's also committed crimes against one of our own."

Everyone was quiet until Monty mentioned that the wolf might be guilty of a crime against one of their pack members.

Several glanced in Anton and Sarah's direction, and Jenna was certain that in deference to them, the other pack members were keeping quiet. There were a few mutterings among them, especially the ones further away from the parents.

"Not only that, but he accused another pack member, Alex's mate, Christina, of committing the crimes. That's a crime in itself. And that's why Alex was willing to take the rap, to protect Christina. That's what our pack members do for each other."

Several nodded.

Jenna was surprised to learn Alex and Christina had mated. She was proud of him for doing so, even if his mother still wasn't happy about it.

Anton said, "We're devastated about this business, first that Alex would take the blame and have to defend himself, and now that Burt has harmed a member of another pack and potentially framed Alex for committing a crime Burt has done. As much as it hurts us to be here, baring our souls, we have to do what's right for the pack. And ultimately, what's right for Burt. His disregard for us shows in his actions. He has to be held accountable."

"He needs to be held accountable by our pack leader," a man said. "He's part of our pack. The alleged crimes were committed against our pack members."

Monty raised his hand for silence. "The serious injury that was done to the deputy was a crime against the Silver pack. Not only that, but for those who are unaware of the situation, the deputy is Alex's half brother. As such, CJ Silver and his pack have welcomed Alex and his family as part of their own. Alex is as much a member of the Silver pack as he is of ours. The Silver family runs Silver Town. They have their own jail, but also have arrangements with a jaguar group that has facilities for long-term incarceration. Burt will be taken care of by our own kind, if it comes to that."

"Jaguars," someone scoffed.

"Yes. Most of us don't have our own facilities to handle a matter like this. As much as we'd like to handle pack matters within the confines of the pack, Burt took on another pack, and it's our job to hand him over to them if we learn he's still in the area. Jenna is here to take him in. If anyone knows where he's staying and doesn't wish to speak up now, you can let me know after the meeting."

Jenna understood why they might feel that way. Like they were a traitor to the pack.

She was surprised that Monty had a pizza party afterward. She needed to meet with Herman's brothers, but to show her support of Monty and his pack, she had a bottled water and a slice of pepperoni pizza.

"Congratulations," she said to Christina, wanting to acknowledge her for the mating.

"Thanks for helping Alex out. I'm sorry I lied about caring where he was when he was working. He told me you questioned him about that."

"I understand the reasoning. You were protecting him."

"I was. I would do anything for him, but, boy, was

I mad he believed Burt's lie. I wish I knew where Burt was. I'd hand him over in a heartbeat. The bastard."

"I understand. Do you think anyone else knows where he is?"

Christina took a sip of her soda and glanced around the room. "They might. They won't tell Monty here in front of everyone."

"I kind of assumed that."

"The older men who are talking to Monty right now are probably talking about anything but. I don't suspect any of them would give Burt safe haven. He's irritated a lot of people. He's only tolerated because everyone likes Anton."

"And Sarah?"

"She still doesn't like that I mated Alex, but she's going to have to come around if she wants to see the grandkids when we have them someday," Christina quickly added. "She's kind of like Burt, rubs a few people the wrong way. Some of our pack members do genuinely like her. Would she hide Burt?" Christina studied Sarah as she spoke to another woman in the group. "Probably. She is always dismissing his antics. This time, he's gone too far."

"I hope things work out between the two of you."

Christina sighed. "For Alex's sake, I do too. I lost my mother when I was young, so it would be nice if we could connect. If she sticks up for Burt after what he did to Alex and me…" Christina shook her head. "And the business with Alex's half brother CJ is unforgivable. Burt could have killed him."

Sarah began wiping the tears off her face, and Jenna felt bad for her. She couldn't imagine what it would be like to have a child who began committing crimes and then had to go to prison. If Burt had been made to pay for his earlier transgressions, would he have learned from his mistakes and mended his ways? Jenna wondered.

Still, from the sound of it, he harbored deeper-seated feelings against Alex, and this was more about that than anything.

No one approached Jenna. She assumed that if anyone did, it would be tantamount to saying they agreed with turning over one of their own to her, and they didn't want to come forth. It was time for her to learn where Herman Schofield was. Hopefully, Monty would get her some leads on where Burt was hiding out. Though she also worried this could backfire, and if someone was hiding him, they might warn him to run.

She gave Christina a hug. "I wish all the best for you and Alex and hope everything works out with you and your new extended family."

"I hope you catch the guy you're after and he doesn't give you any trouble."

"Thanks. I always hope for that. I've got to say goodbye to Monty." Jenna walked over to where he was standing and speaking to the same group of people, who were talking about having a celebration this fall. Christina was probably right. They wouldn't discuss anything about Burt in front of the rest of the pack.

"Hey, Monty, I need to chase down another fugitive, which is why I had to come here today." She glanced at the people he'd been talking to who were still standing there. "No one knows a Herman Schofield, do they? He's not a wolf but lives here."

Everyone shook their heads, and a few muttered no.

"Thanks for having me come to your gathering," Jenna said and offered her hand to Monty.

He gave her a hug. "Thanks for making me wake up about my pack."

Several agreed they were glad he was taking over again and showing some leadership. No one said what she needed to hear—where Burt was hiding out.

"I'm glad for you and your pack," Jenna said and gave him her card again, in case he wanted to give it to anyone, if someone was inclined to contact her. She suspected anyone with information would contact their pack leader, since that's the way it should go.

She left for the auto repair garage where two of Herman's brothers worked. They both were holding wrenches as they stared at her wearing her fugitive recovery agent uniform, and she didn't like their growly expressions. "You probably already know that I'm looking for Herman and need to take him in to stand trial."

"It was a setup," one of the men said, his hands and his shirt greasy. "And even if we knew where he was, we wouldn't be telling the likes of you."

"All right. Thanks." They were hard-looking, muscular, unyielding men. They looked like they could have had some run-ins with people themselves and been the winners of the confrontations. She definitely didn't want to take these guys on.

She left and drove to a service station to get some gas before she checked with Herman's other brother and a girlfriend. She suspected if anyone knew about Burt's whereabouts, Monty or the person would call later, after their pack meeting and lunch ended. They might have even had more of a discussion once she, an outsider, was gone.

She got a call from Sarandon and smiled. "Hey, are you almost home?"

"Yeah. I wish I was there with you. What's going on with you and your case?"

"No luck on finding Herman yet, but Monty called a pack meeting and discussed the business about Burt."

"Hell, that's good news."

"Yeah, no one came forward with information, but I'm looking into where Herman has escaped, and maybe someone will call me or let Monty know privately where Burt is."

"After what Burt did to CJ, I don't want you trying to apprehend him on your own."

"I agree. I'll call the local police if I think I'm going to find him."

"Are you going to stay there for the night if you haven't found Herman?"

"No. It's not that far from home. I'll just return home and come here again tomorrow, if I have leads for either man. Have you had any luck with getting anyone to take your group tours?" She knew he couldn't have or he would have said so already.

"I've got someone to take the white-water rafting. All the guys love doing that. And I contacted everyone on the tour, and they were agreeable."

"Good. That was this summer, right?"

"Yeah."

"Okay, well, that's progress. That gives us a two-week break."

"And I'm coming home."

She smiled. "Good. Oh, got a call coming in. Got to go. I'll call you later."

"Okay, let me know if you have anything."

"I will. Bye, Sarandon. Talk soon." She answered the call from an unknown caller. "Hello?"

"You're the agent who wants to take Burt into custody, right?"

"Yes, and you are?"

"That you don't need to know. Monty's had a rough time of it. We're just glad to see him taking the reins again. Thanks for helping Alex out too. You promise Burt will get a fair deal? That you won't involve the police?"

Now that put her on the spot. She had promised Sarandon she'd call the police if she had to take down Burt. She couldn't lie to this man just to get his information. Her reputation and that of her family's would be hurt in the wolf community.

"You have my word that if Burt comes with me willingly, I'll turn him over to the sheriff's office in Silver Town. Depending on if he's guilty of the other crimes, they'll decide the term of incarceration. He'll be able to shift as a wolf while he's in custody without any issues."

"I have your word you won't try to kill him."

"If he doesn't try to kill me when I go to arrest him, yes."

"He wouldn't do that to you. He's been staying out at his grandfather's old farmhouse. The place hasn't been lived in for seventy years, no running water or electricity, shut off a long time ago. I was running as a wolf in the woods around there last night and smelled his scent mark around the area. Smoke was coming out of the chimney, and his SUV was parked in the woods nearby.

Unless Monty's meeting or someone else tipped him off, I'd check there. No police. Our kind need to take him into custody."

"Can I get some help with it? Some of your wolves to come out and help bring him in?"

"You didn't hear this from me. And if you tell anyone, they could very well tip him off. Not everyone wants to turn him over to another pack. Don't call Monty about it either. He's getting enough flak about it from those same people. We need more of a neutral person, you, to take him in."

"Thanks."

He gave her the directions, telling her GPS wouldn't work. That reminded her of how she'd had the same thing happen while going after Sarandon. At least that had had a happy outcome. She worried about Burt and how he would react.

"No police. We don't need humans butting into our business."

"No police." When she ended the call, she called her mom. "I've got a lead on Burt. A pack member said he was staying at his grandfather's abandoned home. I'm headed there now."

"Did you get ahold of the police?"

She explained to her mother what the man had said to her.

"What if it's a setup?"

"It's the best lead we've got. I have to do this before he runs off." Jenna noted that her mother didn't tell her to call the police again either. She knew how important it was to garner good relations with packs in the area, if they were going to have their cooperation in cases like this.

"I don't like it. Can you ask someone in the pack to go with you?"

"I asked, and he said no. That, if I ask, one of them could tip off Burt."

"When you get there, you call me and keep the line open. I want to know that you're all right."

"Okay, Mom. I'll do that. It's about forty minutes out there, and it's located in the woods." She just hoped she'd have cell reception. She was getting a sat phone, next thing on her agenda.

When she was a couple of miles from the vicinity, she pulled her car off into the woods. Armed and ready, she headed in the direction of the grandfather's farmhouse, but when she finally reached the weathered, two-story building, moss growing on the roof, she saw no sign of Burt's vehicle. Damn it. She didn't want to get close to the house in case Burt returned and smelled her scent. She was afraid he'd run. Then again, he might not return.

She called her mom. "I'm here; he's not. I'm staying in case he returns."

"If he sees your car..."

"It's hidden in the woods. I walked here. As long as he doesn't run through the woods, I should be good. I didn't check out the house, not wanting to leave my scent there. The man said Burt had been using the fireplace, but there's no smoke now. And his vehicle isn't here."

"Call me if he returns."

"I will. If I have to, I'll stay the night in the woods. He might have been tipped off because of Monty's pack meeting and left the area. If not, I need to stay here."

"All right. Just let me know if he shows up."

Jenna should have brought something to drink, but she didn't want to chance walking back to her car and missing Burt if he showed up. She was about to call Sarandon but figured he'd be upset with her for doing this on her own. She sat down and leaned against a tree and listened to the birds singing in the trees until night descended and the air grew colder. Trying not to think about it, she kept fighting with herself about leaving her spot of ground to return to the car, for both her jacket and a bottle of water.

Her thirst finally won out. Except for the crickets chirping, she didn't hear any other sound, so she moved quickly back to her car. As soon as she reached it, she wished she had turned off her overhead light so it wouldn't come on when she opened her car door. She waited, listening, not hearing any sound of anyone, and unlocked her car door. She opened it and quickly grabbed her jacket to put on, as well as a backpack. She shut and locked the door, then headed back to the house.

There was still no one about, and she'd finally reached the place where she'd been watching the house before. No car there. She sat down and pulled out a bottle of water, then observed the house, dozing on and off when no one came. Stakeouts were a pain.

She was just about to drift off again when her phone vibrated in her pocket. *Sarandon.* "Hey," she said, her voice quiet.

"Where are you?"

"On a stakeout. No one here, so I figure I'll leave in the morning or by midafternoon if the guy doesn't show up." She didn't say which guy she meant, but she figured Sarandon would assume it would be Herman or she would have said Burt. And she wasn't telling him she was staying in the woods near an abandoned farmhouse either. At least she had cell reception.

They talked for a while, but she finally said, "I need to go. I'll let you know if anything happens."

"Night, Jenna."

"Night, honey." She ended the call and, about an hour later, nodded off. When she woke, there was still no sign of a car, smoke from the chimney, nothing. She was so disappointed.

Sarandon called her first thing in the morning. "Still on the stakeout?"

"Yeah, I think it's a bust. I'll stay here until noon, then I'm looking into other leads."

"I'm about to take my tour group out, so if you learn anything, let me know."

"Will do. Have fun with your group." She ended the call with him and yawned. "Ugh." She pulled out a granola bar, wishing more than anything that she and Sarandon were at her house, having a nice leisurely breakfast and then a wolf run after that. And making love to him every time in between.

She left her observation spot and was heading deeper in the woods so she could relieve herself when she saw Burt's SUV hidden in the brush. Her heart began to beat harder, and she whipped around in time to see Burt aiming a gun at her and shooting.

And she went down.

———⟋⟍———

The whole time Sarandon was on the butterfly hunt, he was having a hell of a time keeping focused while talking to his guests and showing them all the perfect wildflower spots where butterflies flitted about the flowers in profusion. Usually, he was too busy thinking about what he needed to say on his guided tour, but this time, all he could think of was Jenna, and he worried about whether she was okay. He didn't like that she'd been watching for the guy all night without rest. Catnaps wouldn't do it if she was faced with an aggressive suspect and had to react quickly.

No one had any word about what had happened to Burt either. Sarandon wondered if wolves were giving the guy refuge.

When he got a call from Jenna's mom, he worried right away that something bad had happened. All he heard was, "She's okay." His thoughts went fuzzy, and he felt dizzy.

The people on his guided tour were so busy snapping shots of tiger swallowtails that no one saw his distress.

"Is it a tiger swallowtail?" one of the women asked Sarandon.

"Yes, it is." Then he asked Jenna's mother, "What's happened?"

"Burt shot her."

Sarandon saw red. He was ready to leave right then and there, but he had enough presence of mind to realize he couldn't run out on his tour group. They probably wouldn't find their way back to where they'd left their cars on their own. "You said she's all right?"

"Yes. She was doing surveillance on Burt's grandfather's ranch. She called Monty for help, and he and several of their men went to her aid."

She would have only called them if she'd been hurt so

badly, she couldn't do it on her own. And what the hell? She never should have gone after Burt without police backup, at the very least. She hadn't once said she was after him either. Sarandon had assumed she was going after the other guy. "You said she was okay." Sarandon would kill the son of a bitch.

"She was wearing her bulletproof vest, thank God, or she would have been dead. She's bruised and sore. No broken ribs. I'd hoped you'd come take her to your home where she'll be safe until she's able to work again. She's at our home, recuperating."

"As soon as I can get someone up here to take my place on the tour, I'll be coming for her."

"She'll be glad to hear it. Mate her, Sarandon. Keep her safe."

He knew he'd be giving up his job to help her with hers. He loved what he did, but he loved Jenna more. And he couldn't deny he enjoyed working with her on her cases.

"For now, she's sleeping, or I would have had her talk to you. She'll be thrilled to see you, though she's worried you'll be mad at her."

He was. Hell, no way did he want her out there on her own, facing that bastard. "Tell her I'm coming."

"I will. See you in several hours."

He got on the phone to his brother Brett. "Hey, I've got an emergency. Jenna was shot. Burt shot her. Can you come out and be the guide for the rest of the tour? And find someone to take the next group out? I need to bring Jenna home for safekeeping."

"Yeah, Sarandon. I'm already leaving a note with my boss, and I'm on my way."

"Thanks."

"What are brothers for? I know you've been trying to get someone to take your business over, but no one's stepping forward."

"I've got one guy to take my whitewater rafting group out. Just need to make arrangements for the other tour groups. I have to make sure the people who paid for the tours are agreeable to someone else guiding them."

"We'll get it worked out, Sarandon. If we have to refund money to anyone who wants to cancel because we get a different tour guide for them, then we'll do it. I know you don't want to do that, but Jenna's too important."

Sarandon kept thinking he only had to do this for six months, and then he didn't have any more tours scheduled. He had breaks in between, and he planned to see Jenna every time he had a few days' break.

"We'll take care of it, Brother. The pack will. One way or another, even if we have different wolves taking over different tours. Jake can do the birding tour. He's taken tons of photos of the Colorado birds, butterflies too. I'll put a call out to him to help me with this. I don't know that much about butterflies."

"All right."

"I'm on the road. Be there as soon as I can."

Within the hour, Brett was there, relieving Sarandon of his job. Sarandon had already told his group what had happened. They'd all wished him well and were fine with his news reporter brother taking over, and they were eager to meet Jake.

Brett walked Sarandon to his car. "If you need any help, let us know."

"I'm bringing her here where she'll be safe from Burt or anyone else who might try to hurt her."

"What about Burt?"

Sarandon rubbed his whiskery chin. "I'm going to kill him."

"Call us. Don't do this on your own. We'll be there for you."

"Yeah, I will." If Sarandon ran into Burt on his own, he was taking him out.

He hit the road and couldn't get Jenna out of his mind. He kept calling her number, but she wasn't answering. He knew she had to be sleeping with her cell phone off, but he still wasn't going to stop trying.

Four hours into the trip, he finally got ahold of her. "Hey, honey, how are you feeling?"

"Oh, Sarandon, Mom shouldn't have called you to come and get me. I'm not leaving here to hide away in Silver Town with your big wolf pack."

"Okay. Are you ready to mate?"

There was such a long pause that he knew he should have waited until he got there to ask her and maybe when she was feeling completely herself too. "Jenna?"

She laughed.

He smiled.

"It hurts to laugh."

"I'm sorry."

"I thought we were going to wait until all your tour groups are finished."

"I wanted to make sure you didn't consider some other wolf before I came for you."

"Ha! As if that would happen."

"So, it's a yes? Right?"

"Yeah. It's a yes. Who else would break their neck to find a replacement on their job and then drive all those hours to join me?"

"The wolf who loves you, though asking Brett to take my place wasn't a hardship. We all do things for each other to help out. And I think the people on the tour were eager to ask Brett about the wildest stories he'd reported on. Jake's joining them too, and he knows all about butterflies at least. How are you?"

"Sore, missing you, ready to kill Burt."

"I am too. Tell me what happened. Your mother knew I was busy on this tour so she didn't give me very many details."

"I got an anonymous call yesterday from one of Burt's pack members that led me to Burt's grandfather's abandoned farmhouse."

"Hell, Jenna. I thought you were doing surveillance on Herman and were sitting in your car in town somewhere. Not out in the country alone."

"Well, I didn't think Burt was even there. Then, quite by accident, I discovered his car hidden a long way from the house. I hadn't wanted to do a lot of walking around the area in case he went running as a wolf and discovered I'd been there. I heard him and turned but didn't have enough time to pull out my gun. He shot me, knocked me out, and took off. He might have thought he'd killed me."

"I'll kill him."

"You and me both. My whole family is ready to. I suspect if your family got involved, they would all try to take him down. The only good thing that came out of this, if you can call it that, is that Monty's whole pack united over this issue. They were furious one of their own could have murdered me. If I hadn't been wearing a vest, that's just what he would have done. No one is going to give him a safe place to stay now. They were horrified he would resort to this. So what do we do? Hand him over to the cops?"

"No. We handle this wolf to wolf. The mystery of the passport theft will have to remain that."

"I'm ready."

He wanted to tell her that in no way did he want her near the bastard, but if she was going to be his mate, they were in this together. "What about the man you were supposed to take down before Burt took you out?"

"Herman? I didn't have a chance to speak with his third brother, nor his girlfriend. He's not a wolf, by the way."

"Is anyone from your family looking for the fugitives?"

"Not yet. My dad and sisters are trying to apprehend other fugitives, though they were ready to drop their cases to come to my aid. I told them there was no need. My mate-to-be was coming to help me take them down."

Sarandon smiled. "Hell. Yeah." He hated that she'd been hurt, but he had every intention of taking one fugitive in and the other down—permanently. No one messed with his mate and got away with it. They talked for two hours, and he finally said, "I guess I have a new job and a new home to go to." He wasn't sure if that was what she wanted, but as her mate, he wanted to be with her no matter where she was or what kind of work he had to do. He suspected that if Jake's wife decided to go back to being a bounty hunter, Jake would accompany her, making his photography business a side business.

"You have tours set up for half the year."

"Yeah, but Brett's helping me to get someone else to

step in and iron out any problems we might have. Jake's going to do the birding tour."

"Are you sure? You're not going to miss that?"

"Being in the wide-open spaces? I'll do that with you instead."

"Okay."

"We'll live where you want to live. I love you and want to be with you."

"I wanted to be near my family, but I want to be with you. I'd already decided that if it meant living farther away from my family, I'd do it. You made me fall in love with you. I worried you might not want to be around my family that much."

"Why would you worry about that, Jenna?" He thought he'd shown he really cared for them.

"My previous mate was a lone wolf, no family, and he didn't want to live by them. I was afraid that when we had our child, he wouldn't want to see them either."

"No problems there, honey. I love your family. I've already adopted them."

"My dad thinks you're great. He's already talking about cookouts with you, fishing, and hunting. It worried me that I might not see you again."

Sarandon laughed. "You'll come first. Always."

"He was hoping we'd run as a pack some too. He worries about my sisters running together or alone. I think he's really looking forward to having another male wolf in the family."

"I'll want time alone with you, but running with your family is fine by me." He glanced at the car clock again, wishing the drive wasn't so long. "So you want me to work with you."

"My family will be thrilled. They're excited to have a son. Living next door. You don't have to make all the changes. I don't want you to feel you have to give up everything. I could live in Silver Town with you."

"We can take vacations there and visit with my family. They'll want your family to visit also. They're just as important to my pack."

"Thank you. I had hoped you would say that. I want to start back on this job tomorrow though. I still want to check out the last two leads I have for Herman."

"Are you sure you're feeling well enough?"

"Tomorrow. I'll feel fine by then."

"I'll let you get some more rest. I'll be there in a little bit."

"All right. See you soon."

Ecstatic that Sarandon had asked her to mate with him, Jenna left her room in her mom's house and found her on the phone in the dining room. Her mom glanced up to see Jenna and ended the call. "How are you doing, honey?" She hurried to rise from her chair.

"I'm fine, Mom, but I'm going back to my place."

"You can't. Wait until Sarandon gets here, and he can take you there."

"We're mating. I want to be there when he arrives."

"Oh, heavens. He finally asked you! That's great news. I'll take you to your place right before he gets here. You can't be alone."

Jenna got a glass of water. "Okay."

"You can't mate right away. Not with the way you're feeling," her mom said.

Jenna smiled. She had no intention of holding off. She wanted this mating just as much as Sarandon did.

"What…what about your living arrangements?"

"Don't worry, Mom. He's fallen in love with the family and with me, of course. He wants to be part of our agency, and we're staying right next door."

Her mom was in tears and lightly hugged Jenna.

"It's okay, Mom. When we start having babies, you can take care of them while I'm chasing down fugitives."

"I'm so happy for you. And for us. What about a wedding?"

"We can discuss it later. Since Sarandon's giving up his family in Silver Town, it would be nice to have the wedding there."

"Okay, I agree. You rest up before he gets here. I know you're not going to heed my words about taking it easy tonight. Not that I would either if I were in your shoes."

Jenna agreed and spent the rest of the afternoon sleeping. When she got a call right before Sarandon arrived, she smiled. "I'll see you in just a few minutes, honey," he said.

Her mother hurried to drive her back to her house. "Don't overdo it."

"Mom." Her mom gave her a big sigh, then got out of the car to walk her into the house. "I'm okay, Mom. You really don't have to stay."

"We're not taking any chances."

Both of them were armed with 9 mm pistols as they walked through the house, making sure it was clear. They heard a vehicle in the driveway, and Jenna's mom hurried to see who it was. "Your knight is here. When does he want to start working? What about the business he's in?"

"The pack is taking care of it. I hope you won't be

too rough on him when he applies to work for you, like you were on Dad."

Her mom smiled and lightly hugged Jenna again. "He won't have to apply at all. He's already helped with several of your cases, so he's been vetted. This is cause for a celebration."

When Sarandon pulled up in the driveway, Jenna and her mom met him outside. Her mom gave Sarandon a hug. "Keep her safe and ensure she doesn't overdo it."

"Yes, ma'am." Sarandon gently pulled Jenna into his arms. "You're beautiful."

They waved at her mom and then headed inside Jenna's house. "How are you feeling?"

"Better. Even a couple of hours' rest made me feel much better."

"You have to take it easy. Your mom said."

"There's easy, and there's easy. We're mating, my sexy, hot wolf. And that's not open for discussion." She slipped her hand through his belt loop and pulled him into the house. "After what happened, and what could have happened, I'm not waiting."

As soon as they were inside the house, his hot gaze speared her. She was ready to strip all his clothes off so she could admire his gloriously naked body.

He cupped her face and kissed her forehead, then pulled her into another light embrace.

"I won't break," she assured him. If he was going to delay a mating because he was worried she was hurting, she would scream. She wasn't delaying this for anything.

"You have to know how I feel about this. I don't want to hurt you."

"You won't." She tugged him to the bedroom and began taking off his clothes.

"You aren't in a rush, are you?" He sat on the bed and pulled off his boots.

She removed hers, then slid her shirt over her head. "Aren't you?"

He laughed. "I could hardly think of anything else but being with you again. I'm ready to make up for all that lost time."

He stood, and they helped each other out of the rest of their clothes. Despite being in a rush, he continued to kiss her bare skin, taking it slow, checking her over, assuring himself she was all right. As much as she wanted to hurry things along, she loved how gentle he was with her, how concerned that he didn't hurt her.

His gaze was smoldering as he paused to observe her, and she loved how he could look at her like that—like he could devour her, like she wanted to devour him.

"I want this. You. Me. Together." She took his hands in hers, eager to make him her mate. Nothing was going to stop this from happening now. Not unless Burt walked in the door. She hated Burt for what he'd done to her and everyone else who had suffered at his hands, but she had to admit that if it weren't for him and everything he'd pulled, she and Sarandon probably would never have met. She thought the world of Sarandon, and she couldn't live without him in her life.

"I love you," Sarandon said, kissing her, then lifting her onto the bed.

"I love you right back, Sarandon." She couldn't believe they were doing this, and not six months from now. She couldn't have been happier.

Then he was kissing her again, his cheek rubbing against hers, his hands on her breasts, massaging, warming them. She was melting into the mattress underneath his touch, her blood hot with need, her feminine core screaming for attention. He rubbed her nipple, then moved his mouth lower to suckle it, licking and kissing it. She about came unglued and arched against his hungry touch. "Oh…my…God," she said on a deep, throaty groan.

He lifted his face and frowned. "Are you all—"

She pulled his head back to her breast, directing his actions, breathing out a strangled, "Yes!"

He chuckled.

She combed her fingers through his hair and rubbed her inner thigh against his outer thigh, leaving her scent on him, wanting him deep inside her. He continued to suckle her breast, making her inner core tighten with desperate need. She was trying not to make a sound, fearing he'd think he was hurting her, and she didn't want him to stop for any reason. Or to make her speak and lose her concentration.

He began kissing her mouth, then reached down to cup her mound. She held her breath in heady anticipation, waiting for him to touch her, to bring her to climax.

He slid his finger between the folds and began to stroke. She groaned, her whole body on fire. She felt his full erection stirring against her leg. She dug her fingers into his waist, dying for release, wanting, needing, craving this. Between his expert strokes, the scent of their arousal, and their pheromones cheering them on, she felt the scales of balance tipping in her favor. And then she was splintering into a million ecstatic pieces. Before she could gather her wits, he pressed the tip of his penis against her, seeking entrance, waiting for her agreement. God, he was so good for her.

She swept her hands down his buttocks and tugged at him to penetrate her. "I'm ready," she said in case he needed the encouragement.

He nuzzled her cheek and whispered, "I love you."

"Love you right back." She wanted to tell him to get on with it. Instead, she spread her legs and pulled him to join her, needing this, the union between wolves, the act confirming they had chosen each other and no one else.

He obliged, pushing into her, joining her, thrusting as she rocked back and forth. She slid one of her feet over the back of his leg, caught up in the wonder of making love to her wolf. Her wolf forever and ever.

Sarandon couldn't have loved the she-wolf any more than he did, and though he had worried Jenna would be too sore to make love, she wasn't letting him get out of it. He hoped she wouldn't regret it later. He was glad too, that she was feeling well enough after what Burt had done to her, but he didn't want to think of the bastard and what he had done to Jenna right this moment.

He kissed her sweet, warm mouth, thrusting his cock between her legs, believing heaven couldn't be any better than this. No woman would ever make him feel the way she did. Her eyes were hot with heat and need, and he had every intention of making her come again, with him this time. He licked her lips, and she parted them for him, her fingers stroking his ass, her touch stealing his thoughts, her tongue teasing his. This time, he sucked on her tongue, and she groaned against his mouth.

He pressed deeper, pulling her legs higher, wanting to go as far as he could, feeling her pelvis tighten around his cock. She felt damn good wrapped around him in a loving embrace, and he didn't want this to end. But he was cognizant of her injury, and he didn't want to tax her too much either, especially if she wasn't being completely honest with him about how she was feeling.

"Oh, faster," she said, the words husky and urgent.

He felt the climax coming but held off, straining to give her pleasure for a second time. Then rubbing against her and thrusting again, he felt her spasm, and she cried out, clutching his ass with her fingers. And he came, exploding inside her, the raw, animal pleasure pummeling him in a satiated way.

They were mated wolves now and forever, and he couldn't have been more pleased.

He sank on top of her before he worried he might be hurting her, but then he moved off her and pulled her into his arms. For the longest time, she breathed in his scent, and he caressed her back with his fingertips, lost in the soft and warm feel of her body pressed against his. "Are you okay?"

She licked his chest and rested her chin there, looking up at him. "My mate just sent me to the moon and back. I'd say I was on top of the world."

He smiled down at her. "About the bullet you took."

She rested her head on his chest and sighed. "Since you made love to me, I don't feel anything but delicious afterglow. And"—she stroked his chest—"if you want to do more of this"—she swept her hand down his waist—"I won't stop you."

He chuckled. "I can see you're going to be insatiable."

She looked up at him and frowned. "Aren't you?"

He smiled. "Hell yeah."

"You're such a wolf," she breathed against his chest, then licked him again and kissed him.

"You are too. And all mine."

Early the next morning after making love a couple more times, and way too early for Jenna, her mom called and Jenna figured she had another case.

"I'm so sorry, dear. How are you feeling?"

"I'm fine, really, Mom." It was more that Jenna was still cuddling with Sarandon after making love two more times last night. The bruise on her chest was completely gone. She was just tired from being up half the night with her hot mate. Not that she was complaining, except for having to work today.

"Maybe Sarandon can go after this man while you rest up a bit. You sound tired."

"No, that's okay." Sarandon needed to rest up too, but it had all to do with them being newly mated wolves, for heaven's sake.

"The man's name is Haldon Jones. He skipped out on his bail, and this one isn't paying his court-ordered child support or alimony. Are you sure you can do it?"

"Yes, I'm fine. Send me all the information, and I'll track him down."

Her mom sent her the mug shot and bond information. "I also need you to run to the police department and pick up another application. We're going to start personally picking up these cases so we can smell the suspects in case they run."

"And to learn if they're a wolf," she said, kissing Sarandon's cheek. Neither had made a move to leave the bed. He was awake, listening, running his hand over her bare back.

"All right, dear. I'll let you take care of it."

"We should have it done in record time. Especially since I now have a wolf partner."

"Your sisters are envious. Now they both want one too."

Jenna yawned. "They'll have to find their own. I've also still got to run down Herman."

When they ended the call, she and Sarandon got ready to go.

"No chance for a wolf honeymoon, I take it," Sarandon said, pulling on his shirt.

"All I've got to say," Jenna said, slipping her boots on, "is we need to take care of these cases pronto, so we can get back to looking for Burt. Once we're done with him, maybe we can get a break. Are you sure you can handle working as a fugitive recovery agent without the training?"

"Yeah, I'm still a part-time deputy sheriff anytime Peter needs me to be."

"All right." She thought he would be fine, but she'd still had to ask.

When they arrived at the jail, they got the paperwork for a guy who'd been arrested for writing a couple thousand dollars' worth of bad checks. He offered to pay for his bail bond with a check, and Jenna said no to that. "Cash, postal money order, or certified check only."

Once Jenna got a certified check from him, she and Sarandon ran into Officer Calvin Meissner. "Meet my new husband and partner in apprehending fugitives, Sarandon Silver," she said.

Meissner's jaw dropped for a split second. "So she didn't tase you but married you instead? That's a new one on me." He shook Sarandon's hand. "Congratulations to the both of you. I'm glad to hear you've got more help on this. I heard you caught Jeffries. Good job. We've never been able to locate Burt Dreyfus."

"Neither have we. Maybe he left the country. Oh, and from time to time, we'll be using a scent dog to try to track the fugitives down. We've picked up a couple of them, so you might see us with them when we attempt to apprehend these fugitives."

"Sounds good. We'll talk later. Got another call coming in." Meissner's phone was buzzing, and he answered it.

When Meissner left, Sarandon said to Jenna, "Scent dogs?"

"Wolves. Or dogs that look like wolves. I think we need to take a new approach with some of these fugitives. Especially if they're running in the woods."

"Like Burt?"

"Absolutely. Especially with Burt. The only thing we have to decide is who gets to play wolf."

"Me," Sarandon said, because he was taking Burt down as soon as they could track him.

She nodded and was looking up information on Haldon, who was right there in Colorado Springs. "Haldon has an ex-wife and a couple of kids at a location an hour from here. I thought we'd visit her first to learn if she might know where he's hiding out."

"I'm all for it."

When they spoke to the ex-wife, she mentioned a woman who had dated him after they divorced. "Trixie Bigsby," the ex-wife said. "If she knows what's good for her, she dumped the bum."

They located Trixie and called her up. "Haldon? I broke up with him a couple of weeks ago. He told me I was his soul mate, but I learned he was seeing two other women. Bastard. The drinking and DUIs made me call it quits. If I tell you where you might find him, do I get the reward money?"

They got so many calls like this when they offered a reward for information leading to the apprehension of the suspect. Even though they were always hopeful it was a good tip, the majority were false sightings, mistaken identities, wishful thinking.

"If the information you have on Haldon's whereabouts directly leads to his apprehension, yes," Jenna said.

"Okay, while we were dating, he took me to some of his childhood haunts and said sometimes he still returns to them. He'd go there when he got in trouble at home. He had an abusive stepfather, and his mother didn't protect him. The final reason I called it quits with him was that he was driving with a suspended license because of a couple of DUIs. My dad was a drunken deadbeat, and I could see where our relationship was headed, same as my mom's with my dad. My dad was having affairs with barflies. You name it. I drove by one of the places this afternoon on my way to the grocery store, and I thought I saw him entering a motel room with a disheveled blond. His hair is shaggier and he's wearing a scruffy beard now, but I'm pretty sure it was him."

"Give me the name of the motel and the list of other locations, and we'll check them out," Jenna said.

"You will let me know if you find him, won't you?"

"We will."

"I saw him at the Moonlight Motel on First Street in Colorado Springs. Yeah, I know. You'd think he'd want to get out of the city. He doesn't have a car, totaled it while he was DUI the one time, and he doesn't have any car insurance. I don't know how he can hold down a job, but he's always got one. The other places are motels just as seedy as the one I'm sure I saw him at." She gave Jenna the list of names and locations. "Hey, you're the one looking for Alex Dreyfus, aren't you? Is there a reward for finding him too?"

"Alex Dreyfus? How do you know about him?"

"I work at a bar in Colorado Springs. His brother, Burt, was coming in there, bragging he was a cameraman for a TV show. Had my interest, believe me. That's where I met Haldon. Anyway, I left with Burt after I got off work a couple of nights a week. He said his brother was in a bit of trouble and he had to help him out. That's when I saw the reward offered for his brother, but I never knew where he was, and Burt wouldn't say or didn't know either."

"Alex was cleared of all charges."

"Oh, okay. Good."

"Do you know where Burt is now? Have you seen him recently?" Jenna asked.

"No. He was supposed to meet me tomorrow night at the bar after I get off. Why?"

"Was there someplace special he was taking you?"

"He'd come to my place. Why?"

"If you see him or hear from him, let us know. He's not on our case list, but he's wanted in the case of identity theft and stolen passports, for injuring a deputy sheriff, and for shooting me."

"Holy crap. Are you serious? See? That's the problem I have with guys. I think one's okay, and then I learn he's the worst of the lot." She paused. "If he's not on your list, that means no reward?"

"Oh, there will be a reward. We need to apprehend him before he hurts anyone else. And thank you. We'll let you know what we discover concerning Haldon."

"Good luck."

Jenna was already driving in the direction of the Moonlight Motel. "What do you think the chances are that Burt will try to hook up with Trixie tomorrow night?"

"Slim if he's running scared after trying to kill you, but it's worth checking out."

"Do you think we'll find Haldon at the motel?"

"I sure hope so. At least we have other leads to investigate if this one doesn't pan out. Are you wearing your bulletproof vest?"

"Always. Dad got me a new one, hole-free. We can't call the police in on the situation with Burt," Jenna said.

"Right. Not after what he's pulled. We have to handle this ourselves."

When they reached the one-story, ten-room motel, the sun was hitting the grimy siding. Jenna wondered what it had been like and the kind of clientele that had stayed there when it had been brand new. It looked similar to the one where they had apprehended Jeffries—same approximate age, just as run-down. Three scratched and dinged cars were parked next to the rooms. She went to the office to present the pictures of Haldon to the woman inside and showed the manager her badge. Sarandon stayed outside, listening to their conversation but watching the motel rooms to ensure Haldon didn't leave if he was still here.

"He's staying in room five. Wait, is there a reward for his arrest? There is, isn't there?"

This got dicey. If the manager had called their number to report him, that would be different.

"We have to apprehend him first. Did he register a car?"

"No."

"And was he alone?"

"He was with a blond."

"What was the name he used?"

"Jones." The manager gave her a key to the room.

"Is there a back way out of the rooms?"

"No. The only windows are out front."

"Thank you."

Then Jenna moved outside, and she and Sarandon headed for the room. "I hope he's still there."

When they drew closer to the door, Sarandon said, "I hear someone showering inside."

She hoped it wasn't just the blond and Haldon was gone. She knocked on the door.

No one answered.

She used the key on the door and opened it, but Sarandon quickly moved forward, protecting her. She couldn't appreciate him any more than she did.

"Out of bed now," Sarandon said, advancing on the bed,

and she saw the naked man sprawled across the mattress, the bedspread and sheets tangled up on one side of the bed.

The shower shut off.

The man in the bed didn't move, snoring.

The place reeked of sweat, whiskey, and beer. Two empty whiskey bottles and a couple of six packs of empty beer cans were lying all over the floor.

The door opened to the bathroom, and a blond-haired woman in a towel shrieked to see them standing there.

"Sit on the chair over there," Jenna commanded.

"Who...who..."

"I'm a fugitive recovery agent, and we're taking him in to the police department. Haldon has an arrest warrant out on him."

Sarandon picked up one of the empty whiskey bottles and filled it with water from the bathroom, then returned and poured it on Haldon's face. The guy came up sputtering for breath.

"Get dressed," Sarandon ordered.

"What the hell?" Haldon said, coughing and hacking.

"I'm taking you in to face your charges at trial. Hopefully, you'll be incarcerated this time and not let go," Jenna said. She glanced at the blond. "You don't have any arrest warrants out on you, do you?"

"No...no."

"Come on, man, get it together," Sarandon said to the guy.

Haldon began to pull on some boxers. "What are you doing here?"

"Arresting you," Jenna said. "So we'd prefer you were dressed when we left."

After Haldon had a shirt and jeans on, he slipped his

feet into a pair of flip-flops. Sarandon helped him to his feet, then tied his wrists behind him with plastic ties. "Okay, come on, Haldon. Let's go to jail."

"Is there a reward for his arrest?" the blond asked, looking like she thought she would have a chance at the reward.

"No," Jenna said. And she got the car door for Sarandon. She called the woman who had given them the tip. "We got him, thanks. Once I've turned him over to the police, we'll take care of the reward money."

"Oh, thank you. He was bad news. I'm so glad something good could come of me knowing him."

"I'm glad you knew where he was too. Thanks for all your help." Then Jenna drove to the police department and called her mom. "We've got Haldon. We're headed in to turn him over to the police. And, Mom, this woman gave us the information to take him in." She gave her the ex-girlfriend's name and number. "And the woman in the motel office identified him and the room where he was staying. So she might need some reward money too. Your call."

"I'll take care of it."

Jenna was glad they had caught Haldon, but Burt was still on the loose. "Trixie might be meeting with Burt at the bar where she works, so we're hoping we'll take him down then."

Chapter 20

AFTER THEY DROPPED HALDON OFF AT THE POLICE STATION, Jenna and Sarandon headed back to her house, and all he could think about was how much he craved to make love to his mate. He visualized stroking her into completion and plunging into her hot, wet sheath; his cock was already half-aroused.

"What do you do after you have a case like this when you're so close to home?" Sarandon asked, his voice much huskier than usual. He was glad everything had worked out and no one had gotten hurt.

She eyed him for a minute. "I usually go for a wolf run. It always gives me the feeling of freedom and helps me to shake off the concern I have when I have to take a suspect in. Now that you're here with me, I feel so much better. I don't *need* a wolf run to get it out of my system. Afterward, I would have gone back to Cañon City to look for Herman."

He parked the car in her garage. "I could just make love to you and get rid of the adrenaline rush that way. You know what they say, don't you? Having all that excess adrenaline in your system, if you don't burn it off in physical exercise, can make you jittery."

She chuckled. "Is that why your voice is so rough? It's definitely on the agenda. I still want to run. Don't you?"

"Yeah. And then I'll make love to you." But he was

thinking that making love to her would have to come first. He was too ready for this.

"How could I be so lucky." She leaned over the console and kissed his mouth but slid her hand over his erection, and it jerked under her light touch. She smiled and licked his lips. "Hmm, looks like someone's got other plans. *First.*"

"I'm damn lucky. And hell yeah." No way could Sarandon smell his sexy mate running as a wolf with him, feeling her rubbing against him in a loving way, and not take care of the raging need he had to make love to her beforehand.

Ravishing his beautiful mate, and *then* running with her. He had to keep his priorities straight.

Once they left the car, he snagged her hand and headed into the house. In the bedroom, he removed her holster and pistol.

"Hmm, this reminds me of the first time we met." She removed his holster next.

He laughed. "I was thinking the same thing. And how our foreplay in the leaves at the cabin was a real turn-on, as much as I was trying to keep some control over the notion."

She chuckled. "I noticed."

"Couldn't be helped. All your ordering me about and armed to the teeth, you were sexier than hell." He unfastened her protective vest and cast it to the floor.

"I was hoping you'd want to do this first. Been thinking of this for a while?" She rubbed her hot body against his erection and yanked off his protective vest, dropping it on the floor on top of hers.

He loved it when she stripped him of all his gear.

"Hell yeah. As soon as we dropped off the perp. All I could think about was getting you naked. You're so beautiful, Jenna."

"You're one sexy wolf, Sarandon. I was imagining the same but didn't want you to think that's all I thought of you—sex and more sex, like you were my prized stud wolf."

He chuckled. "Works for me." He settled her on the edge of the bed so he could remove her boots and socks, rubbing his cheek against her knee, smelling her musky aroma. "You're already wet for me, aren't you?" He looked up at her to see her smiling down at him.

"Since I've been thinking about getting you naked and having my wicked way with you."

He smiled at her, took hold of her shoulders, and leaned her back on the bed. He unbuckled her belt, pulled down her pants zipper, then slid her pants off. He rubbed her mons through her wet panties, glad she was just as eager to have sex.

Not expecting it, she left the bed and yanked his shirt out of his jeans, her fingers slipping underneath his shirt and stroking his chest. "Hurry up. You're way behind me."

"We'll remedy that." He tore off his shirt. Then he leaned down to remove his boots and socks.

As soon as he stood tall, she ran her hand over his cock straining against his jeans. He groaned.

"Hmm." She kissed his naked chest, running her hands up his muscles, palming his nipples.

Her touches and kisses stoked the fire burning in his blood. Yeah, no way could he have waited to have her. He pulled off her shirt and unfastened her bra, and then he kneaded her beautiful, bountiful breasts.

He wanted her now, but he was trying not to rush this time, loving the feel of her smooth fingers on his skin and the way her nipples pressed against the palms of his hands.

He ran his hands down her arms while she unfastened his belt and then pulled down his zipper, her fingers caressing his erection. He couldn't last and hurried to pull off her panties. She slid his boxer briefs down his legs, and he kicked them off before he pinned her to the mattress, his wolf, his mate.

Mine.

Sarandon gave her a long, lingering kiss, his touch a drug Jenna didn't want to give up. Ever. Her body was as taut with need as his appeared to be.

He anchored her against him, rubbing his stiff cock against her, and she rubbed her body against him, breathing in his scent and collecting it against her skin.

She swept her hands down his back as he pressed kisses on her cheeks, then her throat, her neck, making her tingle with exquisite need.

He kindled a fire deep inside her, his warm tongue pressing against her lips, seeking entrance. And she let him in. Welcomed him, the sweet, spicy taste of him. The erotic touch of him.

Never had she imagined she'd feel this way with another wolf, so completely taken in. So fiercely passionate. So ready and demanding.

With Sarandon, it was always uninhibited, passionate sex. Having him touch her scorched her as she couldn't stop touching him. Feeling his smooth, heated skin, tracing his hard muscles, she enjoyed his cock rubbing against her leg as he moved to stroke her into oblivion, and she was ready for him too.

Oh God, he was so very good at this. And tormenting her with his strokes. She breathed him in, her sexy mate, her wolf, his pheromones zinging about and tantalizing hers.

Their heartbeats were thundering as he stroked her harder, faster, into a fevered pitch. Now or never. She felt the rise and fall in one tumultuous, cataclysmic moment, and then the waves of climax carrying her out to sea.

Feeling boneless, she wanted him now, every bit of his glorious cock thrusting between her legs. Now.

Jenna was one hell of a seductive wolf. Sarandon was damn lucky Alex had brought them together, and though Sarandon had never believed in fate or destiny, he couldn't deny he felt that meeting Jenna like he had and falling in love had been fated.

He spread her legs apart and entered her slowly, then pulled out and began to thrust. He'd never met a more passionate woman. Never needed one like he needed her.

He kissed her lips. Licking them, then seeking entrance. She parted her lips for him, but when he inserted his tongue to taste her, to caress her, she sucked on it, making him nearly come.

He thrust his cock deeper between her legs, slipping his hands under her buttocks, so she was higher and he could forge even deeper. She clung to him, matching his thrusts, drawing him in and holding on for dear life.

He would never be able to get enough of her, and he

was glad he had an extended lifetime to pleasure her. When she grazed her nails gently down his back, he couldn't last any longer.

He came, thrusting a few more times before grinding out, "You make my world complete."

"As you do mine. I can't imagine not having you in my life since we met."

He pulled off her and lay on his back. She snuggled up to Sarandon. "You're easy to love, you know."

"I feel the same about you."

"I feel totally boneless and wish we could just stay here the rest of the day, just like this."

Hating to mention it, he said, "We have to find Herman."

She sighed. "Yeah, time to put another one behind bars so we can do more of this. Come on, mate of mine. Help me up."

He got out of the bed and pulled her up and into his arms. He snuggled her close, his cock twitching. She smiled, then kissed him slowly on the lips and finally separated from him. "I'm getting something to drink before we run, and then let's go."

"Sounds good to me. Making love to you works up a bit of an appetite too. We can eat when we get home."

He swore he heard something push the wolf door open, and she quickly whispered "Wolf company" to Sarandon before shifting.

No one would come into her house without forewarning unless that someone was trouble.

Sarandon had shifted just as quickly and brushed past her, ready to tear into the wolf. There was only one wolf he believed would come in uninvited.

When he saw the brown wolf this time and smelled his scent, he recognized him from the meeting with him at the Antlers Hotel. *Burt*.

The wolf's brows lifted, his tail stiff, his ears down a little as he saw Sarandon. What did the bastard think? That because Jenna had been trying to locate him on her own, she would be alone right now? Badly injured? Barely able to fight him, if he showed up unannounced?

Burt tried to make it back to the wolf door, but Sarandon pounced on his back and bit him hard.

The wolf let out a yelp. Sarandon wasn't letting the bastard live. When their kind tried to kill humans or wolves, it was a death sentence. Unless there were extenuating circumstances, like self-defense or protecting an innocent. But going after people who were trying to do their job and keep their kind safe?

The wolf was as big as Sarandon, and he twisted and turned to get loose of Sarandon's grip, finally breaking free. He was hurting. Even so, he snapped and snarled, trying to keep Sarandon from attacking again. Thankfully, Jenna waited in the wings, and Sarandon was glad she didn't try to attack. This was his job, unless the wolf managed to get the best of him. Sarandon wasn't about to let him. He lunged in, and the two wolves growled and snapped at each other, trying to grab the other's throat but only managing to clash teeth.

Sarandon tasted his blood, and Burt's. Burt tried to back out the wolf door and Sarandon tried to stop him, but Burt managed to get outside, whipped around, and ran.

For his mate and CJ and Alex, Sarandon couldn't let the bastard go free. He ran like the wind after the retreating wolf, and he heard Jenna running to catch up. He saw her run beside Burt, and Sarandon didn't want her to get anywhere near him until he realized what she was doing. She was running him toward the box canyon. Like Alex, Burt wouldn't know the area that well. He'd only been here the one time.

Sarandon loved his clever mate, though he still didn't want her near the bastard.

As soon as they reached the canyon, Burt looked up and realized his mistake. He had no time to rectify it. He turned, and Sarandon was on him again. Only this time, he tore into Burt before the wolf could fight back. He cut off his windpipe and held on until Burt sank to the ground and shifted.

He was dead.

Before Jenna could race back to her house to tell her mom what had happened, Sarandon saw five male wolves running toward them. *What the hell?*

No way could Sarandon fight off that many wolves, and with only Jenna's mom at her own home next door—even if she could come help out—two females and one male against five hefty males wouldn't be a match they could win.

Then one of the wolves barked at the others, and they all stopped. The black wolf ran forward then, the alpha male of the group. Sarandon could win this battle, even though he was bleeding some. He would do anything to protect Jenna.

The wolf barked at him, and Sarandon smelled his scent as he ran to join them. *Join* them. *Not* fight them. Relieved beyond measure, Sarandon realized the wolf was Monty.

How had he and the others known Burt was here? He wondered if they'd caught wind of where he was headed. Sarandon hoped the pack would understand why he'd had to take such drastic measures.

Monty shifted. "We have other men standing by. Some of my men will return with you and Jenna to let them know where we are. We'll take Burt back with us. I'm sorry it had to come to this."

Sarandon shifted. "How did you know he'd be here?"

"The whole pack has been on the lookout for him. We learned he was meeting some waitress at a bar tonight, but we discovered he's been staying at her house. After what happened to Jenna, we were afraid he might come after her. After he tried to kill her and didn't succeed and it turned the whole pack against him, we were worried he'd want revenge."

"Sorry it had to come to this."

"We smelled his scent at the house. We know you couldn't let him go. We'll take care of him. Thanks for all your help," Monty said.

Sarandon nodded, and the two men shifted. Then he went with Jenna and two of the men. He smelled that one of the men who stayed with Monty was Anton. He was sorry for him most of all.

Jenna kept pressing against Sarandon, showing him her love and support. He licked her muzzle, and they kept loping toward the house. Only now did he feel some pain from the bites Burt had managed to inflict. Nothing really serious that wouldn't heal up in a few days. More irritating than anything.

When they arrived at the house, they found five cars sitting in Jenna's driveway and more men, still in their human form, appearing anxious to learn what had happened. One of the wolves shifted and said, "Burt's dead. He entered Jenna's home to kill her, and Sarandon had to fight him. He didn't have a choice."

"Hell," said the man who had taught the boys to ride motorcycles. He glanced at Sarandon. "I don't blame you one damn bit. As much as I hate to say it, Burt dug his own grave."

"We'll show you where his body is." The man shifted back into his wolf form, and he and the other wolf led the men to the box canyon.

Sarandon followed Jenna into the house through the wolf door, and as soon as they shifted, she was looking him over, tears in her eyes. "God, Sarandon."

"I'm all right. We're all right. The pack is with us on this. They'll take care of him."

"And Alex? What will he think when he learns you killed his brother?" Jenna pulled Sarandon into the bathroom to tend to his wounds.

"If he can't understand that protecting my mate is more important than life itself, it doesn't matter what he thinks."

"True." Once she tenderly cleaned his wounds and bandaged them, kissing each of them, Sarandon pulled her into his arms and kissed her mouth with tenderness.

Jenna's phone rang in the bedroom, and she nearly leaped out of his arms. "Wolf howl. Mom." She rushed into the room, got her phone, and put it on speaker. "We're all right." She glanced at Sarandon as he pulled her into his arms again. He kissed her cheek.

"Monty and some of his pack members are here. Sarandon had to kill Burt."

"Anton called to say they had just arrived at your house but not to come over until they knew it was safe."

"Yes, Burt had come into the house to kill me, but he didn't expect me to have a mate. He wasn't planning on having to face a wolf like Sarandon."

"How is he?"

"Dead. Burt, I mean. Sarandon? A few bite marks. I'll take care of him."

"We don't have to try to locate Herman right away. Let Sarandon rest up."

Sarandon was shaking his head. When he had a mission to do, he did it. A few bites weren't going to stop him.

"Did you tell him what the guy is charged with?" her mother asked.

Jenna looked up at Sarandon, and he frowned down at her.

"Aggravated assault and battery." She smiled a little at Sarandon.

"We'll take him down together," Sarandon said. "We're going to get something to eat, and we'll be on our way."

"Are you sure you're all right?" Victoria asked.

Sarandon smiled. He hadn't had a mother in so long; he was going to love this.

"Yes," Jenna said. "We're a team, and I don't want to do this without him."

When they ended the call, they got dressed and found Monty and his group taking Burt home in a tarp in the back of one of the trucks that had a cover for the bed.

Everyone had shifted back and mostly dressed. They all looked pretty grim about the whole situation.

Sarandon wondered if the man who had told Jenna where to find Burt at his grandfather's farmhouse was here.

He didn't have long to wonder. The older man came over with Monty to speak with them. "I'm so sorry," he said to Jenna. "After Burt shot you and you finally came to enough to call Monty for help, I realized what a mistake I'd made, believing Burt wasn't capable of injuring anyone like that. I just figured CJ had riled him. To try to kill a woman? You were still lying on the ground and barely able to move when we arrived, and you hadn't even drawn your gun. So he wasn't acting out of fear for his life. I can't tell you how much I regret forcing you to go alone and not calling for any backup. I'll do whatever you want to make it up to you."

"Thanks. You don't need to. Your apology is enough," Jenna said graciously.

Monty shook Sarandon's hand. "Don't be a stranger. You're as much family as Alex is."

"Despite what happened here today?" Sarandon asked.

"Hell yeah," said two of the men who were getting ready to leave.

The one said, "You took care of a bad situation none of us wanted to handle."

The other nodded.

"And, Jenna," Monty said, "you're just as much family."

"Thanks, Monty. We'll be headed into your territory looking for another fugitive soon, and when we have the chance, we'll drop by and say hi."

"That would be good." Monty gave her a hug, and then he and the rest of his men left.

"I feel bad for Anton," Jenna said.

Sarandon noticed he'd already left with the man driving the truck carrying Burt's body and hadn't said goodbye. "He'll take time to grieve. I just hope that Alex will understand." He didn't want to lose his brother before he'd even had a chance to know him.

"You know," Jenna said, taking Sarandon's hand and leading him into the house, "you have a sister and her family to get to know better too."

"Right. That *we* do."

"Let's have lunch and go find Herman."

—◦◦◦—

Jenna still felt bad about the situation with Burt, knowing that's how it had to end, glad his pack was willing to forgive. It was still a hard thing to do.

Trying to focus on the task at hand, they drove back to Cañon City to try to track down Herman, letting Monty know they were again chasing down a fugitive in his neck of the woods.

"We want to help."

"Herman Schofield is human."

"And he's wanted for aggravated assault and battery, and your wolf partner has been injured. We want to help. We need to help."

"We don't want to get a bunch of your people arrested if anything goes wrong."

"We'll just be your backup, and you lead."

"All right. We'll be there in an hour. Whoever wants to go with us can, and we'll revisit the garage where two of the guy's brothers work. I have a sneaking suspicion they know where he is, but they weren't about to tell me where."

"Just come here, and you can take your backup with you."

When they finished the call, Jenna couldn't believe the pack was going to help them in this.

"Monty's taken control of his pack, given them a mission, his territory, and they're willing to make amends to you. Sounds like a good deal."

She wiped away tears. "Right. And they want to make amends to you." She glanced at him. "You were injured."

"Not hardly a scratch."

She snorted.

Sarandon got a call from Eric and put it on speaker. "Yeah, Brother?"

"Brett's coordinating this business of finding people to take over your guided tours. Somehow I got roped into taking on the hiking tour."

"Roped in?" Sarandon asked, smiling.

Jenna still didn't get the dynamics between the brothers. Was he kidding? Or not?

"Uh, yeah. My mate said we were doing it. Together. As a team."

Sarandon laughed. "Thanks, Eric. And give Pepper a hug for me. And for Jenna."

"Especially for me," Jenna said.

"I will. Hey, Monty called CJ and said you took Burt down. So, what I want to know is why I'm hearing this from CJ."

Jenna smiled at Sarandon. His older brother would always want to be the first to know what was going on in Sarandon's life. She'd make a mental note of it. Contact Eric first when they learned they were going to have their children.

Sarandon told him about Burt trying to kill Jenna. Twice. That he'd taken him out and that was the end of the matter. "The best news is, not only do we not have to deal with him any longer, but a couple of people from Monty's pack are coming to help us out with our next case. We're on our way there now."

"Just how badly injured are you?" Eric asked, sounding concerned.

"Just a few bite marks. They'll heal quickly."

"They wanted to help out because they're afraid you're not at the top of your game," Eric said.

"They want to help out because they feel badly about what happened to us."

"All right."

Jenna swore Eric was waiting for her to chime in and say Sarandon was fit for duty, but this was between him and Eric.

"Let me know, first, if you have any more life-or-death situations," Eric said, commanding.

Sarandon smiled. "Will do."

"Better."

She chuckled. She loved his brothers.

After they ended the call, Sarandon got a call from Darien.

"Uh-oh," she said.

Sarandon laughed. "Yeah, I should have told him too."

The rest of the way to Cañon City, Jenna listened to Sarandon telling the story over and over: to his other brothers, Brett, and even CJ. Monty's version wasn't detailed enough. Sarandon talked to his cousins Jake and Tom after he explained to Darien what had happened.

Jenna wondered if it would always be this way, even now that he lived away from the pack. She suspected it would. He was a Silver wolf and would always be a Silver wolf, no matter where he lived. She thought it was wonderful to have a family and a pack like that.

When they reached Monty's house, she'd expected to find a couple of men who had volunteered to help. Instead, ten men were standing in the curved driveway, cars parked all along it, and in the center, two of the men had hold of Herman Schofield.

Her jaw dropped, her mind racing as she tried to figure out how that had happened.

"We figured we'd find him for you," Monty said. "That way, Sarandon would have more time to recuperate, and you'd have a break. And if you've got room for a couple more fugitive recovery agents working for your mom, I've got a couple of men who would love to join your force and cover this area."

"They'll have to apply for the positions with my mom and complete the training. If it were me, I'd say you've done a wonderful job. We'll pay the reward money—"

"This one is on us," Monty said, the men agreeing.

One of the men there was Anton. Even he had come through for them.

"Thank you. All of you," Jenna said.

"Thank you," Monty said.

Epilogue

A WEEK LATER, INSTEAD OF THE SPRING FLING JUST BEING A gathering of wolf packs, with Sarandon and Jenna's blessing, Pepper and Eric went all out to make it a combined spring celebration and a wedding.

Jenna couldn't believe that not only was she gaining the Silver Town wolf pack as family, but also Eric and Pepper's Grayling wolf pack. And Alex; his mate; his sister, Faye; and her family came, as well as Monty, who was still the leader of their pack and eager to see some good in the world. And Alex's parents. Jenna was glad to see them all.

Faye was smiling this time and seemed to want to get to know her half brothers and their extended families. Her kids ran to play with kids from the other two packs.

Jenna's mother had hired three of Monty's pack members, and they'd already caught four of the suspects on the run.

And they had all wanted to meet the Silver pack too.

Everyone in the Silver pack treated her family, her parents and sisters, as part of their families too. And they were thrilled.

"Brett told me he found guides for all your tours and was worried you'd be upset no one minded you weren't going to be guiding them any longer," Jenna said.

Sarandon laughed. "He was kidding you. He knows I wouldn't be upset about giving it all up for you."

Jenna's sisters, Suzanne and Crystal, were having a great time dancing with a lot of bachelor wolves, and Jenna worried they might mate a couple of the wolves and end up with one of the other packs.

Sarandon took hold of Jenna and waltzed across the grass to the music. "I thought I wouldn't be able to do this with you until the Victorian Days celebration in Silver Town."

"My family can't wait to do that with your pack. My sisters and Mom have already bought gowns for it."

"They'll have a great time. And don't worry about your sisters leaving your family and your family's business to stay with one of the packs here. All the bachelor males have been warned that if they are interested in either of your sisters, they'll have to live where we live now and be vetted by our pack leaders and your family."

Jenna laughed. "You're kidding."

"Nope. It's a way to ensure we have good relations between the packs."

"My poor sisters." Jenna smiled up at Sarandon. "Good thing you weren't vetted."

"Everyone knew we were perfect together, and I'm as good as they get."

She laughed. "And just as arrogant as usual. I can't agree more that we're just perfect for each other and you're as good as they get—at least for me. I love you, Sarandon. Thanks for being you."

"I love you, honey. I had gone to the cabin to get away and think of new adventure tours. Then I heard a trespasser and meant to send him on his way."

"I was your inspiration for the greatest adventures of your life."

"You are at that."

"Ready to go to the cabin?"

"I thought you'd never ask." Sarandon swept his bride, his mate, into his arms and carried her toward their car, all covered in flowers.

Everyone cheered the bride and groom.

Jenna couldn't have been happier to have found her fugitive-recovery-agent mate and to protect him as he protected her on all their wild fugitive chases.

And Sarandon couldn't have been more pleased to agree that Eric had been right. A mate of Sarandon's own made for the hottest adventure of them all.

Read on for an excerpt of book 2
in Terry Spear's Billionaire Wolf series

Billionaire WOLF FOR Christmas

Coming soon from Sourcebooks Casablanca

GRAY WOLF DR. AIDAN DENALI STARED AT THE BLOOD sample under the microscope and the notes scribbled on paper nearby. He wasn't going to get anywhere with this. Not without new wolves to test. As much as it killed him to do so, he was giving up on his research on finding the cure for the *lupus garou* longevity issues before the Christmas holiday. Maybe his twin brother, Rafe, was right, though Aidan hated to admit it. Maybe joining Rafe and his family early would give Aidan the break he needed, and he might even have some new insight into what was going on for their kind. He could even bounce ideas off his brother and Rafe's mate, Jade. Yet it wasn't like Aidan to consider leaving his research behind for that much time. Not until Jade and her son, Toby, came into their lives. That had made them even more of a family, and he enjoyed the change in dynamics.

Still, Aidan couldn't help but worry that he was

going to fail in his mission when so many people were counting on him. Why couldn't he be more like Rafe? Rafe was successful in all the money deals he'd made. Finding Jade was another success he'd racked up. Not that Aidan envied him for it. He just wished all the time he spent on his work resulted in some headway. As to the matter of the wolves… Well, he had to get out of his lab to pursue female interests. And then what happened? His date invariably would ask about his work and if he was getting anywhere with it. He'd say no and explain the reasons, and then he'd be back to thinking about the issue and forget all about the she-wolf.

Frustrated with his lack of progress in his research, Aidan put away his notes and locked up the lab. When he made his way to the living room of his home, he saw Ted Gallagher, one of his bodyguards, raising his brows in question. Ted was an even-tempered, muscular red-head who could take down the meanest of wolves.

Yeah, Aidan normally never left his lab at this hour. He was known to be a bit obsessed and a workaholic. "I'm going to the chalet earlier than planned."

"Hell, Doc, that's good news. I mean, I guess, if you're not bursting at the seams with news of a cure."

Aidan understood what Ted meant. "I can work on it at the chalet, if I'm not too busy playing with Toby and visiting with my brother and Jade."

As soon as Aidan spoke the words, Ted got a call. "Uh, yeah, this is Dr. Denali's personal assistant." Ted eyed Aidan, waiting to see if he wanted to take the call.

Aidan had told both of his bodyguards to say that if they had to explain who they were. They took his calls while he was in the lab and wouldn't interrupt him unless it was important.

His other bodyguard, Mike Stallings, joined them.

"Sure, just a minute." Ted covered the phone's mouthpiece. "Everett Johnston is calling from the gray wolf pack in Bigfork, Montana. He was originally with the Seattle pack."

Aidan perked up. Anything to do with the Seattle pack interested him, since it was the only wolf pack he'd located that hadn't agreed to allow him to test their blood. "Let me speak with him."

Ted handed the phone over.

"This is Aidan Denali. How may I help you?"

"Hey, Doc, this is Everett Johnston. You checked my blood when you came out to Montana. You tested my mom's and sister's too. But Dr. Holly Gray, who is with the Seattle pack, called my sister, Tara, and told her she was worried about a pack member who had been banished. He's currently living in the Glacier Peak Wilderness. Holly and my sister are friends. They were just talking about him and how Holly keeps searching for him when she can, but she hasn't been able to locate him. I thought, since you have a cabin in the Wilderness, if you could find him, maybe he'd give you a blood sample." Everett cleared his throat. "What I was really hoping is that if you can find him, you could bring him here to live with the Montana pack. I've talked with our pack leaders, and they said they'd be willing to take him in. He's a good guy, and he needs a home with a pack."

Aidan opened his mouth to say he'd be glad to, but Everett continued to talk, sounding worried he might not be able to convince Aidan to look for the lone wolf.

"We know the Seattle pack has refused to allow you to sample their blood. Who knows? Nick Cornwall's blood might give you a break in your research, if you haven't had any success yet. I suspect that all you'd have to do is tell him the Seattle pack refuses to allow you to gather samples of their blood and he'd be agreeable."

Thrilled with the prospect, that's all Aidan needed. The call to action: offer Nick the opportunity to find a home among the wolf packs Aidan knew of, and he'd get him there—and possibly get a blood sample from him too.

"Why did Ronald Grayson banish him from his pack?" Foisting Nick off on a pack if he was a problem wolf could prove troublesome. Aidan wasn't about to do that. He'd take him in and deal with him the best he could instead. Making sure the wolf was fine health-wise would need to be Aidan's first priority. But getting a sample of his blood could be a boon.

"He wasn't banished for any good reason. It really was a shame Ronald kicked him out of the pack. Poor guy lost his mate and was having a difficult time coping. Ronald said he was causing trouble for the pack. I can't imagine anything being further from the truth. If you search for Nick, just be careful. Holly Gray says several members of the Seattle pack are staying at a group of cabins south of the peak and are running in the area this week. She'll be looking for him again. *Alone*. There are grizzlies and wild wolves out there. She shouldn't be by herself. Then again, maybe it would be best to avoid running into their pack and, if possible, go to Glacier Peak Wilderness after they're gone. At one time, Ronald had declared the Wilderness as a free zone for other wolves to visit, but he could have changed his mind. He's like that."

Aidan couldn't believe what a rotten ass Ronald was. "Thanks. I'm free at the moment, but I have a family gathering in a couple of weeks. I need to get this done now, if I'm going to do it before the holidays. I'll try to locate Nick."

"Good luck, Doc. I sure hope you find him. If you do, tell him he's more than welcome to join our pack in Montana."

"Will do. One other thing. Why is he living in the Wilderness? Why not just move out of Seattle and find a home someplace else?"

"He had to sell his home and sold off everything else. At least he's retired and has an income, but he's been so distraught over everything, he just left and is living out there for now. He probably doesn't know where other packs are located. Even if he does, he might feel, with the stigma of being banished, that no one would take him in anyway. Not to mention he's lived all his life in the Seattle area. He's older and more set in his ways. Oh, and I asked Holly if there was a chance you could get the pack leader to change his mind and agree to give blood, but she said no."

That would have been the best Christmas present ever. "Okay, thanks. I'll let you know if I locate Nick and can convince him to allow me to fly him out there."

Aidan ended the call and passed Ted's phone back to him, feeling he had some direction in his research again. And hope.

Ted was frowning. "Must be a combination of good and bad news."

Mike folded his arms across his chest. "Yeah, his intermittent frowns and an elusive smile say so."

"Scratch my last comment about going to the chalet. We're packing for a cold-weather camping trip. We're going to the cabin near the Glacier Peak Wilderness. A lot of equipment is always there: snowshoes, climbing gear, cross-country skis, snow bikes, and I have a lab there. The Seattle pack is staying at the cabins south of there, but we need to locate a wolf they banished from the pack. And possibly convince him to fly with us to meet the Montana pack."

"I'll arrange for transportation," Ted said.

"Actually, you don't have to go with me," Aidan said, heading for his bedroom to pack. He thought that if he ran into Dr. Holly Gray, her pack might not object as much to a lone wolf.

"Like hell we don't." Mike pulled out his phone. "You might just need us this time... Hey, Chet, we need a car dropped off at the private airport near Glacier Peak Wilderness... Just be on standby. If Doc says we need you for an additional guard detail, we'll let you know. Thanks." Mike turned to Aidan. "You sure we don't need Holloway on this mission?"

"No, Hugh's sister is due to have triplets any time, and he told his twin he'd be there for her. We don't need three bodyguards." Aidan didn't think he'd need one.

The Wilderness area was vast, and locating the wolf probably would take much longer than the two weeks they had to search for him, unless Nick wanted them to find him. Aidan couldn't envisage why Ronald had kicked the widowed wolf out of the pack. He couldn't imagine anything worse than losing the comfort of other wolves during a time of deep sorrow. If Nick didn't want to join the pack in Montana, Aidan was certain one of the other packs would be eager to take him in. Though the one in Montana could be a good start for him. Like Everett had said, they had taken in several females who had lost their mates. Who knew where that could lead? In any case, he would fly him to every location he knew until he found the pack Nick felt comfortable with.

As soon as the men had their bags packed and were gathered in the living room, Ted asked, "Do you think the guy will even want to talk with you?"

"If we're lucky and can locate him."

Ted grabbed a few bags and hauled them outside to load in the SUV.

Aidan went to gather anything else he might need from his lab. Every getaway place Rafe had purchased for their use had a room dedicated to Aidan's research. Aidan loved his brother for knowing how important it was to him.

When he went outside, the guys were ready to load into the vehicle. "What about shopping for Christmas presents for your nephew? You said you were going to do that before you left, and there might not be much in the line of shopping out there," Ted said.

"Yeah. Right." Aidan pulled out his cell phone and looked for a shopping mall close to where they'd be staying. "We can drop by a mall on the way, pick up what we need, buy some groceries nearby too, and then drive to the cabin and settle in. Once we've done that, we can start doing a grid search of the area surrounding the volcano and see if Nick's still there."

"What about the Seattle pack?" Mike asked.

"Everett said his former pack considered it a free zone for wolves. We've never had any issues when we've stayed at the cabin before."

"Were they in the vicinity at the time?" Ted asked. Ted and Mike had never been to the cabin before, Aidan realized.

"Maybe not."

Mike snorted. "That pack hates outsider wolves. I bet you if we run into them in the Wilderness, there will be trouble."

"Don't give Doc any ideas. He's liable to scrap with them just to get them to bleed on him so he can test it," Ted joked.

Mike and Aidan laughed.

"Why haven't I thought of that before?" Aidan smiled, but he was serious. It could work.

They drove to the private airport and loaded the plane with all their gear. A car was waiting for them when they landed in Washington. Aidan knew it was helpful to have a wealthy brother—all they had to do was call ahead to make arrangements for anything they needed and it was done.

At the mall, trees in the parking lot were decorated with white Christmas lights, and every parking spot was taken. They drove around and around and around, looking for a free spot, while other cars did the same. Then Aidan saw a sign for valet parking. "There. Valet parking. Go for it."

Inside the mall, Aidan saw that Christmas lights sparkled all around the inside too. He never bothered to decorate his place. There was no need since he hadn't planned to be there. Rafe had always gone all out for Christmas. He held a charity ball at his place every year right after Thanksgiving weekend. That was all the Christmas Aidan ever needed. Just a quiet gift-giving on Christmas morning, and then the brothers and their bachelor friends all did whatever they wanted. Flew off to another location, ran in the woods as wolves somewhere, fished, hiked, exercised in Rafe's gym, partied— whatever they were in the mood for.

This was the first year Rafe had a mate and a son. It wouldn't be quite the same. And Aidan was looking forward to it. Aidan could envision the tyke's wide-eyed expression when he saw all the wrapped packages under the tree. It had been many years ago for them, and Christmases had been homespun affairs, everyone making something special for everyone else. He'd always thought fondly of his mother, who made such a big deal of loving a tea towel he had created for her when her favorite one had caught fire. She used that towel until she died. Rafe had made her a bread box, teasing him that sewing was for girls.

When Aidan had to stitch him up after a wolf fight, Rafe didn't tease anymore.

As he and his bodyguards made their way shoulder to shoulder through the noise and confusion of the crowds, Aidan remembered just how much he didn't like shopping. Aidan had ordered everything else for the family for Christmas, but he'd wanted to pick up some special things for his nephew and had waited too long to do it online. He hadn't expected to see the mall this crowded but reminded himself it was Saturday and getting close to Christmas. He normally purchased most things online and would never go shopping at a mall for *anything* at this time of year.

Acknowledgments

Thanks so much to Donna Fournier for all her brain-storming help throughout the writing process. And to Dottie Jones and Donna Fournier, who are invaluable in helping catch stuff I can't see! I couldn't do it without you. Thanks to Deb Werksmen and the cover artists who make the book so much fun and ready for eager fans. And thanks to my fans who tell me the direction I need to go!

About the Author

Bestselling and award-winning author Terry Spear has written over sixty paranormal romance novels and seven medieval Highland historical romances. Her first werewolf romance, *Heart of the Wolf*, was named a 2008 *Publishers Weekly* Best Book of the Year, and her subsequent titles have garnered high praise and hit the *USA Today* bestseller list. A retired officer of the U.S. Army Reserves, Terry lives in Spring, Texas, where she is working on her next werewolf romance, jaguar shifters, cougar shifters, continuing with her Highland medieval romances, and having fun with her young adult novels. When she's not writing, she's photographing everything that catches her eye, making teddy bears, and playing with her Havanese puppies and her first grandchild. For more information, please visit terryspear.com, or follow her on Twitter @TerrySpear. She is also on Facebook at facebook.com/terry.spear and on Wordpress at terryspear.wordpress.com. Follow Terry for new releases and book deals: bookbub.com/authors/terry-spear.